To Bury Their Parents

**Being the second book of
Because of Her Shadow**
A Novel by Jason Dias

Prologue

She stared at her thumb.

Once, the woman had had a name. It was lost now, forgotten. Her identity was secure, though: she was the emperor. Just Emperor now. She knew what she was and a name was not needed.

Her thumb contained some of her identity. It was dark on one side and light on the other, golden and warm. The nail was white like the inside of an oyster shell. The pad had lines that swirled and twisted like eddies in a tide-pool as the waves go out.

"Emperor, we have brought you a prisoner."

Her guard-captain. He had a name also but, like Emperor, was reduced to a function. His function was to guard her person and follow her orders. Her function was to conquer.

"Who is it?" she said.

"A local resistance fighter. Militia, she calls herself, but her cell were armed with butcher knives."

"Bring her."

Emperor's attention moved off of her thumb and into her room. The floor was tiled, the walls mosaics. She sat in a tall chair with its back to the single door. Her eyes skipped over scenes of conquest told in tiny stones of blue, silver, brown, all cemented together to make a greater whole.

One stone caught her attention. It was perfect. An ovoid of pleasing proportions, green just the hue of the deep sea at sunrise. One perfect stone in an array of perfect stones, each selected for their individual properties.

The door opened again and the prisoner shuffled in, alone. Emperor's ears were keen. Everything about her was keen, sharpened, distilled down to its most basic essence. She stood, knowing the visitor could not see her yet, and came around the chair.

The woman looked down on her, feigning contempt through her fear. Her hauteur was shallow, though, and neither was fear her basic nature. Emperor knew it by looking.

"You are smaller than we imagined," the prisoner said.

"Is your name Militia, or only your function?" Emperor asked.

"What?"

"So many flaws." Emperor approached. She walked behind, viewing the prisoner from all sides. Once her circuit was done, she sat back in her chair.

"I could kill you," the prisoner said.

"You could not kill the thing inside of me. Tell me your name."

"Grund."

"Sounds base. Are you base?" Emperor closed her eyes and let her other senses explore Grund. Inside of her, above her stomach but below her lungs, the blue thing shifted. It never slept and nevertheless it woke now. It moved out, grew, expanded. It reached her skin. It made tendrils, invisible to the prisoner, that reached out and covered the space between them.

"Why did you bring me here?"

"I want to get to know you."

"Why?"

"Some part of you is useful. I will find that part and discard the rest."

Grund offered some complaint, some bit of arrogance that still failed to conceal her terror. Meanwhile, blue tendrils crawled into her nostrils unnoticed. Through her pores. Into her heart and deeper, into the basic nature of her being.

Militia.

She plays at it but she could be it. Too many other concerns. Look here: love for her family. That will never do. Concern for her own safety. Cut it away and what is left? But here is love for what passes for a nation in this part of the world. Hatred for me and also admiration. Nurture both.

Half those thoughts were her own and half belonged to the blue thing that rode along inside of her. She had left many selves behind along the way to this moment and might leave more. But now was not the time to cut away at herself. Militia needed her attention.

She cut. The blue thing cut. Everything unneeded fell away.

"What have you done to me?" The voice was doubled; there were two of her now, and both recoiled in pain. One stood back to her full height in a moment, setting the hurt aside to take stock of the situation. The other hesitated. She let the pain dominate her.

That would be the left-over. The dross.

"Captain."

Emperor's summons was obeyed at once. He stepped into the room with brisk feet. "My Lady?"

"Don't call me that. I am Emperor and no lady. Take this one..." she pointed at the weak woman who had spoken. "Take her and put her in the arena for the next show. Let her fight for her family. Take this one and put a uniform on her. She will defend this city to her last breath. Isn't that right, Militia?"

The new woman looked at her old self with open hatred in her eyes. "I didn't know I was so weak," she said.

To the eye, she seemed exactly as the one Emperor had cut her away from. Same build, same stance, same hands and hair and teeth. Any weakness of body both would have shared. But as the old version was led away, struggling and kicking at Captain, Emperor knew she had perfected what was left.

"Are you Militia, or is that only your role?"

"What's the difference?" the new woman said.

Captain came back in a few moments to lead her away and Emperor returned to contemplating her thumb.

Ransom

Whilla looked at the flower. Her mother wanted the purple ones with fuzzy, thorny stems to boil for tea. Some of the flowers were turning into nettles, so she had to be careful. This one had soft blue petals and a green stem. Its leaves were wide and flat, deeply colored, veiny. They didn't look like stingers. She touched the stem at the top. When it didn't sting her, she plucked it and dropped it into her basket.

Her sister helped. Neea was younger, twelve to Whilla's fifteen. She had a basket in one hand, too. She had woven it herself. It had a long round handle and a wide, flat bottom so she could lay the flowers out in a pile. And she had a bit of cloth for handling the ones that were turning nettle.

Whilla was a pale girl. The frothy white clouds wisping by overhead were not very much whiter than her. She stayed indoors a lot or in the shade because the sun here was really too much for people like her. Her hair was reddish with streaks of blonde; Neea looked just like her only her hair was pure red, copper in the forge-fire, and her skin had lots of big, dark freckles.

They were halfway down the mountain. The flowers were just opening in the morning sun. They didn't mind the sun like Whilla's skin did. If you were patient, you could watch them slowly unfold. But Mother needed the flowers quickly for a poultice. Her wounds still pained her even after ten years. So Whilla picked another flower, laid it in the basket.

"Do we have enough?" Neea called to her sister, from a little farther down the path.

"A few more," Whilla said.

"Perhaps we can help," said a voice from down the hill. Focused on the flowers, the girls had not seen the two men coming. They had bows and knives and heavy packs, sandals dirty with miles of wear. They set down the packs and smiled, but their eyes did not smile. Their eyes hungered. They were brownish men of indeterminate origins. All sorts of people came to the Starfall, usually as pilgrims and sometimes as traders. They came from as far as Lurk or Xun across the sea, and appeared in all varieties from black Xunians, gold Lurkians, the bronze people of the Greenlands and the black or brown people of nearby Hitai.

"Thank you," said little Neea, but her sister was more cautious of strangers.

"No, we're fine," Whilla said. "Come on, Neea, this will be enough after all."

"Do not run off now," said the man. His friend dug in his pack for something. "We have come a long way. How about a welcome?"

"Mang will welcome you in the village. Follow us up if you like." Whilla held her hand out for Neea, who turned to catch up.

The second man found what he wanted: a length of rope with a loop tied in one end. He threw that end almost casually and it fell over Neea's shoulders and snugged tight as he tugged on it. Neea screamed. Her basket fell to the dusty ground, scattering thistles. The wind grabbed them and spread them out in a crazed pattern. The man dragged her backwards and the first man ran forwards. She fell down but shrugged out of the lasso, jumped back to her feet as only children can, and started to run up the hill. But the first man was on top of her now. He grabbed her around the neck from behind, lifted her off her feet, and then there was not much else she could do.

Whilla started to come back down the hill but now the second man had his bow in his hands. "Come closer, child, and we'll see if your blood is as bright as your hair."

"Let her go." Whilla took another step forward, challenging.

"Oh, we will, we will," said the first man. "Come to the rock oasis. You know the one, yes? Every traveler uses it. Bring us each a bronze sword, the ones only your smith can make, and we will be on our way. We won't even entertain ourselves with the little one. Run along home now, tell the village our message. Who did you say would welcome us? Mang was the name? We will see him on our own ground."

"I will come for you," she said boldly, took another stride forward. An arrow appeared between her feet as though it had always been there and Whilla retreated a step, suddenly uncertain.

"See that you do. With our payment."

The two men backed slowly down the path, Neea kicking and thrashing and screaming between them. The village was too far for them to have heard the screaming, leaving Whilla to either follow or run back for help. She stood indecisively for some time, unable to choose between reactions. Everything had been so sudden, unpredictable. After a few moments, though, the girl turned and ran up the hill towards home. Before she was really close enough to be heard, she started to yell.

"Help! They took Neea! Help!"

And, before they had heard Whilla shouting, her friends were on their way out of the village to meet her.

Gareth, Xin Ban and Guarl. Along with Whilla, they were the four living children who had been born on one night fifteen years before, inseparable since age five. The fifth, Vault, had been murdered in childhood in a succession battle he had been too young to know about.

"What's wrong?" Gareth asked.

"Robbers. Bandits. Two men, they took my sister."

"So let's go get them," Xin Ban said. "Get her back."

"I'll get my bow," said Guarl.

"We should just pay them. They asked for swords and they'd give her back," said Whilla.

"I'll go tell Mang and then we can head out," Gareth said. He had the bronze skin and dark hair of a Greenlander and his casual approach to language had infected all his friends. Greenlanders were prone to contracting words, shortening them, slurring them together. South of the Impasse he would look completely average: average height, average weight for his age, features that would not stand out anywhere except for green eyes.

The group split into four, each person going their own way.

***

Guarl went straight to his parents' hut. Pok, his mother, stopped him at the door. Unlike other families, this family spoke their native language at home.

"Are we in some hurry, my son?"

"Yes, Mother, some hurry. I need my bow."

"Why do you need a bow in a hurry, my son?"

Guarl sighed heavily. "I need it in a hurry, mother, and therefore do not have time to explain." He was a tall boy, the tallest of the four friends, and so he hung his head to avoid looming over his mother. His long fingers were wrapped around his bow now. He had dark hair, totally black where his mother's had gray at the temples, and dark narrow eyes.

"When you need a bow in a hurry is precisely the time to explain," his mother said.

"A friend is in need. She has been stolen and is in some danger. I must go to her rescue."

"You alone? What makes you think you will not also need rescue?"

"We are all going."

"Do as you think best," she told him after a pause. "But please do think."

"Thank you, Mother," he said, and ran out of the hut, bow in hand. Pok followed him to the doorway and stood there, watching and wringing her hands. Guarl tried not to see her there, tried not to glance back.

***

Xin Ban went to the long hall where she lived with her mother, and her mother's aunt and uncle. Most people lived communally here. During a siege ten years ago they had all banded together in one home for safety and, when most of the village had been burned down, the long hall was the first building to be reconstructed. Xin Ban's mother, Xin Ban, was one of those who had gotten used to having everyone else around.

Inside was a long, open space running down the middle of the hut with cots along the outside edges. There was a big fire pit in the center with a bronze stove and most cooking was done communally.

Xin Ban tried to get her bow and sword without anyone else noticing, and here was a major weakness of the communal living approach. She managed not to encounter her mother, but eighty other pairs of eyes watched her come in, snatch up what she needed, and slide outside with her head low. Like Guarl she was very tall and kept her head down to try to be less conspicuous. She had thinner lips and a thinner face generally but otherwise they looked like brother and sister. This despite coming from different nations in a very large region known generally as Lurk. She looked up on her way out, at the broken steel sword hung over the door as a trophy or a reminder. It had been worth a great fortune ten years before and was still worth a lot for the steel alone.

Outside the hall she met Chess, coming back from the lake. Chess used to swim there every day but since the siege found it both painful and unnecessary. The god that lived in the lake no longer drove her to it. She was a tall woman in her middle forties, heavily muscled, and just as heavily scarred. Her blond hair had run mostly to white and her blue eyes had faded to almost the same color.

"Where are you hurrying off to?" Chess wanted to know.

"It is not my place to say," Xin Ban replied, and continued to take mincing steps away from the long hall, the very picture of someone trying to look inconspicuous.

"Your place to say? What does that mean?"

"If I told you what I meant, I would have to tell you what I mean not to tell you," Xin Ban said. By now she was far enough away to pretend not to hear further inquiries, which she did with about the same subtlety as she had snuck out of the long hall.

***

Gareth found Mang at the old forge, which was really just a hole in the ground that time had not yet erased. After the siege the whole forge had been relocated, brick by brick, closer to the lake.

"We have a problem," Gareth told him, interrupting some memory or reflection.

Mang stood up and turned to face Gareth. He was Xunian, a small black man with a grayish cast to his features. He had no teeth left due to his habit of chewing narcotic leaves. "What sort of problem?"

"The arming for battle sort of problem," Gareth said. "Neea has been taken by some men and they want a ransom. Two of our special swords."

"We do not have any special swords," Mang replied. "Korina does not make them since the siege. The lake spirit seems not to want them."

"We aren't going to wait," Gareth said. "You should talk to the others. We're going down there to get the girl back."

"Do not be foolish. Go slowly. Let us decide what to risk."

"No time," Gareth said, and ducked into the hut where he lived by himself. It had belonged to his brother and the woman he married, Jeen. Jeen lived in the long hall now, though, and Yohn had died a long time ago. Even though he was too young for his own place, Gareth lived there because nobody else wanted to. Inside he found his brother's bow, made of black wood from the other side of the lake. And then he was off, running back towards the old forge where his friends would meet him by unspoken agreement.

Whilla was there with not just a bow but with her older sister, Kwin. "I am coming with you," Kwin said.

"No you aren't," Gareth told her. "Risk Chess' daughters, all three in one place, plus the granddaughter in your belly? Not on your life."

"I'm going."

"She'll wait on top of the rocks, sneak around to where the Small People watch the camp. She won't take any risks," Whilla said.

"You agree to that?"

"Yes," said Kwin.

***

By now the others were arriving. The five of them strode down the hillside, stringing bows. They went in two loose knots, Gareth and Whilla and her sister, walking in an ever-shifting triad, and then Guarl and Xin Ban behind. Xin Ban's and Guarl's families had warmed up to one another over the years but still had some sort of old national history between them. Guarl and Xin Ban seemed to be determined to make up for all the generations of mistrust in one single generation.

Soon they walked over Neea's lost flowers, now only the basket to mark that they had once been organized. A desert hare sat munching one of the thistles. It did not react as the five went past, perhaps sensing their attention was elsewhere or perhaps merely hoping to blend into the scenery. On an ordinary day it would not have survived so many bows in one place.

The scenery changed through high-altitude pines to patches of giant fern where nothing else could grow, then in the lower parts of the path to gnarly desert willow, maple, the occasional splay-leafed oak. Then gay meadows full of blowing grasses, flowers in yellow and orange, slowly retreating before the Yellow Sea in the distance.

It was most of the day before the five caught their first sight of the oasis. There was a rock wall built up by generations of visitors as thanks for the water. Under the wall was a dry space with a cistern fed by a nearby spring. Two fires burned under the wall.

Here Kwin broke off from the group and took a long looping path towards the top of the rock wall. Hopefully whoever was at the oasis would be too frightened of the Small People to use the wall as a lookout. The remaining four walked straight at the camp.

They should have known when they saw two fires rather than one. There were more than two kidnappers. There were twelve.

Two rode out on small horses, little brown mares that looked both too little to hold the weight of the men riding and like they could run forever and ever, perfectly suited to the dusty flat emptiness of the Yellow Sea.

"That's them," Whilla said. "Those are the two who took her."

Nothing about them looked evil. They didn't have glowing red eyes or twisted limbs or even bad teeth. They were just men of medium build and medium height and maybe medium mind, plain and ordinary and dangerous.

"That's far enough," said one of them. He had a bow over the horn of his saddle.

"I agree," Guarl said. "Stop there." Bravado. He had learned about fighting from people who remembered the war, people who trained every day, but he had never thought he would have to really defend his home.

The two men laughed. The second had a lasso across his lap. "Did you bring our swords?"

"No," Guarl said. "We brought arrows. Send the girl out or we'll let you have them."

"You stupid puppy. Four stupid puppies. Can't you count? Go back and get what we asked for before we decide to entertain ourselves with your child. Or decide she's worth more to the slavers. Little girls like her don't last long in the sun, chipping off rocks for the tombs of kings."

Gareth nocked an arrow. Whilla did the same.

"Draw those bows and you die," the first man said. "And we shall still have our ransom. Turn around now."

Guarl lost patience with the interaction, nocked and drew and fired all in a heartbeat or two. The arrow took the first man in the eye and he tumbled off his horse, onto his back. Dust puffed around him. The little horse didn't seem to notice or really much care. The second man was moving before the first had finished falling. His rope flickered out, snatched Gareth around the neck. This forced him to drop his weapon unspent and grab at the rope as he was dragged off his feet.

The bandit ran his horse back towards his own camp, Gareth strangling behind him, unable to do much but keep the rope from breaking his neck. Guarl started to pursue but no boy is as fast as a desert horse. Xin Ban let off two arrows, both missing as the rider cut back and forth. Whilla caught up to Guarl, put a hand on his arm. "Don't."

The three friends approached now slowly, with measured strides and arrows across their bows. At the camp, men and women snatched up swords and little bronze shields and came to form a line. But a woman came out from behind them, waved them still. "You shot one of my men," she said in an accent heavy with Xunian heritage. She was tall and heavily muscled, dressed in boiled leather armor. A mallet hung from her belt on one side and a slaver's bullwhip from the other. Those things said Hitaian but her barbarian accent and her grey palms said Xunian.

"And we'll shoot you also," Guarl said. "Give us back our people."

"No matter," the woman said as if he had not spoken. "A long time ago, your people broke my sword. That sword was my fortune. I have come to get payment for it. The man you shot is one less to share in my wealth. Still, I cannot have you killing my servants, can I? I shall have to entertain myself with this one my outrider caught in his rope. Trust me, he will be suffering until you return with my payment."

"Give us the girl," Xin Ban said. "Let us take her back to her mother. We'll be back with whatever we have, swords and coins, just give the girl back."

"A token of good faith," the woman said. "Neea, come here."

Neea stood from behind one of the fires, came over meekly. "Can I go?" she asked in a broken little voice.

"Yes, child, go in peace. So long as you promise to tell your leader my name. Do you remember it, child?"

"Yes."

The three took the girl and backed away, poised to fire at any ambush, but the bandits just laughed at them.

***

It was night when Kwin met them in the tall grass, hugging her littlest sister close. "Did they hurt you? Touch you?"

"No," Neea said. "They weren't nice but they didn't hurt me any. I'm hungry. Are we going back for Gareth?"

"No," said Guarl. "We'll have to pay them. Should have done that the first time. Gareth will pay for our mistake."

They trudged back towards home, hoping to arrive there by morning, moving much more slowly than when they had gone out. Close to the foothills, they were met by Mang and Erlo. "You got her," Mang said, smiling toothlessly. "Excellent. Are you hurt? But where is Gareth?"

"They took him," Guarl said. "They took Gareth. They're going to torture him until we get back with what they want."

"We do not have swords," Mang said.

"We brought bags of coin," Erlo added.

"They won't take those, not those alone," Xin Ban said. "What we need is the sword from the long hall, the broken one."

Mang and Erlo looked at one another sidelong. "Did they say a name? Two men, you said, no women?"

"No," Neea said softly. "Their leader is a woman. She said her name was Zhang."

                         ***

It was a long walk back to the oasis. Mang and Erlo were getting close now. "Let us not provoke more violence by showing in force," Mang had suggested, and the others had agreed. Chess had wanted to come but she could hardly walk to the sheepfold and back nowadays, never mind clear down to the edge of the desert.

"We are going to have to do something about those children," Erlo said as they caught sight of the campfires on the horizon. He rubbed his head and wished there was something in his gourd besides water.

"Yes," Mang said back. "They are headstrong, too prone to risks. We will have to marry them off, settle them down. Soon. Even marriage may not be enough."

"They are no more unruly than we were at their age."

"Perhaps true," said Mang, "and perhaps not true. But at their age we did not have destinies. At least not ones to attract prophets from far away. It may be time they were sent out to seek their various fortunes."

"You cannot force something like that. Flax used to say, let them have their own destinies, don't tell them what is foretold. Let them stand or fall or love on their own terms. He wished those fortune tellers had never come and I tend to agree."

"Getting close now. And evening is on us. We might not want to approach too quietly."

From here they could hear someone grunting in pain. Not screaming, but grunting under some repetitive force. Gareth, if Zhang was making good on her promises.

A little closer, and Erlo shouted out, "Zhang. We brought what you wanted, the best we could anyway." The sound of his own raised voice hurt his ears.

"Stop," they heard her say, and the grunting faded into what sounded like sobbing. Zhang came out to meet them, away from her people and their fires and the smells of roasting meat. "Show me what you have brought so I can stop torturing your boy." Where Mang and Erlo had aged, Zhang had seemed only to grow more refined. Thinner and stronger at once, harder and colder.

Mang opened his sack, pulled out the broken pieces of the long, curved sword Zhang had brought to the village ten years before. "One sword, two pieces. Not quite two swords but special. You can live a long time from the sale of the steel alone. Longer if you can find someone to re-forge it for you."

"In the North they could do it," Erlo said. "So well only a seasoned eye would know the difference."

"Is this how you value life in your village? Less than your metals?"

"You saw the lake," Erlo said. "You know it has its own power. It has not made any of what you seek in ten years. We also brought money, all the coin we could scavenge." He held out a sack of money, fist-sized and heavy.

"We never meant you any harm," Mang said. "You could have joined us and lived peacefully."

"You should have killed me. That is the only way I will ever know peace," Zhang said.

"Whatever it is you want, this is all we have. Please, take it, give us back our boy." Erlo proffered the bag of coins still.

"I suppose there is enough money here to have not wasted my time completely. And I suppose broken steel is fair payment for a broken boy. I have had my fun with him. He is all yours now." Dismissively, Zhang turned and walked back towards her people. "Send him," she said.

Gareth came obediently a short time later, staggering and limping. His nose was broken and his lips bloody, one finger pointing off at a weird angle.

"What did they do to you?" Mang said, breathless.

"They... they..."

"It's over now boy," Erlo said. "Come on, let us get as far as we can from this place before they change their minds."

The two men each put one of Gareth's arms around his shoulders and they all but carried him away, until the night was half over.

They were not prepared to make a fire, did not bring any food or water. It was a cold camp they made that night under the stars. But Gareth shivered much more than the heat could account for, even though the men bracketed him with their bodies.

"You hurting?" Erlo asked him.

"Yes."

"You want to get all the hurting done quick or slow?"

"Quick."

"Good." Erlo took the hand with the dislocated finger. Gareth moaned, the pain intensifying, and Erlo grabbed the bent finger, pulled it straight.

"Scream if you need to," Mang said.

"I wouldn't scream for them. I won't do it now."

"If you like," said Erlo. "Next the nose." And Gareth grunted as Erlo set his broken nose as best he could, but did not cry out or scream. "Good?"

"No."

"Good," Erlo said. His hands were shaking and he put them in his lap. He could not hide the sweat standing out on his brow. "Last bit of pain. Ready?"

"Let's get it over with."

"Tell us what they did to you."

Gareth did. He told them everything. He refused to cry out or weep as he spoke. But Mang and Erlo cried in his place when they heard.

When he was done, Gareth stopped shaking a little, hugged his knees close to his chest in the dark. "What I told you, you can never repeat," he said.

"What good does a secret do?" Mang asked. "They have a way of turning sick inside you."

"The others, they'll blame themselves," Gareth said. "I know them. They will suffer everything I suffered, in their minds and memories, they'll blame each other and suffer it forever. They won't be able to see what I see: that I would have traded myself willingly to keep it from happening to Neea. What they did to me... I'll hate Zhang forever for it. But I won't hate my friends. It doesn't seem to yet but one day this will have been worth it."

"Boy, I think today you may be a man. I'll hold your silence." Erlo knew about keeping quiet when quiet was called for. Living with Chess when the god was in her, that had taught him.

"I think it not wise," Mang said.

"But you'll do it," Gareth replied.

"Yes, I suppose you are right. And you must promise to curb your recklessness."

"Maybe."

Then they lay down. Erlo listened to the others sleep. They were restless but he was wakeful. The shakes moved up his arms, settled in his chest. Sweat made him shiver in the cool night air.

I need a drink.

Gareth moaned in the night without waking. Erlo, in the midst of his own suffering, only looked at him with pity.

Nothing inside him knew how to offer help. Not for what he had been through.

***

They started walking again in the morning, Gareth in an increasing agony of deprivation. The going was slow, especially at the times his friends had to half-carry him. He was not heavy but neither were they young. A pack of baboons, Small People, followed them some of the way but never came close enough to seem threatening. They were more curious than aggressive.

Where the land turned from grasses to rocks to rising hills, among small stands of trees and others of ferns, Guarl waited with Xin Ban and Whilla. They had bows, quivers of arrows, but also water skins and packs of food.

Guarl was first to speak. "We're sorry we had to leave you. We're sorry we failed."

Xin Ban and Whilla echoed the sentiment with their faces, no need to say the words.

Gareth had little to say. "We could use some water."

Xin Ban tossed over a skin and Gareth drank it down. Erlo and Mang gratefully accepted skins too, Mang's water dribbling down his chin and onto his chest as he sucked toothlessly.

"You must be hungry," Xin Ban offered, and pulled some hard bread from her pack. Soon they were all sitting and chewing and slurping, almost as if nothing much was different. But everything was different.

"Ready?" Xin Ban asked when the water was gone and the food was eaten. "Let's go back up to the village."

"How's Neea?" Gareth asked, once they were all moving.

"As far as she is concerned, it was a great adventure," Whilla said. "Like one of the stories Chess tells when she's feeling well, or Korina."

"Your mother is very angry with you," Xin Ban said. "Impetuous, she called you, like your father. Or your brother."

"Was it still worth it?" Mang asked.

"Just remember what you agreed to," Gareth said.

They walked into the village more or less together, and went into the long hall. All of the mothers set to work on Gareth's wounds, daubing and pasting and bandaging. At some other time he supposed he might have liked the attention. As it was, he was asleep long before they were done with him.

<u>Swimming</u>

Gareth woke up in the night, weeping softly into his chest.

Mang had insisted he sleep in the long hall, at least for a few days. Gareth, weak and hurting, did not want all the attention but could not find the resolve to say no. He felt unsure of himself. Cautious. Afraid.

It was worth it, he told himself in his mind. *It would have been Neea. It was worth it.*

A contrary thought wanted to enter his mind though, half-formed and bleeding. *I'll get her one day. I'll pay her back.*

It wasn't a thought in words, not so clear, but it was a very strong feeling. It started in his belly and burned up through his tear ducts and radiated out into his fists. He tried to keep them loose but they wanted to clench of their own accord, to burn through the air and break against something, someone.

It would have been Neea.

Gareth slid off his borrowed cot, tiptoed around his sleeping family, past the stove, out into the night. He was not unobserved. It was impossible to go unobserved in the long hall. Someone was always awake, always watching. He heard people snoring, a child talking softly to her sister, a couple loving in the dark. Xin Ban got off her cot, and followed him out, and Whilla too.

Outside, one of the village men - a newer resident out of the Greenlands - kept watch in the night. It was windy outside but the lake didn't know it. The lake was flat, glassy, blue. It always looked the same, light or dark, rain or hail or slanting sun, always the exact same shade of blue. Fish jumped without splashing, boats left no wake, and swimmers sometimes saw strange things under the water - darkness and stars, other things.

Gareth, Xin Ban and Whilla walked down to the lakeshore. The young women could not have seen Gareth's wet cheeks in the dark but they put arms around him anyway, knowing without seeing. Guarl was already lakeside when they got there.

"It's beautiful," he said. "It's always beautiful."

"It was beautiful out in the dark," Gareth remembered, not knowing how. Once, it had been a spinning collection of rocks or ice or something else, out where there was no air and no warmth. And then it had been pushed, shoved towards the world, and where it landed it turned into this lake.

"People died for it, lots of them," Whilla said. Indeed the lake might well have been red rather than blue given the battle that had been fought over it ten years ago.

"I'm dirty," Gareth said. "I wanted to come here and be alone for a while, go in there and try to feel clean."

"What did they do to you?" Whilla asked, soft.

"I don't want to talk about it. I won't talk about it. But I want to be clean. I want to be alone."

"We'll be alone with you," Guarl said. The others nodded.

Gareth nodded too. It made sense to him: these people were almost as much him as he was. Alone meant absent others. So he stripped out of his clothes - a woolen kilt in Hitaian style, a woolen jerkin, wrist bands of embossed leather - and dropped them on the shore. Then he slipped into the water. Guarl dove, Xin Ban jumped, and Whilla sat on the edge and let herself fall in sideways.

As always, the water did not react. It did not bob or turn into waves, surge up or away. The four swam for the middle of the lake with the confidence of young people, no thought for reference points or temperature.

"It will take more than water to clean you," Whilla said between strokes. "Where you feel dirty... it is not your body. I..."

"It will take fire and water and time, and work maybe," Guarl said.

"It's hopeless," Gareth said. "I know it's hopeless. But the way I feel..." He choked up, momentarily lost his stroke, slipped into the water. Under there it was blue, blue. Everything blue was nothing, light the same as no light. Under the surface he was gone, missing, and there was a little peace. Momentary.

Then he was up again, with his friends. Swimming for the center of the lake, feeling the stretch in their muscles, the strength in their arms and legs and torsos. They were strong the way young people were strong, tireless as young people were tireless.

Soon they were there, in the middle, treading water.

"What they did," said Xin Ban, "they did to all of us. They hurt you the worst, and you can try to keep that a secret, but if hurting you pulls you away from us, that hurts us. They did it to you, and what they did to you they did also to me."

"And me," said Whilla. "You didn't want what they did, and I don't want what they're doing. We love you." And that was like saying *I love me*. The only fact making the two things different was that one was missing, the one who should be treading water right there in the space between Xin Ban and Gareth.

"I know how you feel," Guarl said, and that would have been a stupid thing to say except that he could. He could look at his friend's face, or even just lay in his separate house and think, and he knew exactly how Gareth felt. He could feel himself smoldering.

Tears were water and rage was fire, but fire and water were the same thing. They were chaos, standing opposite metal and wood and stone, those things that were peace and stability.

"Let's swim," Gareth said.

"Where?" Xin Ban asked.

"Down there. To the bottom."

"Impossible. Nobody ever found the bottom," Guarl said.

"We never tried. Others did, but never us."

"Let's go, then," said Whilla, and a blink later her head was gone, replaced with kicking feet. Xin Ban followed. Guarl frowned but took a deep breath and followed anyway.

Gareth was last to disappear from all sight.

They swam through the blue, the color that was always the same and never rippled or showed any interest in the world. Xin Ban felt lost, as if her fingers were drawing through nothing, as if she were going nowhere in a world with no points of reference, no objects to approach or move away from. Her breath seemed like it could last forever and as though it might have to. *Could I find the air again if I ran out?*

But something changed, deep in the center of the lake where nobody had reached before. The blue started to fade away, to darken. There was soon nothing at all around them. No water, no light, no air or need for it. They had become unborn.

"I can see the stars," Guarl said, standing on rocky ground. And there they were in all their multitudes. Whilla looked for the constellations her mother had taught her: the bear, the widow, the bow, but they were nowhere to be found.

"The gods are watching," Xin Ban said.

"How many?" Gareth wondered, and they all wondered. They didn't have any words for so many stars, so many gods.

They walked, not talking for a while, not really going anywhere. Traveling was just habit. And then there was the god before them. It was blue, blue as the lake had been. Blue like Chess' eyes were blue, blue as the sky was in the evening, close to the mountains. Three big pieces were turning about each other, slowly. Smaller pieces moved between the bigger ones, no special order to the movements, no real pattern. Dust surrounded the whole thing. It swirled and turned and reflected the light from the far-away gods, from the blue god in its midst.

"Where are we?" Gareth wondered.

"No-where," Xin Ban said.

"In the place where you were never hurt, where you are being hurt always, where we are working it out." Whilla cried a little looking at the god. Her hand wanted to touch it.

"Who's that? On the other side of it?" Guarl pointed, wished he had a sword. But they were all naked, empty of hand.

"It's me," the young man said, and they all knew who he was. Gone more than ten years, gone since before any time they could remember. "Come on. We don't have much time."

What was time, really? None of them knew, but they hurried now, stood surrounding the god. They held hands: Vault to Xin Ban to Guarl to Whilla to Gareth to Vault. The god was there, in the middle of the circle they formed, turning and turning, faster now. Now it was not turning but spinning.

Together as one, all five children stepped into the blue.

***

Xin Ban woke to the sound of whispered conversation all around. Whispers like snakes in dry-fallen leaves, an autumnal susurrus. Something wrong.

When Bianc had died two years ago the sound had been the same: low, soft, and sharp. *Don't wake the children. Decide what to say first. What happened? How did it happen? She was old, it's natural.*

Xin Ban slid off her cot, into some loose clothing, went to see what was happening. Everyone was crowded at one end of the hall, wanting to see through the door but unable to because it was too crowded. And those in the doors were afraid to go out.

Gareth stood in the back, trying to see over the crowd. Xin Ban touched his elbow, pointed to the door at the other end of the hall. Whilla came with them and the three of them went out into the morning. They were tired, bleary-eyed, and the crispness of the morning felt good.

Clean.

They went around the long hall. There was Guarl, waiting for them at the corner nearest the lake. The water was choppy, kicked up by a little breeze. It was gray like algae on granite under a sky as choppy as the water.

The god was gone.

"I thought we dreamed it," Gareth said, too loud.

"Dreamed what?" said his mother from the doorway. "What did you dream?"

"We swam in the lake," he said, "Tried to touch the bottom. I just wanted to feel clean. Down there, we saw the god. It was just some blue rocks. And we touched it. But that had to be a dream, that part had to be a dream."

"Perhaps not," Mang said. "The god is gone. Our lives once again must change. And yours, it seems. You are children no longer."

Korina looked at Gareth. "Father said we had to make our own rituals, our own ways. This seems as good a way as any to be recognized as adults." Korina was Gareth's oldest sister, the forge master, rarely seen away from her fires.

"Yes," Mang said, "yes, as good as any. We think you should go. All four of you, you should go. Whatever the god wants from you can no longer be found in this place. And others will hunt you now. We have been talking, and we think it is time."

"We cannot just send them out," Jimina said, almost shouting.

"Mother, he is right," Gareth said. "We messed up big. We got Neea but lost everything else. Everything else that matters, we lost that. We have to go. I have to go, which is the same thing."

"No-"

"Yes. If that wasn't a dream, then the god told us."

Light splitting into darkness, stepping into shade rather than into rock and that shade falling across their hearts. The world spread out before them like a map and then like the terrain: north and south, at least for starters. And Vault, Vault waiting for them, patient.

"We'll get our things," Xin Ban said softly.

"I have to tell you something first," Jimina said. "I have to tell you what the Gravetender said."

"What did she say, Mother?"

"He, the Gravetender's father before her time, the day after you were born. He said to tell you something. To say, never start a fight but never refuse one, and you will always be the victor. He said this day would come - not in so many words, but we knew. We always have known."

"What will you do?" Guarl said, his parents weeping but standing aside.

"What we have always done," Mang replied. "Fish, farm, raise sheep. I hear the fish jumping - how long since you heard a sound such as this? The splashing of water? But you must go. Today. Now."

"Mother, I don't know what that means, what you said." Gareth hugged her close, kissed her forehead. Another son leaving her world.

"Nobody knows what it means, if it means anything. But we were to tell you, after you failed. After you were hurt. He knew that much."

Gareth nodded, resolute but shaking, went inside to get his things.

Whilla approached her own mother. "I have to go as well."

"You know how to read," Chess said. "The man, the grave-man, he said once you knew how to read you would have to learn how to read. Nonsense probably, we thought it was all nonsense, the kind of magic that seems like magic because we believe it is. But he said to say it."

"Will you swim again?" Whilla did not know why she asked.

"No, child. I hurt too much most days, and the others I will be busy wishing you were here."

Whilla hugged her mother, pulled her tight, and something went out of her. A little blue color like a butterfly seen between the trees. Chess seemed to relax a little bit, some of the tension leaving her brow. "I love you," Chess said. "I had to leave my home once. I came here, and then you were born. Everything I've suffered you make worthwhile. Now go find your fortune, whatever that is. Take my spear with you."

"Are you sure? What if..."

"If I need to use it we are already lost. I will never fight again. Take it."

The spear was from a time when the god in the lake helped them forge metal weapons, when it knew a siege was coming. It had a black wood shaft with a long metal head, a strange red color. That blade could cut steel. "Thank you, Mother."

Xin Ban came out with a bedroll, a bow, a bag of food, and some skins for water. Her mother talked in her ear as they walked, keeping her close. Her father had died on the way here but she had an aunt and an uncle to say goodbye to. They all talked quietly, undemonstrative but very close.

Finally it was time to go. Xin Ban knew this was an exile but it still felt like a fond farewell. They turned at the last point on the path where they could see the lake and marveled at this changed view, at real water sloshing and splashing and changing color as the sky filled with clouds. Waved at their parents and friends and families. And then finally walked away, backwards, preserving the sight as long as they could.

"Why didn't you talk to your parents?" Gareth asked Guarl.

"We've been discussing this for years," he said. "My prophecy, my birthright, was that the seer held me up and turned me in a circle. My parents have always thought this meant I was to travel to far places, to see everywhere. We only had to say goodbye. They were excited."

"My mother wasn't."

"Neither was mine," Xin Ban said. "No more Xin's in our village now."

"Mine either," Whilla said. "She took it pretty well all together. But our people, that's what we do. We grow up and leave home, travel village to village and look for trouble. That's what she always said."

"If Mang was right," said Gareth, "then we won't have to look far for trouble. It's going to find us sooner or later."

"Should we all go together?" Guarl said. "Or should we split up?"

"I want to go to the Greenlands," said Gareth. "I want to find out what happened to my father. I want to collect his sword and maybe bring it back home for Mother or Korina."

"I don't think we have any better ideas so far. Let's all go," said Whilla.

They agreed. Then started the long march down the hill, out of mountain terrain and into grasslands.

Gareth's mind hopped from thought to thought like a bird in a cage. The hurt of leaving home; the pain in his body; the tired soreness behind his eyes; the presence of his friends. Thoughts of his father, lost so long ago, honor lost, body lost.

And the little bit of hope that Zhang would be there, astride some future path, a target for bloody vengeance.

***

Up in the village, Chess wiped away her tears - and she was in good company there. But she felt optimistic. Even almost good. Her pain was less than it had been in a long time. She stretched, cracked joints.

"Perhaps I will go and swim after all," she told herself.

***

Fum worked his way down a short hill, being careful to keep trees between him and his quarry.

Ten years since I walked over the edge of the map and just kept walking.

Almost true. There had been villages, harvests, even some women. But always that lure, that whispering voice from just over the horizon: *follow me and be free!*

He put his back to an oak tree. It was somewhat stunted, the weather this far south not being totally conducive to oaks. Pines tended to fare better. He looked right, edged his face around the bole, and saw them.

Soldiers.

The Southerners he lived with now, these Greenlanders, knew nothing of soldiers or armies. They grew their crops, lived in peace, and told their children tales of Hitaian slavers to compel their good behavior. But there they were, across the field. Men and women with creamy brown skin and red hair, dressed in boiled leather armor. They had an array of fighting gear with them: long and short swords, round shields, long spears. Most of that lay on the ground around them as they swiftly erected a camp for the night.

What threat might soldiers pose to one man alone? Perhaps none at all, perhaps the ultimate threat. But there was no reward with no risk, and he needed to know their intentions.

And I have grown so bored.

Bored with harvests. Bored with family. Bored with peace and prosperity. Bored, even, with the women who came to him seeking his exotic flavor.

He stepped out from around the tree and sauntered towards them. One of the soldiers saw him immediately and set down the logs she carried towards the growing fire pit. She did not reach for any weapons. She raised one hand, palm out, in what he took to be a sign of greeting.

Fum reciprocated exactly and stopped where he was.

The others noticed him now, six people with a stranger suddenly all but among them. They controlled it well but Fum noticed the signs of shock, of mistrust: tight eyes, tight shoulders, lips not quite relaxed.

The first one, the one who had raised her hand, said words Fum could not comprehend. He had picked up the Greenlander speech well enough and he knew both forms of Hitaian but the world was large, full of manners of speech.

"I hope we have some language in common," he said. He used Greenlander, thinking the other tongues unlikely.

"Ah, Greenlander," said one of the men. "Hongian, even. What news, stranger? Come closer, perhaps share our fire."

Once I was a Prince. I never shared fires with soldiers. And this I know: soldiers never invite wanderers to eat their food.

He stayed where he was. "A good crop of plums in West Village. The sugar harvest looks chancy. I hear of locusts in the south."

Two of the soldiers swapped a quick glance.

Ah, he is not the only speaker of Greenlander. Why would foreign soldiers speak the language?

The man said, "Locusts, is it? Come closer. Let us begin as friends."

"Begin? I thought we might just pass in the night, remain strangers. What news have you?"

"Empire," he said. "Glorious empire. Wealth and abundance, miracles of human achievement. But come, perhaps you have more to trade than news. Plums, perhaps?" And the guard stepped forward. He opened his arms just a little, just enough that Fum's eyes should have been drawn to his hands. And in that moment, the woman who had greeted him reached behind her, pulled a long knife from her belt.

"With regrets," Fum said, "I must really be on my way. But I will show you a miracle."

The woman threw the knife. Two more soldiers reached for their weapons. But Fum had disappeared.

Studies

"In the third century of the fourteenth dynasty, King Arionus was, we think, a woman. As does your mother, she wore a golden beard and a man's headdress. It is difficult to verify the assertion after so much time and following the loss of her tomb sometime in the middle fifteenth dynasty. Are you paying attention, Jul?"

Jul was a child of ten, with dark skin and hair, golden palms and soles. He wore a gold kilt as fitted his station. "Why should I?" he asked.

His teacher was a woman of indeterminate age, gray of skin, gray of hair, gray of eyes. Even her voice was gray. "Because the past predicts the future. That which has happened can show us what will happen, if we have eyes to see."

"When I am King I'll have the eyes torn out of all historians, then they can never see, and I will not have to hear it."

"Charming boy. And when might you be King?"

"When I am a man I will be King," he retorted.

"You have not been listening. I need fear no threat of your Kingship. I will be long dead if such a thing comes to pass. Your mother is King, not Queen. You know what that means?"

"It means there is no King to hold the throne."

The teacher smiled. "Good, Jul. It means she rules in her own right. And when does a ruler of Hitai give up the throne to his children?"

"When they die," he said.

"So unless you plan on killing your own mother - would you think such a thing? - she will rule until she dies. Is your family rich?"

"Richer than any person in the kingdom." He might have said in the world, only the kingdom was all the world he knew. Well, except for the village at Starfall, and they had little wealth.

"Tell me, who lives longer: the virtuous poor or the sinful rich?" asked the teacher in her droning, dull, detestable voice.

"There is no sin, only wealth. I am rich so I will live long and long."

"As will your mother, Jul, as will the King. Think on it."

"I choose not to. I hate this lesson, all these lessons. What good are they?"

"If there is no sin, there is no good. These lessons then are neither good nor ill and should curry no hate. Perhaps if I told you a story..."

Jul stood up then. He was tall for his age as the diet of a royal boy would predict. Handsome in a soft-featured, boyish sort of way. "If you wish to keep your tongue, tell me no stories. I am going to visit my puppies."

"Your mother..."

"My mother will have you beaten when she finds out that you threatened me."

The teacher's eyes widened. "What threat have I offered?"

"I have forgotten, but I am sure it will come to me if I am not distracted. Puppies will be just the thing."

All she could do really was watch him go, and sigh. Children did grow up so very fast. It was good for a boy his age to be sly, manipulative, crafty, and cruel. At least if he was going to survive long as a boy in the royal household, and gods forefend as King one day. Never mind being a good ruler, living long enough to be good required deeds worthy of demons from the myths of Old Hitai. An historian should know. So as she watched him go, it was more with wistfulness than with apprehension or disappointment.

***

Jul trotted down the hall, out towards the practice yard. His puppies were in a shed beyond the elephant enclosure. All the slaves and even the guards knew he was meant to be at lessons, but none had the rank to challenge him. Only The Blood could do that and there was precious little left of The Blood. His uncles were dead and he had no aunts, no cousins, no siblings.

He let himself into the shed and all the puppies started to whine, each in its own little wooden cage. He took one out. It snapped at him but he didn't mind. He had pulled all its teeth out and the little thing could not hurt him.

They were wolf puppies, their mother a long-legged wolf from the edges of the desert. She had had a black mane like a horse and black feet, with an otherwise golden coat. Tall enough to see over wild grasses and a fast hunter, though no real match for the cats that lived out there, or even a hyena.

Jul set the puppy on a wooden table and it scooted back away from him. He let it go; there was nowhere in here for it to run, really, and as he had taken its eyes it could not even see to try. He turned around and pulled down a set of bronze pliers from the shelf by the door. They gleamed softly in the scant light from the gap around the door, between some of the planks in the walls.

Since all the teeth were gone, he decided to start taking claws instead.

The door flew open behind him, bounced off cages set too close to it. Turned into a black cut-out by the light was the figure of his mother, instantly recognizable. She wore a golden headdress, a golden beard, a golden kilt, a golden brassiere crisscrossed by leather harnesses. At her hip hung a long steel dirk. She carried the scepter of her office, a bronze cudgel clad in gold and set with green glass from the hills around Starfall.

"It is time for boys to be at their lessons," she said, and her voice would have sounded kindly to any guard or slave passing by. But Jul knew her too well to suspect her of kindliness. He knew he was in some danger now.

"I am at lessons, Mother," he said, trying to sound like a slave who knew he was about to be punished. "I am learning about the anatomy of wolf paws. See how his claw joins to his skin?"

"You are about to learn what it feels like to be whipped like a slave."

"You would not-"

"Do not tell me what I would not. When you are a man I will tell you what I did to become King and you will wonder that you survived childhood. But you will only get that chance if you go now to your lessons."

He put down the pliers. "Yes, mother. But I wanted to play with my puppies."

"You can torture these wolf-children later. It is good to harden your heart to suffering if you want to be King one day. I am proud of you. But if you are not back in your lesson before I arrive there to check on you, I will do worse than beat you. I will put you in a cloth kilt and sit you with the boys and girls of lesser blood."

That would mean beatings from everyone, even slaves. It would mean disgrace and humiliation and no shed full of puppies. "I will go," he said. And he went.

Dusty hallways and shafts of light passed unremarked. The boy hurried, knowing his mother's legs were long and her will capricious. He went past the living quarters, past the throne room, to the stairs up to where Wyrrn waited to bore him further.

He heard footfalls behind him. Jul glanced over one shoulder to see if it was his mother come to put him in a cloth kilt but it was some other woman, a gray woman in priestly garb. He ignored her and slipped up the stairs.

Wyrrn continued a though he had never left. "So you can see by the end of the fourteenth dynasty the rules by which a woman could rule the kingdom were quite well established..." The teacher went on and on as though someone were listening. But all Jul could hear were the whimpers of puppies as he pulled them to pieces, bit by bloody bit.

***

"He is not a bright boy, I am afraid to tell My King," the teacher said.

"Intellect is rarely a virtue of the rulers," Dllyx admitted. "I suspect he is his father's son more than his mother's, and his father always ruled by force of arms over swiftness of wit. Still, there must be some way to get the histories into his mind."

"My King, it might be helpful to know what it is you want him to know, and then just tell him. He does not seem the type of boy to learn by inference."

"A direct approach, Wyrrn?"

"Yes, My King."

Dllyx thought. "Then drop history completely. Teach him how to poison and check for poison. Teach him how to plant sharp objects in fruits. How to distract with a false plot within a false plot while constructing a real one. How the simplest tricks are the most effective."

"Pardon my stupidity, Great King, but do you wish him to kill you?"

"Do you think me stupid enough to be killed?"

"No, My King, please forgive such an allusion. Rather, the histories are replete with kings who allowed themselves to die so that their children could ascend unharmed."

"Ah. No. But let him know I know every trick, every plot, every device. Let him learn to be wary. Let him grow sleepless with worry. In the long run he will benefit. When he is a man he will have to beware every lover and every girl who offers her hand. Even I shall have to send the occasional assassin if for no reason than to maintain appearances or to keep him sharp. If he dies he deserves to."

"As does his teacher?" asked Wyrrn.

Dllyx only smiled. She left without another word or backwards glance, out from the classroom wing and out of the palace. Across the parade ground were the apartments where her father-husband had once kept his pet seer. Mithodroxes, her name had been, a white woman from the northern lands. She had managed to survive slavery in the quarries, digging out rocks to make tombs, until her powers of sight had saved her from that fate.

Dllyx sat in Mithodroxes' old chair, a thing of wicker and neglect. It had been a decade since the shadow of that woman had fallen in these apartments, across this space, over Starfall.

The apartment was as empty now as it had been then. A rough bed of straw now long-rotted, this wicker chair, plain stone walls not even smoothed or dressed. The woman had lived rough even here. She might have eaten the choicest dates and tasted rare wine, eaten honeyed bread, had the best-trained lovers, but she had eschewed all of that to preserve her sight.

I have the whole kingdom, Dllyx thought now. *Everything Mithodroxes turned her back on, denied herself, all of it is mine.* In a story, all of that would bring her no pleasure. But in point of fact it all brought her a great deal of pleasure. As did the knowledge that all her scheming had brought her to this place where she had no need of courage or schemes or cleverness, where she could be as blunt as her father's scepter.

The apartment started to darken as evening crept along outside, so she went to stand on the balcony and watch the gods emerge in the night sky. *Did Mithodroxes see through their eyes?* She had predicted the manner of Dllyx' ascension, had told her as much, and it had landed in her ears like a threat. She had hated Mithodroxes as an enemy. It was still hard to work up much love for the woman but she was long gone, perhaps long-dead.

A guard passed by near Dllyx on her balcony, and she called down to her. "Guard? Arrange in the morning for these apartments to be torn down brick by brick, and each brick smashed and ground into powder. Have the powder scattered handful by handful into the sands of the Yellow Sea."

"Yes, My King," said the guard. She hurried off in a new direction to enact the order.

The night progressed and Dllyx stayed on this balcony outside the palace. She felt calm out here, looking at the palace from outside. This place was quiet. Truthfully it was quiet wherever she wanted it to be, but here the quiet seemed deeper.

Inside, in the King's Chambers, was the bed where her father had made her his wife. The silence in that place was full of the screams she refused him, the fights she refused him. Those chambers were empty, the bed melted down and all its dressing burned, but for her it was still there. She slept in the rooms where she had grown up and called those the King's Chambers now. But those too were full of noises from the past.

Moburu, her elder brother, always full of plots and bravado. His voice was all through the palace. Dead now, body lost in the Gray Sea. He had become a monster, a literal monster before the end.

Bumbu, he had lived with her here too, sometimes came to sleep in her bed. He had been just a baby when her father sent him away, out of the country to keep him alive. And Fum, a young man, was dead at her hand.

Those were the noises of the palace: death and loss. Dllyx was hardly lonely. Any of those lost men would have killed her to get the throne or killed her to keep it. But the sounds of their voices, their machinations, their presence, weighed loudly in the silence of nights like this.

By now it was dark enough to see every god, to count falling stars. None fell the way the god had fallen at Starfall, only made short white lines in the sky.

"I wonder which of them is my father," Dllyx said to herself. "I must be sure to ask the Gravetender."

***

The Gravetender, too, was looking at the night sky and wondering. She had had a name once, just ten years ago, and already it was hard to remember. Now she was just the Gravetender, living life amongst the tombs, building them and keeping them up.

There was a whole plain dotted with them, various constructions of stone. Anything that could be built by stacking blocks together was out here somewhere: beetles and camels, obelisks, stairways that went nowhere or into the sand. In the dark it was hard to imagine all the things she had seen, all the things she had built.

"Did you have a mother?" her son asked her. He should have been asleep hours ago but Gravetenders kept strange hours, needed to know the night sky as well as the terrain, and when she went into the sand this boy would reign here. He would give up his name and take on her title.

"You know, I never asked my father if I had a mother? He always said there were two of us, only two."

"Do I have a father?"

"No," she said. "I lie if someone asks. I say I lay with some guard or other, just a dalliance, but these are lies we tell that we might stay here and work on the plain."

"You mean the tombs?" He was an inquisitive child and the Gravetender hoped this meant he was clever. Her father had always said questions were better than answers.

"Each tomb is important. It carries its occupants into the stars where they live their next life, each according to the way they lived their lives here. I like to think we send them home. But also the whole plain is important. It brings into line many different worlds."

"Your father went to another world."

"Perhaps. But long ago now. Ten years. Many things happened then, a confluence of happenings. Just as this is a confluence of places, where some can walk from one world into our world, or from here into another world. When the stars are just right. But with the right power, it could do something else, also."

The boy thought about it. "What else could it do?"

"I do not know," said the Gravetender. "My father knew but he would not say. He said we would know when the time was right to know. For now we only follow the plan, build the tombs. Lifetime after lifetime, we build the tombs."

"The slaves suffer for this. Children, like me. I have seen them. They hammer and cut and drag. Sometimes they die from the heat. Sometimes they are crushed under rocks. But they suffer."

"Yes. Mithodroxes said that would stop one day, when this place fulfilled its purpose. I asked her if it would be worthwhile and she said it would. Or was that my father?"

"Your father who told you?"

"My father who asked."

"Oh," said the boy.

"So, there is King Ynn. That star there, the bright one. His tomb - the one atop which we sit - its windows point there, tiny tunnels from his crypt through the walls of the tomb. After he died and was placed below, that star came alight in the sky. So there he rests above us, watching his sons and daughters live and strive as he planned all along.

"My father might be anywhere up in that sky. There is no telling. Nor can we know where we will go in the end. Can you use your gift yet? Can you see my last days and know my life?"

"No," said the boy.

"Usually it comes to us when we become men or women rather than boys and girls. At least most strongly."

"And then I will be able to look at a baby fresh-born and know how it will live and what it must do?"

"Live? No. Only how she will die. And what tomb you must build her so that she can find her place among the gods," the Gravetender said. "Come, now. We should inspect some of the tombs tonight. Take up your staff. Since my father's days we must be wary of the dead. So far they seem only to enact some moments of their lives and do not see us or know us, but the past does not always predict the future."

"Yes, Mother."

"And do not call me Mother while we are about all our work."

"Yes, Gravetender."

Night

A peach hung from a low branch. It was fuzzy gray in the moonlight, smelled of summer and sugar and just the slightest bit of wine. *To taste a peach...*

That thought skittered and skidded across the mind that held it, not touching, not impacting. Like the wind over the lake where the god had lived all those years, blue water never disturbed by wind or rain.

Is that what I am? Disturbed?

But he was nothing, had no thoughts, had never tasted a peach or sipped wine.

The peach moved, rocked back and forth on its stem as a small thing landed on it. Disturbing thoughts scattered as doves before a hawk. He watched the bat with eyes that drank in light as a prince drinks wine. The little thing clung to its prize. Tiny teeth razored open gray flesh and the smell of fermenting fruit intensified. It lapped the juice that flowed out.

He could smell the bat, too. Its fur, its saliva. Its blood.

It was warm. A tiny heart beat in a flutter and hot blood coursed through thread-thick veins. He could smell the heart, the veins, the heat.

He was a hunter. A killer. No intention of his could draw his eyes from the little bat. No future plans, no greater good, only the urge to prey.

But he waited. Muscles tensed, ready for the leap. Eyes widened, nose gaped. He crouched in the dark, in a deep shadow.

Voices. Once, he might have understood that they were in some foreign tongue, alien to his ears. Now he spoke no tongue at all, did not comprehend there was a language to not know. He knew only that men came close. Two of them.

They came every night. One had a jar and the other a net. This was their peach, their tree, their orchard. The bats stole from them in the night so they stole the bats. Of a morning, he could smell the soup they made, bats boiled all day in their own broth, and it drove him mad with hunger.

There they were. Two men. They smelled of sweat. They had a fire for light. This was a warm place. Trees bore rich fruit and heavy green leaves, blessed with sun and black soil. The night was pleasant. The men talked, chatted, no fear in them. One netted the bat with a practiced hand. The other killed it, fished it out, and dropped it into the jar. They moved on to the next tree, carrying light and shadow with them. Neither noticed that no bugs chirped here, that the night was silent all around.

When their backs were turned, he raced silently out of his shadow. The man with the net reached up. The other watched, oblivious. He took that one. Plucked, snatched him up, disappeared into high branches with hardly an effort and barely a noise.

The man with the net turned around at the sound of the jar crashing to the ground. The thing in the trees watched him, mouth full of meat, as the man turned in a circle searching for his friend. The smell of blood thickened in the air. The pleasure of it nearly drove away what little mind he had left. And yet he savored the smell of fear wafting from the man below, relished it as his empty belly relished the blood and meat he had taken.

That fear was as fine as a peach, ripe and fat and full of juice. As fine as summer wine. A princely thing.

***

Xin Ban sat up in the darkness. There was a dream behind her eyes. Heart-tripping, blood-speeding. Something had fluttered in her face, something squamous and hurt, and she was the one hurting it. A scream...

Was that the dream, or was that out here in the night?

The stars looked down, silent as they always were. A moon fattened on the horizon, sinking below a rim of waving grass.

"Only a dream," Guarl said.

"You're awake?"

"Just now," he said. He came to sit by her, a dark shape, only the suggestion of a person. His body was warm next to hers, hip-to-hip, facing the moon. "Bad dreams. Fear."

"Only natural, I suppose," Xin Ban said. "Everything has changed. We have always been together, but never alone."

"Yes. Part, but apart. The world was always small. The lake, the forge, sheep and fish. Quail in the hills, green glass below. The Coughers. Beyond that, just the idea that other places were out here."

"Our parents. Our people. Gareth's cats. Remember when they were only kittens?"

"We were only kittens ourselves," Guarl said.

"Yes." Xin Ban edged closer for warmth. A breeze stirred the grass, hissing through it, and far away some animal snorted. "Is it our fault?"

Gareth turned over in his sleep, muttered.

"No," Guarl said. "What they did to him, they did it. We might have stopped it, but only by dying, by getting him killed. He's alive to suffer. That's no good, I guess, but it's the best we can do."

Xin Ban said nothing. Gareth's sleep eased as her mind moved on. *Just kittens,* she thought. *Aren't we still just kittens? We thought we were big, that's the trouble.*

Gareth stirred again, and Xin Ban said, "Is it good enough?"

"What?" Guarl said.

"The best we can do. What if the best we can do is to get hurt? To watch our friends suffer?"

"I don't know," Guarl said. He took her hand, held it in his between his knees.

The wind died away and then came back, one strong gust to shake the grass, to make Xin Ban shiver. In his sleep, Gareth moaned, cried out. His hands came up to fend off some imagined attack. Then he quieted again.

"We owe something," she said.

"Him?"

"Her."

Xin Ban could not see Guarl but she did not have to. She rested her head on his shoulder, a hard, bony pillow, and knew he nodded slowly.

***

There were hours of darkness left yet until morning. Jeen's eyes, though, would not wait for sunlight, and nor would her tears.

She rolled off her cot and fumbled in the dark for clothes. She left them on the floor each night next to the bed, knowing these awakenings were just a part of her life now. She shrugged into a shift, a wool dress, a shawl, then pulled back the wool hanging that separated her space from the other living spaces in the long hall.

The tears stung her eyes, clung to her cheeks. Out here there was enough light to shine through them, flames attached to candles on the hearth. Three, or perhaps only two. They wove together, blurred, sparkled through her grief.

Outside, the stars blurred together just as the flames had. She hauled the door closed behind her, trying to not make too much noise.

"Again?"

A voice from the roof. The last ten years, the village at Starfall had kept a watch. Now they had nothing more to take but the habit was ingrained.

"Again and always," Jeen said.

The watcher said nothing.

Jeen walked along the path that led away from the lake, towards the forge. Korina might be awake in there. She hardly slept, either, preferring to stare into her flames and think of her father, of her poor doomed brother. Or perhaps of nothing at all.

Yohn, Yohn. It was not supposed to happen that way. Fool. My love. Hero.

The grief was fully on her now. She passed the forge, thinking for just a second of looking in, of sharing the sadness. Her husband, Yohn, was Korina's brother. But the thought passed as she passed the forge. Down the hill road, away from the village.

When she was far enough away, she let the sadness out in the form of a wail. A cry of anguish that ululated through canyons and woods, out to where wild things scurried and rutted and strove, through forests of giant impossible ferns.

When it was done, when she could breathe again and her hands did not want to tear at her dress, she sat in the dirt on the path and just wept.

"Every night, more or less, for ten years." Chess had come along behind her, and dropped a hand on Jeen's shoulder. "What kind of love can have inspired such suffering?"

"Is it suffering to grieve?" Jeen said, wiping her face with a sleeve. Sunlight edged over a faraway horizon in advance of the sun itself.

"That sounded like suffering to me," Chess said. "Shall I sit with you?"

"You never have before," Jeen said, offering the space next to her. "Plenty of room on the trail."

"I have heard you go out, and I have seen the way you hold it in all through the day, and even I have heard these terrible pains in the night. Sometimes I think about coming out to you but my body is too weak, too broken. It hurts just to breathe, just to be at all. The weight of the lake spirit... it used me then, when it was done, left me with all this pain. And in the day, well, I do not come to you because I am a coward."

"No."

"Yes. I cannot bear that I do not feel as you do and I am afraid if we talk, rather than you feeling better, I will feel worse. That my spirit will ache as my flesh does."

"But you came," Jeen said, forcing a smile. "I thank you. I know how you suffer, too."

Chess turned her eyes outward to that glowing horizon. "You still love him."

"Of course. More every day. Reckless fool."

"Him and Moburu. I did not know they were the same."

"Yohn was never the same as your friend," Jeen said. She felt angry but pushed that away, kept her voice kind.

"No, not completely. They were both touched by the lake spirit. They both did monstrous things, in the end. They both wondered what it meant to be a man, a good man – though Mo denied that to the end."

"But?"

"But. Moburu embraced his role, his fate. The god made him a jaguar and he became it. Relished it. He said he was set free by the transformation. Yohn, though. He struggled with his role. Felt. Guilt and grief and shame. I wonder if he knew we would one day be sitting on this path together, grieving him."

Jeen stood, brushed dirt off her dress, dusted her hands. "Let me help you up."

"I feel well," Chess said, and stood on her own. Slowly, weakly.

"Nobody grieves Moburu as I grieve Yohn."

"Is that the difference?" Chess said.

"I hope not." The two women looked down the path as though expecting visitors. Nobody came up from the Yellow Sea or the Preserves or the haunted woods. "Walk back with me," Jeen said, and took Chess' hand.

"Yes. Swim with me."

"Swim? Why?"

"I want the company."

"You have not been in the water in years."

"Yes," Chess said. "I have missed it. And it will hurt. But I feel…"

"Better?"

"Yes, but also like I did back then. Like something is coming."

Into the Sand

Mithodroxes stood and stretched. Her house was small: she could touch any of its four walls from where she stood. It smelled of old salt, dry leather, her own sour sweat. Light came in through cracks in walls made of wood salvaged from caravans over the years. And there was a well in the center, a grandiose word for a hole in the ground where water seeped in during the night.

She dropped her small bucket into the hole, hauled it up with a length of twine. The twine frayed around the handle. It would need to be replaced soon. The water was cool, brackish, barely enough to sustain her.

Perfect.

Her bed was a rough bit of leather to sleep on and a rougher bit of wool to keep off the worst of cold at night. She rolled them up and stacked them in one corner as though company were coming. Company had not been here in many years, though, well before she had found this place. She had seen him, in that dark place where God cast her to watch over events. Tall, black, strong. Irretrievably mad. Not as mad as the master of the house, but mad enough.

Easy to stay lost in visions or memories of visions. Another such thing drove her now, though.

Mithodroxes went out of the tumbledown shack where she had lived so long, onto the Yellow Sea. Sand crunched under her sandals and stuck under the straps. Those would need to be replaced soon, too, or else she would wander around the desert bare of foot. The house was full of old cantinas and leather flasks scavenged from those lost in the desert but Mithodroxes had more scruples than the Master. Stealing shoes was as beyond her as slitting throats.

She was barely on the Sea at all. Just half a day's walk into the Tomblands. She looked up from the sand, up from her feet as they trod and trod, and put her eyes into the tombs.

Majestic, some of them, stretching up for the clear blue sky like a thief for a gem. Grandfather's Pyramid, what they called the tomb of Dllyx' father's father, himself the King of

Grandfathers. He had refused to lay down and die in his time. Hythi's Burden: a great pile of stone blocks painted blue, some lesson lost on its occupant and forgotten by the few visitors to this place. A staircase that rose to nowhere, another that dropped into the ground and required constant maintenance to keep clear of sand.

Sand. It stuck to her skin, fine yellow powder like dust. It grated her scalp, thick, heavy granules like tiny versions of the stone blocks she had once cut to feed the Masters' manic tomb-building. It got in her clothes, her sandals, her mouth. Some even stuck in her eyelashes and she resisted the urge to blink it away.

Hardship and deprivation power the sight.

And, chasing so close to that thought they were nearly the same words:

I do not want the sight. I never did.

But God required this of her.

So she trudged her sandy path into the Tomblands, one foot and then the other, through a wind that rose up to cut her and a sun that punished her as it ever did for her light skin, fair hair, faded blue eyes.

Ahead, a stairwell sank down under a squat gray building. Those stones had not come from anywhere nearby. Slave children would have cut them from rocks at the northern end of Hitai's domains. Put them on round stones, spheres that could be tossed in front of the stones, rolled underneath, and collected at the back to start all over. Pushed them and pulled them all the way here, enduring these same sands, this very wind, as well as the lashes of their Masters.

She could hear their cries, could see a child who had fallen, foot crushed, struggling to keep up.

Such a burden, the past. And the future worse.

The stairs waited.

They descended twenty feet to terminate at a great wooden door with bronze bands. Behind it, in the relative cool underground, Cthai stood over her drafting table, her son nearby as he ever was. She had grown to be a thick woman: a heavy waist, round hips, legs that tapered to delicate ankles. Her chin was square, strong, and her brown eyes stared at something far beyond the parchments on her table. They failed to register Mithodroxes at all. Her heavy gold headdress slumped down over her brow. It complimented a golden kilt, the highest possible badge of rank worn sloppily as a morning drunk.

The boy, though, saw her right away. "Mother – Gravetender. A visitor."

Cthai's eyes cleared. "Oh. Who is this, now, to come unannounced? Some desert waif? I have no water for you. Go and see the quartermaster."

"Waif?" Mithodroxes said, almost tempted to smile. But smiling would stretch and crinkle the burns on her face, ever-present, always agonizing. Better to try to forget them. "I suppose so. I knew you father. Tell me, girl, do you still remember your name? I always wondered when your kind forgot your names."

"Name?" Cthai said. "I am the Gravetender. And you seem to be insolent. Such a tongue should not be carried around the Masters. They might snatch it out."

"I am familiar with their scruples," Mithodroxes said, helping herself to a stool. "I have come to check on the progress of the new King's tomb."

Cthai stared at her, mouth open. Her son came to stand by her side. He was too small to see over the stone table, so Mithodroxes could only see the top of his head: curly black hair as yet unknown to the headdress. Soon, though, his mother would start to cover his head, fill it with the mythology of this place. Tales of magic, of destiny, to cover the ultimate purpose of this great, grinding machine.

"I know you," Cthai said, finally. "I should have known when I could not see your death. You carry a shadow around you, a veil made of time. You are the White Witch. Mithodroxes."

"I know who I am," she said. "The tomb?" She looked around the table, drawn to a bit of clay all but hidden among the clutter. The size of a child's fist, a square block of it, red and gray.

"What? Oh, Dllyx' grave? A great stone serpent that bites itself. Poetic, yes? It gives her fits to think on. Half the purpose of this place."

"Not the half, child. Is it ready?"

"That," Cthai said, "I cannot tell you. You know, you must know. I stand aside."

"I, too. I have no part in the petty politics of Hitai."

"Nevertheless... Wait – such a thing falls well within the lines of your shadow. You are not asking me because you do not know. Are you? You are asking me because you have foreseen some effect of the question. This is a communication, some message from your northern bear-god. A prod, to do as it wishes. It will not work."

"No?"

Cthai turned her gaze back to her drafts. "Her son's tomb, now. There's a thing. Three tries to build it and each time, it only collapses. We have not the skill to make what must be made. His is a stone sphere balanced on a stone carved to a thin edge."

"The Great Ones rarely heed such warnings, Cthai."

"Cthai?"

"Your name."

The Gravetender reached under her headdress to scratch her head, a gesture reminiscent of her father. "Of course. Only, I am the Gravetender now. That name belonged to another woman, since gone into the sand."

"To which I must now return," Mithodroxes said. "Weary and burned and none the wiser. The Masters were more merciful than my God." She stood, stretched her aching back, turned for that wooden door back into the heat. "They only lashed me when I did not do my work. Now my work is to suffer the lash. You are wrong, though."

"Yes?" Cthai said, already making mathematical notes on the edge of a page.

"God is no northern bear. That was my sister's mistake." She shut the door behind her, feeling its weight, then mounted back up the steps.

***

"That was odd," the Gravetender said when Mithodroxes was gone.

"Odd," her son repeated.

"We have not had a visit since..." But she could not remember what she had been about to say. A tickle of memory. A boy and some glass, perhaps. How long ago now?

"Mother?"

"Yes, boy?"

"She saw the clay."

The Gravetender's eyes roved around the table, found the little cube. "She did, did she? And how do you know that? Too little to see the table, or her eyes. What did you see?"

"Nothing," he said. "Do I have a name?"

"If you do, I've forgotten it as I have forgotten my own. Did she mention it? Never mind. The clay." She picked it up, dropped it carelessly into her son's hands. But it unsettled her. Gnawed at some recess in her memory.

"We do not build with clay," he said.

"We have not built with it, no. Clay is a strange thing. You mold it and shape it. Stones, those you break down, piece from piece. A form is in them and you cut away everything not that form. Then you pile them up, their forms joining and joining until you have these great mountains of rock, like Grandfather's Pyramid. He had a name too, you know."

"But clay?"

"Yes. Clay, you add on more clay to make the form you want."

"Or just twist it to your needs."

"That too. Clever boy."

He pulled himself up onto his toes to look over the workspace. "Mother? There is no clay in the plans for the King's tomb. Is that what she wanted? Mitho... The White Witch? To see if there was clay in it?"

"No," the Gravetender said, but she was not sure. "No, but there is a lesson in it."

"What lesson?"

"It does not matter," she said. "They never hear the lessons anyway."

***

Jul eased out of bed. A Prince, *the* Prince, he had a room to himself. A bed made of iron and silver, a mattress stuffed with down feathers, a rug from the skins of lions and leopards. His room even had a real door. Gold strapped with iron, it was heavy and secure. A little light crept in underneath from a torch in the hallway.

He put on his gold kilt and nothing else. No sandals, no tunic. Under his mattress, found easily by his chubby little hands, was a long knife. It had a carved bone handle, something sacred that slipped his mind. The blade was long, thin, sharp and smooth on both sides. Bronze but good enough for the job. Steel he could get. Secrets so tall as that, though, were beyond his ability to enforce.

The door opened easily. Counterweights in the wall made his job easy. *Soft pillows, soft rugs, counterweighted door. Mother seeks to keep me soft.*

In the hallway, two guards stood across from his door, the torch steady between them. An ancient of at least forty years stood to the right, a girl barely grown into her leather kilt to the left. She said, "My Prince has a need?"

He stared at her, planning to keep staring until she looked away, but she was too stupid to take the hint. "I'll have you flogged for insolence," he said.

"If it please you, My Prince, only your mother bade me watch you. I should rather be flogged for obeying the King than for looking at the Prince – especially so comely a one as you."

That should have made him smile but it did not. He frowned, concentrating. "Are you going to follow me?" he said.

"Hard to watch you from around corners," the man replied. More insolence – and not so much as an honorific. "'Watch the child', she said. 'Report in the morning.'"

Jul thought even harder. He started to sweat though the night was cool. "Watch? Report? Are you going to interfere?"

The girl smiled. The man just looked away.

"I will be the King one day," Jul said. "Tonight, could be. Will you stand aside?"

"If the King wishes it," the girl said.

Now Jul did smile. "Just stay back and be quiet, then. I will have to be stealthy and your creaking leathers and jingling harnesses are enough to wake the dead."

The girl made a sign over her heart as he said that and, at last, looked away.

Jul turned right and trotted down the hall, forgetting for the time being his own call for quiet. The two guards followed at a discrete distance, surprisingly soft in their movements. He worked his way through the maze of residences, past cloth hangings over walls and in doorways, past the sounds of snoring, breathing, rutting. In one room a baby whimpered and he thought of the puppies out in the kennels. He hoped they whined in their sleep and thought of him.

When I am done with my mother, I might come back for the baby. The King must die fast. But a baby would be better than the puppies.

Into darkened halls, now. His feet knew the way. She called on him often enough to attend her, to listen to some droning speech about honey or heads of cattle or slaves. There, ahead, was her door. Even in the dark it glimmered. All steel, it was, polished to a high sheen that caught light like liquid, swirled it around to wet the eyes.

Two guards stepped out of the shadows into his path. An old woman and a boy hardly older than Jul himself, taller and thinner with a wisp of hair on his lip.

"Stand aside," Jul said. "I have come for my throne."

From behind, the girl said, "My king does not wish it."

At that moment, the steel door opened. His mother came out, dressed in her gold kilt and battle halter, her father's cracked, bloody mace in one hand. "Come for me, have you boy?"

"Yes," he said.

She laughed and the sound made him blush. It was a hateful noise. "Stupid. You know why I never had another baby?"

"No," he said, angry and reddening, feet planted.

"Because I want you to be the King one day, only you are too stupid to cope with sisters or brothers. Ruthless and cruel, but no subtlety in you. You need time to learn it. Time and perhaps a lesson. Ced?"

"Yes, My King?" the girl said.

"Take this boy back to his rooms. Throw his kilt on the floor and lash his back forty times or until he screams. If he screams, lash his feet instead."

"Yes, My King."

He stopped turning red then. All the blood drained from his face, from his head, making him swoon. "You cannot," he said, thinking not of the pain but of the shame. To be beaten by guards, hardly better than slaves...

"You will plot," his mother said, and he barely heard. The knife dropped from his hand and he scrambled backwards, right into the old man's hands. "You will plot and fail. Next time you had best be a lot more clever than this, or else I might just kill you and have another son. If you do much better, I will beat you with my own hands."

"I shall kill you," the boy said. He meant to shout it, but it was more of a whimper, pudgy hands balled into soft fists.

"Indeed you shall. But not soon, I think. Do it," she said, and the girl, Ced, dragged him off to his punishment.

The Forge

Jeen passed by outside.

Korina heard her as she often did, sobbing, muttering to herself in the dark. Sometimes Jeen would pause outside the forge as if debating whether to come in. Sometimes she came and stood in the doorway, not really seeing Korina, perhaps thinking of how to start a conversation.

Yohn was dead. He had died ten years ago. A hero, a martyr, a monster. What more was there to say? Jeen's husband, Korina's brother.

I loved him, Korina told herself. *Jeen lost herself in him.*

The tools of her trade lay around her on the floor. She sat in the middle of the array of tongs, hammers, awls, stranger things. Crucibles and molds. Piles of scrap. The array was orderly, even beautiful to Korina. But they were wasted. Ten years ago, she had refused to make any more implements of war. They were not needed, could not bring prosperity. They could only lead away from light and life. The lake loved them, once, but then Yohn died. Moburu died. Chess... well, she lived, but the god in the lake had abandoned her, left her to suffer the injuries she took in its service. And the god blessed no more weapons.

So she made hinges and oarlocks, fishhooks and latches. Arrowheads for hunting birds.

And they bored her.

The sound of Jeen's grief passed by outside.

Korina scratched her chin. A thin, wispy beard grew there and accumulated soot and grease.

She never changes. Time does not pass for her.

The god in the lake had brought with it features of an earlier time. When things were just one thing, had not diversified into the varied forms of the modern world. When men could also be women, or wolves, or jaguars; from when metal had not split into iron and bronze, tin and copper and zinc; when trees bore more than one fruit. Before past and present had divided. Or life and death.

And Jeen, it seemed, was locked away in a past where the grief was still fresh.

The fires had burned down long ago. Korina ought to have been sleeping only she rarely slept. She sat in the near-dark, only a red glow from one coal in a tin by the door, and reflected on her tools.

***

Chess pulled water, dragged it under her, pushed it behind her. And thus she crept around the lake.

It was hard going. Her muscles were not only weak but stiff. Once, on the long trek down from the Northlands, she had seen a tree stump so old it had turned to stone. Moss grew up one side; the other was buried in a hillside, thirty feet above the ground. She had climbed up to touch it, study it with her fingertips. It had been cold, hard, dead. An artifact.

That was how her muscles felt. Like wood gone to stone. Like dead, cold artifacts.

But she persisted.

The water was water now, not blue magic. It cooled her skin, obscured her vision. It sloshed up into her nose and eyes and clogged her ears. She made waves to add to those that followed the wind.

And she persisted.

A quarter of the way around the lake, exhaustion set in. Dragging herself through the water was too much. Another stroke, two, and she was able to grasp at the side of the lake. With water suddenly set to motion after seventeen years of perfect stillness, already the banks were beginning to erode, to lose their unnatural vertical lines, their less natural circular shape. Chess added to the loss: clumps of earth came away under her hands until she had dragged herself half-out of the water to lay there on the bank, panting.

The smell of smoke had long abandoned her. Once, she had dreamed of war, had practiced for it day and night. She had made of herself a weapon. And when the god was done with her, war left her scarred, slowed, and full of pain.

My daughters. I paid for them.

Soon the panting was done. Chess considered sliding back down into the water and forging ahead but she was all but spent, body aching. She could do a little more, would have to. The thing about climbing naked into the water was one had to return to the point of origin to reclaim one's clothing.

So she set off again, back the way she had come, more clinging to the side and walking hand over hand than actually swimming.

Back where she had come from, a few people had gathered. They watched her progress from the bank, muttering to one another. They seemed to be trying to decide whether to join her in the water.

Not this nonsense again.

It had been that way, years ago. After an attack by a monstrous boar, Chess had become a sort of local hero, with admirers following behind her, emulating everything about her. Her exercise, her training, the way she walked, her style of dress. Everything.

Yohn said it was harmless, that she gave them hope. She never got used to it, though.

Finally, exhausted, she was close enough to hear them talking. "Help me out," she said. Hands came down into the water with her, warm hands full of life and strength. She flopped to the dirt. Her friends and followers dried her, dressed her, helped her to stand. Someone clapped her on the back.

"We missed you," someone said.

"Are you going to rejoin the daily training?"

"Will you swim with us again?"

And then it came clear to her. They had not come out here because she was there. They had never stopped. She had come out to follow her own followers.

***

Korina watched from the forge. She watched Chess splash around in the lake like she had never swam before. Watched the villagers come out for their usual swim and see her out there as if returned from the dead. She was weak, Chess was.

Used up. Her stomach was flabby, her arms given over to scrawn, breasts wasted, knees thick as if with arthritis.

When they hauled her out of that water like the fishers with their daily net, something happened to them. They were energized as she was exhausted. They punched one another on the shoulders, clapped and cheered. Instant camaraderie. For a second, a minute, it was as though no time had passed at all.

The past is now. Life and death are one.

When the crowd had moved on, their daily ablutions completed, Korina went down to the lake. The ground was soft, damp. It felt good under her sandals. Morning air nested in her hair, kept short to stay safe around the forge fires. At the lakeshore, she set her clothes on the shore and slipped into the cold water. There was nowhere to stand so she treaded water while splashing water over her face, her head.

Once, the lake had pulled her under. When the god still lived here, the spirit that whispered in her ear, told her how to stoke the fire and cut the rock and anneal the bronze. It had sucked her under, shown her time and space, darkness, emptiness. In that cold other world, she had seen all the gods in all the worlds staring at her like so many stars, blank eyes empty of interest, starving for warmth.

That was long ago, now. All long ago.

Korina climbed out on the bank. Clean and empty, she stood and looked at her own reflection in the water.

Her face was splotchy, as were her arms. A thousand tiny burns over the years from stray embers, sparks, and ash made her skin a motley. She had thick shoulders and arms and a narrow waist. The rest, she could not see in the water.

Power.

Those heavily muscled arms were power. Trained, built up through years of wielding the hammer, pounding weakness out of metal, pounding strength and purity into it. Bronze at first but iron now, too. Soon, maybe steel. It would take hotter fires, new fixtures: things she would have to build herself, with the strength of her arms and hands.

Hotter fires.

Nothing caught her eye or her mind like fire, like liquid metal, open flame, the low orange glow of a coal.

She glanced at the long hall as she turned to walk back to the forge. Thought briefly of going inside. Sitting with old friends, family, newcomers. Eating fish and bread, laughing, telling stories.

But her mind drifted instead to the old sword that had hung in there, the broken steel thing. The woman who had brought it had reclaimed it now.

We are short one sword.

Suddenly, that did not seem right. It seemed out of balance. Something had changed in this place where past and present clung close to one another. Never mind the loss of the god – she could still feel it out there in the world, somewhere. Never mind that her last brother had gone off to seek something. That sword was suddenly the most important thing in the world.

Korina stared at the long hall, stared a hole through the door. Realized at last that she was standing still. Set her feet back into motion.

Now she tore her eyes away from the hall, a new thought, a new fire in her belly.

Zhang stole our sword. I shall have to make a new one.

***

Fum ran north.

A Prince of the Blood. A trained hunter, politician, tracker and military leader, reduced to running and conjurers' tricks.

He mentally thanked his father one more time for throwing that magician across his path, surer every time he remembered those events that it had all been more than an accident.

He splashed through a creek under mottled shade. Spruce trees creaked in a northerly breeze. The wind blew at his back – not ideal for the hunter but good for the prey. He grasped at a root sticking through the bank and dragged himself up out of the creek. He mostly wanted sleep or at least rest, fatigue thrumming through his muscles and muzzying his thoughts. But not yet.

Here was a place for an ambush.

His tracks through the stream bed would be visible. He could slow down, take the time to pass without detection, but the foreigners were too close behind him. They would think him hurried and careless, though. Running into the water to try to shake off trackers – a childish tactic. He stopped now to work on the tracks he had made up the embankment.

Erasing. Breaking off more soil, smoothing it over. He could have made the track disappear, made himself disappear, but he only scrubbed away the tracks. What was left behind was clear evidence someone had scrubbed away tracks.

Trees clung close to the water, a long double row of them. Anyone lost in this wilderness could find water easily by seeing where these pines grew. Then the land flattened out and tall grasses took over, swaying dun and faded green, spotted with thistles.

Another trail into the grass, with pains taken to conceal it – but not too well.

His lead might grant him another hour and then he would be swarmed by soldiers. The first group had used horns to summon another and now there were twelve of them, scout-armored and infantry-armed, trained to run all day and all night.

Fum found a likely-looking tree back across the water. It was a good piece of work to get down the muddy bank without leaving any marks, or only those marks a non-human presence might make. A bit of tree branch helped: stepping on that left a track in the mud that seemed random and was too shallow for a person to have made. Rocks and roots projecting from the mud also helped but he had to carefully scrape the mud from them. He could feel time ebbing away.

Then up the other bank with extra care, and up the bole of a pine that had good screening: thick cover, other trees along the line of approach. The first branches stuck out from the bole about ten feet off the ground which meant a tricky climb to start. He could go a little faster now, though, because he went up opposite the direction his stalkers would come from. If they followed the trail, they would never investigate this trunk for clues, never come to this side of the tree.

If only I had a weapon.

Fum had started with a bow and a few arrows. Those were lost now, stashed behind a bush miles south of here. He had a knife, a water gourd, a little bit of rope, some twine, and his wits. Even the knife was more suitable for peeling carrots than fighting enemies.

If only I could shoot soldiers in the back with wit.

Nothing to do now, then, but wait. With more time he might have set a snare, some trap to slow the enemy, make them cautious and angry. Paranoid.

Presently, he heard voices. They came on slowly. At first, he was unsure what he heard. It might have been birds or some other random forest noise but it slowly resolved into the strange southern speech he had heard them use before. They seemed to be arguing, three of them. The voices were quiet and controlled but tight. One spoke. Another spoke over her before she was done. There was a pause and then the third and the first started talking at the same time. The second overrode both.

They came along the creek bed, hardly splashing. He could hear their gear clanking and grinding, though, enough noise to wake the trees around them. For his part, Fum all but held his breath and resisted the urge to peek around the trunk of his tree, through the intervening branches, to see them come. His feet dangled from the branch and he held them still, held his whole body frozen.

He heard them reach the point where his false track led into the grass. They debated some more.

Silence.

Silence.

Finally: voices again, the clatter of weapons being passed from hand to hand. They had taken his bait, fallen for his ploy.

They climbed out of the water and took a direct path north, where they knew he must go.

Fum waited for an hour, then another, still as stones and twice as quiet. Then, still careful, he edged out farther onto his branch to peer around. Nothing to see, not from here. He dropped to a lower branch and then to the ground. Stepped around the bole.

Into a soldier.

The man had a spear in one hand, topped with a bronze blade, a short-sword with a nearly triangular blade in the other.

"Hello," Fum said.

The soldier turned his head to the left and took in a breath. Fum had a bit of twine in his hand with hardly a thought. He stepped forward, inside the range of the spear, under that arm, up behind the soldier. The man was tall which was fine. In the time it took him to draw in a breath to shout, Fum had whipped the twine around his neck and pulled it snug.

The cry of alarm turned into a struggling gurgle. Sword and spear forgotten, the soldier grabbed at the string, tried to pull it out of the flesh at his neck. Tried to drag Fum forwards.

Fum kicked him in the back of the knee, dragged him backwards as he fell. Flipped him so the soldier landed on his chest with Fum kneeling on his back, pulling, pulling.

The twine broke.

The soldier gasped for a raging breath, neck purple, muscles bunched.

Fum snatched up the dropped short sword, having to tug it because his prey had landed half on top of it. The man forgot to call for help, being preoccupied with surviving. Fum found himself flipped off the man's back but the soldier did not manage to stand, only to get to his hands and knees for a moment while Fum rolled away.

Fum sprang on him, drove the sword into the back of his head.

Then he flopped onto the ground, decades of pine needles cushioning him, and panted until the gray fog left his vision.

Sometimes wishes were granted. Now Fum had not one but two weapons.

Among the Dead

The clay.

Cthai stared at it. The other things on her table held no importance this morning. Only that little cube of clay.

Where did it come from?

She did not remember putting it there. Had someone come in while she worked on Dllyx' tomb? When the boy had asked after it, it had seemed natural enough. A plan, a lesson, an allegory. She had remembered acquiring it.

Hadn't she?

It sat there amidst the clutter of a drafting space next to a bit of charcoal, an inkwell, a roll of parchment. It was gray or red depending on the light. Smooth, cubic, oily.

And it was bigger today than yesterday.

Hadn't she told the boy that very thing? To build with clay, you took a block and added to it what was needed.

She touched it with one finger. It felt warm, just the same as her own body. Soft and smooth, like the skin of a new-born baby. Like Rejax.

My son's name is Rejax. I shall have to tell him when he comes in from lessons. He will want to know.

Only, had he ever been a newborn baby? Cthai could not remember.

She left the thing there on the table. There was more to do this day.

She went out the door, up the stairs, and into the sand. It blew around, listless, aimless. Not a good allegory for this place of tombs nor for the souls that dwelt here. Only the most driven became Kings in their time. Only those souls inhabited the device. The thing itself, the whole plain, had a purpose. Hardly fitting for sand to eddy around the place on no schedule, with no goal in mind. But Cthai could hardly control the wind.

The walk out to Dllyx' tomb took an hour. The central parts of the great machine were nearly finished now so tombs accumulated around the edges.

I tried to tell her about the machine but she was not ready to hear it yet. When I asked if she had seen my death.

But whose thought was that? It felt comfortable, like it had always been there in her mind. Part of her.

And there was the structure ahead. A coiling hump rose out of dusty yellow sand. It looped around itself, seemed to move as the wind threw sand around it. Finished, past finished. But the lesson of the clay was here, too.

And Dllyx.

She stood on the back of a chariot drawn absurdly by lions. The captain of her guard led them. Xenia. A woman of middle stature, fit and scarred, grayish of skin and dark of hair and eyes. Lions were no fit beasts for a chariot. She came from around the back of the structure, eyeing it carefully, critically. Then Xenia saw the Gravetender; the lions saw her; and with all that focus on her, Dllyx could not help but have her attention diverted.

"Make them pull in a straight line," she said. "They do jerk and twist. Oh, there she is. Gravetender. Why have you made me this horrible thing?"

"The design is greater than any of us, My King," the Gravetender replied, raising her voice to cover the distance.

"It seems like an insult. Xenia, take me closer to her."

"Yes, My King."

The Gravetender did not want her coming much closer. Dllyx seemed to think she was dangerous, and in her own way that was true – but the Gravetender was more concerned about those lions. "Statements in stone are not directed towards living eminences, My King, but to their descendants. These are lessons for those who come after."

"What lesson is my son to take from this thing?" Dllyx said, close enough now that she no longer needed to shout. Her lions kept their focus on the Gravetender but Xenia restrained them with a gesture.

I should prefer a cage over a gesture.

"I do not see their minds, My King."

"Only my death."

"Yes."

"Tell me the manner of it."

The Gravetender refused the urge to laugh. Dllyx was so predictable, so repetitive. This was the same conversation as that long ago visit. *'Is my father's tomb complete? Tell me or else I will kill you.'* The urge died in her chest, though: because that visit had not been with Cthai but Cthai's nameless father. She could hear his voice in the memory, not her own, and she'd been hardly more than a girl at her studies. Out here on this infernal plain.

"You know better than that," she said, trying to ground herself in the moment. "You know we stand aside. I see, I build, and we all live with the consequences of our actions."

"Your father said much the same," Dllyx said, and nudged the lions closer.

Yes, I did.

"Every King and postulant asks such things, My King, and every Gravetender replies the same. We stand aside."

"Do you?"

The Gravetender waited, saying nothing.

Dllyx' eyes eventually left the Gravetender's face, wandered out to the near horizon. It was cluttered with tombs. Fanciful buildings, statuary, piles of old rock. "The Starfall boy. Vault, his name was. My brother killed him and brought home his skin."

"I do recall, My King."

"Your father built him a tomb. Built them all tombs. Five Starfall children. As though they were contenders for my throne. The boy is dead, though. The purpose of the tombs of contenders is to obfuscate, is it not?"

"If only those destined to rule received tombs in their lifetime, this would be a form of expressed prophecy, yes. They and their siblings would know always which of them would live and succeed, and which would suffer an end of their time."

"And you destroy the tombs of those who fail."

"Yes, My King."

Dllyx edged the lions another step closer. The Gravetender could feel their breath now, could all but hear their heartbeats. They were each maned giants, big as oxen, tall enough to look her in the eye. Dun and chestnut brown, the colors of the grasslands, of the sere desert.

"So tell me," Dllyx said. "Tell me why Vault's vault still stands."

The Gravetender smiled, right into the face of the nearest cat. "My King possesses an agile mind, I am sure. Such things are not for me to say. Only that this whole place is instructive for those who care to listen."

"I find that my son and I have this in common: no patience for such lessons. You are all the same, you gravediggers. Always on the very edge of insolence. Always just on the right side of manners, insults implied but unspoken. I wish you would just say what you mean so I could know whether or not to have you beaten."

"Has My King come all this way to the Tomblands to complain her servant is not sufficiently insolent?"

"This self-eating snake of mine. Is it done or not? That you may tell me, yes?"

"Within limits I may, yes. Because, My King, all men know when their time is near. I might say as I please and tell you nothing you did not already know." The lions came one step closer still, leaning in now, trying to smell her. "Done, yes, nearly. Only needs a few extra things. A crown for the snake, a beard, a scepter."

"To show that I ruled. That I was King here in my time."

"Yes, My King."

"Delay them."

The Gravetender shuddered. "The Kings, they always ask this. Always you want more time. But truly, time is yours to make. Time is not out here on the plain but back there in your city, in Hitai, in your bedchambers and your counsel rooms and atop your throne. Time is in the veins of your children."

"I knew you would say such. Send a runner, then. The very moment it is complete, send me a message that I might know my time is up."

"Yes, My King. Only... a finished tomb only shows the possibility of death, not necessarily its imminence."

"Nevertheless..."

The Gravetender scrambled to one side as Dllyx lashed the lions into motion. Xenia gave her a shove to help her stay safe and so the Gravetender watched the King of Hitai leave from the luxury of a berth in the sand, sprawled on her side.

The lions were a statement of some kind, some unsubtle madness to mask Dllyx' native cunning, no doubt. Always had it been so. They hardly were suited to the task of pulling a chariot, though. Their gait at a walk was not smooth, not from the perspective of the yoke. The chariot rocked up and down on the axis of its axle. It swayed from side to side. And the animals needed constant attention from their handler. Altogether a clumsy, uncomfortable ride, so far as the Gravetender could see.

***

"I need a mirror," Cthai said to herself.

The boy heard. He sat atop the table, inking in some lines drawn in charcoal. "Your father said the same."

"And how would you know that? You were not born when he went off into the sand." *Was I pregnant then? Did I stuff some rags around my belly to seem fat?*

He shrugged. "He asked if you could see the manner of his passing."

"I had not come into my power yet."

"You had," he said.

"Strange to argue the past with so new a person. Did I tell you, I remembered your name today?"

"Never mind it," he said. "I will not need it." He spilled a drop of ink, quickly soaked up what he could with a shred of vellum.

"You ought not say such things."

"It is true," he said. "No sense hiding it. You cannot protect me from knowledge of death – not amidst so much evidence of it."

"You sound like him. My father."

"Yes," he said. "So do you."

"In any case. It is not you who needs protection. Never tell what you see. Your words... they imply my time is near. That soon I will go into the sand as my father did and his before him. Then you will be the Gravetender, though your training is hardly begun. And that implication, it goes into my mind, expresses in my actions. You do not tell the future because telling it creates it."

"Yes, Gravetender." He set the quill aside, leaving a mark on the map where none belonged. His attention then turned to the cube of clay. "It grows," he said. "Day by day."

"Yes."

"What will it be? And who adds to it?"

"I cannot say," she said. "Always they ask these questions, boy, and never can we tell them."

<u>Ghosts of the Road</u>

"Tombshade," Guarl said.

"So named for where it grows," said Whilla, recounting some lesson of Jeen's. "But is this place a tomb?"

Guarl crouched in the shadow of a wall. It was a rotten wooden palisade, crude but efficient when it had been built, maybe, but no contender against time. It rose twelve feet above the road, ending in sharpened points now replete with fungal blooms and algae.

Gareth came closer, Xin Ban right behind him. "Not a tomb," he said. "A fort."

"The Xunians?" Guarl said.

"Who else?" said Gareth. "Looks the right age. And nobody local builds like this."

"It stinks," Xin Ban said, covering her mouth.

Whilla said, "Yes. Like rot and mushrooms."

"And worse." Guarl stood, slipping some of the tombshade blooms into his pack. He saw Whilla looking. "You never know," he said. "Could come in handy. Or maybe we can sell it."

"Let's go inside," Gareth said. "The day is nearly over. We can at least have some shelter from the wind." That had been cool and whining all day, lowering spirits.

"I don't want to," said Xin Ban. "The smell. And something else. Like Guarl said."

"We should at least look," Gareth said, and disappeared around the corner, looking for a door. "It's a triangle," he said. "Three sides."

"I know what a triangle is," Whilla said, going around the other way. "Here is a doorway." The door lay in the dirt, rotted into flinders. The remaining wood was thick with fungal growth. Tombshade, Bogrot, Dim's Harrow, others she could not name. Jeen would have known all the names. She stepped gingerly inside.

The walls made deeper shadows in the gathering gloom. She squinted at some shapes in the dirt.

Guarl came up behind her, stepping less carefully. "Nothing grew in here but toadstools," he said.

"Plenty of grass outside," Gareth said, stepping in behind Guarl. Grass everywhere, even on the road. But not in here. Maybe Xin Ban is right."

"Yes," Whilla said. "But we're here now. What are those shapes?"

Fungus mounded over three distinct forms in the dirt. In the shadows, they were just rising humps, half a foot high. Two might have been bodies; one was too long.

"The dead?" Guarl said.

"Animals would have carried them off," said Gareth. "Wouldn't they?"

Xin Ban stood outside the door, not looking in. "Animals have the sense not to go where only toadstools can bloom. They know to stay out of haunted places."

"Don't be-" Gareth started, but then something moved. The long form. It twitched, sat up.

All three backed out of the door, nearly tripping over one another as the impossibly tall man stood. As he rose, the toadstools and rot fell away. He was revealed to be only bones, unscattered by scavengers, held together by nothing. And as the rot fell away, so did time. Flesh clothed the bones once more, and a breastplate, and a tall helmet with a high feather crest. All in all, the figure stood over eight feet tall.

Guarl blocked the doorway with his body, a knife between him and the figure. Gareth readied a bow. Whilla had her mother's spear, the remains of the daylight playing over its dull red blade. Xin Ban hid behind the others, watching as she could between them.

"Will it attack?" Gareth said.

"They told stories of the dead come to life," Whilla said. "At the pool. Jeen and Yohn. There were skeletons. They walked around, but seemed only to enact some event from the past."

The tall man had something in his hand. A half-spear with a black haft and flashy red tassels where the head was joined to it. He held it up as if in challenge. Then an arrow appeared in his leg, shattering the armor and the bone, and he fell back into the mounded heap in which he had been discovered: rotted and broken, toadstools his only marker.

"The Captain," Gareth said, awe in his voice. "My brother shot him. He broke the agreed on rules of combat, so Yohn shot him in the leg. He must have died here."

Whilla said, "I think Yohn shot him with more than an arrow."

"What do you mean?" said Gareth.

"When he took on the plague and ran down the coast, he must have stopped here. Infected these people. These ones died where they lay. The others might have stumbled off."

Gareth stepped away, put his back to the fort. Guarl and Whilla went back inside to root around.

"Are you all right?" Xin Ban asked, putting her hand on his shoulder.

"Yes. I just..."

"It's one thing to hear the stories?"

"Yes," Gareth said. "And another to see the costs. We speak of him like a hero. But these people were not fighters. They were the hurt, the infirm. That's why they died here: too weak to crawl away, too broken."

Guarl and Whilla rejoined them outside the fort now. Whilla said, "He did what had to be done. We're here to feel bad about it. That's what he wanted. You know, guilt is for the living."

Gareth wanted to say his brother might have said the same, only he had been too young to know his brother, too young to know what was at stake. Too young to know he had only the time at hand to listen and love. "I guess."

"Look what I found," Guarl said, and held out the half-spear the giant had held. It still had finger-bones fused to it with mold and lichens. The tassels were gone now and the head was green with corrosion but the haft was good. "Hardened wood. It's still good."

"Good?" Xin Ban said.

"Well, usable. I think you should have it." He held it out to Xin Ban.

She stepped away, hands raised between them. "Don't give that thing to me. Throw it back in there. I heard the stories too, you know. When Jeen and Yohn took bronze weapons and swords from their dead, the dead came all the way to Starfall to reclaim them. Left bony footprints in the dirt."

"I'm not afraid," Guarl said.

"I'll take it," said Gareth. "I want it. Do you mind?"

"No, of course not. Why?" Guarl handed the thing over, gently, like passing a kitten.

"A reminder," Gareth said.

"Of what?" asked Whilla.

"Of the cost," he said. "I guess we'd best keep walking a ways and see if there's anyplace better to sleep. A night on the road seems unappealing."

***

The night was deep now. Guarl and Whilla slept in the tall grass off the road, a fire in some cleared space between them. Gareth and Xin Ban sat on a piece of broken cart left over from the war. Stars provided minimal light. Noise from insects encroached on their peace.

"You don't have to watch with me," Xin Ban said.

"What good is a life where you only do what you have to?"

She stayed quiet, looked across the horizon she could see. Scanning for movement.

"Sorry," Gareth said. "Can't sleep. Nightmares." He had the half-spear across his lap. With his normally-sized frame, it seemed more complete.

"Oh."

"And nightmares I can stand, only when I have them, everyone seems to have them. After that spook house, I don't want to ruin all your rest."

"I'm sorry," Xin Ban said.

"I'm not."

"No? I cry whenever I think of it. We should have..."

"We should have done as we did," Gareth said. "We believed in something. We loved our families. We were willing to risk something – and we did. Something was lost."

"Vague language," she said, "for what they did to you. I'm sorry. Again. I don't want to make you relive it."

"Yeah," he said. After a while: "They hurt me. Deep. Bad. I'll live with that. But I *will* live. And so will Neea. That old fort, and this stick, they're lessons. Reminders."

"Metaphors," Xin Ban offered, remembering another of Jeen's lessons.

"Metaphors, sure. They say, there is always a cost. Can you bear it? Yohn saved us all but there was a cost and that cost is the corpses in that fort, hidden in the grass all around it, scattered about this broken highway we will walk again tomorrow. We can regret. That's a luxury." While he said it, his hand traced fading bruises on his chin, under his lips.

"He did what he had to," Xin Ban said.

Whilla sat up from her bed in the grass. "You two talk louder than Mang snores."

"Sorry," Xin Ban said.

"And you apologize too much," she went on. "But regret isn't everything. I wasn't sure if I should tell you."

"What?" said Gareth.

"Tracks. I found them yesterday. A group of people. Booted. And the door – it did not fall in on its own. It was rotted out, but someone kicked it down. There was a space in the fungus, cleaned by a kick. Someone else came this way."

"Her," said Gareth.

"Lots of people live in the world," Xin Ban said.

"Go back to sleep," he said. "We'll be quiet."

"If you aren't going to sleep," Xin Ban said, "no point in both of us standing watch. I'll lay down, too."

Soon enough, Gareth had the night to himself.

***

Gareth strode along the causeway as though he had rested the night. The others were worse for wear.

"Nightmares," Whilla offered.

"Yeah," Guarl said.

"Next time, just sleep with us," Xin Ban said. "And slow down. We don't have to get there tomorrow."

The pavement here was good, leading down into the marshes. Where the ground went boggy a few miles ahead, Gareth could see the road breaking up. Short stretches of stone fractured into the marsh. Water and grass grew up in the spaces, cattails and willow-ferns. Something out there croaked, a weird noise, loud and threatening.

"Frogs?" Guarl said.

"Crocodiles," Whilla offered. "Breeding, probably. Jeen says the Xunians all but exterminated them out here but the younger ones swam back from upriver when the old ones were gone. Now they're the old ones."

"I wonder how big they get," Xin Ban said.

"Let's don't find out," said Guarl.

Gareth pointed with his spear. Ahead and to the left, off the road. "What's that?"

Fungus protruded above the soil in a patch clear of grass. Still too high for water even at high tide.

"More toadstools," Whilla said. "Or mushrooms."

"Mushrooms we could eat," Guarl said. "Didn't bring enough food to last forever."

"I wouldn't eat those," Xin Ban said. "Not tombshade this time, but still grave goods. Nature's offering."

Gareth stepped off the path, onto the low prairie. It was a hundred steps to the shape. He prodded it with his spear, turned over some old bones, a broken skull. "Animals left this one alone, too," he called. The others had stayed firmly on the causeway as though it offered protection from unseen threats.

"Just leave it," Whilla said. "Let's not disturb them."

Gareth let it be. The corpse could have had a sword they could use, or some coins. More likely the Hitaian patrols that had come through here had taken everything of value. He did not want to rouse any more of the dead, though, even for a profit.

He stepped back onto the road behind Whilla. "They died for something," he said.

"What do you mean?" she said.

"Don't know. Even so, they did."

They passed another such mound, and another. Then they were in the water, walking just above sloshing, salty marsh on the causeway, in places hopping from rock to rock to stay dry. Then, in a spot where the stones had sunk below the level of the tide, everyone got their feet wet, happy for sandals that would quickly dry. Xin Ban took hers off to carry them.

"Slippery," she said. "Algae on the stones."

To the right, cold ocean opened up. To the left, the marsh carried on. Crocodiles sunned themselves a mile or so away, up on what passed for dry land.

"What's that? Another fort?"

Ahead, as far away as the crocodiles, Guarl had spotted a structure rising out of the marsh. One building on stilts, twenty feet high. Others lower but still out of the water. Walls all around, fractured by time but painted red.

"This is where they landed," Gareth said. He pointed all around. "And died. There. There. Here. In the water."

Each place he pointed, no grass grew out of the water. Bones clung in places to the rocks, held in place against the tide by unseen forces.

"Even the fish and crocodiles would not eat them," Xin Ban said. "So sad, to lay where you fall, forever undisturbed. So sad to stay just yourself, not taken into the sky by hawks or buzzards, not taken into lion cubs as mothers' milk."

"I think it's peaceful," Whilla said, but she shuddered.

"Someone is in there," Guarl said.

"After all this time?" said Gareth. "They can't have come back."

They walked on, coming to the shadow of the red wall with wet feet and cold hands. One person sat in the tallest building, sort of a guard-house with a balcony and a rail. He looked Hitaian: grayish skin, dark hair and eyes, undyed wool clothing. He shouted down: "You are not crocodiles." His language confirmed his dress: low Hitaian.

"And you," said Guarl, "are not a Xunian soldier come to invade the Starfall."

"No," he laughed. "Only a park ranger come to count crocodiles. The King is very concerned over damage done by your Xunians. The population, though, is resilient. It is almost as though it never happened. In fact, you are drawing attention. Come up, children, come up and share my fire. Did you bring food? Or better yet, news?"

"Food yes," Gareth said, "if you like stale bread and dried mutton. Our news is staler than our bread, I'm afraid."

"No," said Xin Ban. "He won't have heard about the lake spirit."

"What about the lake spirit?" the man shouted as Guarl mounted his ladder.

"Gone," said Whilla, glancing at Xin Ban then back up at the ranger. "Tell me your name."

"Roap," he said. "Where did it go?"

Xin Ban looked like she was about to answer. Whilla silenced her with a gesture. "We will tell you over a fire as we dry our feet."

Roap laughed. "A bargain," he said.

***

"And then we decided to go," Whilla said, finishing the tale, having mentioned nothing of their involvement beyond that they came from Starfall. "The water was just water. The fish just fish, the air just air. All the heroes could rest. But the young, we were not content to sit by the lake and watch the new waves."

Roap clapped his hands. "Well worth a fire," he said. "And even some tea. I will brew it. News out here is rarer than..."

"Than what?" Gareth said.

"I was going to say fur on a crocodile, only I have seen two like that only this yesterday. The world is changing. Perhaps rare no longer has any meaning."

Guarl said, "Do they still get big? The crocodiles?"

"Not so big as once. Give them time, though. The real monsters, they take a lifetime to grow. You know, you are the second person to ask me in the past few days. You would think people care what happens out here at the edge of the world."

"Let me guess," Xin Ban said. "A group of men led by a woman. A woman with a broken sword."

"How did you know?" Roap said. "They paid for their fire with the tale of how the sword was broken. I believed not a word, but it was a good story. I misliked them, to be truthful. Malice rode that one's shoulders and her crew were worse, just hungry hyenas looking for a piece of meat or a bone to crunch. You're not with them."

"No," said Gareth. "But we might like to catch them up. Which way did they go?"

"As you go," he said. "Towards the Greenlands, the end of the causeway. Be in no hurry to catch them, though. What they would do with meat and bones like yours, you wouldn't like to find out."

"About that," Gareth said. "You know, they gave me a story and I think I owe them something for it."

"Indeed," said Roap. "Do tell."

"On our way back, I think."

Roap laughed. Nobody else did.

History

Jul woke up from a nightmare. Fires. Walking over hot coals, being chased by his mother in her headdress and golden beard, many big men behind her, all with gold and turquoise headdresses.

Awake was hardly better than asleep. The soles of his feet hurt not from his dream but from his punishment. And the room was full of thunder. It rolled off his door, over his rugs, into the softness of his bed, and into his aching head.

No, not thunder.

Someone was knocking on it. Someone strong.

"Come," he said, voice weak with self-pity. And, when they kept knocking, "Open the door, damnit!"

The door creaked open, letting in a cool draft from outside. Jul pushed his feet out from under his furs and let the breeze caress them. Then he looked at the man who filled his doorway.

He was not tall, at least not compared to other men around the palace. Maybe for a peasant. But he was wide, as wide as two men. And old: at least fifty, twice Jul's mother's age. Bald head, lines around his mouth and eyes, broken teeth in his smiling mouth. And a limp.

His skin was dark as Jul's own, palms golden. This marked him as one of The Blood. But his clothes...

"What are you?" Jul said.

The man laughed. "Not what, fool. Who."

"Fool?" Jul started to get indignant.

"Ah, be calm. I am a Prince as you are a Prince, boy. Yes. You have neither sisters nor brothers, have you? You mother could not bear to have to kill them, or watch you do it. You've never met someone so high in The Blood as you, have you?" He laughed again.

"A Prince? Really? I do not believe you. All my mother's family are dead. And you are too old."

"Too old to be a prince? I suppose you're right, boy. I've been away. Slaving, trading. Exiled. Your father's brother, not yours or your mother's. See these furs? Ice bear, this one." He pointed to his cloak, an extreme affectation in this hot place. "Wolf here." The skins that covered his chest and arms. "Plain cow for the leggings and boots. Good Northern steel in the scabbards." He wore several knives and swords – in the presence of the heir.

"My father? You knew him?"

"Oh yes," he said, coming in. He sat on the end of Jul's bed. It sank under his weight. His eyebrows raised, and raised more as he glanced at Jul's feet. "Your mother did this to you?"

"Punishment," he said. "Slaves did it."

"Oh. Well, your father was no better, in the end. It was exile for me, or else death. That's the way of it here. And make no mistake, boy: those are your choices, too. You kill her and you do it her way, or else she'll murder you out of hand. She won't like it, no, but she'll do it."

"You came to tell me that? I have ten years. This much I know."

"Well," the man said. "A smart boy, then. You will know to keep me a secret, if you're that smart."

"She doesn't know you've come back?"

"She thinks I'm dead. They all do. I played them a game. A lifetime ago. Now I'm just a poor trader named Chans. Haha. Soon, though, maybe I'll be Ergol once again. Ergol with the club foot." He reached under his fur shirt and pulled out a pouch, tied around his neck with a strip of leather. "Bones, boy. Ankle bones. Whole thing hinges on these."

While Jul's eyes were on the bag, the Chans' other hand slipped to his waist, loosened a knife. He pulled it, tossed it onto the boy's chest. It dropped into his lap.

"Always watch both hands," Chans said. "Never look where you're told to look."

"I won't." He took the knife in one hand, found it to be sized and balanced for a child. Steel, rippling in the light. "Good knife."

"Worth more than your ass," Chans said, and laughed at Jul's shocked look. "Told you, I'm a common sort, have been since before your mother's mother snuck into her father's bed. Oh yes, more secrets, boy. She told you your father was her father, didn't she? Stupid cow. She never saw it. I saw it. Or my spies did. No matter. You can shake this place up, if you want to. I'll help. Only, don't tell anyone about me yet."

"I won't," Jul said.

"I'll be off now. Guards will be by this way soon and if they find me here, they'll ask some questions I can only answer with murder. It isn't time yet for any murder."

Jul did not want him to go. Only a few minutes, but more words, more honesty than he had ever known. A peer, even an ancient one, was something he had missed from his life and never known. But Chans was up and gone before Jul could mount much of a protest.

***

One steel penny was a small enough price, so Chans paid it willingly.

Guards discovered him just leaving the residences. "Looking for the quartermaster," he said, but the guards wanted none of his talk. They were two women, tall, dark, silent. Their hands lingered near sword-hilts. When they nodded him towards the right, he went that way willingly.

Xenia had a small office. A closet-sized room, a wood table, a wooden chair. Some quills and inkpots, strips of vellum for counting, rolls of parchment for scribing. They stuffed him in there, blocked the exit with their own bodies. "You look common. We have a whipping post down in the servants' quarters and plenty of servants with strong arms."

"Oh," he said. "I was only lost. Perhaps the punishment for being lost would be a mite less if a man dropped a few coins on his way out?"

"Silver?" Xenia said, eyebrows raising.

"I'd not insult you with silver. Maybe gold..."

"For five gold coins, I can have you tied up outside and beaten by these mutes. Their arms are stronger but their status is higher. And at least they do not brag."

"I am an old man, and humbly sorry for wandering into the wrong part of your palace. Of course this is your space to protect, and you must. But also strength and power like yours leave room for mercy, especially for the aged and infirm. My ankle-bones, they pain me, and a whipping would just slow me more when I need to be fast."

Xenia just smiled. Her eyes narrowed like a cat pretending to sleep.

"I have steel, of course."

Now she patted a dirk that lay across her chest on a sash.

"Not the steel I meant." He reached into a pocket for a steel penny. The guards tensed but not too much, not to the point of drawing their bronze short swords, and they relaxed when the coin plinked onto the wooden table. If he was right, they heard nothing; but Xenia sat back in her chair, braced her feet up on the table, and waved them all away.

Then Chans was back outside the walls, and quickly outside the palace. There was plenty of money spread around his pockets and purses. Plenty of coins to buy a place to sleep, a woman for company, a nice jug of wine.

And information.

But first, he needed to visit the Tomblands.

From the palace, the tombs were a good bit of travel. He walked the mile between the palace and the city on a road of crushed white stone. It was quick going, although he had not missed Old Father Sun up in the north. The heat and light beat on his face, his shoulders, cut through his fur disguise and made him sweat. By the time he reached the edge of town, he stank and glistened, like one of the rot-smelling fruits they liked to the east in the lands of Lurk.

"They stink to keep the monkeys away," a trader had told him once. A tiny man, only the size of a child, with a huge head. "They stink to say, 'do not eat me.'"

In Chans' opinion, it was wise to ever listen to such messages.

Through the edge of the city, past the shops that catered to the wealthy. Over a stone bridge, a river running slow beneath it. Soon it would flood, nearly touching the bottom of the bridge, but for now it seemed a weak thing, hardly more than the flow of a man's piss in the snow.

Then out through the Sun Gate.

That damned thing nearly burned his eyes out when he looked at it. All polished up to catch the light, to let people know they left the lands of mortal women and men and set to walk the paths of the Gods.

But what was out there? Half a day away, through gritty sand and rock, near to the edge of the Yellow sea, why, there were only graves.

Massive graves, and spectacular, sure. Towering, some of them, others tunneling. Always fascinating, sometimes instructive, even humorous. But graves all the same. Each housed a corpse and some housed the dead servants of long-dead masters. A few held whole battalions of the dead, modified to have the heads of crocodiles or lions or birds, to fight some imagined enemy in the sky.

But they were all dead.

If he remembered just right, rather than being pure, they all stank of spices and salt.

But there was a tomb he had to see. To visit, to touch.

The Gravetender had made it for him a long time ago. In truth, it should be in pieces now, the component parts spread out among newer projects. He had lost his bid for the Kingdom. His brother had won – and with mercy, no less, if banishment on pain of death could be called mercy. Truthfully, such was hardly the worst Ynn had ever done.

But Chans thought it would still be out there. His own final resting place, rotting gently under the sun in this place of death and sand. And he needed to see it.

***

Dllyx stood just as Xenia came into the throne room. She lingered on the dais just a moment, until she was close, before coming down. She was not quite so tall as her guard-captain so she liked to retain that elevation as long as she could. "Walk with me," she said.

"Yes, My King."

The two strode out of the audience room and down a passage towards the residences. Windows opened on the left onto a hot day, a close sun, the heat and dust safely on the other side of plaster and expensive glass.

"How may I serve?" Xenia said.

"I want to keep you close," Dllyx told her. She touched the other woman's hand. "I trust you. I want you always on hand. Keep dangerous surprises nearby."

"Lions, My King? Jackals?"

"Yes. I hear tales of a strange man wandering the residences." She kept her pace even, her voice flat.

"A trader," Xenia said, matching Dllyx as she could. "Furs, children, steel. He has been dealt with."

"If he comes back, bring me his hands and feet."

"Yes, My King. Lions are not subtle; they may be somewhat shorter than you imagine."

"Gnawed or not, bring them." They came to a crossing of paths. An archway led out into the sun to the left where pleasant gardens awaited royal pleasure. Straight ahead lay the proving grounds where soldiers and animals both practiced their predatory skills. To the right lay the residences. Dllyx went that way and Xenia kept pace. "Another thing."

"Yes, My King?"

"I need a crew with picks and ropes. We will go into the Tomblands soon, perhaps on short notice. Some monuments want defacing. Have them ready."

"Will twenty do, My King?"

"Perfect. And make sure they are ready to get blood on their hands. There may be resistance. I hope there is."

Xenia stayed quiet.

Dllyx reached the place she wanted: a staircase that rose above the apartments, into a small room full of parchments and vellum. It stank like a rendering plant up there. She jogged up the steps. At the top, she cracked the door and listened. Wyrrn droned on in there about some damned thing.

"He felt around on the floor for the hammer but he could not reach it. His friend was too heavy, and too strong. A worthy warrior, your father named him, each time he told the tale. He had no choice but to take out the man's eyes with his thumbs, then break into his brain. Behind the eye sockets the bone is thin and weak, you see. Even with no weapons it is easily broken. And the brain is the seat of life. The embalmers think it is of no consequence, something extra the gods gave us – but no man can live with no brain."

Jul was silent. Dllyx pushed in further, expecting to see him gazing out of a window or down at his feet, but he sat on a cushion near the teacher. His eyes were wide and his mouth half-open. She ducked back out, unnoticed, not wanting to break whatever strange enchantment this was.

Wyrrn went on. "He took with one hand and gave with the other. Decate was your father's only friend, the only man he ever loved or trusted. They fought together, warred, caroused as young men do. To kill him by his own hand was the highest honor. Decate's place in the stories was assured and he was to be buried at the right hand of your Father when Ynn's time came. But to rob him of his eyes...

"All through the afterlife, Decate must stumble along at Ynn's side. Eager to protect, to offer good counsel, but unable to see dangers before they arise. Salvation and damnation in one act."

Tell the boy how Ynn raped his only daughter, Dllyx thought, but pushed that away. It was ugly. Too much. He was interested; let him be. A little hero-worship might be just what the boy needed. And besides, ruling this place was a job for the cruel.

Bait

Nik stumbled across the remains.

Of course they had all known the orchard was no longer safe. They went out in pairs then, when that didn't work, in threes. Then only in the brightest parts of the day. Still, though, every few days someone went missing.

Where did they all go?

It seemed like magic. Bad magic.

But here were parts. Of whom, Nik could not say. Bones crunched under his sandal and he stopped, backed up, knelt to investigate. The two women with him halted. They had spears ready, tipped with their best bronze heads.

In the dirt, he found small bones, maybe fingers. A few bits of rib. But they did not seem random, not scattered as a scavenger would leave them. And the more he stared, the more a smell found its way out of his undermind, into his real thoughts.

Death.

It was always there, always nagging at consciousness in this little village by the orchard.

The small bones led in a straight line to larger bones, hidden partially in grass that grew up wherever trees cast no shadows. Those bigger bones to larger still. Ribs to the short bones from limbs, to the longer ones, vertebra interspersed in a repeating pattern. At the end, twenty or so feet from the start of the trail, lay a skull.

Human.

The smell was stronger still. The woman behind and to Nik's right covered her mouth and nose with one hand. The other leaned between her own knees and retched.

Past the skull, something dark glistened in the harsh daylight. Beyond it, something wet seemed to move as the trees above made dapples of light that played through the relative darkness.

"I do not want to look," Nik said.

"Nobody wants to look," said the woman with the hand over her face.

"I already lost my last meal," said the other. Wim, her name was. Short, stocky, brave. Good with a blowgun or a bow. "I will go."

"No," Nik said. "You brought the spear. I will look. You protect me. It will be nearby."

"What will?" Wim said, but Nik knew she knew, so he said nothing back.

Two steps. Three. The things on the ground were pieces of whoever's bones these were. Strips of skin at first. Then parts from inside. Eyes. Liver. Kidneys. Heart. Lungs. Entrails. Many smaller things he did not recognize and did not want to. Finally, at the end of that path, the brain.

"Who was this?" he said. But there was no way to tell.

"Five people gone," Wim said, "and this could be any. We know now they are dead."

"What could do this?" said the other woman. Rul. Tall, thick-boned. No teeth in front – she liked to fight. "An animal?"

"A pattern," Nik said. "Animals do not sort through bones and organs. Do they?"

"Baboons?" Wim suggested.

"A cat," Rul said. "My father kept a cat as a pet. To keep the place free of vermin. He fed her table scraps. And every day, she would bring something home, into the room. A mouse. A bird. Sometimes a snake. And she would carve it up into pieces, spread them around. 'Look,' she might have said. 'See how I earn my keep.'"

"A cat," Nik said, trying the words out. "A gigantic cat, bigger than a woman, silent as nightfall. And it wants us to be proud of it?"

"Not proud," said Wim. "Afraid."

Above, in the trees, there was a noise. Almost a growl. Nik thought it sounded a little like laughter. His bladder let go. Hot urine spilled down his leg, stained the front of his loincloth. "I am afraid," he said, whimpering.

"I am afraid," Wim affirmed.

They both stumbled backwards, towards the meeting shack where they had chosen to live communally until this threat was resolved. Walls of grass and palm frond were hardly protection but it would make them feel safer. Nik, seeing nothing in the trees and knowing his eyes could only fail him, turned to walk forwards and make better time.

"Rul?" he said.

Wim spun, too, a full circle. Staring, glaring into the shadows of peach trees, into the branches, at the sky. "Rul? Where are you?"

This was how it always happened. There and then gone. No amount of protection, no number of watchers made a difference. Nik started to run, knowing his legs must fail him just as his eyes had. The thing, the cat, whatever it was... if it wanted him, it would take him. The speed of mortal legs might as well be palm fronds and grass.

"What could do this?" Wim said. "What could take her from between us?"

Nik, breathing heavily as he sprinted, called back over his shoulder: "Something evil."

***

Korina set the last bit of metal into the crucible. It was a big crucible, as big as both her hands spread out wide. A lot of metal sat in it. Steel coins, bronze fittings, a touch of gold. Some tin, some copper. Silver studs from men's ears. Randomly, as an afterthought, some of the green glass Yohn had collected, a thing given her as a gift after his first outing.

An absurd combination of things in truth. If alloyed in a natural fire, under usual conditions, the thing she made would be next to useless. Both soft and brittle, full of impurities.

The fire was hot enough. She used a pole to slide the crucible through a slot, then shut the hatch. The bellows awaited and she plied them, dirty, smelly things made of leather and wood. They breathed fresh air on the coals. The gods of fire and chaos liked fresh air, liked to burn it. The place sweltered.

Korina's skin glittered in the firelight that escaped around the edges of the oven chamber. Bits of metal, tiny flakes, had embedded themselves in her skin over the years until she came to look like a piece of her own work. Dark, strong, awaiting a good polish.

With the door shut, Korina could not watch the fires burn or the metals melt together. That was a loss. The best things in life were behind the shield of stone and earth and metal that kept the fires from her skin. Molten iron would be a thing to see. Molten rock would be better, but no fire she could make would burn so hot. She tried to picture them in her head, the bits of scrap and coin, a fortune, going soft. Shimmering on the edge of cohesion, suddenly losing form as a bubble of soap bursts, drooping into a red-white pool.

When the time seemed right, she opened the hatch, hooked the stone crucible with the pole, and dragged it out.

Now was a delicate time. She had to use tongs, protect herself behind a leather shield, to pour the metal into its mold. A rectangle in stone, eight inches by three by three deep.

As usual, she spilled none of it. The glowing fluid came quickly to rest at its lowest stable point, filling the mold perfectly. And there it began to cool.

Korina set aside her protections and came as close as the heat would allow. Squatted on her heels. Watched.

The light of it reflected in her eyes.

***

Far away, Nik pleaded with the head-woman of the village. "You have to come away with me. You all have to come. It is no animal out there, no bear or tiger. It is nothing we have seen. It is no ghost or ancestor to be appeased. It is evil. And it will kill us one by one until we are all dead."

"If we leave, we starve," the woman said. Like all the head-women, she was bigger than Nik. Tree-tenders like him hardly ate more than the bats they could catch. The royalty ate fruit and honey, meat and mead. "All our trees are here. All our crops. Our farms. Mangos, peaches, bananas."

"I know it," Nik said. "And when you are dead, what will you eat then? Come away, come away! Come away and live! We can take seeds..."

She would not hear him. "Go if you like. If you go, stay away. We have no need for cowards among the trees."

He backed up, shocked. "Banished?"

"If you wish it."

"If I leave, others will follow. Who will collect your fruits then? Who will keep you fed?"

"Then stay."

"Not possible. Not... Send me away, but not banished."

"What do you mean?" she said. She shook her head, a gesture of interest that rattled the silver jewelry around her neck, dangling from her ears.

"A quest."

"An errand? Like the old people?"

"Just that," Nik said. He sat down on the bamboo floor with his legs crossed, awaiting the anointment as in the stories. Head bowed, he said, "Send me to find rescue. Send me to bring help. If you will not come away, we must find some power who can fight this thing."

"If you like," the head-woman repeated. She took a short knife from her belt. It was stained from acidic fruit juices, black and green. She used it to slice her thumb. Blood welled up, and that she rubbed over her palms until they were slick. "You are tasked. Sent on an errand. Bring us a hero, Niklotolous Bactro. Bring us a hero, become a hero." As she spoke, she rubbed the blood into his oily black hair.

He remembered his mother touching his head like that. When she had lived, she would rub palm-oil into his scalp. Then she would sharpen her shears, plop a bowl over his head, and cut off all the hair that stuck out. Now he did all that himself, his mother having passed on.

She never saw these evil times, he thought. *A blessing to die while the world was good?*

Then she was done, more ritual words mumbled. He had not been listening.

"Time to go," she said, and turned to a bowl of fruit on her bamboo table. She picked a nice fat peach and took a bite. Juice dribbled down her chin, dripped onto her cleavage.

Nik quickly gathered his few possessions from the common house. A spear, a blowgun with a few feathered darts, a sling. A net bag with some food in it – bats. Then he walked away from the orchard that had always been his home, fare-welling nobody, telling none of his mission.

I will never see them again. When I come back, they will all be dead, cut apart, arranged among the trees.

From high up among the narrow branches where spiders grew large enough to capture birds, a great black cat watched him go.

***

Fum wished his brother were here. Moburu had always loved a good fight. Then again, eleven to two was hardly better odds than eleven to one, and Mo would likely insist on doing this thing honorably: calling out each soldier person-to-person, trusting they would have an honor code that valued being butchered by one of the world's foremost warriors.

Not a one of these soldiers could have stood against his brother, Fum was confident. But neither would they line up for slaughter.

They ran north, doing nothing to cover their tracks or take any care. Fum followed from a distance of about a mile. Out here, the land was knee-deep grasses and gigantic anthills, a few outcroppings of rocks or copses of trees. He kept low, back aching, knees twinging. When a soldier looked back, he dropped even lower and froze.

Deer and antelope had eyes made to look for flat horizons. If he were chasing a gazelle, it would have seen him six times today. But he pursued humans. Their eyes were made for seeing what they expected to see. In this case, wild nothing. So long as he presented no human silhouette, he would be safe.

Except that the troupe before him angled now towards a copse of willow trees, the kind shaped like fountains. Branches erupted from central trunks to rise high into the air and then splash back down to the ground in green and golden arches, leaves spilling in mad disarray, in tumultuous order. Twelve feet tall, thirty or so trees. Enough for eleven people to disappear from view.

What might they do with privacy?

Two of them turned around at once. They set their spears and scanned in Fum's direction, away, back again. He dropped and froze. This was no mere glance over the shoulder now but some tactic. The rest of the troupe kept running. Fifty feet from the copse. Twenty. Then they were gone, rushed into cover. The two watchers remained.

Human eyes were made to see what they wanted. Fum had seen complacency. Used to easy victories, he had thought he was winning. And now enemy eyes watched the land between him and them. Human eyes would see more than only human forms but any movement at all.

Long ago, when he was just five years old, the palace naturalist had taught him how to pin insects to boards. She had a board as tall as Fum had been with hundreds of little insects stuck to it, impaled by tiny bronze nails. Collection and study. They were beautiful in their way but Fum's heart had been soft then. The necessities of palace life had not sunk in, not all the way, and he thought what it must be like for the bug she had him stick to his own board.

A moth, plump and hairy, with beautiful wings the color of sand. It made no sound, no human shriek of pain, only beat its wings until it realized it was dead.

Now I know. Now I am the moth, pinned in place not with a tiny nail but by human eyes.

The day aged. Noon had been hours ago. Out here on the plains, days wore on and on. The horizons seemed close enough if one only turned in a circle, but the distance from one to the other at the pace of the sun seemed interminable. Fum knew patience was his only plan.

The eye would see movement. If he moved, then the pursuit would turn again. He would once more be the prey. So he hunkered down, muscles screaming now as he incremented towards the ground at the pace of a slug – or an indifferent sun. Only the dark could win the day for him.

The soldiers did not move except to turn their heads. An hour passed, and another. The two hours felt like days and only the passage of the sun told of it passing at all. A thing learned in the palace, though, was patience.

When one reached for an orange, one did so gently, with care, after checking the skin for marks. To peel it was an act of great caution. Then it must be sliced. Slowly, deliberately. The Prince who casually popped fruit into his mouth without looking for needles, smelling for poisons, well, such Princes died young. Plans set into motion might take years to arrive at their fruition, or be merely distractions from plans that took decades.

Thus when dark finally came the two soldiers had long ago grown tired of their watches and backed towards the trees, taken seats where they could find them. And Fum, though fatigued, was still ready for action.

There was a moon this night. Slender, but enough for gross movements to be betrayed. The watchers might be replaced by now with fresher eyes. So he stayed low and moved slowly. Directly towards the copse. He let his water gourd drop into the grass, tied his rope around his arm to keep it from catching or rustling.

Lateral movement might be seen even in such weak light. But a thing creeping closer might not move at all, only grow slowly in the view of the watcher. In bright light, a dangerous tactic. In the dim...

Fum thought again of Moburu. If he had his brother's prowess he could just charge into the copse and lay about himself, hacking and stabbing.

And then what?

Then more soldiers would come, wondering what had befallen their brethren.

Here was a level of warfare Mo had never comprehended: the psychological victory. *Still, I could use his muscles now.*

The sun was two hours gone by the time he was close enough to hear voices. They were low, barely more than whispers. Without knowing the language, he guessed it was standard camp chatter. *The food is terrible and there is not enough of it.* That sort of thing. Banter, play. Minimizing danger, exaggerating the worth of the group. Things to keep the night at bay.

Closer still. Soon, the trees dominated his vision, just a black hump before him. He focused on silence, crept ever forwards. Finally, he was close enough to see as well as hear.

Two sentries, both facing his way. One moved her head, scanning the far horizon. The other was still as the moon but he heard her breathing, used his ears to guide his eyes to her dark form against the dark trees.

Close enough for some kind of strike. But what?

Moving with grotesque slowness, he let his cloak fall from his shoulders. In front of the two sentries, using every trick he had learned to evade detection, he tied the sword across the spear to make a rough cross, fixed his cloak to it, tied the corners tight to the bottom so it would not flap. He planted it in the sentries' line of sight, just thirty yards in front of them.

Then he withdrew a few yards and skirted the copse, a wide enough distance that his aching slowness was risky but possible. By the time the moon had set the copse was behind him, the sounds of snoring and whispering giving him a sense of direction for a time. And when the sun rose, he was dead asleep in a copse of his own, bedded down like a fox under a willow.

Ropes

A man lay in the tall grass.

The causeway was behind them. The way into the forest, into the Greenlands, was inland. The road did not go that way. Gareth had stopped and waved goodbye to the road three days ago, then turned occasionally to see how long it took to disappear from his vision.

Only a few hundred strides. Then this trackless grassland had sprung up out of the marsh.

Yesterday they had passed a house. It had a barn and a heavy wooden fence that looked like it got repaired frequently. The slats did not all match and some were broken, nailed back together. The place smelled funny, something Gareth did not recognize.

Now there were no buildings to be seen. Ahead lay the tree line, the boundary between what Hitai could claim as her preserves on their most ambitious day, and what the Greenlanders might die to defend. This was the edge of the map and, in effect, unsettled, unoccupied land that kept the two nations at peace.

Gareth saw the man first. The tall grass made it hard to see anything at a distance but they followed a rough trail of bent-down, trampled-down stalks. A pathway, almost, with grass growing up tall and brown as high as any of them. Gareth went first, then Whilla, Guarl, and Xin Ban. Along that path, straight ahead, lay the human form.

"He might still be alive," Gareth said.

"Who?" said Whilla, right behind him.

He stopped, moved to one side so she could see.

"Oh. Man in the path. Looks dead," she told Guarl behind her.

Gareth had his half-spear in his hands. There was just no other good way to carry it. He walked forwards, keeping the sharp end between him and the fallen person. Whilla followed with her spear. Close behind him, she was able to keep the point well out ahead of him.

"We know this man," he said when they were within a few feet. "The man with the lasso. He dragged me from his horse."

"Haven't seen any hoof prints," Guarl said. "Or scat."

"Lions," the man said, croaking. "Lions killed the horses. We killed the lions. Hyenas ate the whole mess. Killed... Oh, three good men."

"What happened to you?" Gareth said, taking a cautious knee beside the man.

"She stabbed me," he said. He had his hands over his ribs on one side. Black blood caked his fingers. Nothing new seemed to seep out. Flies stuck to his skin, big and small ones.

"Fewer men to share with," Gareth remembered.

"Her very words," the man said. "Or close enough. I don't hardly remember now. I remember you."

"You should," Whilla said. "It was only days ago."

"He's dying," said Guarl. "His mind is going. On to whatever comes next. Maybe he will see the gods, in the sky. In the dark."

"Dark..." The man sucked in a breath. "Dying, yes. Too much to ask mercy. She stabbed me in the chest. I'll live another day, maybe. Or the hyenas will come back, rip my guts out. She wants that. They spend their time here, fill their bellies, they don't dog her trail anymore."

"Mercy?" Gareth said.

"After what she did to you. What we let her do. It was too much. We're just honest thieves. Me and Loram. Didn't want to get into no killings. No... whatever that was. Torture. Got a soul, I do. Murky, but mine. No, what we let her do..."

"Doesn't matter," Gareth said. The man started to talk but he went right over him. "It doesn't matter. It was for something, and that matters more."

"Tell yourself," the man said. "Make it true. I heard you whimpering."

"You did worse than that to me," Gareth said. Then he showed the man the half-spear. "You made me a killer."

"I did?"

"Yes. Your friend. Loram? I shot him, didn't I? In the eye. Fell off his horse, dead. You'll see him soon."

Whilla muttered to Guarl. Xin Ban covered her eyes, lowered her head.

"Yes," the man said. "Mercy. My name is Homa. And I beg it. I beg mercy. Use it. Use that spear. It's black enough for this."

Gareth ran his hands over the man's body. Through his pockets, under his shirt. Took away an empty purse, a dull bronze knife he probably ate with. Under his body, Gareth found the slender length of rope tied into a loop.

"You could have done it yourself," he said. "With this knife, or this rope."

"Rope's too long and I've no tree, besides. Knife's too dull. And anyway, I am a coward. You know that. Worse, worse."

"Worse than cowardice?" Gareth said, standing. He affixed the rope to his own belt, handed the knife to Whilla.

"Worse, yes. Mercy. You have to have mercy for me as I've none for myself."

Gareth spat into the tall grass. There was nothing in his mind, nothing at all. No fear, no rage, no satisfaction. It did not even occur to him to wonder what he should do. He only stared down at this living thing, at the flies that came and went from the clots on his fingers.

Whilla stepped forward. She put the point of her spear against the man's neck.

"No," Guarl said.

"Don't," said Xin Ban.

"One of us has to," Whilla said. "We can't just leave him out here for the animals. He begged. I'd want you to. I'd hope you could."

"We could try to carry him with us," Xin Ban said. "Gareth is strong. You are strong."

"Never make it," the man said. "Dead soon. Ah, it hurts. Did I tell you?"

"Together, then," Guarl said. "All together. Don't take this on yourself." He put his hand on the butt end of the spear. Looked to Xin Ban.

She shook her head, flashed her teeth. Scared, disgusted. "Don't ask me to."

"Then she's a killer on her own," Guarl protested. "Her and Gareth, they'll carry it all. For us. I won't let them carry this for me. I'll carry it myself. Together. With them."

"Then I'll be a killer," Xin Ban said, crying.

Gareth turned his eyes away from the dying man. "You already are. We are all the same. The second I let that arrow go, we all became killers. You know that. Let's finish this." He took hold of Whilla's spear low down, near the point.

Choking on tears, Xin Ban came around. She held Gareth's hands, not really touching the spear.

They did not need to count or talk. When they were ready, they all pushed at once. And the man died under their hands.

Tears filled up Gareth's eyes. He had cried for what he had lost, for his innocence. Mostly at night, when the others thought he was sleeping. He had cried for what had been done to him but mostly for what he had done, for killing that man. His punishment, it had seemed, was his due. You kill, you suffer.

But now he did not cry for himself. He cried for Guarl. For brave Whilla. And most of all for Xin Ban.

I'm sorry you have to be me. I don't deserve you and you don't deserve this.

***

"Camp?" Gareth said, eyeing the sky. There was still daylight left.

"That's the Greenlands," Xin Ban said. "Fresh ground. New place. I feel like we should stop here and cross in the morning."

"Why?" Gareth said, touching his chin. He thought he knew why. The darkness in there made him nervous, but not too nervous to recall how it had felt to slide the point of Whilla's spear into that man's body. His own pain and shame reared up as if it could protect him from the memory.

"Why?" Xin Ban said. "Well, maybe you think it's a mad idea, but I just don't want to carry what we did into there. I want to start over fresh, on a new day."

Whilla put her hand on Xin Ban's shoulder. "That's not crazy," she said.

Gareth thought: *we will still be guilty in the morning*. He kept the notion to himself. His friend certainly knew it already.

Xin Ban made a fire. Guarl cleared grass away from the edges. Ample fuel lay within easy reach; Whilla gathered dead wood without going among the trees.

Those were a wall of darkness rising starkly up out of the savannah. There was hardly any transition. Here were sere tan grasses in a waving sea, as far back as they could look. Here were the trees poking a hundred feet up, higher, in nearly a straight line. And if the grass shortened closer to the trees, turned green, it was hard to notice against so severe a boundary.

Dusk dropped down around them as the fire rose up. Xin Ban coaxed it with dry grass and tinder, twigs and then thicker branches and finally a log. Whilla brought more logs and put too many on so that their fire must have been a beacon for miles upon miles.

Gareth put the fire at his back, let it warm him as he stared off across the grass, into the night. Towards home.

"I wonder what they're doing," Guarl said from beside him.

"Telling the young ones tales in the long hall," Xin Ban said. "The Blind Master and the Bronzeworker, the stories we loved most." She sat by the blaze with her feet nearest, stretched away from the heat. She looked not towards home but into the heart of the fire. "And Korina is smelting something, starting something despite the hour."

"She never rests," said Whilla. "Maybe we will forget what rest is, too. Crossing the Preserves, tracking through this forest. In search of..."

"My father," Gareth said. "And his sword. Her sword."

"He made her a sword and she brought it here," Guarl said, repeating an old story as though they were in the long hall with the attention of young children. Kittens. "It was her pass, her token. A trade. They let her go on to the lands beyond and, in exchange, they found out where he had gone."

"He was a good man," Gareth said.

"They said he wasn't," Whilla said. And this was all part of the old story, too.

Then, something new: "Are we good?" That was Xin Ban.

"I don't know," said Guarl. "What does it mean to be good? Or bad? We killed that man. We might have tried at least. What if he was wrong?"

"You make choices," Gareth said. "You choose up. Sometimes you're right, sometimes wrong. Was that dead man good or bad? Who can say? Did he want to steal or did he have to? He took your sister, Whilla. We can hate him for that. But what else did life offer him?"

"He felt bad for seeing you hurt," Xin Ban said. "Does that mean he was good? We felt bad for killing him. Are we?"

Whilla stood next to Gareth and looked where he looked. Stars glimmered weakly and smoke tantalized her nose. "We did what we had to do."

"And maybe he did, too," Gareth said. "Maybe my father just did what he had to. Just like us, like that dead man. Like Yohn."

They all thought about it.

"Like Chess," Whilla offered. "My mother never wanted to be what she became."

"Like Moburu," said Guarl. "The little ones never sleep when we tell them about him. I can only sleep because Yohn saw him die. Lived long enough to say so."

"Yeah," said Gareth. Such talk troubled him: to be like Moburu just from doing what was needed, to lose remorse. "Is remorse what it means to be good?"

"Your father felt it," Xin Ban said. "Your mother complained every day that he felt it too deeply. That she lost him to it. He wandered the village, sat at the forge stroking his face, worrying over it. That's why he made the sword. Not to save Jac. To save himself."

No-one talked after that. Crickets began to sing in the dark and that seemed all the comment that was needed.

***

Xin Ban wiped her face with her hands, wishing for a spring of clean water. Wishing for the unchanging lake that had finally betrayed them by not being immortal. There were a few swallows in her water skin and she sucked at them, wanting more, wanting enough to submerge in. To wallow, to float.

Sun rushed across the grasslands. She watched it rise then watched her companions struggle into wakefulness. It had been a long night.

Gareth made his water, then came back and said, "I dreamed someone passed us by in the night."

"Someone did," Xin Ban responded, looking away.

"You didn't wake us? Why?"

I was afraid you would kill them. "Just one person. A small man. He thought he was quiet but he was not. He was frightened of us. I watched him watch us for a while. I wondered if he would come to us. He seemed to need something. To want something. He only went away, out of the woods, into the grass."

"He could be out there," Gareth said. "Looking for something. Waiting for us to sleep again."

"I don't think so," said Whilla. "He will never have a better chance than last night. Three asleep, one awake."

Gareth stared out into the grass as though he could see the man, check his progress. There were buzzards in the sky, circling, hunting. In the distance, giraffes stretched over the horizon, black against a pale blue sky, and something trumpeted.

"We should go," Guarl said. He thumped Gareth on the shoulder. "The future isn't back there. It's in here. In these woods, or through them."

"I guess you're right," Gareth said. The four loaded up their things, shouldered packs, and crossed out of the past.

Dawn had hardly touched the inside of the woods. Here at the edge, they were unforested, raw, wild. Trees with heavy leaves dropped acorns all around so every step was crunchy and satisfying. Fallen leaves and twigs added a springy cushion. And a smell pervaded the place, several smells all melanged into one.

Leaves and life. Greenness. Filtered sunshine. Bark, moss. Rotting vegetation and deep, black soil.

These were the smells of the woods, so different from the Preserves.

"It frightens me," Gareth said.

Xin Ban smiled. "Me too. A new place, a new future. The village was always the same, until it wasn't."

"Right," Gareth said. "It frightens me that the trunks of these trees grow so close together. We might lose our way."

"Or find it," Guarl said. "After all, we have small idea where we are heading. Into what."

"And behind any tree could be a monster from one of Jeen's old stories. She did love to frighten us, didn't she?" Gareth scrubbed his hair back from his face. "And Bianc was worse. Her mother's stories would give Moburu nightmares."

"All the past," Whilla said. "All those tales are behind us now. Ahead, just the dark in the shadows of trees. Something moves in the branches."

Xin Ban looked up as she trod, plodded along, feet half-dragging in the accumulated waste of the forest. "The wind," she said.

"Monkeys," Guarl said. "I see them." He pointed. "There. And there. They keep pace. Watch us."

"I wonder if they're like the Small People," Gareth said.

"Not so clever, I don't think," said Xin Ban. She smiled, but she was worried. She could not see them, could not say if they might be dangerous. But she did see fruits, high above. Something yellow and almost conical. Maybe mangoes.

"Stop," Whilla whispered.

Xin Ban realized she had forgotten to watch where she was going. She might have strode into a tree or into a gulley or tripped over a branch. She halted in place and looked ahead. Whilla pointed at something right in their path.

It was a tall, four-legged animal. Gray, curly hair covered its body, a color uncommon to the animals of the prairie or the high mountains. It looked like a hyena or a jackal but taller, slender.

"Wolf?" Gareth muttered.

"No," Guarl said. "His face is the wrong shape. Some kind of dog, though."

The dog stood side-on to them and watched, head turned, tongue lolling out. After a few moments, it turned and trotted away, quickly vanishing into the trees. As it went, the forest began to grow loud with the sounds of birds, insects, life in the trees, as if the place had been holding its breath until the dog was gone.

"A dog like that," Xin Ban said. "I wonder if it means there are people nearby. He looked made for hunting."

"Nobody makes dogs," Gareth said.

"They do," Xin Ban insisted. She started walking again and the others followed, caught up. "They make them over time by breeding this one to that until the animal has the form they want. The Kings of Hitai do it. They made cheetahs and greyhounds. Why not others?"

"Could you make a man like this?" Gareth said. "A woman?"

"Why would you want to?" she said.

Then a woman stepped into their way, twenty yards ahead. She wore soft clothing: pants, a tunic, a shawl. The day was too warm for such things. They matched the colors all around: deep green and brown, gold and soft red. She had copper skin like Gareth's, dark eyes, black hair that crept out from under her hood.

"Slavers?" she said in the high tongue of Hitai. "Child-stealers from Hitai are not welcome here. Rotho will chase you away."

He heard his name and bounded out of the woods, twigs and leaves stuck in his fur, to stand by his master's side. He seemed to grin as he panted.

"We're not Hitaian," Gareth said in the same language. "Look. We're all different."

"My mistake," the woman said. "They call me Ludia. Rotho you know. There are others. Watchers, walkers. But you are just children yourselves."

"Gareth," he said. "This is Guarl, Whilla, Xin Ban. And we're alone now. Looking for someone. Maybe you saw her. A strong woman. Dangerous, armed."

"And why would you want to find such as her?" Ludia said. Rotho stopped grinning, mouth snapping shut. His stance became tense.

"We owe her something," Xin Ban said.

"Money?" said Ludia. "Service?"

"Justice," said Xin Ban.

"Strange story." The dog relaxed. Ludia seemed to do the same. "But if it's justice you're after, you'll want to talk to the magister."

The four advanced until they were alongside Ludia, who led the way deeper, darker into the woods. Gareth said, "You did not answer whether you had seen her."

"We saw her," Ludia said. "I did not but my mates did. We watch, and we see. She wanted to go through. We might have sent her back. Had the look of a slaver about her but she was not one. Barely spoke the tongue. And she did not seem to want to be told what to do."

"You did not send her back?" Guarl said. "So what did you do?"

"Led her ahead, around the towns, out of the woods on the other side. Made her think it was her own woodcraft that got her through."

"Why?" said Gareth.

"Not hunters, us," she said. "Nor fighters. Just watchers. And if I were a hunter like you, I'd not have any interest in catching that one."

"You could lead us to where she went," Xin Ban said. "But you won't now, will you?"

"No," she said. "No, you are much too interesting, children. The magister you want, and the magister you will meet."

Xin Ban frowned. "You keep calling us children but you're barely older than me. I'm a woman but for a marriage."

Gareth came alongside and squeezed Xin Ban's arm. "It's good," he said. "We can find out about my father. Then we can go on and do the other thing."

Xin Ban smiled. It was a habit, a reflex. Her feeling, though, was something between dread and anticipation.

Metal

She started at dawn, a rare night of sleep behind her.

The green glass had scorched, charred, blackened, but had not melted. It was perhaps incapable of melting.

Korina dumped the ingot out of the mold. The vermidion had floated to the top and so was invisible now on the other side of the ingot. The metal made a satisfying sound as it dropped to the bronze anvil, low and ringing, a pure note. She intended to make it ring many more times.

Her hammer was steel, obtained at great expense in trade. An investment. If she could work iron, it would pay for itself many times over. The first job was to flatten out the ingot into a long rectangular plate. She hit it twice: hard-soft. Strike-bounce. The sound was good, the feeling unfamiliar. Bronze gave way quickly but this new alloy was solid and strong. It barely dented and did not fracture.

She hit it again. Tap-bounce. Again. Repeated a hundred times.

The ingot started to stretch, warming under the hammer, elongating and thinning. The going was slow, slow. But Korina was patient. Most people went to the long hall to eat when the sun was high in the sky but Korina kept working, kept hammering. Now the metal had stretched out to a shape that seemed vaguely like a blade: long and flat. The vermidion had splintered and ground, resolved into dust, spread in a smear across part of the bar.

She picked it up and tried to fold it in half with her hands. Even hammer-warmed, it was too strong for that. She had to put it half-over the anvil and beat it down into a right angle, then set it with the angle pointing up and hammered the angle closed.

One.

Outside, the fishers brought in their catch. Korina did not notice. She kept hammering, sweating, breathing in a slow meditation. Tap-bounce, tap-bounce, tap-bounce. Again. Don't stop, let the metal warm, don't let it cool or rest. She hammered the two layers together, back into the same long, flat shape. Now the dust of the green glass was distributed more or less throughout the bar.

At the long-hall, villagers lit fires to make their evening meal. The sun touched the mountains, those weird, layer-blended rocks, and light began to leave the sky.

She folded the bar over again and started over.

Through the night, gaining confidence, the metal learning what she wanted, she folded it three more times.

When the sun rose again, she stepped from the forge, enticed by the smell of bread. A rare treat, made with flour acquired in trades. A hard loaf sat in a brown wicker basket, covered with a bit of wool. There was butter, too, and a bit of roasted fish.

An offering. Probably the Xin family. They treated her like the ghost of a relative, the honored dead to be appeased and respected with gifts of food. And she was like that: hardly seen, solitary, mythological.

In any case, the bread tasted good. Strength re-entered her tiring arms and shoulders. The fish brought warmth, clarity of mind.

And back to work.

That day she folded and re-hammered the bar four more times, twice dead cold and twice after heating it to an orange glow in the forge-fire. The last time, she sprinkled it with ashes from the coals.

The next day, Korina rested. She ate the offerings brought by villagers, bathed in the lake water, and slept. If she dreamed, she did not remember.

Then, the work again.

Now the blade needed to be shaped. That meant working out the shape of a tang at one end, its length twice the width of her right hand. She used no molds, no shears, only the hammer, coaxing out the shape she wanted with compression-heat and artful tapping, making flat shapes with the anvil, the flat side of the hammer. Then the blade itself, three fingers wide at the bottom, one finger thick, tapering to two fingers at the end and the thickness of parchment. She put a point on it, regretting the deadliness but admiring the beauty. When her sweat fell on the blade, she did not wipe it away.

It was nearly done now.

Korina brought in wood to stoke the fire. There was another meal in a basket by the door and she brought it in, thought about eating.

An offering.

Logs clattered into the forge. It was too hot to stack them. She had a metal rod to move them around with, push them back. Then charcoal made in the hills north of the village and reserved for special work. Roasting whole animals on feast days, smelting ores.

Again, she sat back to watch the wall, to imagine the fire raging inside.

I miss the old days.

Not the war, although the threat of death had added something to life. An urgency, a need to love fiercely. But the fires, the simplicity of bronze, the easy company of her father. Yohn. Bianc. Bero, her apprentice, gone off now to his own life in Hitai, wedded and proudly a father.

Her stomach talked to her. Chattered and twisted. The smell of food reminded her she was only human, not a spirit, not an ancestor. Just a woman.

She picked up the basket. The fire was hot now. It raged through the wall, baked, wafted heat across the forge. She sweated and contemplated the covered meal. At last, she opened the hatch. Put the basket on the floor. Pushed it inside with the metal rod.

An offering.

She watched through the opening as the basket quickly took flame, as the wool withered away, floated off as white ash. As the bread blackened, burst into golden fire. Soon, the whole thing was just a black smear on the already sooty floor.

It was time.

She put the metal bar into the forge, now clearly a sword and nothing else, nearly robbed of any other potential. She pushed it in, let it rest in the greasy soot, watched it.

Her skin started to turn pink. The flecks of bronze and soot embedded in her began to respond to the fire, to hold heat and give it to deeper layers of skin. Then she began to redden.

So did the sword.

When it glowed a bright red like crisp apples ready for biting, she dragged it close with the pole, then took it up with her tongs. She had to carry it far out from her body: the thing wanted to burn her up. The heat was like a light too bright to look at, like a truth that, once learned, would destroy the mind that held it.

Panting and sobbing, unaware of tears rushing over her face, she carried the blade out of the forge, down the short path to the lake.

Time.

For Jeen, it had all but stood still. The griefs of yesterday were still fresh and hot: magnificently burning, glowing things like this sword. They cut her each day and kept her warm at night. If time could be still for her, if this lake spirit that made different things the same could even make the present one with the past, then it could come and take this one last sacrifice. It could come and steal the heat out of this weapon, replace it with a blessing.

She knelt. Held the sword out over the water. Slowly let her arm drop.

Lake water sizzled and spat, steamed. It had never done so before, when it was just a flat blue plane. Korina liked it, heard music in the dance of water rushing to become air, bubbling up and over the blade.

It slowed and stopped. There was a great deal of water and only this one tiny bit of hot steel. The temperature exchange was rapid, almost sudden.

When the blade came free of the water, she kept her eyes closed, not ready to see the result. Would it have some strange color, imbued with a primal essence, reduced from iron and brass and copper, tin, gold and silver to just *metal*?

She set it on the ground in front of her. Opened her eyes slowly.

It had a hard shine obscured by accumulated soot. It would need to be cleaned and polished. The color was silvery but darker than silver, darker than steel.

But plain, ordinary, unblessed.

And never mind. The lake had put nothing into the blade but it had put everything into her. Into her shoulders, arms, hands that could shred stone, a drive to finish what she started. The drive to stand for hours or days or weeks to hammer out a project, to rage at it, to become a master.

Time to finish shaping the blade.

***

"Where is Father?" Kwinderallion gritted the words out between tight teeth. The pain of childbirth was on her. She panted and waited for the next wave of sensation to move through her body.

Chess held her hand tighter. "Menfolk rarely watch the birth. He is likely with Trimb, sitting on the dock with their feet in the water."

Kwin could see through a gap in the door to the pier. Yohn's hut, more recently Gareth's, was badly in need of repair. She could see a knot of men out there but none of them looked like her father.

More of the strange feeling that was part pain, part pressure, and also something else. It was like her body did not belong entirely to her. Some of it had belonged to the baby now for three seasons – a space in her belly, at least – but now her body contracted without her willing it to. She could feel the head down there, pushing, squeezed out by this alien will that controller her body.

"It moves," she said.

"Good," her mother said. Her attention seemed to be pulled away, though.

Between contractions, Kwin said, "Is this what it was like for you, Mother? I feel so strange."

"At the time of labor, the gods help us because we do not know what to do. Especially for the first child. This is summer now, the end of summer. In our own tongue, Kwinikala. Kwinikala helps you push."

"Kwinikala. I was summer-born, too."

"Yes."

Another wave of effortless effort. Then she gritted her teeth and bore down, hard, hard, and stopped. "The baby is almost born."

"Do not stop, Kwin. Keep pushing. The baby will tell you when – oh yes, like that. Again. Again." Chess let go of Kwin's hand and moved down between her knees. "I can see the top of Baby's head. A little more effort, now. A little more. Push! Again!"

The pain was huge; the sensation of being controlled slipped away and Kwin pushed on her own, grunting with the effort. It was like lifting the heaviest sled up by the runners except the work was deep inside her body, not in her legs. And in a way it felt good, pleasurable.

Then it was done.

Chess held up a wet red little thing and Kwin squeezed her eyes shut, wanting to look and also needing a moment of rest. Only a moment. She felt so strange! The hand that had touched her womb was gone and behind it had left emptiness. Kwin was flattened, hollowed.

She cried and did not know why. Joy and sorrow seemed at once the same thing. Confronted with a choice, she chose the joy.

"The baby..."

"A girl," Mother said. "Here. Hold her. I need to cut your cord."

A little tug and that was done. Kwin put the child against her chest. The baby's skin felt hot. She wriggled then went still, perhaps as exhausted as her new mother.

"What will you call her?" Chess asked.

"I do not know, Mother. Trimb left it to me as if this were Sorub and the old ways mattered."

"Perhaps they do."

"You know, I do not even know your whole name? Here, they only call you Chess."

Chess turned to peer out the gap in the door then back at her daughter, at her granddaughter. "The day I was born, it was the end of spring, and the start of the cooling times. The starving times. That year there was snow. The latest snow we could remember. It fell on sprouting grains and killed them. That is my name: snow late in spring. In our language, Chessnagalicaricon."

Kwin had eyes now only for her new babe. Light from the gap in the door fell over the child's face. She wiped womb leavings from her face with a corner of the bedsheet. "How would I say, 'spring in the summer?'"

Chess sucked her teeth for a moment. "You just said it."

"In Hitaian," Kwin said. "I mean at home. In the north."

"This is home." When Kwin sighed, Chess went on, "I know what you mean. Be patient with an old woman. Chessnakwin."

"Can I name her that? Chessnakwin?"

"She is yours to name," Mother said.

"Thank you, Mother. Could you bring them now? Trimb and Father?"

"Yes." She went to the door and creaked it open. "Kwin. I am very proud and happy. I will be back soon to cuddle my granddaughter. But first..."

"Rest," Kwin said.

"Yes."

"I know what this cost you. To be awake, to stand with me for so long."

"I hope you never know that."

***

A steep path led up into the mountains. One side fell away into a view of the Yellow Sea in the distance, scrubby green meadows between, dead trees directly below. Conifers had been replaced, overcome by giant ferns with orange berries the size of fists and curling cones the length of Nik's forearm. The ferns looked like they might arrest a fall. He elected not to try them out.

At the top of the path lay a small monument. A cairn made of all different kinds of rocks and dotted with old relics. A shattered arrowhead. A bit of leather scrap. Things Nik did not recognize. The thing made him shiver, though.

Is there a body within?

Through some scrubby trees that hated the altitude and past the ruins of an old forge, and he was in the village. There were houses all around, some in styles he recognized. Woven reeds or thin planks, thatched rooves sometimes on thatched walls. Hanging fabrics for doors or just open spaces, not much need here for privacy or security, not much cold to manage.

And a long hall, half-finished. Started with thatched siding, slowly being rebuilt with log walls, chinked in with clay. Straw roofing over only the front few feet, almost fully replaced with tiles from clay.

There was a new forge by the lake that dominated the village. The noise of it rang in his head. Ting-ting, ting-ting, ting-ting. How could anyone stand it?

He glanced at a boat on the lake, long as four men, six aboard. It was near the shore, just pulling in next to a pier attached to the long hall. One of the men in the boat stood up, making the rest curse.

"Bactro?" he shouted. "Nik Bactro?"

His cousin, Hlom. Nik waved, tried to force a smile. It felt good to be out of the grasslands, in a place where other people lived. Away from the hyenas that had followed him for miles, days. From the lions that he knew were always close, though he never saw them.

"Hurry," Nik yelled back. "We need help."

Hlom clambered out of the boat, waving off his share of the work. "Help? What has gone wrong?"

"Something evil has come to our village, cousin. Something ghostly and hungry. They sent me to find a hero."

"And you came here?" Hlom said. "I ran away from there five years ago rather than marry your niece. What sort of hero does that make me?"

"But we both knew the stories of this place," he said. Now Hlom was close enough to touch and Nik embraced him. "This is a place where heroes are hammered out. My ears say they must be making another one."

"What? Oh, their forge-master is a mad-woman. Never one to put off work for minor things such as sleep or food. At least they made her stop hammering at night. Well, until these last few days."

"Hammering. It must be a torment. Weece is dead."

"Weece?"

The other men from the boat finished unloading their catch into barrels and baskets and started to gather around. "If you had married her, you would be bereaved. And Kalta. Marim. Lood. There is a monster, something, it takes us whether we watch or not. It can steal a man from between two of his brothers while they watch him, and they will not see. We do not find bodies, most times. When we do, the bodies are taunts, messages we understand too clearly: be afraid."

One of the village men was a white giant with red hair shot with gray, one arm only a stump. He roared something in a language Nik did not know, some giant-speech.

Could this one help us? A one-armed giant with a fiery mane?

"You need to speak to the woman," Hlom said.

"Is she a hero?"

"She was." Then he said something to the giant.

It did not soothe but seemed to excite him, to incite him. He shouted more, the words hurting Nik's ears.

"This beast must be ready to do murder. Do you speak its wicked tongue?"

"Beast?" Hlom took him by the elbow to lead him toward the long hall. There would soon be food and mead to speed the work of the day. "You mean Ham? He speaks Hitaian. We all do here. Too many tongues to manage, otherwise. He just wants to know what you're blathering about. Nice man."

"Can he fight?"

"Who knows? He can fish, though. And brag. Not so well as Erlo but well enough. Come, into the hall with you." And to the red giant he mumbled some more words. Nik understood none of them. One sounded like a name, though: Chess.

***

Chess rooted around under the bed. Little Neea had her own space now, on a smaller cot near the doorway. Their billet was near the front doors, a nod to Chess' infirmity.

Erlo, still on the bed she dug under, objected. "What are you doing?"

"It is the middle of the day, you lout," she said. "What are *you* doing, lying here full of mead while your first daughter gives birth to your granddaughter?"

"Trying to drown my sorrows."

"They learned to swim long ago," she said. She had what she needed: a mesh bag deep enough for food and a thin blanket. "I cannot say why your neighbors put up with you. Out of respect for me, maybe. When did you last help with the work?"

"I mended the nets. Two days ago."

"Ten."

"It seems shorter."

Chess stayed down on her haunches, looked her husband in the eye. "Time moves quickly when you sleep it away."

"You are one to accuse," he said, looking away. In the dark of their little space, it was hard to tell if he flushed or not.

Chess hoped so. "I understand," she said. "I really do, husband. I have laid abed since the war. All the life went out of me. What was left was pain, and sleeping helped the moments drift by. At first you came to comfort. When you could not, you just held my hand, stood by while I drifted away."

"You lost yourself in that battle," he said. "I lost you. I've just been here looking for you."

"I am not in that mug," she said.

"Bitch."

But he smiled when he said it. She said, "Well, the time for rest is over. A man came in from the Greenlands today."

"So? Did he bring marriageable daughters who need inspecting? Beer for trade?"

"No. He brought a ghost. And I am going with him to sort it out."

Erlo sat up, indignant, but then shut his eyes and held his head. "You are in no fit shape to walk down the hill, never mind chase ghosts. All but a ghost yourself, wife. Come to bed. Let me hold you again."

"You will have to let me go, husband. You have done your share of grieving, yes you have. You chased the babies while I became a weapon. And if I have lost my sharpness, well, I need it back. I have to go."

"I am coming with you, then."

"No. You will watch after Neea. After Kwin and her daughter. Shameful man – you have not even gone to discover her name yet. The last of our other daughters has gone away. Did you notice? Neea needs you. You need to be the man you were."

He threw his mug against the wall. This end of the hall was still thatch; it made a sad, rustling sound and rolled to the plank floor. "Not again with this. I lost you once."

"And I never came back," she said.

She left him there, struggling to get into his breeches. Nik waited at the door. He had a pack on his back and a dour face. *I hardly look like the hero he needs,* she thought. *I understand.*

Chess grabbed food from the hearthstone in the center of the hall. Water skins from a peg by the doors. Nothing else. "We go," she told Nik. He spoke none of the language but seemed to understand, going with her through the heavy wooden doors.

Jeen waited outside, leaning against a railing. "You can't go," she said.

"Do not try to stop me. I have to do this."

"Stop you?" Jeen said. "You did not let me finish. You cannot go alone."

Then Chess noticed Jeen had a pack, too. Hers looked fat and heavy, as big as Jeen herself. Chess wanted to object. But Jeen had nobody. Bianc was buried behind the sheepfold, a gentle death from wet lungs at a goodly age. Bero was his own man now, far away in the city. A man of standing and respect. And Yohn...

"Come, then," Chess said.

They turned to go and were halted again. Korina stood in her path, an object in her hands. It was wrapped loosely in a wool blanket, white and blue. "You will need this," she said, her voice low, eyes on the ground between them.

The thing, swaddled up as it was, looked like a baby. A tiny new Chess here to accuse the old one. Of abandonment, or weakness, or maybe worse.

But it was not a child at all. "A sword?" Chess said. "I could hardly swing one. A miracle I can even walk. These last few years--"

But Korina cut her off. "Not you. Her." She presented the thing to Jeen.

Jeen's surprise threw light over her face. Chess wanted to laugh, but instead helped throw back the blanket from the sword.

It lay there on Korina's hands, on the blanket. Light rippled off it as off the lake, slate gray as the sky, as the water. A black leather handle waited under a wide bronze guard. The sword was long, straight, double-edged. Freckled, flecked with tiny green points that caught the sun.

"It is beautiful," Jeen said. "It terrifies me."

"I hope so," said Korina. "It is made for one thing: to kill. Killing should frighten you. You should soil your clothes, scream, run into your house. Wait there for time to kill you with a clean soul."

"Thank you," Jeen said. She took the sword in her left hand. "It is light," she said. "It feels natural."

"Yes," Korina said.

"Is there a scabbard?"

"No. A thing like this... I want you to carry it bare all the way to where you are going. Always. It is sharp. It will cut you many times along the way. You will drop it, feel the burden of it. Know it. When the time comes, decide."

"All right," Jeen said. "I love you, Korina."

"I know," she said. "I want to love you, too, Jeen. My brother..." Those were all the words she seemed to have left. Korina swept away like a boat under oars, lurching into motion, slowing, lurching again.

"Grim words," Chess said.

"What if Moburu had said the same to you? Or Flax? Ten years ago, what if they had told you?"

"I did not hear them," Chess said. She set off, Jeen to her right and little Nik between them, her daughter's daughter ever farther behind.

***

Fum cracked his eyes to let in bright morning light. A shaft fell right between the branches and leaves to land on his face.

A shaft of light.

He had gone from having no weapons to having two, then back to zero. Because, in the end, spears and swords were for people willing to risk being hit back. They were Moburu's weapons, not Fum's – and probably did more good stirring up the enemy.

He guessed the hour to be somewhat after dawn, much shy of noon. He had to piss but needed to scout a little first – no good to stalk through the night only to be seen in the bright light of day. So Fum rolled over, crawled to the edge of his thicket, and parted the branches just enough to peer back the way he had come.

Four soldiers strode north. They argued as they came, all four animated and angry.

Where were the other seven?

Two women, two men. He recognized one as the first he had talked to. She had carried wood. One of the men had spoken good Greenlander. They seemed to be the leaders. The man had on Fum's cloak.

I always liked that cloak. I hope I do not get it too bloody reclaiming it.

The soldiers did not scan for tracks, did not beat the bushes. Grasslands started to ebb into woods here, making it only a few more days to the villages of the Greenlands. To beat every bush would take a lifetime.

When they had passed by, he watched a while longer for the remaining troops. Eventually it seemed they would not follow, not soon, so Fum wandered away from his new temporary home and let his bladder go.

He reflected on how he had awakened: to a shaft of light.

A shaft.

Under a willow tree.

Willow was not the best wood for a bow, but it would get the job done. Ideally, it would reinforce another wood. Compounding, if he remembered correctly. With his knife, his leftover twine and some time, he could make a single-wood bow even his brother would have to respect.

Well, maybe not Mo. Mo would just snort contempt and stick you with his javelin.

He found a likely sapling. Branches were too flexible and tended to be already bent but this tree was long and straight. Wind rustled the leaves around him as he cut it carefully at the base; the sound was as though the world were hushing him. *You are a disturbance. Be at peace.* With a little patience, the tree came free: nine feet tall and about five inches thick.

Not so simple as cutting a bough and throwing a string on it. That is what Moburu had thought. He remembered a day in the fields, playing as children were meant to play. Moburu, always the warrior, strayed too close to the tar pits in search of wood to make a practice sword. Fum might have pushed him in. The smell was awful. The tar itself stank indescribably, but it tended to catch animals. Mo reached for a stick in the sucking, steaming tar. A few feet deeper in a deer lay half in and half out, the sweet meaty smell of its roasting beneath the tar compounded by the horror of the unsubmerged half rotting.

Would Moburu have stank that way?

Too late to find out.

My thoughts dwell on my brother.

While thoughts dwelt, though, hands were busy. He stripped the branches off his trunk then set to carving away bark. It was the work of a few hours to clean away outer layers of wood, revealing the heart of the tree. Sticky work, hot work. Hunger set in and Fum considered venturing out to set snares. With a bow, though, he could secure food easily.

The core made a stave six feet tall. His knife grew blunt, slowing the process of shaping it just so, and dark had befallen him before that task was done. With a stomach aching with hunger, Fum found a likely bit of rock and set to sharpening his knife.

The next day, he finished shaping the stave. It was thick in the middle, tapered at the ends, with notches for his string. It needed to cure then in the sun. The weather cooperated. While it sat, he wandered into the next grove of trees to set some snares.

One stinky man. I owe everything to one stinky man. What was his name?

Fum was bothered that he could not remember the name of the man who had taught him to set snares, and so much more than that. They had floated together up the river from the salt flats, past the preserves, into the heart of Hitai's farmlands. Then they had floated through time, an idyll. Trapping crocodiles and worse, drinking wine, being their own men.

If not for that time, Fum might have tried to live in the palace with his sister, might have tried to wrest away her throne.

Magicians and trappers. What have they made me?

A few twists of twine, a bit of luck and patience. His stomach growled, ached, grumbled like a dog that thinks its master has forgotten it. Palace life had inured him to hunger, but what a luxury to be hungry because there was no food – rather than being surrounded by food that could not be eaten for fear of poison.

While he was there, he scanned around for anything straight enough to make arrows. One fallen branch was long and straight enough. With patience, he could split it, carve out four or five good shafts. Leaves would do for fletching so long as he did not expect his arrows to last long.

Patience. Endurance. Craft and skill.

I would have been a good king – like my father. Dllyx was a monster as much as Moburu. Both of them were all appetite and no hunger. He taught me to be a free man, a thoughtful man. Hence I could never wish to rule Hitai.

There was still work to be done. Fum rested one more night in his little willow grove and left the next morning as a hunter.

In the sunshine, armed by his own craft and on the hunt once more, it came to him.

Kwili. The trapper's name was Kwili.

Mummified

Priests. I hate priests.

Dllyx sat on the throne, Xenia a step down and to the right. She wished Ngali, the cheetah that had won her the throne, sat by her other side. She would send it to eat these petitioners.

"I am Myrsa," one said.

Dllyx catalogued the name but knew she would forget in a few hours. She had met this one before, of course, had met all of them before. They clamored for her time, for her to issue orders, to drive people to their temples, for shares of taxes.

The priest continued. "You have come to no rituals since you were anointed. You have visited no temples."

"You are a whore, yes?" Dllyx said, keeping her voice light, as though being a whore were of no consequence.

The priest's eyes narrowed. Her eight companions held their faces impassive.

Be subtle, Dllyx thought. *Isolate her.*

Myrsa said, "Your father-"

"Raped me."

She flushed a little, just around the collar of her woolen robe – a ridiculous affectation in this heat. "Your father attended the rituals. He even came to do his holy duty at the temple of Caiph."

"Well, for obvious reasons, your godly concubines hold no interest for me. None of your rituals do. I am anointed and now I need you for nothing else."

Another of them spoke, a wheezing old man with powdery hair, sweating through his own woolens. "The education of The Blood has always been part of our duties."

"He has a teacher," Dllyx snapped.

"Yes, My Qu- My King. Only, his religious education is what we mean."

He says 'we' to spread the blame. Well, they all stand here with him. Let them share it.

"Jul will be the next King of Hitai. He will sit on this throne when I am through with it. And I will not let you muddle his mind before then."

"My Qu-"

"Call me that again and I'll have you castrated. Or are you already castrated? Damned priests, so hard to keep track of which one has which silly superstition."

The old man backed away one step, mouth open, ashen skin going a shade lighter. "We mean no offense. But, My, erm, King... The Blood has always ruled with the consent of the priesthood. How do you know the wishes of the gods without our advice?"

"We are the Gods, fool," she said, and stood in front of her throne. *If only for Ngali.* Her hand ached to give the order to hunt. "Now get out. The next priest I see gets a woolen kilt and berth in the slave quarters."

When they were gone, Xenia came up the step that separated them. "My King. An admirable show of strength and ferocity. There can be no mistake that they will get nothing from you. Is it wise, though, to anger them?"

"All part of the plan," Dllyx said. "Father, dear dead father, left things unfinished here. I am the King and I will rule this place alone. No priests to intercede between me and my people."

"You hate them," Xenia said, resting one hand on the hilt of her short sword.

"Yes."

"Tell me."

"Why do you think my father made me his wife?"

Xenia swallowed. "Tradition? You were the last of his Blood left to him? Simple lust?"

"No," Dllyx said. "The priests said he had to. They said no woman could rule in her own right, not without a Bloody husband. He raped me every night until I was quick with his new heir because the priests made him do it."

***

This is my tomb.

Chans stood in front of the monument for the first time in... oh, long and long. He had changed greatly since then. The tomb had also changed.

It was a white hump, a semi-abstract shape, almost a hemisphere. It swirled up out of the brownish sand to stand against the sky, confused with the white clouds behind it. *He saw it. Back then, he saw it.* His hand touched the bag of bones at his chest.

A door opened, a rectangle of darkness to the right. Chans went there. Looked inside. A child greeted him. Eight or nine years old, decked out in exotic headwear, a golden kilt and sash.

"What's this?" Chans said. "A boy?"

"I remember you," the child said.

"I don't think so."

"Oh, yes. I built a great ankle-bone just in case you forgot."

"I see it. You are standing in it. Should I come inside?"

"Of course," the boy said. "And down the steps. The corpse is still here, Great One."

"Great? No, I am just a poor trader, a slaver."

The boy laughed. "I said I remember. You cannot fool an old man."

"A devil from the sand? Out of some mad old story? Will you spin away in a dervish with my soul?"

"Oh, no," he said. "That is what this tomb is for."

Down steep, narrow steps not made for a body like Chans'. Into the crypt below the sand. Cool air, muggy and tight, caressed what skin Chans had left to the elements. In the center of a round room sat a coffin. Plain wood, unadorned, big enough for two men but holding the remains of only one. "The proof I need?"

"Still here, still here. The tomb is really all of that, would you not say?"

"Yes. Except for her. For Dllyx. I think she will not abide by the rules."

"Rules?" said the boy. "Desert rules here. Cheetah rules. Jackal rules."

"Riddles. No, I see it clearly enough. Kill or die, yes? Murder, eat, and run when you must."

"Just so." The boy jumped up onto the plinth that held the coffin and pulled off the top. It was not even nailed down.

The mummy inside seemed deflated. Once, Chans had been a big man. Wide. Thick. Strong. Now he was dead. Withered and hollow. The artists had tried to puff out his chest, his belly, but they had failed. It was only a corpse that was too wide but empty of life.

I am Chans.

No, I have only acted his part. And I shall keep acting for a little while longer. Until the time is right.

I am Ergol.

***

The library room smelled funny and it was close with the heat of the day. The teacher was saying something about chariots. Chariots and war. Jul should have been interested. The teacher should have made it interesting. But she did not speak of the threshing blades on the wheels, how they must have spattered the enemy with their own gore. How blood must have rained down into the open mouths of screaming men. No, nor of how the wooden wheels were rimmed with bronze that crushed bones, savaged guts.

He imagined a different smell than tanned hides and vellum and parchment, different than the sweet-sour sweat of the not-mother woman who spoke. He thought of the smell of blood and rank guts. Of terror.

Slowly, he realized she was no longer talking at all.

He looked at her, and she looked at him.

"Daydreaming, are we?"

"Hardly my fault," he said. He fidgeted on his stool, uncomfortable from another humiliation. "You should teach better."

"You asked of your father," she said. "His father sent him out with these new weapons, that he had kept secret. And your father drove his chariot with his own secret: carefully bred oxen, years in the making."

"Tell me of the men he killed."

"I think you have spent all our time imagining them," she said. She had on a linen dress that looked awful for the heat. She wiped her hands on it, near the knees. "Breeding was important to your father."

Jul's eyes went wide. "Of course. He was a man, with a hero's hungers."

"Not the act," the teacher laughed. "The science. How to produce desirable traits in the offspring of given animals."

"I told you to tell me about his brother and sisters."

"I am," she said.

Jul crossed his arms and frowned. "I am getting angry."

"Good. It will help you focus. Now listen. He knew that if you bred two big oxen, their calves would be even larger. If you bred a smart jackal with a smart jackal, the resulting litter would be clever indeed. But if you curtail the breeding population to a few individuals, not only their best traits are passed along. And in the palace, brother is bred to sister. None else have the rank to marry Gods."

"He married his own daughter. He made me. He must have thought that she and he had something to give a child."

The teacher waited a little. Then she said, "His own children were all very different. Dllyx: strong, patient, direct, dishonest. Moburu: tall and able, strong but not so solid as his father, quick to rage and unpredictable. Bumbu who never grew old enough to know, not here in the palace. Exiled, sent away to live, to survive."

"And one more," Jul said.

"Just so. Fum."

"Clever. Quick-witted but weak, without the will to kill his brothers. Soft. He died on the proving grounds. I have an aunt, then, who is my mother. A baby uncle sent away and probably eaten by hyenas. If none tell him he is a prince at all, he will stay away. Uncle Moburu, who died fighting for the Starfallers he hated. But what of Father's siblings? All dead, you said."

"There is a puzzle here, boy, if you care to see it."

He stood now, paced to the door. "Call me that again and I'll have your tongue out with cold tongs. What puzzle?"

"He let her ascend," she said, uncowed. "Your sister. He let her take his throne without murdering her own siblings. Without murdering him. He murdered himself. An honorable death in combat, yes, so you have heard. But an unwinnable fight."

Jul thought about it but nothing came. "His sisters. One rode out into the desert to die. The other he married. She died in childbirth. Bumbu killed her. His brother, Ergol. Murdered in an ambush on his way north after slaves. Ergol the club-foot."

"Enough for now," the teacher said. She wiped her hands again. When she sweated, it beaded in the fine, dark hairs over her lip. "Imagine, though. Imagine if you loved the animals your mother keeps. Imagine if the cruelty of your father were not matched by the cruelty of your mother, surpassed by it. Your cruelty comes from them both but your lack of love only from her. Imagine if you were not compelled to torture them, if you did not lust after the tastes of their pain."

He opened the door to go. "I would rather imagine you were a rabbit kitten. Just big enough to fit in my hand. I wonder if I could take off all your legs a bit at a time without you dying."

As usual, she did not react at all to his threats. "If you loved them, what would you do, boy? Brothers, sisters, daughters and sons. What would you do if you loved them all the same?"

Jul left, not at all understanding, knowing there was something in the lesson that he could not see. It hardly mattered, though. There was something Wyrrn did not know. He need not solve the riddles because Ergol had come to visit him. Ergol did not trouble him with lessons but only gave him answers.

What kind of animal would Ergol be?

That question did not please him as he skipped down the stairs, out of the nasty heat of the library. He preferred to wonder about his mother.

A lamb. Dllyx would be a lamb. And Ergol could help me roast her to death.

***

A summons. To the King's own chamber.

Not good news.

Wyrrn changed quickly out of her linen dress into a leather kilt and sash as befit her rank. She strapped on no weapons, being of far too low a station for that. Her kinky black hair went up in a bun. No jewelry, plain sandals.

There was no glass to look in. Wyrrn knew she was not even nervous about her appearance, only about her survival. *Well, I always knew this work would end in my murder.*

The servant quarters were tight, cramped. One floor below was hardly worse only the people down there were slaves, property, not skilled tradespeople. In Hitai the distinction was quite fine. Being an educated person, Wyrrn had a room to herself. Hardly wider than her cot which itself was hardly wider than her body, bare stone with graffiti left over from some previous occupant, still it was hers alone.

She brushed past the linen hangings that were her only privacy. Then she changed her mind and reached back inside.

Her rank was low but there was one talisman that marked her out from the masses. Her hand found a quill. It was used, the end brown with ink much the color of dried blood.

With that in her left hand, she strode down a narrow hall, to the staircase, up towards the residences. Up there, the hallways were wider, cleaner. Murals replaced crude, semi-literate graffiti. Pictures of gods and Gods, lessons lost on the cruel people who ruled this place.

When the stranger had come to her quarters, the big man with a bad smell and strange clothing, interest and lack of rank had compelled her to invite him in. The stories he told about Ynn were either a fantasy born of fever dreams, a divine inspiration, or the tales of someone who had lived through those times.

He had the look of Blood about him: dark, fine, big-bodied. Good teeth. But only the victors had likenesses around the palace to compare to.

I should have sent him away. Not listened to him. She knows. She must know.

She stopped at Dllyx' door. Waited, took a heavy breath. Finally, she knocked.

"Enter." Dllyx sounded far away.

Wyrrn opened the door. It swung inwards heavily, not counterweighted. The room was dimly lit by two tallow candles, far away, on opposite sides of Dllyx. She sat in a wooden chair with a straight back. By her side was a stuffed cheetah. Even from here, Wyrrn could smell it.

"How may I serve?" she said. And she thought: *my passion for the histories has undone me.*

"In your usual way," Dllyx replied. "But first, shut the door."

Wyrrn complied, stood with her back against it. "What would you know, My King?"

"Come closer, woman. I am not about to harm you. I need your knowledge, your counsel. Jul says you teased him with riddles today. Offended him. Oh, do not worry. I know you try, yes. But he got all of his father's stupid stubbornness."

Wyrrn shuffled closer, the feather in her hand like a scepter. "He will see when he wishes, My King. And then you do not need the likes of me to counsel you to caution."

"No," Dllyx confirmed. "No, I need to know of the Gravetenders."

"There is only one," she said, correcting by habit.

"I have known two. And there is a third being raised. A child."

"Yes. Yes, My King. But only one who wears the headdress, holds the title."

"Who confers it?" Dllyx said, soft, gentle.

"Confers? Who?" She looked around as if the answer could be found on the floor. "They inherit it. Son from mother from father. One dies, the other takes it up."

"Do they not belong to me?"

"By way of the priests, by ritual, by tradition."

"Are the priests mine?"

"No, My King," said Wyrrn, and regretted that right away. "They belong to the gods. Not even a God-King may act against the wishes of the priests. Not for long."

Dllyx smiled. "Has a King ever executed a Gravetender? Replaced them?"

"No, My King."

"Could she?"

"A better question for the priests, I think. The gods-"

"-have no place in the matters of Gods," Dllyx finished for her. "Now. Who are these people and where did they come from? Always two of them, an adult and their child. Never three, never one. Always the same skin and hair and eyes no matter how they must interbreed with local people. Always the same voice and speech. Always the same magic of seeing the future."

"May as well ask after your own people, My King. The answer is the same."

"We come from the same place?"

"No," Wyrrn said. "No, My King. Nobody knows. The Great Ones, the New Hitaians record that they arose in some far-away land to the south, that they walked here as an entire people. Why? After a defeat or a calamity? They do not say, only that they came proudly. And the first thing they saw was the Tomblands. They saw it. They knew what it meant: immortality. They wanted it, My King. And they took it.

"But the Tomblands are not south of the city. They are west. Coming from anywhere but the west, the tombs would be the last thing they saw."

"What does that have to do with it?" Dllyx said, but she leaned forward, eyes avid.

"There are no lands to the south where people like yours abide. There are no lands on this world that scholars can name with people like yours, language like yours." She wanted to take a step back, to have the door against her skin again. "But when they arrived from wherever they came from, the

Gravetenders were already here. They had already built the tomb of the first New Hitaian King. He was so enamored of his resting place that he retained them, accepted them forever and for all time. It is written."

"They live, then, on the sufferance of a man long dead."

"A God, My King, who dwells now in the eternal sky."

Dllyx laughed. "Go, Wyrrn. Go, my historian. Sleep assured that I will not let my son murder you. You have too much value. Such wisdom. It is not to be wasted on children any longer, I think."

"Thank you, My King," Wyrrn said, and backed up to the door. She tried to push it open, found she could not. Then she remembered that it opened inwards. A second later, Wyrrn was squeezing out into the fresh, cool air of the hallway.

"A last thing," Dllyx called. "Can you draw, Wyrrn? Best to get some practice." She laughed again, and Wyrrn ran, stumbling, back to the safety of the servants' quarters. In her haste, she forgot to shut the King's door.

His Father's Sword

It rested in a stand on a shelf over the hearth. It was green like polished jade, all one color. Pure. The light loved it, glowed in it. The top edge was straight and the bottom curved so that the sword seemed like an oversized knife, just so long as a man's forearm.

Gareth stared at it. His eyes fastened on it and would not move away.

The rest of the room seemed irrelevant. A reed mat covered plain wooden boards for a floor. Log walls were dressed with off-white, smooth plaster. Overhead, a beam ceiling oppressed the space. A long, low table, the door at this end, the magister at the far end.

In front of the hearth, in front of the sword.

He stood as they entered. A graying, balding man with bags under his eyes. His smile revealed good teeth, though: straight, even, small. "Visitors from Hitai," he said.

"The Starfall," said Guarl.

The magister looked at them more carefully. "Not god-chasers, then. Born there?"

"Yes," Guarl said.

Gareth barely heard.

The sword had no scabbard. The more he stared, the more he could see the features in the blade. He had watched Flax and Korina make so many things, he knew just what to look for. No ripples in the metal to indicate folding. This piece had been hot-forged, molded. Hammer marks, probably invisible to the untrained eye. And a hallmark.

His father's mark.

"And what brings four young Starfallers to the Greenlands? The scenery? Business? This?" He spoke Hitaian, the high form spoken in the Starfall. He seemed to notice Gareth's gaze and turned to take the weapon down from the mantle. "Here. Touch it, if you like."

Gareth came forward. The magister held it out flat on two hands. Gareth reached for the handle. It seemed to take an age for his hand to cover the distance. And when he was close enough to take it, time seemed to stop completely. He could not force his hand to touch the grip.

"A sad story comes with this," the magister said. "Murder and worse. A fugitive. Ah, but I see you already know."

"My father," Gareth said.

"You have his look."

Xin Ban and Whilla came forward, one to each side, and touched his shoulders. "This is why we came," Xin Ban said. "We have to know."

"Is it my place to tell this tale?" the magister said.

"Who else?" said Whilla. "Please, don't be afraid of us. This is not a mission of vengeance. We know what he was accused of. We know how that sword came to be here."

The magister turned to put the sword back on the mantle. Gareth had not touched it. "As I said, you have his look. I know, he was your father. You loved him. Saw only the best side of the man. Around here, though... Well, infamy is not too strong a word."

"Did he do it? What they said he did?" Gareth shut his eyes, took his friends' hands.

"Yes, boy," the magister said. "Yes, I'm afraid it is true."

"Rape and murder."

"Yes. All of it."

"Tell me," Gareth said.

"You should take a seat." Then he started the story.

***

His name was Roach, and he was no magister. Not then.

The Sword hung low in the night sky. It was as big as a thumb held at arms' length, standing up from the horizon. White.

No, not white. Blue. If he stared at it long enough, hard enough, it was blue.

And this night, that's all he wanted to do: get lost in staring at the far-away star, the god falling to the world. Because the present was too painful to deal with.

He dragged himself back to the moment, to the hard ground under his feet. A hard gravel path between dark houses looming in a darker forest. The city of Hong. He crunched along the path, away from the city offices and towards the site of the murder.

A man and a woman, both dead. A crowd stood around them, mostly in their nightclothes: felt trousers, robes and hats to keep off the cold. They muttered, low and humming. When they heard his boots on the gravel they went quiet and opened a path.

The woman was closest. She lay on her back. There were bits of stone stuck to her face and neck. She had died on her front and someone had turned her over. To help, perhaps only to see. Her feet pointed towards Roach, her arms splayed, mouth open.

Reeba.

Still on his face lay her promised. Dobe had a spear in his back, sticking up at an angle, low to high on his body. No ambiguity here. Nobody had tried to help because it was perfectly clear he was beyond help. Another week and they would have been wedded before the gods.

"Who saw it happen?" Roach said, and two people from around the edges of the crowd pulled away to sneak off into the shadows. "Who can say who did this?" Two more. "We need your help to catch this murderer."

"Nobody saw," said his neighbor. She was more than thirty years old, a widow. "Nobody saw it happen. They came from the tavern. Full of ale. Jube and Dale drank with them. These two left for home. We heard her scream. When we came out, this is how they were."

"Who rolled her over?" Roach asked, but the few remaining witnesses had nothing to say about that. They each named a different person. "Was she already dead or did she die while you tried to help her?"

More non-answers. These people did not know.

But the neighbor surprised him. "We covered her," she said.

He looked back at the corpse. She was dressed but not covered. "What do you mean?"

"Her skirts were pulled up. Bare to the world. We protected her modesty."

"What else?" he said.

"There was blood. There."

He knew where she meant. Such things did not happen here, not commonly, but the implications were still clear. "Not much chance of keeping these things secret," he said.

She grunted.

"Of course. So, ask around, will you? Spread it around. Say we found some piece of proof. A track in the gravel, a smell the dogs can take. Say the dogs lost the track but not the scent. That we will bring the dogs house to house until they tell us who."

"Lies?" she said.

"It would be worse than lying to let this go."

Wrand arrived with a cloth bag full of supplies. "Two," she said. "They did not tell me there were two. I only brought the winding cloth for one."

"I am going back towards the barber. I'll tell your apprentice to bring more."

"Selt is dim but he can manage." Wrand knelt by Reeba's body first. The eyes were still open, slowly clouding. Stars reflected in them, moistened by her tears. Wrand pushed the lids shut with two fingers and dropped stones on them to keep them shut. Then she lit a candle to make wax to seal them. She glanced up, saw Roach still watching. "You needed something more?" she said.

"She was..." he started, but could not come up with what she was to him. Not exactly, not in a way that mitigated this scene. Not in a way that added any hope. So he made it a statement. "She was."

Wrand nodded at that and went back to work. "Heard finer sentiments," she murmured. "More poetic, more tearful. But no better eulogy."

Roach set off, back towards the center of town. There was no more to do here. He woke the apprentice and the gravedigger, set them to their sad tasks, then started knocking on every door to ask questions. *Did you see? Who was there? Where were you? Let me see your shoes.*

The sun dawned with no wisdom added, nothing learned. He came at last to the forge – a busy place in this burgeoning city in the woods. People constantly needed things made or mended. Already a few gathered outside, waiting for Flax to open his door, to begin taking orders. Orders were from sunup to breakfast each day, first service to first in line.

But no smoke came from the forge chimney. No noise. The place had an empty feeling and it made the skin crawl on Roach's forearms, on the back of his neck.

He knocked on the door, already knowing that was useless. The door opened easily and the view inside Flax' kitchen told the whole story. The place had been ransacked, things taken nearly at random. The knives were gone but the spoons left behind. Bowls but not cups. In the sitting room, the chairs were gone from around the table.

The table would not fit on a cart.

Out back, through the sleeping room and behind the forge, Flax' pen told the rest of the story. The ox was gone and the cart, too.

Not a good cart for fleeing town. Flat, two wheels only, no walls. They would have piled everything in the middle and hoped for the best. Not the actions of an innocent man, to leave a prospering forge in the night with his children, his gravid wife.

Roach all but ran back to the jail where he worked his days. Upstairs was the magister's room.

***

"This room," Roach said, "which came to me after Frands died. Eight years ago. When your father returned here... It stirred up a lot of old feelings. People came to see him in his cell, you know. Dozens. They all brought things he had made them. Tossed them on the ground outside and spit on them. Cursed him. Called him names, evil things I shall not repeat for you.

"Well, Frands did as he had to. He gave Flax a trial, as fair as he could. I gave all my evidence."

"And then?" Gareth said, staring at this man, this magister.

"And then we hanged him. From the tree outside. When he stopped kicking, I cut him down myself – the last bit of work his little sword ever did. We buried him outside the cemetery, outside of town, with all the bits of bronzework. Unmarked grave, I'm afraid. That is what criminals get here. Sorry, boy."

"I want to see," Gareth said.

"He said it's unmarked," Guarl said, taking Gareth's arm to lead him off.

"He did it himself. Didn't you, Roach?" Gareth would not be moved. "You put him in the ground with your own hands. You let the gravedigger shovel the dirt, but you put him in it."

"Why do you think that?" Roach said, a half-smile on his lips. He leaned against the mantle.

"Because of the woman. Because of Reeba. She was yours before she settled on Dobe. And she did not stop loving you when she went with him. You did not stop loving her."

Roach sighed. "I confess it."

"So take me. Take me there. Take *us* there. What he was to you, well, he was something else to other people. A father to me. A good father. An uncle to all these others. A hero to our village. We'd never have survived without him. And I need to see."

"All right," Roach said. "Meet me outside. We'll go there now."

Swing

"Not like that," Chess said, and levered herself up from the hard ground. The causeway seemed to glow in the twilight, to eat the light and heat from their fire. To the west the ground dropped suddenly away to reveal the sea – a real sea, not a misnamed desert – gray as its name. Clouds veiled the stars and a little wind stirred the fire, stirred her hair.

Jeen adjusted her stance, feet closer together, hands farther apart on the sword's grip. Then she slashed again, clumsy and slow. Nik sat a few feet away, staring out at the darkening water.

"Better," Chess said. "But you have to use your wrists also. And turn your body. Let me show you." Jeen turned to hand her the sword. "No, you keep it. I am all done with swords, I think. I feel better, yes, but only well enough to keep hold of my walking stick." That was black rose from a monstrous tree at the base of the hills, a thing with flowers the size of lions' manes in colors like blood and rust. The bees that clung to them were worse.

"I feel awkward," Jeen said.

"The movements are new. I hope they never feel natural."

"It will not come lightly," Jeen said. "Killing. But I would hope for some grace."

"Yes. Now, like this." She stood behind Jeen, put her hands on Jeen's hands, her arms over Jeen's arms. Then she moved her friend through the slash, low to high, blade angled just right. It was slow but fluid, a turning motion that used the legs, hips, torso; arms and wrists imparted the final killing force.

"Like a dance," Jeen said.

"You'd not be the first to say so," Chess said. "And when it works it ends in a penetration." She stepped away to let Jeen practice the motion on her own.

Jeen thought for a minute and then blushed. "Crude!" she said, trying not to giggle.

Chess almost smiled, but then she reflected on how seldom she smiled and the moment was gone. "The truths of life are crude. Without penetration there are no new people, and we do so need new people. To replace the ones lost to swords and arrows and fires. And without war, without killing, how do we protect our babies? I wish I were home with my Neea. With Kwin and her new little Chess. They need me. I have scarce lived in Neea's lifetime. Will she even miss me?"

"Of course she will," Jeen said. "Oh, I mean..."

"It is well. I am not hurt by her hurt. It means she loves her mother, despite all. That is worth living for."

"Why did you come?" Jeen launched another clumsy swipe, almost losing the sword.

"Because of him."

"He hurt you, yes?"

"Well, he disappointed me. I had more hope for him. He was like a brother, like an uncle. Taught me a lot. Without him, we would have lost our war. Yes." She sat back down, aching, tired. The fire felt good. "I loved him, you know. Like a family member. Lost, tormented, still family. That is why I came."

Jeen set the sword down on its tip, one hand on the pommel to balance it. "You came because he meant something to you."

"I came because his torment is real. As real as my hopes for him. You brought the sword. But the lake spirit is in me again, I know it is – otherwise I could not even hobble along as we are going. And the spirit is not driving me to war. I smell no smoke, hear no ringing swords. It wants something else of me."

"What?" Jeen said.

"I do not know."

The last of the sun dropped into the sea and, close to hand, an owl called out.

***

Erlo climbed from bed, his head ringing, mouth dry, bladder full. The noise from the main room was intolerable.

Six days. Chess had been gone for six days. And he had kept none of his promises to her. Their space was dark, the hangings still drawn, and smelled of bodies too close. Worse: it smelled like a sick-room.

"Father?"

Neea. Precious, precocious Neea whose mother had died and yet not been buried, whose father had become a sot, with no sisters left to care for her. "Yes, child?"

"Father, why do we sleep so much? I do not like to sleep so much."

"Jeen left with Chess and nobody else has the heart for lessons. Let me go and piss and then we can sleep some more."

"I want to play, or learn," she said. "We could go to the sheepfold and you could show me how to tend them."

"Easy, girl. You sit by the stile and rest your eyes until you hear them bleating, and then you go frighten off the jackals or the monkeys or whatever else has spooked them. Now let me go and drain off all this mead or else I'll begin to drown."

"I want to go and see my sister and her baby. An aunt is not to sleep all the time."

He stumbled out, fixing his clothes as he went, biting back a curse the girl did not deserve. "Go on, then. She can use your help. Just stay there with her."

Neea ran off with a backwards glance. Was that hurt in her eyes?

I hurt so many, and I hardly even try.

In the main hall where children should be at lessons there was instead the roaring hum of younglings left to their own entertainments. They played, ran, shouted, fought. Little Rajacks held down his even littler brother, trying to make him eat some old fish bones. Sail, one of Brum's girls, just stood in the middle of the room, crying.

Erlo got away from all of that, out under a sun that stood too high in the sky – half the day gone already. The light beat at his eyes, offensive and hard. He walked to the outhouse with his eyes half closed.

A boat was coming in. Four men including his old friend Ham. "Erlo, come look at this beastie we fished up. Three heads and three tails."

Another of the fishers punched Ham on the shoulder. "That's three eels, and each of them has more brains than you."

"We could use another pair of hands," Ham said, laughing. "Get your lazy old carcass out here and live some."

"Got to drain my own eel," Erlo said, shambling on. When his needs were relieved, the boat was back out, fish piled in barrels by the pier.

Another missed opportunity and him not too broken up by that.

On the way back in, he saw women on the roof. Slowly, slowly, thatch came off to be replaced with tiles. Women passed tiles up and others fit them together.

Fire in the thatch. The roof burning, the smell of it acrid. He remembered. Ten years ago and it was like yesterday.

"We could use you," one of the women said.

He did not recognize her. She looked a little like that Xunian woman who had come with her mouth full of threats. She'd wanted to steal the god, to murder his wife. Well, the god was gone and so was Chess and all that was left was the memory of burning straw, the pulse in his chest that would not go away until he doused the fires with mead.

And two daughters.

But he could not face them.

He glanced around, looking for Mang. He wasn't on the roof, wasn't in the boat. The old man was always in the middle of some work. But the thought could not hang on long, not in the stew of self-pity and hangover inside Erlo's head. "I'm sick," he said, and went back into the hall.

The noise was so loud now it was almost the same as silence. His head rang, sweat popped up on his lip, and he felt a thing he had been pushing away almost since the day he met Chess.

Contempt.

I am not a good man.

The noise, the roar, the chaos of children with nothing useful to do. The sickness was real. It was behind his eyes, in his closing fists.

"Quiet!" he finally roared, standing in the doorway like Chess had once stood across the path outside. He did not know if the roar was aimed at the children or at the noise in his head, the buzz of self-hate that never really went away.

Why do we sleep so much? Because being awake hurts and sleep is the only cure. Chess, Chess. If only you had died all the way.

"Quiet," he repeated into the new silence. Softly now, gently. An invocation, a description, a gratitude. "I need you to be quiet."

Not everyone was at work. People came out of their little rooms alongside the main hall, parents of these children, aunts or uncles or grandparents. One had sewing in his hand, another wool that she was carding. *What's the noise? Who shouts? Is there danger?* The mumbles were low, urgent. *Something new?*

"Father?" Neea again, a basket in her hands. "I wanted to go pick some flowers."

"No, no flowers, by all the gods. But they need help with the nets. And the roof. And in the sheepfold. Bram needs help to card that wool. What are we doing here? What are we all doing?"

"The children need a teacher," someone said. Agreement wandered around the room, visiting many mouths and shaking heads.

"Then someone teach them," Erlo said.

"Father? You are someone."

"I know nothing," he said. "Nothing but bragging and farting. My head hurts and I am ill, ill in my heart. I am sorry to be your father, Neea. So sorry. You should have better."

"I don't have better," she said. She came closer. All the children came closer.

Erlo thought of the rafts outside, when the sick, dying men and women rowed from across the lake to shoot arrows into the village in defense of the Starfall. He wanted to run, to panic. To be sick.

"Father, I have you."

The other children said it, too. "I have you, Erlo. I have you." Closer, and then they were touching his hands, pressing in on him.

There was nowhere to go but outside, and only terror waited there. Nowhere to go.

His hands trembled. He put them on his legs to still them. The knot that lived in his stomach now clenched even tighter. If he had eaten today, he would certainly have retched.

"No," he said. "No, I cannot teach you. I know nothing."

"Please?" One child said the word and it gained an echo, a quiet reverberation that tossed it back and forth around the room. It was somehow worse than the noise. Insidious.

He needed a drink.

And, for the first time in many seasons, he put that need aside. It was heavy; it hardly moved. But he had been strong before. He could remember it.

"Please? Please?"

"No. I cannot teach you. But you can teach me. Only sit down there, all of you. Take out your sand trays and your styluses. I always thought reading was like magic, always wanted to learn it. Show me how. Quietly."

They rushed to comply, eager, needing their routine as he needed his sleep and mead. Maybe it quieted some self-hate in their own minds, Erlo did not know. He only knew they had all gone quiet – the children and his own terrible mind.

***

A new thing in a place where little ever changed.

Korina set down her tongs and her hammer, let the bar cool even though it would be better to shape it now. Reheating it would take time and fuel and maybe change its nature. But it would only be a hinge.

She stepped out of the forge. Water burbled and sloshed to her right, slowly eroding the banks as wind propelled it. A fish jumped, splashed. She glanced at the boat out there hunting for fish. Four men stood in it, facing the long hall.

She looked there, too. Women on the roof, none of them working. They all looked down into the place they were building. Outside, people stared at the doors, at the walls. Korina turned in a circle, saw everyone looking there.

The only sounds came from nature. The wind over the water. Far-away sheep bleating. A hawk overhead.

Then the moment passed. On the roof, people crouched back to work with their heads together, whispering. Korina could see their mouths moving but could not hear the words. On the lake, the men sat back down into the boat. Ham tugged on the net, muttered to the man in front of him. Their murmurs walked over the water, vague human sounds stripped of meaning.

What had brought her out here? Why had she set down her tools and joined the other villagers in gawking at the long hall?

Whatever it was, she needed to see. Her curiosity was not slaked.

The path ground under her heels, a crunchy, snickering sound. The air pushed down on her, parted grudgingly from her way, tangled in her hair. Then the doors. Big, wooden, heavy. Defensible. She pulled them open, both of them, knowing what she would look like from inside: a powerful form made dark by the light behind.

Inside, thirty small children ranging from four years to twelve crowded around Erlo. He had one of Jeen's little sand trays in front of him, and a stick, and the children laughed while he clumsily failed to make letters.

What is this?

Neea was by him, tucked under one arm. She reached out and help him move the stick so that the form in the sand looked almost like the form in front of all the other children.

Other villagers sat in front of their hangings. They did their lap-tasks each with one eye on the lessons.

Erlo? I had forgotten him. I had forgotten he survived the war.

And, on the trail of that thought, a new one. A cold thought that made her back pop into sweat, that smelled like ashes.

I am lonely.

Once Bero left to start his own life the forge fell to her alone. And alone she lived. Father gone, mother abandoned to her own griefs, Yohn dead and Flax dead and something inside herself dead. Her heart was too broken even to notice that Gareth was still there, just as lost and lonely as she was.

Making the metal was not enough. Hammering pins and hinges and plates, pouring metal into molds for nails was not enough. She watched the children write another letter and laugh as Erlo tried to copy it, grimacing and biting his lip, and she knew.

She went back to her forge and set the bar aside. It would never do. Another hinge in a place so replete with hinges, a bit of trade-bait in a place that hardly had material needs now. What she wanted to do was make a tool. A hammer, a set of long tongs for very hot work. More than that, than the tools she had made already in her aspirations to steel. The point of the work was no longer the work, the products she made.

A change had come to the village, something new in a place that rarely saw anything new. It was time to bring on an apprentice.

***

Mang's hut had changed little over the years. Light came in through thatched walls that would need to be remade soon, through a roof that hardly kept out the rain when rain came. Light all around.

He lay on his cot, staring at the walls, at the ceiling. Thinking of the living things they had been cut from, pressed into this second life as conveniences for a person. Green fern-fronds now dried out and crispy, stalks hardened, sap dried. He wondered if these ferns, these giant aberrations, had dropped berries or cones into waiting soil before being stripped of their fronds.

Outside, silence descended like a stooping hawk, making him aware of the signs of life by muffling them. Hammers, oars in oarlocks, children playing when perhaps they should be at lessons. Somewhere a baby cried.

I could stand, go outside. Feel the wind on my face. Think into this sudden silence.

But he remained on his cot, a thin blanket of undyed wool over his legs.

He thought of his home. Not this place, not these mountains and this lake and those people. Not the war that had made a home of here. An earlier time. An origin.

Pandau, it was called. A country ruled by two sisters, old beyond counting, laws carved into two pillars outside their mansion. Long-horned cattle called in the fields outside, memories into the real silence, crushing it. The light was brighter there, the sun closer. Always burning. Night was scarce relief from the heat. And, in the night, when the cattle went still and the mosquitos were lured away with smoky candles, there was love.

Horum.

I loved you as best I could.

He remembered a night hotter than this real day when he was not alone in his cot, when Horum lay beside him, both their legs caught up in the blanket neither of them needed.

The two sisters had killed him. For some petty offense, not for his love of Mang. Not that they said.

I was not made for women.

"Here, chew this leaf. It will help with the pain."

An old voice. What voice? What person?

"*They were wrong to have you thrashed, man. I do not believe their stories anyway. What man would lay with a man? You with so many cattle, so many goats. So many offers of young brides. Who could sort through them all?*"

Offering comfort. An aunt. She stitched up his face where they'd hit him on the cheek, where the skin had split open like an orange. Given him leaves for the pain in his jaw. He'd come away with two teeth fewer, back teeth so his smile was still pretty. Oh, so long ago.

"*The seer says there will be a comet. What a thing to see.*"

The leaves, the pain, the loss. He hadn't heard her, not then. A comet, when his love was even then being hoisted onto a platform for the vultures and eagles to carry into the sky?

Outside, life resumed as suddenly as it had ceased. But the present moment had lost its hold on Mang. He absently slipped a leaf into his mouth, crushed it with his teeth. The taste was sour and sweet. That first one, the one his aunt pushed between bruised lips, it had been bitter. He'd wanted to spit it out.

"The taste gets better when you see how it saves the pain."

She'd been right, of course. And different places had different leaves, all tasting just a little different, all tasting just the same: like solace.

A week, and he'd thought he was safe. *Just be careful, just stay alone.* But then a new marriage offer and of course he'd said no. What did a man need with a girl? A man not made for women? When he'd gone home and found a dead sheep in his bed, then he'd known.

"A comet. What a thing to see."

Something to see, yes. And somewhere to go. Far away, exiled but unmurdered. So much dirt had passed under his feet. New dirt, new places. The sea, the magnificent sea. Ships, tar, ropes, shanties, thatch made of giant ferns that had no place in the world. And the same air everywhere.

He lay in his cot as life rolled on outside and lamented that he was alone.

"The taste gets better when..."

Her voice, incessant. It followed him from that faraway place and time. He was too tired to wave it away, too tired to cough or spit.

I should join the Coughers in their camp. They know what to do with the dying.

Her voice. The same voice in the same air. The ground always changed and the walls and the faces, but it was one air all over the world, one blanket that covered everything beneath one sky.

"The taste gets better..."

Mang had a taste for solitude. He might have loved Moburu. The man had been magnificent and his hurts, his vulnerabilities, they aroused the nurturer in Mang. Might Moburu's fate have been different if Mang had confessed it? Or would these new people have been just like the old – no hearts for men not made for women? Would Moburu himself have spat on him, cast him down? Of course there was no way to ask, and so he lay here alone.

Under one air.

Horum had lain beside him once, body to body. Then they'd murdered him and offered him to the sky. He'd dried up, carried off bite by bite to feed nestlings, insects. Plants. Made into nothing, into the air itself.

One air, everywhere.

"The taste..."

Oh, my aunt. I've grown so old alone, so lonely. Now you come to offer comfort again. Gone so long... Are you alive, or are you with me too, in the one air under one sky?

Sitting up was a chore but he managed it. Little gray dots filled up his vision and he hung his head until they passed, then got to his feet and waited again. Outside his hut, life went on.

Comfort

None of them had ever been in a city before. Not since a family trip to Hitai when Gareth was very small. They had gawked and gaped their way to the magister's office and they did the same as Roach led them north through town.

There were buildings of wood and stone, some two or even three floors high. Gareth winced as he walked into each shadow, oppressed by this dark in the middle of a bright day. Trees had risen over them all the way here, through the Greenlands, but had not seemed to loom the way these structures did.

I am going to the grave of my father.

The city went on and on. Here the character changed from stone and wood to mostly wood. There, tile rooves gave way to a strange thatch made of pine needles. He expected to see cats hiding in the thatch or lining the broad, paved lane, but there were none.

There were people all over.

Most everyone here looked like Gareth: middle stature, good shoulders, skin like bronze. Dark hair and good teeth. His green eyes marked him out as different: a gift from the lake spirit. Everyone here had coal-dark eyes in open, curious faces. One or two were of Xunian origin.

The lane narrowed even as the buildings shrank and edged away. Here the lane became a path between two fields full of flowering onions, each field a hundred-pace square.

Every step brings me closer to him.

Past the fields, through a stretch of woods, and there was a house all of bricks. It was half as big as the long hall at home and smoke streamed from a high chimney.

"The death house," Roach said, unasked.

Xin Ban wondered, "A whole house for the dead? I washed my aunt with my own hands and dressed her and brushed out her hair. My mother found three strong neighbors to carry her out to the pasture and we buried her in the sheepfold."

"Here," Roach said, "all the dead are brought to this place. The family may wash and dress them or not – we prefer not. Disease can spread from the dead to the living. The sick-dead we burn. The others we bury there, in those fields, keeping the field fallow for twenty years. Then we plant them with crops and clear a new field. You see the markers."

Gareth strained to see past the death-house that tried to fill his whole vision, mind chewing over memories of the Tomblands: not mere houses and fields but a whole land dedicated to corpses.

But only special corpses.

In the fields where Roach pointed he could make out little stakes. He imagined each would be carved with a name. Past the death-house, the fields stretched out to either side for one hundred paces. And past those, the forest.

Dark and deciduous, green, lush and lively. Wind whispered through leaves and made branches ache and groan. Gareth imagined he could visit here another time and be calmed but now the sounds and colors pinched at his nerves.

"Out here," Roach said, "we bury those we do not wish to remember. Not many. Murder and other violences happen here only seldom. The fields we plant so we know that the bodies of our dead, the spirits, come back as food to nourish us. Here we put trees so the dishonored dead can disperse into the wild world. The trees still protect us. A screen from enemies, life for our wild neighbors, wood for fires and building."

"Which one?" Gareth said. His friends drew closer around him. Even as they did, he knew which one.

Ten years ago. One tree was tall enough but not too tall. A spruce, straight and strong, branches laden with thick green needles and nodes that would soon be pine cones. Grass grew between the trees but under the spruce was barren. No needles, no cones.

"That's him," Roach said. "His tree, there. Another ten years and we can cut it for lumber."

Gareth looked again, this time seeing a few dead stumps. "A marker."

"Yes."

Xin Ban said, "Are you sure you want to do this?"

"Yes," he said, knowing she already knew. "Come with me."

"I will." They all did. All his friends trod over the thick, tangled grass with him until they were near the tree. Roach stayed behind, on the path.

Gareth put out one hand. The bark pressed in knobs and ribbons against his calluses. Sharp, sticky with sap. The air tasted of it, of evergreens at the end of summer, of the wind and the colors.

His throat closed up; Gareth choked and spluttered, coughed back tears. Fell to his knees, hand still against the bark.

"Father. Father!"

His head dropped and wet grief rolled off his face to water the tree. Around him, his friends made a triangle. Xin Ban held hands with Guarl and Whilla, facing away, facing into the world while he looked out of it, into his own hurt.

He stayed there a long time. Nobody moved or talked, not even Roach.

When he finally stood up, empty and weak, he pushed into the triangle to make it a square. He took Whilla's hand and Xin Ban's, all four now facing into the world.

"No," Guarl said after a moment. "This is not right." He dropped Whilla's hand and moved away, making a space where a fifth person could stand.

"I will not join you," Roach said.

"Not for you," said Guarl.

And that was right. There was still that fifth person who belonged with them. Somewhere in the world, somewhere out here beyond the Greenlands, Vault still waited.

***

"What will you do now?" Roach said.

They were back in his office, sitting around his table. Gareth had his head down.

"Stay," said Whilla. "Or go."

"We have to continue on our way," Xin Ban said. Guarl nodded.

"We have to find her," Gareth said, sitting up.

"Who?" said Roach. "Jac?"

All four were surprised. Their mouths and eyes widened. "Of course," Gareth said. "He is alive, and he is with her. We just stood among the dead and counted him among the living."

Roach said, "That is not who you meant, though. You thought of someone else. And I think it is trouble. Go. Go on and find Jac and her daughter and her son. Justice is done here and you have seen it. You will make your peace with what Flax was in the end, and you will maybe choose to be otherwise."

He looked like he had more to say but Gareth stopped him. "I still don't believe it."

Roach sighed. "Even so, move on. There is no more to be done here. And take this – it has sat here long enough like an antler taken from a prize stag." He stood and took down the sword from the mantle, let it drop in front of Xin Ban. "When you find Jac, give it back to her. Give it to the boy you are looking for. It was never hers, never Flax'. It was always his."

"We will," Xin Ban said.

A noise came from downstairs.

"You cannot come in here unbidden! Stay back and I will ask ahead of you." A Greenlander voice.

"No time," said a voice in Hitaian. Gareth recognized it but could not place it.

"What?" Whilla said. "It can't be..."

Then he knew. He knew because she knew. "Chess? Your mother, here? Why?"

People stamped up the stairs, some fast and some more slowly. A Greenlander guard came in first, the woman who had met them in the woods. "They will not be stopped," she said, "but do not seem hostile."

Jeen came next. Gareth had to stare a minute to recognize her, then shoved aside the banal thought that he must not have done well enough on his studies so that she chased him across the world with more work to do. Then Chess, who seemed as surprised to see her daughter as Whilla to see her.

Whilla rushed into her arms and gripped her tight. "Mother – but how did you get here? With your wounds..."

"The god has work yet for me, child," she said.

Then Gareth saw the sword in Jeen's hand. Even so armed she did not seem imposing or hostile; she held it awkwardly, like one might hold a snake.

One more person came up: a small, sallow man wearing just a loincloth and sandals.

"What is this about?" Roach said. "A villager and more slaver-strangers?"

"Too late," the sallow man said. "Too late. We came too late. The spirit killed every child and woman and man, ate their livers, left them for us to find."

"What are you talking about?" Roach said.

Chess looked right at Gareth. "Moburu has come back," she said. "And he will come here next."

***

Chess and Jeen had a few coins between them and those bought a room in a local drinking house. Gareth had never climbed a staircase before the magister's office and watched Jeen go up first. He followed awkwardly, one hand on the wall, as far as he could get from the escalating drop-off to his right. Down there, men and women drank wine and ale out of wooden bowls and ate fowl roasted in a fireplace in the middle of the room.

The whole place smelled of sap and ashes.

At the top of the stairs, a dark hall held four real doors. Jeen led into the nearest on the left. Gareth slipped in behind her, then Whilla, Guarl, Xin Ban, Chess. There were two narrow beds under shuttered windows, wicker frames with stuffed mattresses.

The young ones looked to each other. Xin Ban spoke for them: "We never slept on something like that. We'll use the floor. We like it."

Chess nodded. "Best not get used to such luxuries. And stow those weapons. Strangers have stared at us every step of the way here."

Jeen slid her sword under the bed with a sigh. Gareth thought it sounded grateful. He had a bow and his half-spear; they joined her sword. Whilla had her mother's full-spear with the red point and tassels. It made a passable walking-stick. She stuck that under the bed, too.

"Moburu?" Gareth said.

"Yes," said Chess. "The man with us. His name was Nik. Something longer than that but just Nik to us. He spoke none of our tongues. A cousin in the Starfall told us what he said. A monster in the orchard. Something that could go unseen and unheard. Taking people at will, slowly, one by one."

"So?" said Gareth. "Many monsters in the world now." He looked at his hands.

"When Moburu was cast into jaguar form by the lake spirit, this is what he did. The Xunians camped outside our village. He snatched them up, one by one, to terrorize them. It worked."

"He died a long time ago," Xin Ban said. "A Hitaian lady told us. Yohn himself saw him die. He stayed alive just to say so."

"Yes," Chess said. "Yes, this is so. But Yohn is not here to answer questions. What he saw in his last moments..."

Jeen turned to a window and fiddled with the fastener. Her face was tight, almost fragile. "He never lied. But he was so sick, so lost."

"Why would he come here? Moburu?" said Whilla, sitting on the floor in one corner. The walls were plaster over wood, cold, smooth. Her white skin reflected the white walls, making her appear spectral in shifting shadows from candles in wall sconces.

Chess said, "Because we are here. Me, her."

"Revenge?" Gareth said. "For what?"

"Nothing," Chess said back, sitting on the bed nearest the door. She groaned a little through clenched teeth. "Not revenge. Only, he is an animal now. When he left, he was hardly the man he had been. Now I think he is only the cat, the hunter. The lake spirit abandoned him as it abandoned me, set him adrift in the world. With nowhere to go, well, he just lost his way. Lost himself. But something in him must know we will come. And he will seek out what he knows."

"How do you know?" Gareth asked, anger rising in his chest.

"I know," she said. "Is that not enough for you, boy?"

Now he puffed out his chest and stood up straight, fist clenching. But Guarl came and put a hand on his arm.

"She is right," Guarl said. "She has many years of life more than us. Listen to her."

Gareth blew out a breath. "Good, then," he said. "Well. But I need a walk. My head is full of grief. And that man's story seems rotten."

"Nik?" Jeen said.

"No, Roach."

Chess frowned. "An inauspicious name. Who is that?"

"The magister," Xin Ban supplied. She started to tell Roach's tale while Gareth slipped out of the door and back down the stairs.

Whilla followed him as far as the door. "Don't go out there," she said. "Stay with us. If Moburu is here..."

"Then he doesn't know who I am. And if the stories are right, nothing I do can hurt him. No safer here than anywhere." He stopped her protest with a raised finger. "I'll come back soon. I promise. Just need to clear my head. Please?"

Whilla sighed and relented.

Gareth left the drinking house for the cool night of the city of Hong.

Memories

The Gravetender admired her work.

The crown was perfect. It shone in the high, direct sunlight, platinum and vermidion tossing shards of illumination down onto the sand. It was just a little painful to look at as though it were a sun in its own right.

It commanded the attention.

Clay. Remember the clay.

The work came easily. It always had. But other things were harder to keep track of lately. She was distracted. Thoughts blew through her head like sand across the desert, forming dunes here and eddies there and cyclonic little devils. Sweeping up time, leaving behind death.

I had a name. What was it? My father knew it, once.

Or was she my mother?

I never asked if I had a mother.

I am not myself.

And there it was, lying in the light just as the crown did: so bright it was almost its own source of light. She was not herself. Not in a way an ill person might say. Not as in, *I feel unwell, not as hale as usual.* But as in, *these thoughts do not all belong to me.*

Temporary problems. The work remained. This project in front of her was barely even a cog in something far grander, and that in a civilization with no knowledge of cogs.

These primitives barely comprehend the wheel. I tried to teach them better.

But she hadn't, had she? Someone else had.

"Runner," she said, dashing those thoughts aside with a swipe of a mental hand. "Message for the queen."

A messenger had stepped forward from a shadow. Always ready, if not eager. But when she said "queen," he stepped back again, unsure.

"What is it?" she said.

"No queen, Great One. She will rip out my tongue."

"Ah, yes. She styles herself King. Hubris, really, all of it."

The man came closer again, head down as though the sky had a physical weight and he could hardly bear it. "Is this what you wish me to say, Great One?" His olive skin was turning patchy red as though the light burned as well as weighed on him.

"Of course not. She would kill us both." *Is there some escape from that fate now? Was there ever?* "Tell her I have done as commanded. Her tomb is complete. I will visit to deliver the news in person, only in a day or three. It is a long walk and I grow old and weary. Soon I will go into the sand."

The messenger looked at her with eyes wide. But he said, "Yes, Great One," and sidled off to do as she said.

Not the sand, though, she thought then. *No, not for me.*

A giant scepter sat within the coils of the snake-shaped tomb. The serpent had no hands to grasp it. It was not so gaudy as the crown but would suffice. When statues were moved, their extremities were the most vulnerable: penises and noses and fingertips. The scepter would make an easy and tempting target. And the beard, hung from a strap over the snake's head, would soon fall into disrepair even if Dllyx did not act as the Gravetender expected.

All is ready, then. The works are ready. Only I am not prepared. All these years, all this work, and I am not prepared.

Wind pushed sand around the Tomblands as it always did and the Gravetender retreated to her office to wait.

***

The boy played with the clay. It was as big as his head now, and no longer a cube. It felt warm despite the cool down here. And if he listened...

"Put that aside, boy," his mother said. Her eyes took in the room smoothly but then danced back to the clay. To the mural that covered the wall behind him. To the table. She licked her lips. "Put it away. It is no thing to play with."

"Yes, Mother."

"I am not your mother."

"Yes, Gravetender." But he did not set the clay down, and she did not notice. His mother went to the table and stared at the plans there. All of them, piled and scattered and strewn. The small tombs and the large, the main map, the sub-maps. Food tallies, worker dispositions, lists of ages and names. The boy watched her stare. "Mother?"

She grunted in response, not looking, not moving.

"Mother, I wish to walk the graves."

"Learn well," she said. "Soon, boy, soon this will all fall to you."

He took the clay with him. Through the door, up the steps, into the waning light of day. Sand and wind, dry air and dry noise. If he concentrated, he could smell tannin and spices amidst the stink of flint.

The clay did not mind, but he knew it would be far too dry for it up here in the wind. It wanted somewhere cool and moist, dim. The office was no longer safe but other places would be.

It took a long time to find what he wanted. Stairs down with barely any marker above the sand. An old grave. One of the first Hitaians lay here, the ashen ones from before the time of the New Hitaians. When Dllyx' people had marched out of the desert, the first one had been here a thousand years already, building roads and tombs, monuments and machines.

They knew a thing or two about cogs. And mathematics, celestial mechanics. Magic.

He did not need magic now, only a little luck. The thing in his hand would fulfill its purpose, complete its life cycle. All it needed was time and space.

Down the stairs. Sand tried to bury the place and workers came but rarely to this part of the Tomblands with brooms and brushes and shovels. He slip-stepped down to the bottom, to the huge double doors that served as the real monument here. Graven things of bronze showed terrible scenes: murder, impalings, worse. And the doors were made to open outwards.

He broke the seal with his hand. The clay circle snapped cleanly in half and dropped into the dust at his feet. A precaution, not to keep anyone out but to serve as an alarm. Dllyx' people would not think to check such things. Then he shoved his little fingers between the two doors, gripped the leftmost, and heaved.

The counterweights had endured. The door moved an inch, two, then crunched to a stop. Too much sand down here at the bottom of the steps.

He could fix that. He dug the sand out from behind the door with one hand, the other cradling the clay, piled sand in front of the other door. Just enough to get a few more inches. Just enough that his head would fit into the space. Then the rest of his body followed.

Inside, stacks of grain sat in rotting bags. Mice had been at them over the centuries and their waste had introduced moisture and rot. The place stank of beer and death. The bags ringed a plinth big enough for three coffins. Some old king from when the kings were not gods. From when these tombs were for the people, not for the dead. His wife to one side, an unfortunate child to the other, each buried with him.

So sad for one to die before their time.

He climbed up onto the plinth, setting the clay up there first so he could use both hands. The child's coffin he ignored. "You will never be a child, I regret," he told the clay. "No time for such niceties." The woman's coffin looked promising: minimal rot and that dry, and a mummy that looked like it would come out in mostly one piece. The king's coffin was in better shape, made of better wood with more skilled lacquering. He lifted the lid and peeked inside.

Tomb robbers had been at this one. The mummy was all broken up, scattered within the box. Bones stuck up here and there and droppings showed that mice had found something of value here. Maybe if he were small enough he could crawl away along their scent-trails and find little nests all stuffed with mummy-wrappings.

The woman, then.

He lifted her out with tender care, set her in the king's box, and closed the lid over her. She weighed almost nothing.

"I hope your heart weighed less," he muttered, thinking of the grotesque mural in his office. "Mine is heavy, I confess."

Then he dusted out the woman's coffin the best he could. It might have been easier just to upend it but it might not stay together if he did that. It seemed as light as the mummy, dried out and wasted.

Finally, the clay. It looked small indeed there in the middle of the box. Vulnerable. It tugged at his affections. But this was the best he could do: a coffin for a cradle.

Mother might have missed him by now. It was time to hurry. Even she could only remain distractedly maudlin for so long. So he covered the box with its feather-weight lid, jumped down, and hit the door.

Wind or the weight of sand had pushed it shut. He shoved against it and those first two inches again came easily, and again terminated in a crunching stop against a barrier of sand. He pushed harder, using his weight.

I used to be much heavier.

The door moved, but not enough.

The boy stuck out his hand, his arm. Put his head against the crack and forced himself through, made an opening as he went, grasping for the last of the light. Behind him, in the dark, something moved.

A dry sound like sand through fabric.

Probably a mouse come to smell the clay.

Nonetheless, his urge to be gone came on stronger. He struggled now, panted, pushed, panicked. This was no place to be caught. No place to die.

Then the sand gave it up. The door creaked open one more inch and he was out, out into the end of the day, into the flinty smell of desert.

I wonder if that is what it is like to be born?

***

Blood leaked from her nose into her mouth, hot and sharp. She knew fear then, knew it really. Intimately, like a lover.

Have I ever had a lover?

The Gravetender groaned her way off her knees back into a standing position, stomach clenched from the fist that had landed there, and spat out a tooth. More hot blood came with it.

Dllyx stood above her, tall and resplendent in her silver kilt. No, not silver; white gold. She had elevated herself above even the Kings, then, created a rank just for herself. Her hands were empty, open. Inviting. But behind her stood two guards. Big men with heavy fists, massive, round shoulders. One held a gigantic spear.

Twelve feet long and as thick as a leg at the base with a long, splintery tip and a crossbar four feet down. The Gravetender wondered if that might be for a banner, but she knew it was not.

The guards behind her hit her in the back of her knees and she dropped again, skin into sand, palms down. "The accused remain penitent," one of them said.

"You came without your lions, My King," the Gravetender said. Blood dripped into the sand from her face and was gone. "I knew your threats were empty."

Dllyx smiled. "For treachery, for interference in the politics of Hitai, and for betrayal, you are sentenced to be executed."

"Treachery and betrayal are the same thing," the Gravetender said. "And should the trial not come before the sentence?"

"We had the trial before we came. Easier that way."

The Gravetender tried to turn, to look down her stairs, into her office. They had come while she slept, an uneasy act, something fated and unnecessary. She had not seen if the boy was there or if he had run off.

"The office?" Dllyx said, making her voice sad. "What you plot down there is against the interests of the Kingdom of Hitai. It will not continue. Guards, burn it."

A low-oxygen environment, absent any chimneys and made mostly of stone did not seem an ideal site for a bonfire but she held her tongue on those points. Dllyx would understand none of it anyway.

The Gravetender raised her eyes to see who else had come for the show. There was Dllyx and her two guards. The two behind the Gravetender. Four more, all armed with spears. *Eight soldiers, only*. She spat again. Behind them, a rank of priests. The dance cult and the poisoners, the breeders and the sinners. More. All in ceremonial attire as though to attend a wedding. Or a funeral.

"What do you think of all this?" she said, looking at the head poisoner. He was a dark man of small height and sallow, shallow eyes.

He took this as a cue to address Dllyx. "Do you mean to murder the Gravetender?" he said. "Such a thing has never been done, cannot be done. The Gravetender is at the heart of the accord between the Kings and the Gods."

"Burd," Dllyx said, addressing one of the back row of guards.

He reached into the sand and lofted another great spear, the twin of the first in every way. He planted the end on the ground and grinned.

"I brought two spears, Rept."

"One for the young one?" he said. "Atrocious. An atrocity."

"They never take a good threat the first time," Dllyx told Burd. Then, to Rept, "You could take his place. Only a conspirator would defend a treacher. The quickest survive an hour. The slowest... I have seen a strong man last a week. How long would you contemplate your loyalty?"

"Oh," the priest said, and took a step back. They all did, color draining from them until they looked less like a squadron of peacocks ready to strut through a mating dance and more like a yard of dusty chickens.

"Good, then," Dllyx said.

The smell of smoke drifted up from the office. The Gravetender supposed there must be even more guards or lackeys down there. It was all about the same, though: she had no strength to resist. Even the Tomblands Guard were sworn to the King, not to the tombs or their tender. All that was left to do was die. And that filled her with dread, with the fear that had been slowly gnawing her thoughts into ribbons.

How will she do it?

Being dead was hardly frightening. But dying...

"Bring her," Dllyx said, and then she led a march across the sand. Towards her own tomb.

Well, that was expected.

Behind the priests, almost hiding and revealed as everyone changed positions to follow, was a small, grayish woman of too many years. She had a plain shift with ink stains on the sleeves, a silver kirtle strapped on over the top of it. Ceremonial gear she had never worn, a new rank for which she was unqualified. She avoided making eye contact with the Gravetender, seeming to prefer the view of the tombs.

All of it is death. Out there or in here. But avert your eyes, do, if it pleases you.

A larger mob waited at the tomb. The Gravetender amused herself by dragging her feet, refusing to walk, but the guards had plenty of strength to drag her. She bought only a moment more of existence, into which she thrust knowledge of these new women and men.

Wreckers.

They had hammers and bars, ropes and pulleys.

The Gravetender knew each one of them. They had helped demolish more than one obsolete tomb out here. She wanted to laugh and was grateful to the fear and nausea that made such laughter impossible. No reason to give away the game.

The guards tossed her down a hundred feet from the snake tomb. Her face almost went into a hole dug there, a circular pit a few inches in diameter. She could not see the bottom. While she looked, contemplating this new mystery, they stabbed her in the back.

The pain was a revelation. An incredible thing that drove out all thought, all sense, all reason. So huge that it was meaningless. Her body screamed and tensed and tried to struggle but her mind could not hold so much agony. Face contorted and spine bent, she just went away.

The spear stuck through her middle, from next to her spine and out through her navel – or where a human would have a navel. She could not look down to see it, this new thing, because they hoisted the spear upright with her atop it. She slid to the crossbar, down the widening spear. It ripped open her insides to make way for itself. Then she hung on the spear, head and feet down, abdomen up. Blood and gore leaked down the pole.

The pole went into the hole in the ground perfectly. All that was left to do was turn her so she could see the wrecking crew go to work, upside down. Blood leaked out of her throat, up her nose, into her eyes, but she watched. From this painless/pained place, she watched.

They took down the scepter first. So predictable. Then the beard. The going was hard: the Gravetender's work was solid. An hour, two hours. She started to stink of congealed blood and offal, of ruptured bowels, and that distance from her own body began to fade into workaday suffering, the aching of death.

Unbearable.

The crew seemed to want to stop, seemed ready to pack up. Only Dllyx herself pointed at the crown, shouted some words the Gravetender could not understand through the veils of stink and suffering and light that grew around her. Then they tossed ropes around it, around the crown, and pulled it into pieces.

Dllyx came to her then, looked her in the face, eye to eye. She looked so strange from this angle, inhuman, monstrous.

"Not finished without the crown, is it? I will go there in my own time. You should have helped me. When I am ready to go, my servants will rebuild it. Her, my new Gravetender." She pointed at the inky woman. "She will put the crown back on its head and this monument will stand here for all time. It will say I lived. I ruled here. Me."

The Gravetender tried to talk but she could barely even breathe. The stake was through her guts, through her abdominal wall, and those muscles stretched her diaphragm. More blood bubbled from her mouth, her nostrils.

"Disgusting," Dllyx said. "You know, I almost believed you were some sort of gods in your own right. But look at you: all too mortal. I am glad you are still alive, though, that you can die slowly. Because you have a hope left. I know it. I know that hope. It has rotted my family for years, generations."

The Gravetender started to turn. Men put their hands on the pole beneath her. She could feel it vibrate with each touch, shake through her bones and organs. She screamed, a weak, airless sound, as her face swung away from the tomb.

Her son stood there, two men holding him. Two more had that second spear behind him.

"No fear," he said. "Your name is Cthai. Cthai. Your name is..."

"Now," Dllyx said. "Now, watch your last hope die."

Duel

Warm night air played around Gareth's face and clothes, ran fingers through his hair. The city was unexpectedly noisy in the early dark. Behind him, the rooming and drinking house was alive with song and conversation, the clatter of dishes and cups. Ahead, people walked the dusty avenues in strange styles of clothing.

Gareth had never seen a hooded cloak before. They gave passing people a sinister feel. *Why would you want to hide your face?*

He set out in the direction most of the people went. Two women held hands and kept their heads down. A tall woman and a short man hurried by, excusing themselves as they went, well inside each other's space. More strangers and more and more, a dozen, two dozen. More strangers than he had seen before today. They went down narrow alleys, into houses with signs out front or without, or just ambled along.

Ahead came a strange sound like ten swarms of bees. He could not quite see over the heads of the taller people but gathered there was a crowd further along this path. The buzzing was the sound of raised voices, of low mutters and murmurs escalated to be heard over other such noise.

He hurried, excited to see another new thing, his dragging grief left momentarily behind. He slid in between people, into the wall they made with their flesh, until he could see what they were looking at.

Two men. One tall and the other average, dressed in leathers and armed with bronze swords. Each had a woman behind him.

"You called out the fight," one of the women said, "so he chooses the weapons. You know that's how it works here, Jarl."

"But swords are so everyday," he said back. He glanced around the crowd and smiled as he said it. "No showmanship in swords. What about nets or throwing axes?"

"Swords," the other man said, and tested the edge of his own blade against his thumb. It did not draw blood but it would probably do.

A disturbance in the disturbance: a figure broke into the circle across from Gareth. A familiar face. "Fighting in my streets? I try so hard to civilize you."

"The forms are in place, Roach," said the woman with the showman. "Everything legal."

"A dispute over a drinking bill? Or a woman?" Roach said, hands on hips. He looked both exasperated and amused. "Killing business or only boredom?"

"Oh, boredom, of course," the showman said, testing his weapon on the air: slash-thrust, slash-thrust.

"Well," Roach said, "try not to hurt anyone. And if there's a killing, be sure to register it with the constable. Don't want any strange corpses found in the morning. Bad for business."

The crowd laughed. Gareth turned to watch Roach exit the scene and scratched at his face.

Legal murder? Fighting for fun?

The fight began while he was off in his mind, trying to ponder out the meaning of all this. Sounds of bronze on bronze brought him back, reminiscent of Korina's forge back home. Flax' forge. Bronze swords made a special sound like nothing else, ringing and deep.

The two men battered at each other, blocking overhand chops and roundhouse swings, neither especially elegant. The smaller bumped into the showman, forcing him against the crowd near where Gareth stood. People pushed him back into the rough ring and the fight went on until the showman scored a hit with his dull sword.

He struck against the handguard of his opponent's weapon with a horrible noise, a broken noise. The showman's sword shivered violently and he dropped it to the dirt, shaking his hand. But his enemy also dropped his sword, and two fingers with it.

Gareth's Greenlander was quite good. His father and mother had taught him. But it seemed they had left out some choice words. Gareth imagined they were mostly profanities.

He thought about helping but nobody else did. Around him, strangers laughed and pointed, and the group began to disperse into the night, the fun concluded. Gareth did not think to wander with them and soon was alone with the two fighters and their seconds.

"Swords," the showman mumbled. Then, more firmly, "That'll be gold then, Master Wilkes. Five coins, you wagered."

"Be decent," the other man said through his teeth. His companion was busily bandaging his hand. "My fingers, you wretched scoundrel. How am I to work?"

"Too drunk to feel the pain, it seems. Too bad. And you ought to have considered all that before you decided to come play with swords. My gold, please." Then he seemed to notice Gareth standing there with his mouth open. "You have a problem, boy?"

"I don't think so," he said, heart seeming to come alive.

"Not from around here, I take it. Well, here's a piece of advice good the world over: it isn't polite to stare."

"Yes."

"So? Off with you. Unless you care to make a wager?"

"Um..." Gareth blushed and looked away, not sure what he was supposed to do – or even to think about. But he was in the habit of walking by now and his feet took over, carrying him past the two men and their friends, into darker streets. Then they took him back. Without knowing why he did it, he went back to the showman. "I have a question," he said.

The man looked surprised. "Is it one of honor? Because I could use some more beer money."

"No. I notice you seem to be a good age."

The man laughed. "Maybe *I* will have a question of honor. Only that does not sound like a question."

Gareth wanted to laugh, too, so friendly was the man's smile. "It's only... There was a murder here. A long time ago. A real one, not a fight. A woman and her man, stabbed, her raped. Would you remember it? Would you know where it happened?"

"No," the showman said, turning back to his friends.

"Thank you in any case."

"But I know who would know," he said without turning back. "Go to the Hanging Sevens. A drinking house. Three streets behind you. Ask for Milla One-Tooth. Old Milla knows everything."

"Thank you," Gareth said, and set off walking.

The man continued at his back, a grin in his voice: "Only don't tell her I sent you. I still owe them money."

***

Whilla sat with her mother on the little bed. Crickets chirped outside and the sounds of people began to fade. "How can you be here?" she said. "Really?"

"Cannot say," Chess said back, softly because the others all slept or pretended to, Jeen in the other bed, Guarl and Xin Ban tangled together on the floor like long-legged puppies. "The day you left, when you touched me, I felt something. It took days to grow but even then I knew what it was. It was like the first time the lake spirit spoke to me but also unlike. I felt..."

"Better?"

"Yes, better. As though there were hope. Like I had slid into the water with wounds that should have festered and murdered me and slid out with a chance at life. Only the smoke did not come, the sounds of swords and death."

Whilla stayed quiet a moment. She traced an old scar on her mother's bicep, one of a great many. "It saved you out for something. The battle was done whether you lived or not. It needed you to go on."

"Perhaps," Chess said.

"I wish I could restore you to what you were. They all say you were magnificent."

"I think I still am. Who else has so many scars to show? Each one is a victory, a kind of honor. Back at home in the north, well, so many stories and honors would bring many offers."

"Offers?" Whilla said, then she understood and blushed. "Oh. But I mean, I wish I could take away your pain, your fatigue."

"Yes, girl. Yes. I might even want that myself. But it was a price I paid, and willingly. I have this to endure so you can live. You and your friends and Erlo, your sisters, all the others. This was the cost of life."

"Even so."

"Yes," Chess said, and sighed. Whilla heard it and felt it, felt her mother's ribs expand and release in her embrace.

She touched Chess' arm again, more fully this time, her whole hand smoothing out the skin. Her eyes closed as she thought of how much she loved her mother, how proud she was, how glad she was here. They would have to part again, Whilla knew that, but to be able to say goodbye once more was beautiful.

Goodbye.

A hard word, a loaded word. A harder thought.

Tears came with it, as hard and loaded as the word. They stung their way out from under her eyes to hang from her eyelashes like raindrops under an eave. No sobs, no piteous noises, just the knowledge that love hurts sometimes. Her mother had scars gained from loving, real, physical scars that could never be erased, and those were a kind of honor. And Whilla's tears, they were an honor, too.

One of them dropped from her eye to splash against her arm. It was cold by now from the air, the heat of her body dissipated away. When it touched, her eyes opened.

Blue light wafted from her hand, the one touching her mother's arm, as the heat had left her tear: into the air, never to be known. Blue light that was not light, that struck the eyes but did not impart a glow to anything else.

"Did you..." But her mother's eyes were closed. Chess only basked in the love of her daughter, too tired to do anything else.

"What, dear?"

"Nothing, Mother. You should rest. So much walking, and so fast to have caught up to us here."

"Not so fast. We came a straighter way. You will have taken the causeway, to look for relics of past battles, as boys are wont to do."

"Still, you must wish for sleep," Whilla said, standing, not believing her mother's explanation. Something else. Gods and purposes.

"I feel more awake than ever," Chess said. "Something in the air. I hardly ache now. I could almost take up my spear and go out to look for monstrous pigs in the lanes below."

"Do you wish it?" Whilla started to kneel, to draw the spear from its place under the bed.

Chess put a hand on her arm. "No. No, such is for the young, girl. It is for you to learn now. Perhaps I will sleep after all. Here, lay with me. There is room, just here."

To sleep once more with her mother close – close and more awake than she had been in years... But her sisters were still far away, and her father. "No," Whilla said, feeling the sadness of her own smile. "My place is with them now." She put out the candles and got onto the floor, pressing up against Xin Ban. The other girl sighed in her sleep and moved to make more room against her body.

"Gareth," Guarl said, perhaps in a dream.

"He is safe," Whilla whispered.

"No," Guarl whispered back. "He is dangerous."

That should have disturbed her but it did not. It was a thought she had without knowing, now put into words in the weird twilight between dreaming and waking, and it fit there. She looked at it as she might look at a candle-flame: interested but not entranced. Then sleep rolled over her.

***

The place was ordinary. Worse, it was a stupid thing to try to do in the dark: to examine the site of the murder decades afterwards, kneeling in gravel by a bronze memorial while mosquitos tried to murder him.

Another one landed on his hand. He heard it, a tiny *whing*ing sound, slapped it away. He put one hand on the monument to feel for letters.

It was cold. The little bronze post smelled of ice and metal, a scent that ached in his teeth. Flinty gravel underfoot, almost certainly new since the killings, and grass on a nearby verge. There was an alley behind him and a lane ahead with houses that smelled of sap and brick dust: also newer than the murder.

Where would the two young lovers have been walking? That way would lead away from the city, into fields and then the woods that surrounded Hong.

He traced out letters on the post. This was how Jeen had taught him to read and write, tracing letters in sand with a stick, one by one until he knew them all, then word by word. The post said:

Reeba
Reflections and love
Offered as food
For what else can sustain the dead?

Gareth found those to be strange sentiments. He stood to consider them. While he thought, a light fell on his back.

"Old signpost, old message. Young man in the dark. You bring a new one?"

"A new what?" Gareth said, turning, calm.

"New message." The speaker was an older woman, seamed and gray, toothless. She wore good cotton dyed in bright colors, those visible in the glare of her lantern. Three candles burned within.

"No," Gareth said. "Only questions."

"Bad business," she said. She came closer, looked up at him. "Very bad. Jarl said you were curious, and that's bad enough."

"The curiosity, or that Jarl said it?"

"Oh, he's a piece of mischief, that's right," she said, and her chuckle sounded like a squirrel declaring its territory. "Come along with me, child. We'll have us a walk along the lane.

You're a handsome one. I can pretend I'm still young and pretty if you pretend the same."

Gareth blushed and wondered if her candles were bright enough for her to see it. But he took her arm and they strolled along. "Is this how it was then? Two young lovers arm in arm, walking away from town?"

"Toss some hard brew into it and yes, I suppose it was."

"No packs or carts, no animals. Not to leave, then."

"Oh no, no. They were not married yet, see." She walked slowly, pushed up against Gareth so that he could imagine just how it was. He found himself aroused and even more embarrassed. She went on, "Round here, young folks are not allowed to tumble one another until they've their own house. Rooms won't let to them, parents won't allow it. But they was eager, as young ones are. You are eager, aren't you?"

"Of course," he said. "The night is warm. The crickets sing to us, and the locusts, too. Somewhere the owls preen and the pigeons hide in the boles of trees and everything is ripe for romance."

"Listen to you talk," she said. "The night is cold and my bones are old. But I remember, yes I do. It was as you say. Just so." They passed between some houses into a spot even darker than the rest of the night. "Just there, Henried would have baled his hay. Lazy man would have left it out for the night. Should have taken it all in but he lost his sons that year, all four of them. Well. Warm place for young lovers on a nice night."

An assignation, Jeen would have called it. But she was a princess of sorts, prone to big words with heavy meanings. "Someone followed them. They were going here, to this field, to love. And someone caught them."

"Oh, yes."

"You saw it."

"Could be that I did. Except I didn't. I saw someone running away though, after."

"You were here, too."

"Yes," she said. "I confess it, I was. Bit too old for bedding down in the hay, that's right, even then. Not too old for stealing sheep, though."

Gareth stopped and she stopped with him. They stood arm in arm under the moonless sky in the shadow of two houses. He thought, mind turning as slowly as the unseen stars above. Then, "May I have your lamp?"

"Yes, boy." She gave it to him.

It had a wire handle that looped over the top. The wire was hot from her hand, hot from the candles. He held it up until he could see her face, really see it. Lines, creases, gullies carved out by time and care. Baggy eyes, brown under white brows, hair gone mostly to silver. And a mark on her forehead. "You come out at night when people can't see your face well enough."

"And I have a hood. Around my shoulders here, see?"

"Yes."

There was a mark on her face, over her eyebrows, under her hairline. A brand, a scar from an old burn.

He said, "When you are caught stealing sheep, they mark you here, don't they?"

"Yes."

"Beasts."

"Steal a sheep, steal a life. That's how it goes, boy. Never mind you're too poor yourself to eat. Take the food off someone else's board. Lucky they only marked me. I only stole the once. Well, not counting the times they never caught me – but never after that." She smiled.

Her grin had no impact on Gareth at all. He felt tears pushing from behind his eyes, hot, passionate tears. "I'm sorry," he said, and gave back the lantern.

"You didn't do it. And I've made my way since, yes. So now you know why I was out here."

"And why you said nothing. Which just leaves what you saw."

She turned away, set down the lamp. "Never told a soul, not until Jarl come to town. Fighter, he is, bragger. Had a brother like him, years ago. Hard. Ruthless, even, maybe bad. A lover down deep, a lover, a poet, hurt and afraid. Well, and he had himself a son. They said you come back, boy, and it was like he come back from the dead. Never knew him much myself, but I knew him when I saw him."

Gareth's heart had sunk down to hit stomach, down to his groin, and it was going lower. Reality had taken a sudden turn. Reason and emotion skirmished in his head with sounds like the duel earlier in the night. "You knew him."

"I did. And when he run off with blood on his hands, well, I couldn't tell, you know? I couldn't say. Family. But he saved me the trouble, didn't he? Run away. Not just from the murder but from the whole town. From his life. Thought he was safe only he come back later, years later. Got himself strung up."

"He did it," Gareth said. "You're saying he really did it."

"Unless there's some other reason for him to run from two dead people, all covered in blood, in the night, and then pack up and leave the next morrow."

"And you're saying you're..."

"Best to forget that, son," the woman said, and picked up her lantern. She took a step and then another, out towards the darkness past all these new houses. "Didn't no good ever come of having me around. Thief. That's what they called me. Was only hungry, only hungry."

He took a step of his own, a big one. Caught her and turned her around to look into her face. "Family." He looked again at the shape of her eyes, at the shadows of her cheeks, the rounded chin. But the dark won: there was not enough light to see, and he did not want to embarrass her again with the lantern. "You're family."

"You owe nothing," she said, and pulled away. "Hangman cleared all the debts, boy. Well, and I said my piece. Clears the rest, don't it?" This time she kept walking, and Gareth let her.

He stood, mind racing, heart dead at his feet. Time ground past and past. Finally his mind cleared enough to wonder, and he tossed a question after her: "But where will you go?" Only she was long gone by then, invisibly far away. All that was left to do was to return to his friends, his family.

On the way back, he stopped at the bronze post once more, touched it again, felt it all over for writing. That weird message he pondered while his hands worked. And they found something. A lip on the back side from the epitaph, a bevel. His finger traced inside of it, found another engraving. One word. It was hard to read with his hand: small, cramped, hardly room to move. But he concentrated, tried again and again, patience lifted by despair.

One word.

Roach.

Works

Wyrrn stood on a rich carpet thrown over dusty brown gravel. Over her head, silk sheets caught the wind and tried to flap, rattling the poles that held them. Four poles, one square, one carpet. The silks shone pink and red and yellow under the sky, letting in enough light to hurt her eyes even were the four sides not open to sun and wind.

She had a table, chest-high, with a few bits of parchment and ink. Her old dress still rode her shoulders, augmented now with a kilt and the headdress torn from the last Gravetender's corpse.

Ten days ago, I was afraid of Jul having me murdered. Or his mother doing it. Now I have no fear of such – my station has worsened. No sense fearing the inevitable.

Only she did fear. The dress clung to her back in a wet pool along her spine. Her palms were too damp to touch the parchments without ruining them. And there was not a soul around to speak to or plot with. No guards, no assistants, not so much as a messenger hidden in the shade to await her orders. Only the wind and dust.

Only the dead.

"*I promised you, did I not?*" Dllyx had said. "*And here it is. All this place is a blank parchment awaiting drops of ink from your pen. Dream it up and a horde of slaves will descend to make it happen.*"

Dllyx' laughter still seemed to echo back and forth from the walls of tombs all around, chattering, maniacal.

"I am no Gravetender," Wyrrn said, and wondered if it were early days yet to start talking to herself. Madness was as certain as death only she hoped to stave it off a while longer. So, back to the drawing.

Only she was as terrible at drawing as she had suspected. Some blotchy ink lines graced the page but nothing that looked like anything. And there was no inspiration. Whose tomb was she meant to be building, anyway?

"Nobody's."

Her own voice surprised her again, but it was right.

"I am here to accomplish nothing. If she wanted work done, she could have left the old Gravetender out here. But without plans, what will the slaves do? Go home, I suppose."

It would be simple. She could just walk over to the quarry, a day or so north, and march up to the High Master or whatever they called the chief of slave-runners, and tell them to send all the children away. A pocketful of grain and a flask of water and off you all go.

But she did not do that.

Wyrrn tried another line. The ink just would not flow from the pen as it did from her quill. It spotted and clumped and ruined the parchment. And still no shapes or forms or purpose came to mind.

"Ah," she said, this time ready for her own words. "A gift. I no longer fear my own death or the manner of it. She's already killed me."

***

A fresh morning. Wyrrn had slept in the open tent on a silk rug. Her scalp itched; as she woke, she scratched sand from her hair, dusted it from her palms. This was no way to live.

But, for a dead person, she imagined she was doing rather well. A little dirt in her hair was a minor inconvenience next to having her organs scooped out into jars and her limbs restrained with varnished rags.

Food was a problem. She made a crude toilet in the sand, scrubbed her hands with sand, rubbed sand both real and metaphorical from her eyes, then worried about her grumbling stomach. Dllyx had made no provision for sustenance or even water, only a metal pen, some bare parchments, a touch of weak shade.

The slave camps would have food. Or the barracks. Guards wandered the Tomblands erratically, and they were people. People ate food.

In the end, curiosity won out. Soldiers were interesting; they figured in almost any history she could remember reading. They fought and died, rose up kings and brought them low. But slaves...

Out here, the slaves were but children. And the histories barely mentioned them.

So, the slave camps. An hour north through blowing sand, past a rising sun that made her squint into the wind. The monuments stabbed at her consciousness, old things and older that she struggled to associate with the names of the revered dead – and the reviled. Old Grandfather was easy enough to see, his great pyramid a monument to his longevity. But where was Ynn, his son? And who dwelt under that thing shaped like half a globe? She tucked the headdress under one arm. Silly thing, heavy and hot.

The walk went quickly with so many delicious questions to distract from her thirst and hunger, from sand that rattled around in the bottom of her sandals no matter how many times she shook them out, no matter how carefully she trod. She heard the camps before she could see them: the noise of bronze and wood tools on stone were like music. The sound of the Tomblands that would slowly impress on her mind, that would come to signify this sun, these colors, this heat.

Then the sight. A wooden fence around a quarry that moved over time, drifting ever westward along the seam of red rock this particular camp mined. Red dust blowing east on the wind as though running from the sun. And children, hordes of them, all ages, bent to the work. They used antlers or bronze chisels or wooden mallets, strings or wires. Some used plain strength to haul rocks around on their backs. Small children as young as a few years, older ones close to adulthood, everything between.

Every one had too much sun in their face. Every bare back showed signs of the lash.

When Wyrrn drifted into the camp, climbing over the crude fence, three Masters turned their eyes to her. One, a tall woman with thin lips and a long nose, hurried over. "This place is for slaves," she said, glancing at Wyrrn's silver kilt. "You are no slave."

"A Great One now, I suppose," Wyrrn said. "Lately a slave. Really just a thirsty woman."

"How did you come to this place?" the Master said. She tapped her short lash against her leather kilt – lower rank than Wyrrn. "You walked across the desert?"

"The King bade me come. She gave me this hat but neither food nor water. I can hardly eat the hat."

Now the Master noticed the headdress under Wyrrn's arm. "But that is the Gravetender's headdress."

"Quite," Wyrrn said. "I suppose I should wear it, only it is very heavy and the day already so warm. Out in my tent and among the tombs, there was no-one to see."

"You are the Gravetender."

"Quite," Wyrrn repeated. "So, is there water to be had here? Food? What do Masters do for food?"

The Master dropped her eyes – then fell to her knees. "You did not... I... Please, forgive, Great One. Forgive. You must have me beaten, I know that, but please..."

"Oh, stand up. Just show me where there is water."

"Yes, Great One," the Master said, climbing to her feet. "This way. A cooling shed, the best we have. King Ynn himself came once – a momentous day that was. To this very shed." She led the way. "That day marked the rise of Mithodroxes. She had her first vision that same day he came to visit. And Lud was here, the Great Overseer, almost a king himself."

Wyrrn listened to the woman ramble and rattle until she opened the door to a low stone building, gray where most of the stone here was red. Inside was cool and damp. Water trickled into a cistern, the noise making Wyrrn want to piss again despite being desert-dry inside and out.

A stone bench ran around the outside. She sat, put her feet up on the lip of the cistern. Sand slid out of her shoes, out of her clothes and hair. The Master found a metal cup, dipped water, gave it to Wyrrn with a deep reverence. Silently, she backed out of the place.

Cool, wet, shady. Wyrrn drank water. Slowly, enjoying each sip. It tasted of stone, sand, the cup – but also of life and of dark places underground. What sorts of story could water like this tell? How many parchments could it fill with wise words?

The Master came back after the cup was empty. She was laden with food wrapped in linen, making Wyrrn think of the denizens of the various tombs all around. But the Master unwrapped yellow bread with olives baked into it, a small loaf of hard cheese, and a bowl of moist dates.

"Great One, will you be staying long? Sometimes they come, the new Gravetenders... And they go again, and we never see them. But they are... and you are..."

"Your anxiety is misplaced, I think," Wyrrn said. "Two days ago, I was a slave. An historian, a teacher of children. Now I have this hat and this silver kilt. Strange rank. I am here as a joke, a punishment of sorts. She even demoted me as she promoted me: the last Gravetender's kilt was gold. I am Outcast. I do not intend to punish anybody. Thank you for the food."

The Master bowed her way out.

Wyrrn ate food in the dark, chewing each bite with intense thought. The bread was the best thing she had ever tasted, fatty and soft, salty, with a crust that almost crunched in her teeth. But she thought little of her fortunes. Bread was for the living and she was just a spirit, a ghost. A revenant that had not yet realized it was time to lay down and be still.

Her attention was on the noises outside. Children grunting with effort. Tools and rocks. A young person feeling the lash, crying out but not begging.

All this to make those things outside. Men and women fit the stones but children cut them. Slaves.

She stood, brushed crumbs off her clothing, and went back into the sunlight. Masters rushed to make everyone busy, probably to impress her with their efficiency. She cornered one, a man with three brown teeth in his mouth and skin that marked him as an outlander.

"What happens when they grow up?" she said.

"Great One?"

"I know that," she said. "Look, I will put the hat back on to save the confusion. Well? What happens to them?"

"They... The ones who die are thrown into the desert or built into the walls or burned and mixed into mortar. The ones who live, they cannot work these quarries any longer. They... Some are sold. To other slavers, to the peoples that gave them up. Some are moved. Into temples, or farms, or the palace. Those are the lucky ones, Great One. Most, they go on to be the main workers of the Tomblands. The fitters and breakers, haulers, climbers."

"I understand," Wyrrn said. It seemed obvious once he said it. Those adults had to come from somewhere. "And the children. Where do they come from?"

"We buy them, Great One," he said, turning away and looking down.

"From?"

"Sometimes foreigners sell us their children. They are poor, cannot keep them. Sometimes gangs rove the outlands and bring them back in chains. We do not ask how they were taken, by sale or force. Merchants gather them by the river."

Wyrrn watched two children haul a rock much too big for them. It slid across little round stones a third child raced to throw in front of it, running behind to gather the stones back up only to toss them in front of the rock once more. One wrong step, one slip, and any of the three children could have their leg shattered under the block. They had rope burns on their hands so deep the hands seemed deformed.

"Harsh lives," she said.

"Yes, Great One. Sometimes... The last Gravetender asked us to lighten their loads, to take only slaves accustomed to sun. Work slowed and we went back to this way, this more brutal way. We teach these children to endure, use their youth, and the tombs get built."

"Why?" Wyrrn said, mostly to herself. The Master started to answer but she waved him silent. The question needed to hang in the air. It had followed her out of the cooling shed and it needed to be known.

What purpose is served by all this?

The histories did not say. It was known that, before these new Hitaians who styled themselves as God-Kings, the Tomblands were made by professional laborers. They worked out of love, part of a national project. But this, this atrocity, had started sometime before the advent of the God-Kings. They did not bring it but found it. Wanted it. Took it.

Why?

Something about this place was worth all the suffering, justified it. Not tombs for the dead, no. Not immortality for a select few. Something grander. If only she had her scrolls, her histories.

"Do you keep records here?" she said, the words erupting out her mouth from someplace deeper.

"Records, Great One?"

"Papers. Tallies. Histories."

"Only accountings, Great One. Grain usage, water rations, productivity over time, slave titles. Nothing of interest to a Gravetender, surely."

"Yes," Wyrrn said. "Exactly of interest, to me. And I wish to see this machine in action. This quarry, the masons, the draggers and crafters, the architects. I wish you to build me something and right away."

"Of course," the Master said, bowing deeply. "What is your desire? Only name it."

"I need a workplace. Here. A room with no windows, with a cool, dry space for documents."

"We keep our accounts in the grain silo, Great One," the servant said, bowing deeper.

"That will never do. I will reside there until my temple is finished. Make it spare, a place for work."

The Master bowed so deep his hair touched the sand. "A temple?"

"Yes. A temple to history. To the ancestors, if you like."

He ran off to begin to make her dream a thing of sand and stone. And there was a grin on his face as he left.

At least someone is happy. Perhaps things will be well, after all.

***

Jul found a note in front of his door. It was partly lodged under a rug; he saw the edge and wondered at it.

Has the teacher returned so soon from her exile?

Who else would slip parchment paper under his door? Almost no-one else could read or write.

Mother?

His heart quickened and sweat stood out on his upper lip. Why would she give him a note? For no reason that could possibly be good. The bruises were not yet healed from his last beating.

He shifted from foot to foot, his walk down to the stables forgotten, the note like an asp in his path. Only one way to defeat the snake: pick it up and read it.

Only he did not want to.

Jul pushed open the door and contemplated the hallway. He could just step over it, leave it buried under the rug, pretend not to have seen it. Ignore it. Only then it would nag at him the way the teacher had nagged at him, forcing him to have knowledge.

Your father was a brute, a savage. You are the last product of his sadism. He murdered his own siblings and exiled his children. Your mother is worse, only more subtle. She will have you killed soon and begin again. And there is a note, a note, a note.

Finally, he knelt down and touched it with one finger. Ran his nail around the ragged edge. Then he snatched it up, petulant, lower lip out as though his mother had interrupted him playing with his puppies.

The writing inside was large and inexpert. Not the teacher, then. No more lessons for him, not ever. And not his mother, whose letters were well-formed even if her words were only partly literate. A mystery. A puzzle.

He read the words, mouth moving, shaping them into meanings.

Ignore the stables. The foals do not need your affections and your mother watches to see if you will love one of them. But I hear that they are training a cheetah today and using live bait.

A slave was caught stealing from the granary. The servants plan to bet on how far she can get. Such information is very valuable.
Your friend.

He read it twice more, scanning for some meaning beyond *your mother watches.* Those words took up most of his inner sight, made it hard to even wonder at the rest of the note.

Your mother watches.

The lives of servants and slaves meant nothing, nothing at all. What profit was there in knowing they would bet on such a thing? Wagers were for those who had small lives and hoped for more. What more could a Prince wish for? He could not win a dead mother, not betting on races, especially ones with such sure outcomes.

Your friend.

But he had no friends, only slaves and servants.

Except for one.

He took the note with him, pulling the door closed behind him, and headed out for the proving grounds. At the first torch, he took some fire along. It rode well on the parchment, smoking and glowing until the parchment was gone. Wherever it went, the flames went with it.

Chans was there, standing among the servants, dressed as one. He was too big to be a servant. Short but wide, a family trait Jul had yet to inherit. Dressed in wool with wooden sandals. A useless disguise, really. His back showed where his shirt hung away from his neck, and there were no markings there, no scars. His hair was long but clean, and overall he gave off an air of health and wellness, of confidence. He lacked the desperation of a servant.

Jul came to stand with him. Together, they looked down a long track to the animal pen, dirt with grass growing up in the verges. The fence was only four feet high, posts six feet apart with wooden slats nailed horizontally between them. Just a guide, nothing to keep a dangerous animal from the spectators but training.

"I got your note."

"Obviously," Chans said. "And do be subtle, will you?"

Jul smiled, thinking how subtle he could be. Chans was dressed as a servant; Jul could have him beaten or killed any time he was displeased. But he was not displeased, and that was a strange feeling. Chans spoke as an equal, as a mentor, and he did not know how to feel about it.

"She comes."

Jul glanced about, confidence shattered like the illusion it was – but Chans did not mean his mother. He meant the poor hapless slave.

The gate opened at the far end of the track and a naked woman spilled out of it. She screamed and fought, tried to get back into the pen, but people with spears forced her out. She fell again, into the moist dirt.

She turned and examined her path ahead: five hundred feet of worn track ending in a blank wall, the palace wall. Fence lay to either side, lined with servants, the crowd growing thicker moment over moment.

"She will try to force her way through the crowd," Jul said.

"She is a slave," Chans countered. "She will take the easy path, the fatal path."

"We will see."

The woman stood on wobbly legs, a foal fresh from the womb, finding her legs.

"A gold penny on it," Chans said.

"Betting is for fools."

"Losing is for fools. Winning is for those with the heart and mind to see hard truths. Will you win, or die?"

Jul kept his mouth shut and his eyes on the woman.

Behind her, a noise in the pen. A cage had opened and the cheetah was in there, against the gate. Waiting. Growling. It coughed, battered the bamboo bars that kept it from its prey.

The slave ran between the fences, dashing for the far wall, a frightened, mindless animal. The pen opened and the cheetah erupted, faster than breath, faster than thought. It took her down in a tangle, clamped fangs on her throat.

"I did not lose," Jul said. "I knew better than to bet."

"You also did not win."

"Neither did you," he said, a smile teasing the corners of his lips.

"You have me there," Chans said, also grinning. "You spoke to your teacher about your father."

Servants, formerly intent on the sport, noticed who was among them and quickly found other places to be. Within moments, just Jul and Chans loitered at the fence. Servants walked between them to retrieve the cat – not a job Jul envied.

"She thought I had changed my heart and grown an interest in history. But I learned all about him. A monster, he was."

"In his way," the other Prince said. "Yes, monstrous. He meant to kill me. I think. But he gave me a chance to get away. A Chans, to get away." He laughed at that. "I think Chans was supposed to go on, to live as me – a gift to his guard-captain, who he blinded and murdered on his way to his father. But perhaps... He had a soft heart, you know. In the end, he let his sister go into exile, let me go into ambiguity."

"Meaning what?" Jul said, spitting through the slats onto the track.

"Who knows? Only Ynn, the old devil, and he's not here to speak of it, is he?"

"But you are. What do you want, old man?"

Chans put his back to the fence as the cheetah prowled past, a handler on each side. "Only to help you," he said.

"Help. Me. Things do not work that way, man. Not here. Here we cultivate our blood then murder everyone who shares it. It is the family way."

"Ynn tried to change that. I would change it, too. But your mother stands in the way. I could remove her."

That would help me, yes it would. A known monster for an unknown monster. Some bargain. Only I know my mother will kill me soon, or make me wish she had. Can this man be worse?

"Then I would be King here. I would rule this place," Jul said.

"In time."

"As I thought. I will think on it."

"Think fast," Chans said. "And well. Win, or die. Only, while you are thinking, I need to meet some priests."

"Priests?" Jul started to walk back towards the palace, out of the sun. "What for?" He thought of the woman watching him under the stairwell. Wherever he went, he could remember priests nearby. Not making contact, only watching.

"Just tell them you wish to speak with them all, to pick one. As King, you will be their patron. They will fall over themselves to win favor from the presumptive King of Hitai. And when they come, you will present me."

"I will," Jul said, smiling again. "By the Gods and the gods, I will."

Chans squeezed his shoulder and smiled back. "Time to disappear again. But know I am watching over you just as she is. I will not let her kill you. Your trials are nearly over, Nephew."

***

Chans did not wait for Jul to arrange a meeting. In the north, where water flowed freely and rested in great lakes, sometimes people liked to bathe in it or even to swim. And the water could be cold but tolerable, or cold enough to kill. Thus in that icy place they had a phrase for what he meant to do: testing the water.

The city of Hitai stank today. A taxidermist near the palace accounted for much of the odor. It was a long, flat building with plaster walls and no windows. Carcasses came in by river barge. A dozen salvagers sorted now through piles of crocodiles, tossing the rotted ones into the water and keeping those that had arrived mostly undamaged. Sharp knives took off the skins expertly and butchers waited for the rest.

In this place, nothing went to waste. In the water, poor people of grayish castes sat in rowboats. They used long-handled nets to snatch up the rotted carcasses rejected by the salvagers. Those could be made into fish bait, boiled for stew by the poorest, stripped for leather that did not need to be cosmetically pleasing. Even the teeth would wind up serving in tools.

Life in Hitai, Chans thought. *Life everywhere.*

Not all of the stink came off the taxidermist. The river itself reeked of spilled dye and sewage. All along the streets were people selling food. Roasted scorpion, snake on skewers, rats or pigeons. As the neighborhood grew poorer, the vendors stopped saying what sort of meat was in their offerings.

A cat came out of an alley, as tan as the walls around it. It looked at Chans with its tail up and its eyes on his. Hoping, perhaps, for a treat. Chans looked but otherwise ignored it, intent on getting his business done and then perhaps retreating to the countryside for a few days, away from the stink.

The temple he wanted was not subtle. It stuck up from this poor neighborhood, a tiered pyramid forty feet high in a wattle-and-daub sort of place. Conspicuous wealth in a conspicuously poor part of town.

Steps went up one side of the pyramid. He climbed them slowly, keeping pain off his face by rote and habit, hardly even tempted to wince after all these years of pretending wholeness. At the top, minutes later, his reward was relief from the sun. He had not realized he was sweating and he smelled as bad as the town.

The smell inside the small room at the top was cleaner but no more pleasant: incense and wood smoke and, under that, something musky. Reptilian, even.

These are all the smells of home – the cooking, the spices, incense and smoke, even death. When did I become a foreigner?

Two women sat in the shade, one older but both well beyond the appointed lifespan of a common Hitaian. They wore white samite. A fire burned on a bronze plate in the middle of the room and benches lined the four walls.

Lurkian, Chans assessed, glancing at the plate. *Worth more than slaves and does not need feeding.*

The women eyed him as he eyed them. He knew how he would look to them: like a stranger.

"This place honors Caiph," the older of the two women said. "Caiph is for those of The Blood."

"A long walk from the palace," Chans said. He put his fists on his hips.

"You do not look to have come from there," the old one said. Her companion looked even more closely, though.

"He does have a look about him, this one. Look beyond the garb, Sister Ormea."

"Oh, I see what you mean."

Chans watched them watching him. Then, "If you look any more closely, your eyes will strip the garb off my hide."

"A rough speech, too," the elder said. "As if from a man long away. But run, Sister Mand. Bring up the High One. If there is stripping to be done, let her eyes do such work."

Mand got up from her bench. She tossed a handful of something fragrant on the fire. Then she slipped out a door hidden in the shadows where Chans had thought there was a bench.

"Sit," Ormea told him. "You've no kilt to tell your rank so I shan't call you Great, but I will make you welcome. Myrsa will know how to dispose of you."

"What if I did not come to be disposed of?" he said.

"Men never do. Always some other purpose to speak of. In the end, though, we must have our offerings."

Mand returned via the hidden door, another woman in her wake. Of middle years, with dark gray skin and tight, graying hair. Her kilt was silver, her sash gold.

"The Blood rules over Hitai," Chans said, standing. "But who rules over The Blood?"

"Blasphemy," the new woman said. "I am Myrsa and I serve Caiph." She came closer, touched his arm, walked around him. Chans had to step away from the bench to let her behind him. One finger trailed across his back, his other shoulder, his chest. "I know your type."

"Let us talk," Chans said. "Send these ones away."

"Oh, I do not take offerings myself. Too old for such. And there is blood, and there is Blood. The Blood is unruled and yet the blood requires guidance."

Chans thought he heard the distinctions but might have been wrong. His ear for his own tongue was not so strong as once. "I offer not gold... or blood. Send these women away from here and I will tell you secrets."

Myrsa waved vaguely and the two others left, smirking.

Chans blushed a little, surprised at his own reaction. Myrsa sat down, crossing one leg over the other, and patted the space next to her on the bench. Chans complied but left some room between them.

"You may have fewer secrets than you think," she said. "My Prince."

"Your Prince has only ten years. Other Princes, well, you would have to bring them back from the dead."

"Such a thing has not been done," she said. "Do you know how?"

"Does the King abuse you?"

"Your mind is skittish. A horse in tall grass, not knowing where the lions are. A problem with your type." She edged closer and again put a hand on Chans' arm. "We lost your line. All of it."

"You have lost me in that tall grass," Chans said. "But I could bring back your Prince. Would that please you?"

"The King will not come here," she said, and Chans felt more lost than ever. There was a game here whose pieces he could not see. "And a woman is of little use to us. We do prefer our Kings to have beards of their own. Much more productive."

"She has a son," Chans offered, feeling blind.

"Yes."

"Does she keep him from you?"

"Oh, yes. And he is not able to make his offerings. Not yet. She hates him, you know. Dllyx the woman hates the boy more than anything. His father is her father, a blood contamination it will take generations to correct. But if we had access to the boy..."

Chans took her hand and held it still. It had wandered to his chest, trying to slip inside his shirt. "What is happening here?"

"Oh, you were too young when you left us. You could be happy here, you know. No need for vengeance, no need to mount a throne. Caiph needs offerings. We serve The Blood. Ynn saw it, saw the need. Stay."

"My nephew... great-nephew, really. He will come to you. Bring an offering. Will you support him over his mother?"

"Politics, and treason," Myrsa said. She withdrew her hand from his body, turned to put her back to the wall. "But if you can protect the boy until he is of age, well. You will send him to us in the right time. And until then, you will rectify your brother's errors. If you are squeamish about breeding, there can be no union."

He blushed again. "That is what you want from me? Easily enough given." He grabbed her shoulders to bring her close, too rough, too awkward, shame on his face.

"Not me," she laughed. "With one carefully chosen to retain the best of you. Downstairs, in the temple."

He let her go. Stood, turned his back on her. "That's all? Why didn't you just say it?"

"I like when your speech grows common. Common is candid. Why, you say? Well, because your brother hated us. And while we know your body well enough here, your mind is not yet known. Will you be disgusted as was Ynn, or hostile as Dllyx, or engage us casually as have so many generations?"

"I need you," Chans said, "and you need me. For now, that would seem to conclude our negotiations."

"We would have certain proofs, of course."

"Of course," he said, and then he strode out of the shade and into the harsh sunshine, back into the stink of the city.

Time

Sun pried its way between the shutters to fall across Jeen's bed, over her face. She woke, stretched, pushed herself into a sitting position. Her feet touched an arm as she turned to stand, and she leaned over to see whose.

Xin Ban, Guarl and Whilla lay in a tangled pile down there. And Gareth lay across the doorway, snoring.

Chess was awake, too. "Morning still comes too early, whether to the Starfall or the Preserves or to this place. It has no decency to wait on old women."

Jeen smiled, then laughed. "Not so old," she said.

"I have seen forty summers."

"Not you, old woman. Me."

They both laughed now, and most of the young ones woke. Gareth just turned over and groaned.

"There is a monster to catch," Chess said. "I suppose the day is not too long after all. We should start."

"But how?" Jeen said.

"Find the bodies, I suppose."

The roomkeeper had hot food downstairs: eggs in their shells and burnt bread with butter, weak tea and strong ale. Jeen gave him the last of her coins to make sure the children ate. Then she put her sword down on the table in front of her: a sure invitation to strangers to sit elsewhere.

With crumbs on her chin, she said, "Do you really think he will come here?"

"Yes. A feeling. The spirit has moved us to this place. Where else would it move him?"

"A confrontation." She touched the sword, used a finger to wander the outline of the hilt, the guard.

"Time is different here," Chess said. She leaned back and belched, washed down the belch with ale.

Jeen tried to puzzle out how the comment applied to the conversation. Confrontations, time... Nothing came.

"Grief," Chess said. "Leaving the Starfall has put time between you and Yohn. It has been days since you wept over him."

Jeen thought now, her eyes slipping shut. The idea was as shocking as cold water, as surprising as the skeleton that had stood up to offer its service all that time ago. The dead walked, and grief moved on. She called up his face and found it as clear as ever: kind, narrow, dark, haunted. Would his face fade from her memory? Would she begin to lose him as she lost her grief?

"They live outside in their time," Chess said, "and they live inside in ours. That is how it has ever been. Soon you will stop looking for him, stop noticing every moment that he is not with you. Because he will be with you: taken out of the world but taken into the heart. Fully, completely, finally joined in a way your wedding could never manage."

Jeen opened her eyes and lurched to her feet, fresh grief like a rockfall over her heart. She snatched up the sword and staggered out the nearest door – the back door into a small yard bordered by stables and a fence.

"Are you running?" Chess said, voice kind.

"Yes."

"Senseless."

"I know."

"So, use that sword instead. Guard up. Feet apart. Good. Feel the stance, the weight of the world against your feet, the air on your arms. Now move. Slash. Throat, eyes, guts. Good."

Chess worked her for an hour or more until Jeen's clothes reeked of sweat, until her lungs begged for air and her arms for rest. The grief sat on her shoulders as if to watch and, while it grew no lighter, she grew stronger.

"I think I can bear it," Jeen said, leaning on the sword.

"I know you can, dear. I only brought it up because I knew you could. Yesterday or the day before or earlier, I did not know. Today, I knew. You will think on it and it will hurt, then you will live and it will hurt less, and one day you will think on it and smile and laugh. Were there not good times? Love? Happiness, even?"

"Yes. Thank you."

She was about to say more. About sisterhood, about the Cougher that Yohn had loved. But a noise came from the alley behind the stables. A scream.

Jeen did not think and Chess moved even faster. Both were out through the gate and into the alley before the scream had died. There in the dirt lane stood two women with baskets of clothes on their hips. Ahead of them, spread across the path, were the remains of a living thing.

"Clothes and shoes," Chess said. "Human prey."

Jeen was more interested in the women. She got between them and the kill. They looked at her sword, at her face, and backed away. "I am here," she said. "I will protect you." But she spoke Old Ilitaian, which only frightened them more. She tried Greenlander but she could really only write it, not speak it. And besides, the women were already running now, laundry scattered in the mucky gravel of the lane.

"Not much left," Chess said. "He ate this one, almost all of her. This mess is a message."

"He will be easy to find, after all," Jeen said.

"Yes. He wants us to find him."

***

"What did you find out there?" Whilla said, sitting on Jeen's bed. She strapped on her shoes with leather thongs that wrapped around her legs past the ankle.

Gareth leaned against the door, holding his head. "Questions," he said. "A gravestone with her name on it, the one he killed. And Roach's name, too, hidden on it. A woman who claimed to be an aunt. Sword-fighters in the street, men with so many fingers they can shrug off the loss of a few."

"Make sense," Guarl said. "And move. Jeen said there would be food for us downstairs. After today, we will have to work for our breakfast."

Gareth stood aside, then followed the others out, down the stairs. The roomkeeper saw them coming and started to reload the table, taking away Jeen's and Chess' used cups and plates.

"That's the most sense I can make," Gareth said. "A strange place full of strangers." But he went on to detail the night, step by step, all the while eating bread and eggs. "And then I came back here," he said. "I got lost in the dark. Took hours just to find it. It looked different in daylight."

"Dueling?" Xin Ban said. "Fighting over honor?"

"Or for money, it seems," Gareth said. "Anyone can challenge anyone. The challenger forfeits the right to choose weapons. The challenged can decline. Once they choose the form of the duel, they can't back down."

"And they kill each other?" Xin Ban said, eyes wide.

"No. Maybe they fight to first blood or something else. But people die. Roach was there. He said so. He didn't see me, though."

Whilla did not know why, but that thought was a comfort. The way he had stood aside at the grave site, the way he had presumed an invitation into their circle, made her reluctant to trust him. "Anyway. We have to decide what to do now. Zhang must be days ahead of us, maybe more. And we don't know where she's going from here. Or if she knows we're behind her. And we got what we came for. You know what happened to your father. We stood at his grave and made our peace."

"Moburu," Xin Ban said.

"Not our problem," Guarl said. "We can't fight something like that."

"We're the only ones who can," Xin Ban said, turning to face Whilla. She pointed at the spear laying along the table just where Jeen's sword had been. "The stories say no weapon can hurt him. No blade, no arrow, no word, no sword. Only metal blessed by the lake spirit."

"Give it back to Chess, then," Guarl said.

"She wouldn't take it," Whilla said, blushing. "I wanted to, but she said she is done with violence."

"She's going to try to talk to him?" Gareth said. "Or let Jeen protect her?"

"We have to stay," Xin Ban said. "Stand and fight if we can."

"Zhang will get away," Whilla said.

Gareth said, "We stay, then. Zhang be damned. There's more here than..."

A scream from behind the yard cut through whatever he said next. The four of them froze, Guarl in the act of pushing bread into his mouth, Xin Ban with an ale flagon halfway to her lips. Then Whilla broke the tableau. She snatched up the spear and they all four bundled out the back door, armed and frightened.

***

The animal watched from a high roof. Below him, families huddled a little closer around their hearths, thinking of the day's work ahead but reluctant to leave their safe little rooms. He sat in the shadow of a brick chimney on the cool tiles, warmed by their human fear.

Chess did not see him, nor Jeen, nor any of the people who had been only children when last he had a human thought. Their eyes never rose to the rooves. His eyes never left the one he had come for.

Her scent had drifted into the orchard one night. Her scent or a memory of it. It came as a challenge, a challenge to purpose.

Jaguars knew no purpose. Only the taste of blood.

But they did not know the taste of fear, either. So what did make him?

And these were questions on the wind, challenges that ought never to have occurred to him. They drifted into the village, now just a place full of bones that the forest would quickly reclaim, erase, all the carefully husbandry lost in the tangle of life living as it will. Bats now ate the fruit meant for men and no nets descended on them.

Once he had been like that orchard. He existed; he was orderly; he fit into some larger scheme, some larger purpose. Once that purpose was gone, though, he drifted away. Reclaimed by the wilderness, wild. His tail flicked away a buzzing insect that became too curious. His mind could not flick away these ideas that intruded on his basic, thoughtless existence.

Below, the two women argued quietly. One of the boys crouched to examine the soil. The other scanned around the area, eyes finally wandering higher than eye level. The girls stood sentinel, one facing each way the lane ran. All peripheral. He had come for none of them.

His stare was all for the sword Jeen carried.

Order

Jul waited in the hot room where Wyrrn had tried to teach him history and reading and languages. The scrolls and parchments stank as they ever did, a high-pitched rotten smell, long-ago death. One narrow window let in the heat of the day. There was one table and two chairs, neither comfortable. Jul chose to stand, to pace, a fresh crop of bruises making the hard wooden seats uninviting.

Rept was first to arrive. He bowed deeply in the doorway. "My Prince. I am honored by your summons. I last saw you on your naming day."

Jul looked up at the man, a wizened, bent fellow at least as old as his mother's uncle. He smelled of sandalwood oil and whatever grease made the remnants of his hair shiny. A silver kilt marked him as high among The Blood. "Be welcome," he said, the words feeling clumsy in his mouth. "Indeed it has been too long. My mother, the King, has kept us apart."

Rept's eyes widened. He took the seat Jul offered him but then stood again, hands behind his back, when Jul did not also sit.

Too bold? Jul thought. *Too direct? Is he so used to lies he cannot hear truth?* But he said, "Be easy, man. I wish a friendship. No good to start that with muddled words. Sit."

Rept sat.

Another priest arrived, saw Rept sitting and Jul standing. Her eyes also widened. "Myrsa," she said. "My Prince, I bring the blessings of Caiph."

"The blessings of whores," Rept said. His words were bitter but he forced them through a smile.

Jul glanced between the two. "This is not why we are here," he said. "Be at peace. I will need all of you, together."

"Of course, My Prince," Rept said. "Please forgive."

Myrsa sat across the table from Rept, again at Jul's request. "There are more coming. Every major sect should send a priest. When we are all together, I will have words for you. Favor for you all."

Over the course of half an hour, the room filled with sweaty faith-leaders, eight in all. They came from the dancers, the prostitutes, the readers, followers of the sun-god, the astrologers, the animal worshipers, the traditional panoply of Hitaian gods, and even one from the Old Hitaian faiths. The room was crowded with women and men and Jul sweated heavily.

When I am King, perhaps I will lead a march north. Wyrrn always said it was cooler there.

But he said, "Be welcome and be at peace." Again, the words tasted awkward and heavy, but his uncle had given them to him to say. "My man will bring bread and wine. Be my guests."

Rept found his voice again. "My Prince, you alluded that we have been kept away from you not by your choice?"

"Yes," he said. "My mother tried to keep me from your influence. I can see that you like to fight. Like jackal puppies over their mother's teats. No, be easy. For too long has this been the way of it. I would bring change."

The Old Hitaian priestess spoke. "Treason," she said. "Your mother will have us flayed – no, impaled – just for being here." But she made no move to leave.

Jul noted her. Small, too slender, not as old as some of the others. She had tiny hands, dark hair, black eyes. Ash-gray skin. "I am too weak yet to oppose her," Jul said. He knew he was giving away no secrets. For a hundred generations the young made war on their parents; for a hundred generations, the King's greatest desire was to be murdered by their children. "But I have a new ally. One who can protect you. Protect us all."

A mutter wandered around the room, a buzz of words. Jul caught none of them but felt their tone.

Fear.

Rept again. "No King ever openly threatened to murder a priest. Always the Kings have served with the consent of the Priesthood, always have given their favor." He looked oddly at

Myrsa with that remark. "Always have they honored the old ways."

"The Gravetender," Jul said.

"And a promise to impale any who dissented," said Chans from the doorway. His form filled the whole space and, when he came in, all eyes attached to him. He had a deep wine flagon in one hand and a basket of bread in the other. Behind him, invisible until Chans stood clear of the doorway, an elderly woman carried a tray of cups. "Drink with me," he said. "Eat with me."

Jul watched them respond, his gaze drifting around the room. The Old Hitaian woman seemed fearful and confused. Rept masked his feelings. Most of the priests were like these two. But Myrsa sat back, relaxed, and smiled.

"My uncle," Jul said, too loud. "My mother's uncle, Ergol. Myrsa smiled more broadly.

"He was killed," the astrologer said. "Old Ynn the Softhearted exiled him to the north to hunt slaves then had a change of heart. Sent soldiers to ambush him on the road."

"Yes," Chans said. "He also sent a decoy with me. I still wear his name. Chans, he was called. The soldiers were meant to kill me and leave Chans to take my name, to live out his days as a prince in the north. They killed him. I took his name and lived. But I've come back."

Myrsa stared at Chans' feet. Jul noticed her stare and followed it, but saw nothing of interest. Chans wore heavy boots in a place where sandals were more common but all his garb was outlandish.

The others noticed Jul's stare and their eyes lowered, too, until the whole room gazed at Chans' boots. Even Chans looked down at them.

"This is your question, yes? You know," he said, pointing to Myrsa. "You know Ergol had one good foot, the other misshapen. You know Chans did not."

Myrsa shook her head in agreement. "And one thing more. The astrologer knows. Kemma."

Kemma spoke. "When the corpse came back, it was put into the house without the bones of one foot. Mutilated. The soldiers who brought it, they said they shot him from afar with an arrow, picked him out of his retinue. A good shot. But by the time they came for the body, it was in pieces, with a piece missing."

"The boot," Rept said.

Chans said, "Yes. And more."

People began to set down their cups, noticing only then that the servant had slipped away, taking her tray with her.

"If you will allow me one of these chairs," Chans said, "I will oblige you." Myrsa stood and he took her seat, handing her the pouch from around his neck as he did so. Then he unlaced his right boot, leaned back, and pulled it off with a grunt.

His foot was wrapped in bandages, a mummy freed from its box. He crossed the foot over his left knee and began to unwrap it. As he did, bits of metal dropped from the wrappings.

Splints and braces.

When the unwrapping was done, the horror was revealed. The foot was a mangled wreck. Half of it was missing, hacked off in some long-ago surgery. Two toes remained: the great toe and its neighbor. They were fused together. Altogether, this half a foot had the approximate size and shape of an average man's whole foot.

"I did not know," Jul said, covering his mouth with his hands.

"Nobody knew," Chans said. "That was the point, Nephew. I did what I had to for my survival. I mourned the boy but I took his name. I mourned the limb but I cut it away, burned the remains with hot steel and hard wine. I limped away from Hitai."

The priests were quiet. Then Myrsa seemed to remember the pouch in her hands. She shook it. "Bones?" she said. "Your bones?"

The servant came back but did not bring her tray. "The King," she said, and moved aside.

Rept stood, face going slack. The others, already standing, straightened. Some glanced around for an exit but there was none. Chans remained seated.

Dllyx entered through the doorway, plenty of room around her form. She did not have to duck even with her headdress on. In one hand she carried her father's scepter, a dirty thing, cracked and broken.

***

Korina sat in the long hall. An ingot rested in front of her, and a heavy hammer. A girl sat on the edge of the hearth with her.

She had fourteen summers. She was tall and pretty with nice teeth. She had big hands, which was a good sign.

"Take the hammer," Korina said. "Use it to flatten out this bar."

The girl picked up the hammer and pushed the ingot around into a position she liked. "Is it very hot in the forge?" she said.

"Very. And smoky. Loud. Lonely."

The girl frowned, jabbed half-heartedly at the metal. The hammer clinked and bounced. The whole bar, not held in place, also bounced. It flipped over with a clatter. "A profession," she said. "A calling."

"For the right person."

"A home. Maybe a family."

What boy would want you? Now you are young and succulent. Soon all your nails will be broken and your hair full of soot. Soon you will have eyes only for the fires and no time to dandle a child on your hip.

"Try again." Korina did not know if she meant the girl's answer or her hammering.

But the girl held the bar still and beat at it once more. She used her strength this time. The hammer bounced, sending a shock up her arm. Korina had felt it enough times to know it when the girl dropped the hammer. "Ow."

"Too hard," Korina said. "Hit it just hard enough. Firmly. When it bounces, work with it. The bounce saves your energy."

"I'm not strong enough," the girl said.

So I fear. "You could be. Here, watch me."

Korina took the hammer. She began to beat the ingot. A small crowd gathered, youngsters mostly, those not assigned yet to apprentice. Nearly all had already failed this test. Her arm rose and fell fast, tapping more than beating, warming the metal. "The strength is not in the force of the blows but in keeping them up. This is a long march, not a sprint to the finish. The work takes patience. Determination." Slowly, as it warmed, the metal grew more malleable. It began to distort. "Enough," she said. "Here. You do it."

The girl tried. Korina gave her that much. In the end, though, she only bruised her knuckles. The bronze grew cool under her ministrations, cold and stubborn. And the noise it made was wrong. It should have rang out, chimed, sang with her. But the note was sour.

Another day wasted. Fourteen children and none apt for the work.

Later, back at the forge that was her real home, she let herself despair.

I need an apprentice. None here can make the metal sing the right note.

There was only one answer to such a question and she hated it. Even the long hall was too far from home, even a bath in the lake too much time away from her work. The fires were not her friends but her lovers. The molten metal was not a thing to be worked but her blood.

I am not strong enough to go away from this place.

She had a bag, a canvas thing left as a gift one morning from some grateful villager. They had even dyed it. Black and heavy, stitched well enough to carry tools without breaking. It sat unused at the bottom of a tool bin under hammers and awls and shapers, under a file and a rasp.

I am not strong enough.

But she dug out the bag, because such a question really had just one answer.

The forge had more than enough tools for working bronze. She left those. She had spent the past months making new tools. Tools for working steel. Those she packed with care into the canvas bag. They clinked as she hefted it. A heavy thing. Too heavy. But the forge needed an apprentice. She was not strong enough to leave this place in search of one.

But I could be.

***

Erlo stood outside Mang's hut. It was squalid and smelled of sickness. He feared to call out or to try the door. Erlo knew about sickness.

He was damp from the lake. Ten days since his last taste of mead. Finally clean, vomit washed away, sour sweat washed away, the stench of weakness and pity washed away.

But here, at Mang's place, his own new-found cleanliness allowed him to smell the sickness.

"Mang, old goat. Open up the door."

He was there quickly. Mang seemed to have shrunken an inch or two lately.

Erlo, seeing his friend face to face, suddenly had nothing to say. He grasped around in his mind for some words. "Didn't see you on the nets or in the thatches. Worried over you."

"Been tired," Mang said around a mouthful of leaves. "Maybe ill, a fever. I feel better today."

"Good. I am glad."

"You look terrible. Have hardly seen you at all since..." He did not finish. Both men knew since what.

"I've been ill myself. For ten years, I've been ill, maybe longer than that. Chess, she..."

Mang's face drooped. "She was a hero. They will sing songs of her long after we're forgotten."

"What?"

"You were fortunate to know her. I might not be strong enough to help you dig but get some mead and I shall help you mourn."

"What?" Erlo's mind was again empty.

"Took her ten years to go. I hope she's at peace now."

"She isn't dead," Erlo squeezed out suddenly. "She's left me to go adventuring again. Left me with a child. A grandchild. Mang, you haven't met... She woke up of a sudden, shook off the spell that had kept her slumbering and weak but did nothing for mine, for my hurts. And she took up some errand chasing after monsters."

Mang's face twisted, his grief confused with surprise and embarrassment. Then he laughed, a low sound, choppy, that ended in a fit of coughing. Tears squeezed out of his eyes. Erlo held him until he got himself in under control, one hand on the lintel to steady himself.

"I ought to have come sooner," Erlo said.

"You might not have found me here," Mang replied.

"Where else?"

"Delirium, self-pity, nostalgia."

"I know that place," Erlo said. "No more mead for me. These people need us, Mang. The war is over but the fighting is not done. We are being tried by peace as harshly as we were by war and I do not know that we are winning."

"Regrets. Losses. The mourning has become part of us. It lives next to all our hearts. But Chess has woken up, you say. And you are waking. Go back to them, Erlo. I will be along. Maybe tomorrow or the day after. I feel good. I am glad you came." Mang slipped back into his place leaving the door to the vagaries of the wind.

Erlo stood up a little straighter. *There is work to be done here and it falls to me.* He raised his voice as though Mang had gone far away and not three paces back to his little cot. "It is not me they need. I am not the tool for this job."

Mang answered with a voice already muzzy with impending sleep. "When a hole needs digging, you look around for a shovel. But if you have no shovel, you dig with your hands."

Erlo left, back into the village proper. The sun seemed a little brighter, tomorrow a little more hopeful. Unease tickled at his stomach and it felt like a fear-thought, a mead-thought. *Drink me away, sleep through it.* So he clung to the hope and let the fear pass by as a stranger.

***

"Treason," Dllyx said. She spoke angrily but inside she was very pleased. "I tried to teach you, boy. I tried to teach you to be subtle. This time I may have to kill you. The lesson just is not taking."

Chans spoke to the servant. "Thank you, Bissa. You have done well."

Dllyx glanced at the woman and frowned. Then she brightened. "Some type of trap. You think I came alone." Now she laughed. "Forty guards await my cry. And they brought just enough stakes for all of you. Except my son. Something else for him, I think."

"In the bag," Chans said as if Dllyx had not spoken.

She frowned again then controlled her face. *Why is he not afraid?*

Myrsa emptied the pouch into one hand.

Bones.

"Not mine," Chans said. "Chans' bones. And there is still more. His tomb."

The priests muttered. Dllyx felt forgotten, ignored. Rage crept up from her belly. "Old bones will not save you, stranger. You will die screaming, but only after you have seen each of these priests die. You came into my palace..."

He cut her off.

"My palace, girl. Your father never completed the rites of ascension. His rule was illegal. He came to his father with a lie in his mouth. Tam lives on, somewhere. And so does Ergol. Me. Let us go to his tomb and you will see those bones match his corpse's missing foot. This proof you have already seen." He pointed at his own crippled foot. "And that last thing."

"The tomb itself," the astrologer said.

"Destroyed years ago," Dllyx said, but she said it past a lump of fear in her throat. *Was it? Was it destroyed? Or did the*

Gravetender neglect it as she did Vault's tomb, the tombs of all those Starfall children?

Xenia came up the stairs behind her. She had a bronze sword in her hand, glittering streakily in the light from the window. "My King?" he said. "Your orders?"

Dllyx started to speak but now one of the priests overrode her. "There is no King at this time," Rept said. "We have evidence that the King serves us illegally, that a better heir is extant. This is he. We will ride into the desert for the last of the evidence. Now."

"You cannot," Dllyx said. "Captain, kill all these traitors. Kill them now."

Xenia looked from her to the priest and back again. "My King?"

Then people were moving. Rept crossed the space, took Xenia by the arm like an old friend. Led her away, down the steps. Others took Dllyx just as gently, herding more than leading, a small mass of people moving through a narrow space. Confused guards waited below. When the group pushed through them, they only followed. Dllyx did not cry out, did not shout or order, as carried along as the rest.

***

Fum had a clear shot. In the twilight, the woman stood near the top of a rise so that half her body was revealed against a purpling sky. She wore a light bronze breastplate and shin guards, leather strips hanging from her belt, and an assortment of weaponry. From this range – about sixty feet – he could reliably put an arrow into her neck or face.

Except there were fifty more just like her on the other side of the rise. He could hear them sawing wood and hammering poles into the ground. A stockade. They rushed north during the daylight but took the time to fortify every night, leaving behind them a string of half-guarded outposts.

Fum had left his grove of trees with his new bow and his untried arrows, striking not north but south. These invaders had sent four soldiers north perhaps to divert him, to keep him looking the wrong way. His question: where had the rest of the troupe gone? And why?

And here was the answer. Fum had perhaps been too good at evading them. They might have suspected organized resistance, the presence of an army. So they had run south to bring up reinforcements.

He put the arrow back in his makeshift quiver and backed away into tall grass. Some hunting animal growled nearby – a serval cat, maybe, smelling a mate. *Good. It will keep those ones cautious, behind their walls.*

He might have wished he had never stumbled across their advance force to begin with, or never announced himself. Every step so far seemed to have escalated matters, accelerated an invasion he was sure would have happened in any event. Such thinking was useless, though. The only relevant question left was, *what now?*

A wood palisade, made with fresh-cut, sappy pine would burn as if fueled by Hael's own fires.

Then they would know they were opposed, perhaps overestimate the attacking force, bring more soldiers than they needed.

It would be fun.

Yes. Life had been dull in some ways. Nobody trying to murder him. No thrones to contend over, or pretend to as a matter of form. Nothing to live up to. Freedom ultimately meant getting enough to eat and watching your campfire did not spread to your bedroll. Ultimately, freedom was pretty banal.

I want more of it.

Yes, lovely banality. So no ultimately futile acts of resistance. Not tonight. His head was full of information now, and he still had a family to consider. Time to run home with what he had.

He backed farther into the grass. Dark fell slowly over the land and he was grateful for its cover. The animal growled again, this time off to his left. Closer.

And another, right ahead of him as he turned to go.

Then a weighted net dropped over his body and soldiers popped up out of the grass, as good a magic trick as he himself might have orchestrated. Six of them. Armed, sharp, but seemingly in good humor in the darkness. They laughed at him.

One, a tall man hardly more than a shadow, said, "This is him. They said he was a hawk but he is hardly more than a rabbit after all."

It was clear those words were for Fum's benefit – otherwise why speak them in Greenlander? "A rabbit indeed," he murmured. "Well, surrender seems prudent, considering the circumstances. Just tell me I'm not bound to be skinned and dropped in your stewpot."

Only the speaker laughed. The rest probably did not understand his words. "Come along quietly and we will all be grateful for a little rest. You have made a lot of trouble for us, little rabbit. And for what? One over-zealous soldier jumps at her own shadow and then the whole army is on the march. Tell me, rabbit, what have you for trade?"

Soldiers had him on his feet now, unbound so far but well-guarded. His weapons, of course, were out of his hands. "Only information, I should say. And courtesy, of course."

"We will see," said the soldier. "Let us start with names. I am Nivek."

Fortunes

Three ships stood off the jetty. Cold, smelly water filled up the half-mile between Zhang and the ships. As far as she could swim unburdened, an impossible task with her fortune in bags around her feet.

"Plague," said a little man at her elbow. Most of the people here seemed small. This one was particularly wiry, brown, and fast-talking.

Plague was a word she knew. Zhang had followed her Commander around the world, from port to port, land to land. She hated the sea. Even now, the smell turned her stomach, and the noise of waves smashing together and timbers creaking made her imagine the ground raising and lowering under her feet, the horizon twisting and tilting. But so much travel made one alert to certain words.

"On the ships or in the town?" she said. She used Jumiel, the language of her home. The man shook his head and chewed his toothless gums. She tried Wist, the language her troupe had used, and Hitaian even though that language fit her mouth only poorly. He knew none of it.

He let out some words in his oily, fast-talking language. Pointed out to sea. Then he wandered off, leaving Zhang alone on the pier.

Hells and damnation.

She had spent the last ten years here building a fortune so she could go home and retire. Every soldier's dream, that was, and none she knew ever managed it. She wanted to be the first.

But plague, now, that was something else.

Zhang turned away from the water, not quite ready to admit to herself that she was relieved to stay land-borne a little longer. Warehouses lined the docks here, buildings of brick and stone in a place where most structures were made of wood. They were painted and elaborate, but also shabby: the paint flaked away in the salty air.

Behind them, a row of flop-houses stood against a gray sky. Sailors and poorer merchants could share rooms and eat from a communal pot of stew, and visit the prostitutes in the houses one row closer to town.

Zhang's bags were heavy, though. With gold. Steel. Vermidion and silver. A decade of plunder from the weak and unwary. And the sword across her back was worth a fortune, even shattered in two. Much too heavy a collection of things to risk in a shared room.

So she walked past the flophouses. Between the brothels. One woman called down from a second-story window, words Zhang did not understand, and Zhang reflected she must seem a man in her boiled breastplate, leather kilt, leather greaves. The whore above would not be the first to make that error.

Farther into town, two grand houses stood almost back to back. Here the paint was kept immaculate. Mosaics graced the outer walls and gardens surrounded the inner. Birds called from cages in high windows. White smoke wisped across a careless sky from the various chimneys.

Here, richer merchants and sea captains would hire rooms of their own. Rooms with security. Zhang picked a house at random and went to the gate. Three large guards watched her through arrow slits, frowning. One asked a question but Zhang did not understand the words.

She hardly needed to. The question would be common enough, and she had the answer.

She rattled a coin purse, pulled out a fat copper piece, a souvenir from Lurk. She flipped it through the arrow-slit. One of the guards caught it and the three looked at it closely. They seemed no less suspicious, so she dumped some more coins into her palm. Silver. Gold.

Steel.

They went right back into the purse. Too rich for guards on a gate. Too rich for Zhang, truthfully. But now they knew she was the right kind of person for this place.

The gate opened with hardly a sound. Zhang strode up the path between sculpted gardens, eyes on the grand door in front of her. It was wood, painted red, with a mosaic set into its lower panels: a blue rose.

That was a good enough name for the place.

**

"We can help," Whilla said. She had her spear against her body but it seemed more like it held her up.

A constable had come to the scene. The body was gone now, hauled away in muslin sheets to be buried. And no tracks led off from the scene, no blood trails, nothing to point to where the monster waited.

"I feel strongly," Chess said. "I feel the mind of the spirit on my tongue. There is nothing for you to do here, child. Your destiny is elsewhere. That spear is not for Moburu."

"Then what is it for?" Whilla looked around at her friends as she asked, wanting their support, but their eyes were all on the south.

"I do not know. Whilla, I cannot say. But not for this place. I love you." Chess took Jeen's hand and the two walked along the path, and then off into a copse of trees. Their eyes watched the ground.

"They can't make us go," Whilla said.

Gareth said, "No. They can't. But she thinks you put her in danger."

"Really?" She thought about it. They all thought about it. "You could be right. Moburu could use me – any of us – to get to her."

"We can't leave," Guarl said. "Not with any honor. Too much danger here and our families in it. And unfinished business. But we will have to stay guarded. And we can still look around."

"What if it doesn't want her at all?" Xin Ban said, looking at the trees. There were birds all around. Colorful, noisy, excited. Parrots sat in a nearby tree chattering in songs that sounded almost like words.

"Who else?" Gareth said. "We were just babies then. The animal would not know us."

"I don't know," Xin Ban said. "Maybe it wants Jeen. Or maybe it is all a chance. We see meaning in something where there is no meaning."

Whilla followed Xin Ban's eyes to the parrots. To sparrows on the ground, seeming to rest under a tree. Then she looked harder. Starlings, all pressed together on a limb, raucous and loud. Crows on a rooftop. Caws that sounded outraged.

In the sky, nothing. A few gray clouds, disinterested.

Gareth looked, too, and Guarl.

"The birds," Whilla said.

"None of them are eating," Guarl said.

"Or preening," said Gareth.

"Jeen taught us this," Xin Ban said. "The language of the woods. Letters written in animals and birds."

"They are watching something. Warning each other. Waiting." Whilla turned in a slow circle, looking now for places without birds. They huddled under the low wall between the stable and the path. Under the bushes, in the trees. On the stable roof. But the high roof one door over, the stick house full of families...

"Over there," Whilla said. The others looked where she looked.

"On the roof," said Gareth. "In the shade. Is that..."

"Could be," said Guarl.

Gareth set down his half-spear without taking his eyes from the chimney. Unslung his bow and strung it, still without changing his gaze. When he nocked an arrow, a shadow moved from under the chimney, slid away over the top of the roof, down the other side.

"Should we warn Chess and Jeen?" Whilla said.

"Of course," Gareth said. "Though they went the other way."

***

"They will try to follow us," Jeen said. "They want to help."

"Yes," Chess said. "Cruel to leave them to their fates. I did not even tell Whilla about her new niece. But they must make their own way. They must." Chess led Jeen through an alley, a narrow, dark space with cold stone on one side and cool wood on the other. Then she changed direction, turning right on a street lined with merchants, left through another alley.

"Are you trying to lose them?" Jeen said. "You should save your strength."

"Yes," Chess said. "He watched us. From a rooftop. Did you see?"

"No. Why did you not say?"

"Let him think we do not know. Draw him away from them. He will care nothing for them."

"Are you certain?" Jeen said.

"I wish I were. It is me he wants." Chess stopped behind a wool dyer that smelled like the outhouse at Starfall village. She breathed heavily.

Jeen took her arm, brought her close. "Will he come here?"

"Doubtful. He will follow. Leave us gifts wherever we stay. Torment us."

"Why?"

"What he is," Chess panted.

"So what will we do?"

"I had not thought so far ahead. Get our children out of danger. Wait and see."

Jeen sighed, leaned against a wall. The roof was ten or more feet overhead but she imagined it much lower. She imagined something up there, a dark shape, a shadow too dark even for this gloomy day. The sword in her hand seemed heavy. Jeen's fingers ached from holding it. "We will have to trap him. Give him what he wants, take him when he comes for it."

"What he wants is victims. To make the living fear. To make us feel helpless."

"Yes," Jeen said. "Nik, the orchard-keeper. He told us the monster likes to strike like a breeze, unfelt, taking a man from between two friends without their seeing or hearing."

"He will come close, then."

"So why," Jeen said, "did you see him on the roof? If he can hide so well, how could you find him?"

"Two answers," Chess replied, pulling her arm away to stand on her own. Her breath was easier now. "One: I looked for where there was nothing to see. No birds, no squirrels, nothing moving. And I saw his eyes in the shadow, peering back at us. I *felt* him there."

"And two?"

"He wanted me to."

Jeen's grip on the sword tightened. "I do not like it here," she said. "Under this overhang. It feels like the kind of place he likes to hunt."

"I know," said Chess.

Jeen tasted fear in her mouth. It was clear and metallic, bright, unwelcome.

Am I the bait in the trap?

Verdict

Wyrrn watched the crew put the last stone in place. Her building was complete.

A woman with a tool made of ostrich feathers dusted the seams clean. A man with a rag and a vial of oil shined up the outside. It was just as she had ordered: a low, square building of simple gray stone with a flat roof and two rooms. Slaves already carried scrolls and parchments from their inadequate granary home to the shelves built into the walls of the large room. More slaves carried in a long table, wood with a stone top.

The other room was only a cell, a hammock to sleep in and a chair for Wyrrn's tired body. A door in front opened onto the main room, the library, with the cell through an opening on the left.

It will suffice.

She went in. The shade fell across her face and body. It felt heavy. Cool.

Good.

Already the library had a smell. For now, a flinty odor. Sand and cut stone, oil and varnish. The wooden shelves glowed with it. And, over all that, the sour smell of dried skins that would eventually overtake this place.

In a moment, the table got its own chair, a wicker thing with some padding for comfort. Wyrrn sat in that. The slaves busied themselves around her. She ignored them and they ignored her.

Good. Now for the work.

The documents were as dull as the desert sky. She had made a start, beginning a rough catalogue, while waiting for this building to be finished. The Gravetenders had been terrible record-keepers and much of their writings had become nests for mice, chewed into strips and carried off. What remained had been a nonsensical pile, a chaos, a mouse's nest itself.

But now it was organized roughly by time period. She sat facing the door, with her cell to the right. To the left of the door, those documents were the newest. Shelves stretched from floor to ceiling, four rows. They went around all four walls to touch the cell door. And those to the right of that door were the oldest.

She stood, took a careful handful of those, and spread them on the table before her. Incomplete parchments. Weathered, chewed, rotted. But still, they told a story.

Here were orders for tools. Chisels made of antlers, mallets of sandalwood. Here, an inventory. It was not all readable but included tubs of grain, oil for cooking, wood for fires, leather thongs for shoes.

Interesting.

Each strip of leather was specified to be three feet long.

She took off her own shoes. They tied around her ankles and up her calves with fabric strips, not leather but the same idea. Laid out on the table, the fabric ties seemed quite long. But Wyrrn was an historian, not a drafter. That lesson she had learned quickly. How long was it?

"Someone bring me a measuring stick."

The slaves were all gone now. Wyrrn looked around the room, surprised to see it empty.

Damn.

Outside, back under the punishing sun, she found the Master who had told her about this cache of documents. Ramble, his name was. "Bring me a measuring tool," she said.

"Of course, Great One," Ramble said, bowing. "What scale?"

"Scale? Not to weigh, for length."

"Yes, Great One. Only, to measure how much length?"

"If I knew that, why would I need a tool to measure?"

"I am only a servant," Ramble said. "The Great Ones can mock as they like." He affected a mild pout.

"Mock?" She spat. "I am the one as feels mocked. I need to know how long three feet is."

"Ah. Forgive, Great One. We have tools to measure the width of a grain of sand – the seams between stones must be tighter. We have tools to measure the distance between monuments. And we have tools to measure things the size of stone blocks and people. If I had brought you any but the latter, I should have been beaten. Please, I will bring you what you need."

Bemused, Wyrrn returned to her workroom. More documents suggested someone had requested incense. Sixty barrels of it. She set that fragment aside, thinking she might have missed something in the dialect. What tomb could require so much incense? Or was it for the living?

Ramble arrived with a stick and set it on the table.

"So?" Wyrrn said.

"Please, Great One?"

"So how do I use the thing?"

"Ah." He pointed to notches along the wood. "One foot. Two feet. Three feet. On this side, inches."

"So if I lay it like this... And stretch this bit of material like so... then when this end starts at the bottom of the stick and this end at this notch..."

"Three feet," Ramble said. "To the inch."

"Curious. How many Masters are there?"

"Sixteen."

"For a workforce of..."

"Six hundred twenty children," he said.

Wyrrn tapped her teeth. "How many shoes does a Master wear out in a year?"

"I have been here eight years, Great One. These shoes were new the day I arrived."

"Curious indeed." She shuffled documents around, went back to the order for leather thongs. Double-checked her work. "So to what possible use could our forebears have put eight thousand sandal ties?" She dipped a quill in ink, wrote directly on the table-top. Arithmetic was not her favorite pursuit but she had read much of it. Sixteen Masters for six-hundred-odd children was about 35 slaves per master. Eight thousand shoes meant four thousand Masters, and that number was tenebrous, difficult to grasp. The number of slaves they might have controlled exceeded her ability to count. She estimated it at more than the population of Hitai.

When she looked up, Ramble still stood, staring down at her. "Great One?" he said.

"I need you no longer," she said. "You have been very helpful. Now go and see that some stones get cut. Or whatever you do here."

"Yes, Great One. Only... we have nothing new to build."

"Do not trouble me now. If I am right, well, never mind."

"Yes, Great One."

The man shambled out of her rooms unnoticed. Wyrrn was already back into the documents, dripping ink all over the table as she tallied and noted.

***

It was one day to the Tomblands. Much time for thought, for shame and self-reflection.

It took as far as the Sun Gate for Xenia's thoughts to cohere enough to make sense of. She had come up the steps expecting priestly conspirators and one of Dllyx's cousins acting the prince, a simple enough insurrection. But she had seen the boy and that strange man, the one with the noble face and the outlander garb.

Chans looked so much like the man he claimed for a brother that Xenia felt conflicting loyalty. Not to the old King, no, nothing like that. She had backed Dllyx and won. But a loyalty to her own skin, her own self-preservation. Ynn had been a monster far more fearsome than the elephant they had hunted, than any twisted thing to come out of the Starfall.

And then, before she could strike with the sword or summon the guards up the stairs, the situation was over. A simple walk, some easy questions. A trip into the desert. The chance to enact violence seemed passed.

The Sun Gate loomed ahead, passed over her, receded into the distance.

I could still salvage this.

She walked between two priests. They were unarmed. Weak. One was an old woman, puffing and blowing from the exertion of so simple a thing as walking. They could offer no real resistance.

She pulled her sword from its scabbard, checked the edge. The man on her other side touched her wrist.

"Time for that later, daughter. For now we walk under the sun. Many chances for the living. Once dead, no more chances."

"The sun is not god," she replied, but she put up the weapon. Ahead, Dllyx turned to glower at her. But the sun-priest was correct. She could enact violence at any time and meet little resistance. That left possibilities. Perhaps they could eliminate the priesthoods entirely. Or perhaps there was some other way to profit.

The old woman by her fell back and Chans stepped into her place. She was taller but his presence still seemed looming and ominous. He filled enough space for three of her. If not for his age, she would fear his possible martial prowess.

"She is your friend," he said.

"I owe her my life," Xenia said, and she meant it. If not for Dllyx' faith, Xenia would still be a cat-wrangler in the menagerie. Or perhaps her mad brother would have killed her out of hand. But she also did not mean it. What good was money if loyalty got you killed? Murder the priests here, maybe one or two get away, maybe there are witnesses. Then they come for you in the dark, with poison.

"More than a friend, then. I understand. You have twenty soldiers. I have a boy and some scholars. Quill pens and paper shields. So far, you have restrained yourself from violence. Why?"

Xenia glanced sidelong at him. "Violence is mine to unleash when I desire. I could kill you now, all of you. My King wishes me to do so and she will punish me later. I know it. But the violence is mine alone. I have all the power now, all of it. I choose to let you live a little longer. My King is secure. There is no danger here."

"Well said," Chans offered. "You do not doubt her legitimacy."

"That is not relevant. She is my King. I will die for her." She wondered if she were trying to convince Chans, or Dllyx, or herself. Dllyx had made her rich, this was true. The graft alone from her office as Captain of the Guard was more wealth than she had ever hoped for.

"Loyal. Like a dog."

She spat at his feet. "Dogs only follow orders out of fear. What are you trying to do?"

"Walking pains me so. I only wish to pass the time and you are good to look upon. The gods favored my eyes when they made you."

She touched the sword. "Speak plainly. And not of that." But her back straightened. A chance to be even a dalliance for a King might be worth more than the captaincy.

He laughed. There was joy in the sound and an easiness Xenia had missed around the palace. "A shame to come home. I was free out there. Riding through the north, reaving and trading, making a fortune. All the time I had a fortune waiting for me here but I hardly want it."

"So why come back?"

"Honor and obligation. Ynn was a beast. Heartless. They said he was soft-hearted but they did not know him. He set himself a goal and crushed everyone between him and that goal. If he spared me it was not for me, but only to spare his own feelings. So he could feel upright. Vengeance is my duty."

Xenia thought as she trudged. She wiped sand from her cheeks, watched the horizon turning brown as the sun crept towards it through a haze of blowing dust. "We will walk through the night."

"The dark will purify us."

"Those who are impure."

Chans laughed again. "This place rightfully belongs to me. But I won't harm her. Your Princess... she can live in peace. If you start violence, know that half your soldiers will turn on you. They have lived with the priests their whole lives. They go to the temples, all of them. Each is loyal to the gods and the men who speak for them. When the blood grows hot they will rally. Unify. But your Dllyx will be dead by then."

"You are just right," Xenia said. When Chans seemed about to speak again, she went on: "Vengeance is a duty."

***

Back in the desert. Dllyx hated it here: hated the sun that stuck to her skin like hot jam; hated the sand that got into everything; hated the dust in her eyelashes and the grit between her teeth; hated the tombs that spoke of a life lived after dying while her life awaited back in Hitai.

I am the King.

But somehow here she was, plodding along in the middle of a pack of priests, Chans leading the way with her son on his shoulders. Guards followed placidly, a pack of thirty of them, more arriving all the time. The peregrination was slow so they caught up easily.

They had brought their impaling implements. And they would not hear her words.

"I am the King. I command here. I command you. Kill these traitors, these rebels."

"Please, My King... My... If they are wrong, we will follow your commands. But if they are right, then every death we deal at your hands is a murder."

She had talked and goaded and prodded all the way from the Sun Gate but now she was out of breath. The guards were well trained, and as implacable as the sun in his sky. Even Xenia was of no help, offering sour looks but no action. Dllyx willed her to order a strike. But if they would not obey the King, what chance an up-jumped cat handler?

"Not far now," Chans bellowed from the front of the group. "Another mile, maybe less."

He looked barbaric in his outlander garb, with his leather boots and fur jacket, canvas trousers and belt. No Prince of the Blood would clothe themselves so. It was impossible.

What about Fum? Her memory nagged. *Fum bought himself a cloak like a Greenlander and paraded around town in that.*

Fum, her own brother. He had died by violence. Her violence. He was buried out here somewhere, too, until his tomb was torn down. And then the mummy was sent to...

Where? For what?

And then she had to see, to know. She had to see all the tombs, where they had stood, to be sure all those she thought were dead really were gone from this world. Her Father's tomb, Ynn the Tender-hearted, lay far behind them but she wanted to run there, to rip open the heavy doors, to throw off the lid of his coffin. He'd had no tender heart for his daughter, no. She had suffered at his hands and she would see his corpse.

She wanted to scream.

"Here," Chans said. "You see it now at the edge of the sky."

"The horizon," Dllyx called. "Dirty foreigner to not even know the word for where the land meets the sky."

Chans only laughed. "If I am foreign or dirty, it is because my family failed to do their duty. Should have killed me like a proper brother."

The tomb came closer, ground sliding away behind her as she trudged. Too quickly. Here was a tomb she had no wish to see, a corpse that would not ease her troubles.

"It is just the tomb of some old forgotten ruler," she said. "One of the old ones. The peasants of this land would remember his name."

The priests around her mumbled. Rept said, "A brave try, Lady, but futile. The age of the stones shows in the seams, around the edges. They are too crisp and bright to be very old. Sand rasps them away."

"My King," Dllyx said.

"Perhaps again one day," Rept replied, "but for now, perhaps not."

Then they were upon the tomb. Then descending the steps. Finally ducking into the shade. Unfairly, the cool of the crypt offered Dllyx no relief from her sweating. The astrologer took out the mummy and dumped out the bag of bones next to its missing right foot. He ordered them, fit them together. Sighed and waffled and muttered.

"Yes," he said. "Yes, I should say these bones belong with this body. It is the lower ends of the shin-bones that tell the story, really. Here, this shard..."

"Traitor!" Dllyx shouted, pushing through to the front of the crowd of people around Ergol's dais. "I'll have you impaled. Burned alive."

Chans laughed. "Such are the prerogatives of a King, or sometimes a Prince. But you... Poor Dllyx. Your father was no King at all, and so you are neither."

"We cannot take the word of a priest," Dllyx said. That she resorted to reason said something of her mental state. "Priests are all liars and this one has everything to gain. We need an independent arbiter. I will abide by nothing less."

"Shame you had the Gravetender killed, then," Chans said, smirking. Jul, standing next to her uncle, looked up at him with a look in his eyes she had never seen before.

Rept said, "What shall we do with her, My King?"

Dllyx stared at him, her mouth all ready to answer, only he did not mean her. How could he?

"The stakes?" Myrsa suggested.

Xenia, there among the crowd but seeming inert, useless, came to life then. She only put a hand on Myrsa's arm and frowned, but it was enough.

"No," said Chans.

Dllyx started to back out of the room but there were too many of them. The way was blocked. She turned around, pushed, finally scratched at a man's eyes. She got hold of some flesh, bloodied her nails, but another man stepped into his place.

A guard.

"Help me," she told him.

"Not the stakes," Chans said. Only his name was not really Chans, was it? It was Ergol. The poor bastard in the coffin had two good feet. "She remains one of The Blood, family. We cannot treat The Blood with such discourtesy, can we?"

She tried again to escape, now dropping low and diving forward. She made some headway, squirming between people, but someone grabbed her by the belt and hauled her upright.

Chans laughed again. "She has always wanted to earn herself a tomb out here, a royal tomb complete with a stairway into the afterlife. Let her have it."

Dllyx started to scream.

***

The snake lay in the sand where she had left it. Bits of broken stone lay all around. A giant scepter, a crown, both shattered and scattered. Soot marred one wall where breakers had tried to burn the thing.

"It is not finished," Dllyx said, struggling. A strong man held her right arm and a stronger one held her left, fingers digging into her muscles. That hurt and right now she wanted it to hurt. Because what they meant to do next was going to feel like nothing. An empty eternity.

"Of course it is finished," Chans said. "The silly hat and the stave were extras. And the beard. The Gravetender told me. She had them put on there just so when you tore them off the crypt would be finished. Ha. You finished your own tomb. Said something about a lesson in clay, did the Gravetender. The little one."

"Clay? And on these words you will..."

Rept touched her. On the shoulder, just above one of the guards' hands. "A blessing, Lady," he said.

The guards dragged her forwards. There was a little door in the base of the monument and she should have seen that from the start, seen that it was much too small to fit a whole ceremonial coffin into, never mind a sarcophagus. It was just big enough for a small woman, if she ducked her head.

A third guard opened the door and the two on her arms rushed her forwards. She had two choices: duck and fall into the dark, or try to remain upright and brain herself on the lintel. Either choice was death.

I will live a little longer.

The door slammed shut behind her. It sounded like finality. Dllyx could hear them outside still for a few moments, talking, laughing, but the walls took the meaning out of their words.

Then she was alone in the dark.

Entombed.

The door had no give to it. Even if it had, she could now hear people piling stones against it, the wreckage her breakers had made.

This place had been built to offer immortality. She had earned that much by outwitting her brothers, by surviving her father, by bearing a son. The trouble with immortality was none of the Kings had ever been alive when they were entombed. Only the dead were truly deathless.

Dllyx refused to weep or even to rage. She chose to live another moment, and then another.

She crouched lower and felt around. In truth, the door was not perfectly fitted. It let in the merest amount of light and with that she could see something on the curved wall to the right of the door frame.

A torch. And, in a space in the wall sconce, a flint and steel. She struck sparks inexpertly until the torch took and now she had a crude light. If necessary, that light could also get her out of this life: she would burn before she starved.

The chamber curved around like the body of the snake outside. Left or right. Right turned out to be a dead end but left led to a flight of stairs, down into the earth. With nothing else to do, she climbed them.

There was one more chamber, just one. It held a comfortable chair on a dais, and something stacked all around the outer walls. Pots, urns. Amphorae.

Her shoulder itched.

She opened one of the urns and found it full of dried fruit. Another was full of bread. The amphorae held wine. Death-gifts to sustain her in the afterlife. Only she knew that the Gravetender knew how she was to die. The chair with no coffin, that told the rest of the story. She was to have a long time in which to contemplate her failings.

Or possibly to hope.

With time, she might dig her way out of here, might be rescued.

Her shoulder burned now, and she used the torch to cast some light on it. There were black marks where the guards had manhandled her. And one more, higher up. A black smudge.

And a tiny pin-prick. She had not noticed, not with all the pressure on her arms. A pickpocket's trick.

Poison.

I can still get out. I will break down the door. Make a tool, something.

But she could feel her strength ebbing, and ebbing quickly. Her heart started to speed up as she panicked and that only spread the poison faster, made her weaker. Her choice became suddenly urgent: to reach for the wall to steady herself, or to try to fall into the chair on the dais, to take her rightful place in this tableau.

Dllyx stumbled and fell, landing at the base of the dais. She hit her head. Blood trickled from the top of her head, into her hair, to puddle on the neat stone floor. And from down here she could see that the bottom step of the dais bore an inscription, scribed vertically so that it lined up perfectly with her new perspective. It was a long message, a note just for her in letters no taller than one of her eye teeth.

The snake in which you lie does not represent the manner of your life, My King, but the manner of your death: by treachery and poison. I wish you well of it. Unfortunate for you that the poison merely paralyzes rather than kills. I fear you are to starve to death after all, surrounded by food and wine. Ever is this the way of your people.

Money

"I'm hungry." Whilla wished for a blanket. The night here was shockingly cold for someone raised in the temperate foothills around Hitai.

"We're all hungry," Gareth said, and slid closer. They lay on the ground between two brick buildings, protected from the light but cool breezes. All four had their backs to the brick walls and their feet out before them, Gareth and Whilla on one side, their feet tangled with Xin Ban's and Guarl's on the other.

"How do people live here?" Guarl said. "Do they let each other go hungry?"

"Money," Gareth said.

Xin Ban looked up, shivering, as close as she could get to Guarl. "Money stands for trade, then you can trade anything for anything. Chickens, work, food."

"How to get money?" Gareth said.

"Trade work for it," Xin Ban replied. "And time."

"Time," Whilla said. "We seem to have a lot of that. If only we could eat it."

"It is too cold for this," Gareth said. "Here. You should all be together. Whilla, slide over to that side. Keep warm."

"Where are you going?" Whilla said as Gareth stood. "You're right. We should all be together."

She stood, too.

Gareth looked surprised. "I wasn't going far. Just to see if there is anything nearby we can use. Who else is out tonight."

"Then I'm coming, too," Xin Ban said. "Nobody goes alone. Not with Moburu out there. He won't be asleep tonight. Who knows – he could be watching right now."

Gareth looked up at the roofline.

"She's right," Whilla said. Her spear stood a little straighter.

"I can look after myself," Gareth said.

"I know you can," said Whilla. "And if he came while you were away, we would need you. Come on, then, let's look around."

"I hope he does find us. Get this over with." Gareth sighed but moved out with the rest of the group.

"You don't mean that," Whilla said, but she knew he did.

There were so many buildings it still made Willa dizzy. Because forest pushed in on all sides, they were sometimes tall to save space. Not like Hitai, where they were low and flat and heavy. And not like the village where good building materials were scarce. At the Starfall, they mostly shared one space for efficiency – and community.

They walked, breath fogging the air in front of them. Whilla scanned the rooftops. They all did. She imagined that the thing Moburu had become would be totally invisible, though, against the dark sky. There were only a few stars, weak and pallid.

"What's that?" Gareth said, and her heart raced. But he wasn't looking at the sky. His eyes were pointed between two of the tall houses the Greenlanders built to house three or four families. There was washing strung between them. Blankets, breeches, jerkins.

We could borrow the blankets, Whilla thought. *No, you mean steal them.* She blushed even though she hadn't spoken.

"Does it count if you don't say it out loud?" Xin Ban said. "I thought it, too."

"Not that," Gareth said. "On the ground. In the back."

A little light from the windows, the same light that showed the laundry, glanced off something on the ground in the darkest part of the alley. A bundle of rags or trash. Trash was a real problem here, something Whilla had never seen before.

But it didn't smell like trash.

"Hello?" she said, stepping into the dark-dark space. Her voice was quiet and friendly but she led with the tip of her spear. The others crowded behind her, weapons out. "Hello?"

No response.

She got close enough to prod the object with the spear. It was soft and heavy. Disturbing.

"I think it's a person," she said.

Gareth got in there on his knees. "Yeah," he said. "A dead person. Died of the cold, probably. Tonight. No animals, no blood. He has blankets."

Whilla shuddered and told herself it was the breeze.

Xin Ban said, "Me too. I might rather be cold than wrap myself in a dead man's blankets."

"Not sure we can pretend to such ethics," Guarl said.

"He also has a few coins. I'm taking them." Gareth rooted around some more. "And boots. They aren't great but maybe better than sandals.

"We should leave him," Whilla said. "Maybe he has a family who could use that money."

"If he had a family," Gareth said, "they wouldn't have left him to die outside in the cold. Hungry. I can feel all his ribs. Here, touch his face – this man was thin, much too thin."

"I believe you," Whilla said, not wishing to join Gareth in touching the corpse – although, as he had touched it, she already had in a way. *What they did to you, they did to all of us.* Which of them had said that? It was true. Whilla's own sense of safety, of violation, of grief and rage, were all tied up in what had happened to him.

"Wait," Xin Ban said. "Wait. You said you met a woman. An aunt. Family."

"No family of ours," Gareth said. "She offered no help and no particular affection. We share blood, maybe, but she's not family."

"How can you say that?" Xin Ban said.

Gareth just pointed at the corpse. Whilla could not see him but in some ways she was him. She knew. "Because we're starving and freezing in the night, like him," Gareth said. "Here. Take these blankets. Who wants the boots?"

They ended up fitting Gareth best, so he wore them. The coins amounted to twelve bits of bronze. What that might buy, Whilla could not say.

"Whatever it is, we can share it," she said. "Let's finish our business in this place and get back into the free lands between cities where we don't need money. I prefer when *work* stands for work."

***

Zhang sat at a table by herself. It was round, just large enough for her breakfast. There was another chair across from her but it was stacked with her bags and gear. A window to her right gave her a view of the harbor. The three useless ships out there had been joined by a fourth.

"Out of Consent," said a captain from one table over. She glanced at the woman, thinking she had been addressed, but the captain had a guest. Merchant, by the coat and hat and jeweled fingers.

"Plague in Grond," the merchant said. He leaned back in his chair, glanced towards Zhang.

Zhang made sure she was looking back out the window when he looked. She could see his reflection in the window-glass in any event.

"Bulldag would do the same," the captain said. "Keep everyone safe, worry about profits later. Money is for the living."

Bulldag. That explained why Zhang could understand the conversation. That was the nearest port on the Xun side of the Gray Sea. Not her home, but closer than this place. She glanced again at dark skin, tight, curly hair, black-brown eyes. Folk from her own country. But she also saw bellies and soft hands.

"You have business here?" the merchant said, this time unmistakably to Zhang.

"My business here is done," she said, putting her gaze back to the window. "Meant to leave on one of those boats."

"Ships," said the captain.

Zhang looked again. The captain had soft hands. She hadn't pulled on a rope in so long her callouses were all gone. Zhang looked at her own hands: worn, seamed, thick with scars and tough skin. But she felt soft.

The morning had brought a hot bath and a servant with oil and lotion. Another had brushed out her short hair. Still another had helped her dress in clothes that had been boiled, scented and dried overnight.

Soft.

I mean to retire. Perhaps I can become fat and weak like these ones, in the end. But not today.

"No ships out of this harbor," the merchant said. "Not for two more months, or three if the storms come early."

"No way home, then."

"And not much chance of doing any good business," the captain said.

"Not so fast," the merchant replied. "What are you taking home, Lady?"

Zhang choked on her tea. "Lady?" she spluttered. "No lady, me. An adventurer. Here are the rewards of twenty years of soldiering. That, and getting out alive."

"If I may, soldier," the merchant said, "so much to carry such a long way... Coin is lighter. Gemstones lighter still."

"And I assume you wish to make a trade."

"Of course," he said. "I shall make a small profit on the value of your goods – assuming they are better than grisly conquest trophies – and you shall have the ease of carrying money rather than bulky packages."

"Perhaps I like my heavy things," she said.

"Indeed. But think on this: how can you safeguard all these bags when you sleep? How can you hide them if you need to be away?"

Zhang laughed. She turned the chair sideways with one foot. "Have a look, make an offer."

Later, she trudged away from the guest house with a purse full of gold, her broken sword, slave's mallet and slaver's bullwhip the only things left for her to carry. And with the money on her person, she had an idea that the sword could be fixed. Her fortune, restored.

The houses grew increasingly opulent as she climbed the hill, and the view of the harbor behind her more and more grand. The air was clear, salty, and damp. But the smell of wood smoke and charcoal were just detectable.

This was a small harbor, but every harbor she had ever seen had certain amenities. From the top of the hill, near the manor-house probably occupied by some kind of governor, she could look at the whole town as though it were a map.

There was a ropemaker. A sailmaker. Woodworks. Brothel. Too many drinking houses to really count.

And a smith.

Back down the hill, following the trail of smoke. She pushed in through a heavy wood door banded with bronze into a hot waiting room. Furniture said this was a place where a lot of money changed hands: soft cushions, fabrics in red and gold, a curtain to keep the worst of the heat and smoke in the back rooms where it belonged. Before long, a harried-looking man came through that curtain to find her waiting. He poured water from a bronze ewer she had taken to be just for show, quaffed it, and then looked her over.

"Xun?" he said.

"Yes."

"My Xun is weak, apologize," the man said. "Business you have?"

She unpacked the broken sword and held it out to him. "You can re-forge this, yes? Make the two parts into one?"

He took one of the pieces, turned it over in his hand. The shard from the point, not the handle. "Sharp," he said. "Steel?" That was a Greenlander word; Xunians had no name for steel. "Not can forge steel. Bronze here only. Shame."

"Damn."

"Forge hot good, Hong."

"You are right," she said. "Your Xunian is weak. But I understand." She left the smith there to forge his nautical bits and pieces and climbed the hill out of town for hopefully the last time. The road led back towards Hong. Away from home. But with two or three months until she could take ship, what else was there to do?

***

"Here," Gareth said. A sign hung overhead, creaking in the wind. The words were Greenlander: "The steaming pot." A crude painting matched the words. Inside, a singer did what singers do and, even at this late hour, Gareth could hear conversation.

"They will have food?" Xin Ban said.

"The price is the question," Guarl said.

They went in all together, out of the dark and into a hall hardly lighter. Tallow candles sat on every second table. Those tables were sparsely populated, night-people preferring the shadows. The singer Gareth had taken to be a woman was a boy his own age, brown as all Greenlanders were brown, short and thin. He had a flute but did not play it. His song about lost love had little to do with the people here.

There was a plank at one end of the room and a woman stood behind it, a pile of wooden cups in front of her. She looked hard. Eyes, face, shoulders, fists, all tight and wary. She watched the four young ones come in and Gareth could not tell what she might be thinking. Two bow-staves hung on the wall behind her. Unstrung, the uninitiated might not have known what they were – just a pair of sticks.

He walked up to her as though he belonged in this place. Conversation hushed as he passed and the strangers here all watched him while pretending not to.

"The sign outside says you have food," he said to the woman behind the plank.

"Your Greenlander stinks," she said. "Which is fine. So does the food. You have coins?"

"Some," he said. "We could work for more. We're all young and strong."

"Could sell us your youth here. Some willing customers in this lot. I'd be happy to tell you who. But you've not that look about you. How many is this?" Gareth had set his coins on the counter and she spread them with her fingers. "A pot of stew, this'll get you, and a mug of ale. You'll all have to share it. You want more, well, did your parents teach you love-play?"

He blushed. "Not the sort of work we had in mind."

"Shame," said the woman. "You are pretty. Green eyes on a Greenlander. You're one of us, yes? Been away? Thought you must've been slaved out. You've that accent on your speech. Go and sit. I'll bring you something."

He pointed to a table and his friends came with him. At the plank, a tall man turned to watch him go. Gareth felt the man's eyes on him. He looked back. Then he looked again.

The man was a giant. Seven feet tall or near enough, thin, rangy. Not dressed like the others here, either: he had leather all over his body, brown leather with copper plate sewn into parts of it. And also a wooden sword at one hip where these other people went unarmed.

"Mulch," said another man, scooting in next to Gareth at his table.

"Gareth," Gareth said. "That's Xin Ban, Whilla, and Guarl."

"I'm Hobe," the man said.

"So who's Mulch?"

"The tall one watching you. Troublemaker. Likes to start fights. You will be careful. Been a long time since we seen slavers through here."

"We're not," said Whilla. "Nor slaves. Just travelers."

"As you say," Hobe said. "And watch yourselves anyway." He scraped his chair back into his own shadow.

The woman brought a bowl of stew. It was a big bowl and the stew smelled better than she had suggested. She had even stuck a bit of stale black bread in it. The tankard was smaller and the ale watery. "Thank you," Gareth said.

She said nothing, only went back to her space at the plank.

"I think she is being generous," Whilla said. "Tomorrow, we will need more coins if we wish to eat."

"That's my table," the tall man said, looming over Gareth.

"I don't think it is," Gareth said.

"We don't want any trouble," offered Guarl.

Mulch smirked. "Then get off my table. Go sit outside. Outlanders."

"They make those swords like that here?" Gareth said. "Lacquered wood? That's Hitaian style, isn't it? For caravan guards and other peasants who can't afford bronze. Is that what you are?"

"What would you know of it, boy?" He leaned in and still loomed.

"I know it makes you as foreign as we are. At least my mother came from here, and knew my father."

"You picking a fight?" Mulch said.

Whilla put a hand on Gareth's arm. "What are you doing? That's not what we're here for."

Trust me, he thought. "Not doing anything. Just giving Mulch what he wants – trouble."

Mulch stood up and looked Gareth over. Gareth made sure his spear was obvious in the middle of the table. Whilla's was in her hand. The bow stave was less obvious, just a stick over his back.

"You aren't going to jam that spear in him, are you?" Guarl said. "You know what happened last time."

Xin Ban looked between Gareth and Guarl, eyes wide. Her look repeated Whilla's question.

Trust me.

"Spear?" Mulch said. "You like to fight, then."

"No, not at all," Gareth said. "You're frightening me, and my friends. We'll just go. Come on. Let him have his table."

Mulch said, "Not so fast. Duel. You insulted my parentage. I invoke right of honor. Duel."

"Don't be a fool," the woman called from the bar. "Choosing fights with children. You still owe me money and now you're going to get hauled in by the constable."

"Dueling is legal," Gareth said. "Right?"

Mulch turned and roared back at the woman. "Legal, Ratric. Hear that? Boy's a scholar. No constable for me. And I'll pay you with his boots." He turned back to Gareth. "Pick up your spear, boy, and let's go get you killed."

"Spear? I think otherwise." Gareth stood, slowly. The others backed off. Whilla's white skin had turned even paler. Xin Ban had on a worried frown and even Guarl's knuckles were white. "You called for a duel, and I accept. That means I pick the weapons, right?"

All around, silence had fallen. Even the singer was quiet, standing on his stool with his head lowered and arms across his body as though protecting his modesty.

"Not spears?" Mulch said.

"No. Bows." Gareth pulled his off his back and strung it quickly.

"I've no bow," Mulch said. "You can't call a weapon I don't have."

"I do," Ratric said. She turned and took down one of the bows from the wall behind her. "Don't have a string, but I have a bow."

"Here's a string," said Hobe. He fished in his pocket. "Was hunting rabbits just this morning. Here, Mulch."

"Bows." Mulch took the stave and thought. "Bows."

Gareth watched him thinking. "You can't use a bow? I would as soon not fight at all. Not too late to back out, is it? I'll let you go with no damage to your honor."

Hobe cackled. "Oh no, that's not how it works. He asked, you accepted, weapons are in hand. Nothing to do now but get out there."

Gareth put on his best scared face. "Nothing for it, then. First blood, Mulch?"

Mulch smiled then. "We'll see, boy."

Outside. The night was still cold, the breeze still gentle and cool. People from the drinking house lined the lane. Hobe marched Gareth a hundred paces to the right. Others marched Mulch a hundred to the left.

Gareth said, "He's not used to being called out, is he? Wins by intimidation."

"Right you are boy," Hobe said.

"And when he fights, he wins with strength and reach. That sword."

"Right again."

"He has no idea what to do with a bow."

"We'll see," Hobe said. "Don't underestimate him."

They stopped. Gareth turned to see Mulch waiting for him, bow in hand. Someone handed him an arrow. "Ready to die, boy?"

"Not really. I don't think you know how to use that bow, though."

"I can use it. Just you stand still." Mulch laid the arrow across it and started to draw. It slipped off the string, dropped to the ground. Cursing, Mulch picked the arrow back up and tried again. This time the string slipped from his grasp, slapped the hand holding the bow, and he dropped the whole mess.

People laughed. Low at first, furtive. Then louder. Mulch made eye contact with each and they stopped laughing, but still smirked.

"Want to be next?" Mulch said.

Gareth called, "I want to be first. Worry about next when you've shot me. I don't think you can, though." Gareth drew an arrow from his quiver. He nocked and drew smoothly, like Yohn had taught him to an age ago. His black wood bow felt like silk. This is what it was made for, and him too.

"You're right." Mulch got the arrow nocked and the string pulled back a little. He pointed it at the ground a few feet in front of him. "I apologize. This was a bad idea. Let me buy you a drink, a bite of food for your friends." He let the arrow go into the dirt.

Hobe yelled, "Too late. You know that."

Gareth aimed and loosed. The arrow whistled across the distance in a second and struck the tall man in the throat. Mulch fell down without a sound, without a twitch.

Silence.

People turned to look at the dead man, smirks and smiles falling away. Then they glanced back at Gareth, just brief touches with their eyes, before scuttling away.

"I know you had to shoot him, boy, but did you have to kill him?" Hobe wiped his face with one hand.

"Yes." Gareth unstrung his bow and started the long walk to the new corpse he had made.

Xin Ban caught him as he went by, grabbed onto his elbow. "You killed him."

"I know."

"Why?"

"Because I had to, Xin Ban."

Whilla said, "That was reckless."

"Not really. Remember what my mother said. About not picking fights."

"Prophecy?" Whilla shut her eyes, rubbed her temples.

"More than that. Nobody will trouble us again. Not tonight." Gareth finished the walk, knelt down by Mulch. "All his things are mine now, right?"

Ratric was there, standing over him. "That's the law," she said.

"This lacquer sword worth something?"

"About what he owes me."

"It's yours, then."

"Come back inside," she said. "I'll feed you and yours. I owe you for putting him down. We all do. He's been a menace. Hanging around the place for days, trying to fight everyone. What he owed was the least of it. I can make money again with him gone."

Inside, back at their table, Hobe slapped Gareth on the back. "She's right. Sorry I said what I said. Your choice whether to have mercy. He'd have had none for you. Listen, let me get you something, too. We all owe you."

There was food on the table now, enough for all of them, and little glasses of something much stronger than watery ale. Gareth opened his mouth to talk but it was Guarl who spoke.

"We don't need anything else. Not to eat or drink. What we need is information."

Hobe laughed. "Even better. That don't cost me anything." He crossed his arms and sat back.

Whilla said, "A friend of ours came through here years ago. He was only a child. But he would have seemed a slaver to you. He and his mother, a sister. A Hitaian mother and two children. And they brought a sword with them. It was that sword that told your magister where to find Flax, the murderer."

Gareth shot her a look then. Her words hurt even though they were true.

Hobe said, "I'd know nothing of that, not a thing."

"Waste of time then," Guarl said.

"No, not so fast." Hobe leaned back even farther. "Said I don't know. But I know who would."

Later, huddled under a bed that Ratric let them use for the rest of the night, Whilla poked Gareth in the back. "You killed a man to test out a prophecy? I was terrified for you. And more killing. Can this be good?"

"They said if I did not start the fight I could not lose it. He started it, I did not lose. Sorry you were frightened. I was too, if we're being honest. Scared out of all sense. But it had to be done."

"It did not," Xin Ban said. "We could have left quietly."

"And frozen to death outside. It's time to make our way," Gareth said. "That means doing whatever needs doing. Even if it's ugly. And now we have a direction, someone to talk to about Vault."

"Vault," Guarl said. Everyone whispered his name and the argument was set aside for a time.

Coins

Getting to Sorub in the north was not so easy as just finding north and walking that way. The land was complicated and journeys of such magnitude took patience and planning.

But Korina could be patient.

In her tool bag were coins she had made herself. Gold for major needs, tin for minor. One steel coin for emergencies. They were all blank: rulers' faces graced coins from all around but her home was an unruled place. She had a few days' of food and water in wrapped packages and skins, and a bit of oiled canvas in case of rain.

The village of Starfall was behind her now, the hills looming up over her shoulder as she trudged down the path. She looked down over the edge onto the tops of tall, dead trees and the huge ferns that had replaced them.

If I leaped from the edge, would they catch me? Is this a quicker way down the mountain?

Some other woman might have tried it or just yearned for it but Korina was a smith: she knew the dangers in short-cuts.

In less time than she had thought, she came to the oasis, the last marker before the Yellow Sea. Her course would take her past that rock wall and the well it guarded and then into the desert, skirting north around the Tomblands before veering true north. Most people would camp here even though there was light left in the sky, saving up energy for the next day's toils.

But Korina felt good. Strong. Her legs were not used to so much walking yet she was still young and robust, well-fed and well-conditioned. She left the oasis behind her, plodded on past the point where sere brown grass gave way to dust, to fine yellow sand, to desolation. Soon, the mountains were lost in haze somewhere behind her and even the oasis had sunk below the horizon.

She saw a post ahead. Four feet tall, wood weathered to plain gray, barely visible as the wind kicked up fine powder. When she reached it, there would be another at the limits of her vision; and when she reached that, another, all the way to the Tomblands. Out here, there were no other markers. On a clear day one could see those tombs as a low smudge on the horizon but heat would obscure it, dust would obscure it as it did today.

Korina did not mean to go to that haunted place, though. So she put the marker slightly to her right. When she came abreast of it, a hundred yards off, the other was just visible. That she kept to her right, too, and passed it with two hundred yards distance. By the fifth marker, they were lost to sight and she navigated on intuition.

Then the sun set.

The dark seemed sudden, although of course Korina had walked in gloaming for an hour or more, straining to see something besides sand, the low horizon, and the empty sky. When the bats came out, proving that something lived out here worth eating, she had watched without slowing her pace, rapt.

And now, this seemingly sudden dark.

There was nothing to do but get comfortable. Light from the stars above crashed down all around and a sallow moon rode the edge of the sky. Nearly enough light to keep walking by, but that was another short-cut. The job required patience, diligence. So she sat on the flat ground and rummaged in her bag for food and drink. Then, sated, she spread the canvas over her body, weighted it with sand, and stared up at the stars until sleep came.

In the morning, after more food, more water, and a crude toilet, it was time to walk again. The sand had filled her sandals yesterday and wore at her feet. Today, they were sore, painful, and she knew by the end of the day they might crack and bleed. But cracking and bleeding meant thicker, tougher skin later. Her hands testified to that fact. So she kept on.

The sun itself had to serve as her marker now. It traced a predictable line through the sky and it was simple enough to keep on a path just to the north of east. Noon was the hardest time: the heat was brutal and the sun stood exactly overhead, offering no clues. Korina just hunkered down then, nursing her tired feet, sheltered by her canvas.

More water, more food, back to walking. Her bag was lighter than when she started, that was something, and now she had a shadow to walk towards, keeping it slightly to her right.

Within another hour, she knew she had a problem. Her feet hurt more than her hands ever had, so much that she did not even feel the blood flowing from skin sanded away to nothing. She only knew about that when a twinge of pain caused her to look down. The color of blood was a shock out here where even the sky seemed a dusty yellow.

Weak now, stronger later. Hammer the bronze, beat strength into it.

Only her feet were not bronze.

A few more steps and they went out from under her, refusing to bear her weight any longer. Leaving her prone, alone, far away from any other person, only the sun for company.

Korina sat there in the sand. Water from one of her skins, precious and clean, rinsed out the wounds. Her daily bread had been wrapped in linen and that did fine for bandages. All there was left to do then was rest and heal. So she sheltered under her canvas from sun and wind, eyes drawn north as if she could see her final goal out there somewhere, across this desert and wastes of other kinds.

Movement caught her eye from the right, from the northeast. Her vision ticked over that way, focused, caught the object. Small, wavering in heat-shimmer.

Could be anything. Hare, maybe.

But it wasn't anything. Korina knew that. It was one thing. A person. And that person was coming towards her.

***

Wyrrn pushed aside the last vellum scroll. The story was clear now. And it was all about money.

"Ramble, I need you."

The man had taken to waiting outside her rooms as if he were a personal servant. Made her feel intruded on, although she did like the convenience. *I could get used to running slaves.*

Ramble, of course, was a servant rather than a slave. A Master. And that was the story in the scrolls.

"Yes, Great One?" he said, edging into view in the doorway.

"How old is this place?"

"Too old to say, Great One." He came all the way into the room and stood by the table across from Wyrrn.

"How long have the Hitaians made Gods of their Kings?"

"Long and long, Great One."

"And how long have there been slaves on the plain?"

Ramble squinted, thinking. "When the New People came up from the south and conquered Old Hitai, all who were free became slaves. They are Gods but people are just meat. Some we call Masters, some servants, others slaves, but every being who is not God is a slave."

"You are incorrect," Wyrrn said. "There have been slaves for one-hundred twenty-two years."

The squint dropped from his face. Now Ramble affected surprise. "For so long, Great One? Five generations, or even six... No living person witnessed the start of this."

"But they wrote it down," she said, leaning back in her seat. It creaked. "These records are the words and thoughts of those who came before. They never wrote directly about the start of slaving but they did write about money."

"Money, Great One?"

"Oh, yes. These monuments cost a great deal of money. The old people, my people, well, they engaged in these things as a sort of local pride. They loved their kings and their kings loved them. Being king was a duty, not a position, and the people took turns at it. Strange to think on, now. Back then, the projects were modest. People volunteered because they wanted to enshrine their leaders, to honor their service."

"And what changed, Great One?"

Wyrrn shut her eyes and put a hand on her forehead. "The new ones came. The conquerors. A thousand years ago, they came. They saw the monuments and they wanted them. At first, the people were happy to oblige. But the monuments grew more and more grand, fanciful. Here, these scrolls." She touched a pile without opening her eyes. "These detail payments to a labor force. A significant labor force."

"But the money ran out," Ramble said. "Nobody can spend money without bringing it in."

"Wrong again. The money was mostly spent in the city. It came back. Taxes, prosperity. And trade, wars of conquest, more money than could be counted."

"What, then?"

"This pile. Income, no expenses on labor. Greed."

"Simple greed, Great One?"

"Oh yes," she said. "Simple bloody greed. The Masters found they could buy people. Cheaper than renting. Adults at first, but children were cheaper, expendable, and more malleable. Not as efficient but easily controlled. And they found something else, too."

"Do tell."

"They liked being in control. When there were slaves, there were Masters. No longer craft-masters but masters over other people. Every new Gravetender tries to soften conditions but the Masters push back against her.

"That stops now."

"Indeed." Ramble crossed his arms.

"Yes. There is more than enough money to hire adults to do this work. I have the evidence here. And here." She touched her forehead. "That is what we will do and I will hear no word about it. These children outside. Set them free, today. Those who wish we will see escorted home. Those who wish can stay and work, for pay, in the shade."

"Yes, Great One," Ramble said, and he turned to go. He stopped in the doorway for a moment as if he would talk but then just kept going.

***

"You have a metal mind," the woman said, when it was clear she was a woman.

To Korina, she seemed familiar, as if a visitor from a dream too many nights old to know clearly. "Yes," she said.

"But not a metal body, it seems." She came closer, striding out of the dust. The wind seemed to die around her, leaving this phantasm in an area of calm. She seemed tall for a Hitaian, and clearly not a Hitaian. White-ish linens covered her limbs and ruined silks her torso. Her face was sunburned, as ruined as the silks, thick with scabs. Her hair lacked any color at all: white and dirty, sparse around her scalp.

"Are you her?" Korina said. "My brother's new mother, his little wife, they used to tell tales of the Blind Master who haunts this desert."

"No," the woman said, "but I live in her house. Let me have a look at those wounds."

"Not blind, then."

"And no Master. Not as you mean it. No, too much sight in these eyes, even now."

"The witch," Korina said. "You are the White Witch, the King's seer."

"Guilty. Since the King died, though, and his daughter put on a beard, well, I find myself between employers. God always has work for hands like mine, so let us to that. You do not look so bad off. If you can walk a mile or so you can have rest, a sip—well, relief from the wind."

"I brought shelter," Korina said, rattling her canvas. Sand sifted off and more dust wafted into the witch's hair.

She stood. "You are a stubborn one, I know. Come anyway. We both know you will." Then she turned and started back the way she had come, striding and somehow also not covering much ground, purposeful but diffuse.

"I was just a girl," Korina said. "When you came to inspect the children. Hardly more than a baby."

"I know." The woman turned to speak over her shoulder. "Blameless, you are. The guilt for all that has happened belongs to me. It's mine, all of it. I want it that way. Come along, now. We can speak of guilt, of shame, of pain and perseverance. Of what makes iron separate from steel."

"Steel?"

"Yes. Only come in out of the wind."

Korina scrambled upright and shook the worst of the dust off her canvas. When it was stowed in her bag, she trotted after the witch. Suddenly, she was quite far away, like distance was subjective. Greater here, shorter there. Korina hurried to catch up on feet that betrayed her.

"I do not remember your name. Shall I call you Witch?"

"Mithodroxes," the woman said. "Flax was your father, Jimina your mother. Yohn, poor doomed boy, and Poli who died of a cough before finding a husband to keep her. And the other one. We will not speak of him."

"No?"

"No."

There was soft silence then as they walked. Sounds impinged on it but did not quite break it: the scrape of cloth against cloth, against flesh; of sand under sandals; of air sizzling through nostrils not made for such heat.

The swirling winds parted like curtains to reveal a structure. Wood whitened by continuous sun, weathered smooth. Bits and pieces stolen from dead wagons, abandoned desert junk.

Korina said, "That is a house?"

"Arguably."

"And you live there?"

"As much as this is a house, what I do is living." Mithodroxes ducked through a short doorway covered by a leather flap that looked newer than the rest of it. Her shoulders brushed against water flasks on the wall and set them to rattling.

Korina wanted to touch her own flasks but they were safely tucked inside her bag. No way to touch them easily, and no reason to.

Mithodroxes said, "Do not worry, child. I shall not steal your water or your flasks."

"There is room to sit."

"And you should. There, if you like." She pointed to a pile of old rags, scraps of fabrics much like the wood outside: salvaged, stolen, pushed into this new purpose.

"I am not a one for comforts," Korina said.

Mithodroxes laughed. "Then that pile of cloth is perfect for you. Me, I shall sit by the door. Hotter there."

"Hotter?"

"God is cruel, child. Cruel. His purpose is grand, yes, but where the great walk..."

"The meek do well to avoid notice," Korina finished. "The Blind Master really lived here?"

"An obsession of yours? A fear? Be peaceful. There are no ghosts. Well, there were no ghosts, but as your lake spirit does its work, perhaps. Still, I have seen no things here, night or day. She died a long time ago and her body is less than dust now. The past is all dust."

Korina tried to get more comfortable. The rags were, as promised, not much of a luxury. "I have food."

"Save it. You will need it. I rarely eat."

Indeed, Mithodroxes was beyond thin. She looked like a skeleton dressed in rags, an emaciated mummy escaped from the tombs. "The cruelty of your gods again?"

"I will visit none of that on you. You are to go north, yes. Out of this desert, far and far, to a place where water freezes in the sky and falls to the world softer than those rags, gently, with a noise like... Ah, you will hear it for yourself. I never shall. It is my home you go to, or near enough."

"You wish to come with me? I had not sought companionship."

"No." Mithodroxes looked up, pointed.

"God?"

"Yes."

"So what will I find near enough your home?"

"Pain," Mithodroxes said. "But that you know. Toil, and that, too, you know. And the apprentice you seek. Closer than you imagined, and no need to walk so far – though you will have to go all that way to learn it."

"My feet hurt," Korina said. "Perhaps I can sleep in the shade."

Mithodroxes laughed again revealing a grin short a few teeth, the rest with gums pulled back so they seemed overlong, grotesque. "Heal for a day and I will show you how to dress your feet for sand-walking."

Korina glanced at Mithodroxes' feet for the first time. They were linen-clad as the rest of her was, only more tightly bound. No loose tags of cloth to flap and flutter.

"One more thing," Mithodroxes said. "The thing that brings us together."

"What is it?"

"Some of them will come back, child. And you will forge a crown. A crown to seal the past behind us."

Korina laughed now. "Riddles and riddles. I see why you live out here in this miserable place. What King could stand such advice at this?"

Mithodroxes just looked out between the leather flap and the door frame.

***

Fum was tired. Footsore, mostly. There was a difference between wandering the countryside as an explorer and marching across the land in the company of soldiers. At least they did not ask him to keep step with them.

Every day was the same. Wake, eat, march, eat, sleep, begin again. The food was dry and cold and so was the conversation, by and large. He was starting to think about escaping. It would be easy, given his light guard and the skills he had collected.

"A few more days," Nivek said.

He sounds sympathetic, Fum thought. *Not that I trust him.* "Truly the land is vast beyond comprehension." *And your army strange.* Hitai was a land of two peoples and those divided by castes. Old and New Hitaians hardly shared power or roles. But Nivek, at first just a shadow in the dark, had become an anomaly in the light of day. Brown skin, black hair, kohl-black eyes. Broad hands and feet. His Greenlander was so good because he was a Greenlander himself.

"Big enough for everyone," Nivek said.

Right.

The land was changing around them. Woods had yielded to grasslands which now slowly rose into foothills. Rocky crops grew out of gray soil to strive slowly for the sky. Ahead, to the south, the mountains took a bite out of the horizon.

"Before those mountains?" Fum said.

"Just on the other side."

"I am quite sure I have seen enough," Fum said. "Your hospitality exceeds my capacity for repayment."

"Freely given," Nivek said, smiling. He seemed not at all tired. Day after day, miles reeled out under his heels and he went on and on, unchanged, unflagging.

"Perhaps not freely accepted. What would you do if I stopped walking? Turned around to face home?"

"Watch you go, I suppose," Nivek said.

"Really?" Fum did stop, practically panting.

"Of course. Turn and go if you like. These fifty other soldiers, though... well, they are under the impression you killed one of their own. They should quite like to have a conversation about that. Given you have no languages in common, I expect that conversation might involve some hand signs and raised voices."

"Oh." Fum tried to shake off his fatigue and failed. And he was careful to make sure Nivek saw him fail. The sweat on his face was obvious, and the blister on his left foot was no fake. "Then let us hurry on, shall we?"

"After you," Nivek said, half bowing.

Fum sighed and carried on. "I suppose I should be grateful for my skin. Your protection is not un-noted."

"I would like you flay you myself, honestly," Nivek said, striding easily.

"I should worry?"

"Not much. My Emperor was clear that she wanted to meet you personally."

"Emperor? I am afraid I do not know that word."

Nivek smiled again. "No word for it in Greenlander. Lords rule lands, kings rule lords, and emperors rule kings."

"Ah. You mean gods. Or Gods."

Nivek frowned a question.

"Oh. Those are two words in my own language but only one in Greenlander. The former are the abstract beings that rule over fates and destinies. The latter are Kings risen to immortal stations."

"Ah. No, not those. Just a ruler."

Perhaps I should keep following this band. It seems there is something new to learn after all.

And besides, he was troubled by a force that did not only conquer other peoples but absorbed them, made them its own. This band of fifty soldiers was mostly pale: women and men with beige skin dyed pink with too much sun, hair in brown and red and yellow. But one person in five was brown. The bronze of the forest peoples of the Greenlands and the darker hues of Xunians, the brassy colors of Lurkians.

All speaking one language, wearing one style of clothing, marching in lock-step towards a confrontation with the Greenlands. *And, beyond that...*

Dawn

Gareth stood in the doorway. Cool morning dew settled on his face, on his bare chest. Behind him, in the little room they had rented together, his friends stirred from a troubled sleep.

"Close the door," Xin Ban said. "Too cold."

Guarl grunted agreement.

"Roach knows something." He came inside and closed up the door, put his back against it. "He wants us gone."

"Just an accident," Whilla said, motioning him aside. "I need the outhouse. That's outside. So move."

"Take your spear," Xin Ban said, passing it up from the floor.

"I forgot," she said.

"Don't," Gareth said. "I will come with you."

"I know how to pee," Whilla said.

"And I know how to watch for trouble."

She sighed.

"It was just an accident," Guarl said. "Hong is a big place but not so big we will never see him again."

Roach had come around after the duel and sat in the drinking house the next morning. When they had come out of their borrowed room, he was there with some casual questions. Nothing about dueling but about moving on. *Where will you go? What will you do? How soon will you leave? How can I help you to be on your way?*

"He knows something," Gareth repeated, and followed Whilla outside.

Guarl came as far as the doorway. Xin Ban stood behind him and shivered. Guarl said, "And how would you find out what he knows? Even if you found out, what then?"

"I don't know," Gareth said.

Whilla came out of the outhouse and scanned around for danger. The yard, the tree above them, rooves. "No more duels," she said. "We have money for a few more nights at this place, food for a few more days. Then we move on. No matter what."

"I'm getting good at it," Gareth said.

"Too dangerous," said Guarl and Xin Ban at once. He went on alone: "Next time you provoke a duel, Xin Ban is going to stand in for you."

"You can't-"

"If you don't care about yourself," Guarl went on, "you still care enough to not risk her. So that's the way it is."

Gareth sighed, went back in the little room. "Maybe you're right. Anyway, I'd like to check on the forge. See who runs it now. What they do with it. Maybe I have another lost relative."

"Selfish," Guarl said.

"Better than dueling," Xin Ban said, pushing the door shut behind Whilla. "And we've little else to do. Tracking Moburu turns out to be the biggest waste of time."

"The forge, then," Guarl said, and Gareth put a hand on his shoulder.

"Thanks."

***

"This is a waste of time," Jeen said. She leaned against a stone wall just taller than herself. There were trees around but none overhead, and no tall rooves.

"He is here somewhere," Chess said.

"No new bodies."

"He is here."

"No tracks. No spoor. No sightings. No rumors."

Chess grunted, stood up from the track she was examining. "Just a dog. One of their wolf-hunting hounds by the size."

"What if he went home?" Jeen said.

"Nothing there for him."

"But what if?"

"Then I suppose they're all dead. None in the village could stop Moburu, or whatever he has become. We are here. And if he went to Hitai, well, let him. His sister is as sadistic as their father ever was. Maybe he can rule the kingdom with some honesty, as a predator."

Jeen found a lump in her throat. There were hot tears behind her eyes and they wanted to come out to feel the breeze. "I do not want to do this more. I do not want to be here with you."

"Then go home," Chess said, turning away. Then she turned back. "No. Do not go. I am sorry, sorry. Frustrated, worried, sorry."

Jeen cried openly now. "I wish this sword was good for something. I want to hit something with it. Him, you, this sadness that stalks me."

Chess took a step back. "It is still bad, I know. But better, yes? Your grief grows as well as my body."

She sniffed, wiped at her eyes. "We should walk. Keep looking. There is nothing to find under this wall."

Chess obliged. They strolled through the village, close to the outskirts now. Nights sleeping rough left them looking wild and dirty. Jeen's fingers were sooty and smelled of the hare they had roasted last night.

"The smith is this way," Chess said.

"Where Yohn's family lived, before the Starfall?"

Chess saw Jeen wince. "Sorry."

"No, I want to see it. I will cry not. Not *cry*. I promise."

"Time is going backwards now. Your Hitaian has not roughened in years."

Jeen turned around quickly as if surprised. She heard something, or smelled it, or just thought it. But there was nothing, just the wall, the gray sky, a tiny spider sailing by on a silken sail.

"What?" Chess said, wary, poised.

"Nervous," Jeen said.

"Good."

***

Back in Hong.

I hate going backwards.

Zhang reflected on how much of the soldier's life was about going forwards and not backwards. Miles and miles, enough to encircle the world, and ever forwards. Unless you were losing.

And I hate this town.

There was nothing really wrong with it. Sleepy, peaceful, prosperous. Clean in its way, pleasant even. Nobody had particularly tried to kill her here. But it was not home. It was another thing in her way, a delay, a consequence of misfortune. It was a misfortune.

Still, there was ale and mead and even brandy. Though it was early yet, she found a drinking house whose keeper was not sleeping. With some finger-talk she got herself a wooden chair outside where she could watch the road and a little draft of liquid heat.

She did not hate the brandy.

People began to pass by in the road outside. Out for their daily bread, for their labors, or just to be out, they all gave her a good bit of space. She laughed inside, delighting at their fear. They were right to be afraid. Her sword was wrapped in oilcloth to keep off the damp and yet even had it been bare, it could not have been more obvious what she was. Broken sword, broken soldier, more dangerous than a rabid dog or a wounded lion.

The house-keeper wandered out and pointed at her mug. *More?*

Zhang thought for a second before handing the cup up and getting to her feet. If people were moving around there was a chance she could get her business started, and started was closer to finished, and finished meant she could walk back to the south where the ships called.

People left her as much room to walk in as they had room to sit in. That felt good. Except that as she walked, she slowly grew convinced someone was watching her. It started as an itch on the right side of her nose that would not go away, then a pressure on her back, then the rising of her hackles. Instincts honed by decades as the predator alerted her that she was prey, and she knew enough to listen.

When she looked around, though, there was nothing to see. Just people going about their daily business, small, brown people in their drab clothes with the dull lives she hated and envied.

And a smell.

Low. Musky. Imagination, almost, only not. She had smelled it before. Her mind raced, and her eyes checked the high places. Nothing.

The smell was gone now, and the feeling of being watched. She still stood there in the road like a mad person, trying to remember, willing herself to remember. A singular scent.

Zhang's eyes were drawn again to the high places. Rooftops. After her failure at the Starfall, she had lived in Hitai for a while, hiring out as a guard or a fighter. She fit in well with her dark skin and lack of compunctions, and the language came to her easily enough. And in Hitai, every ledge held a cat.

No cats here.

Some people kept dogs. She had seen them her last trip through, big, rangy things bred for killing their wilder cousins. But no cats.

Cats.

The idea made no sense, and the next memory in line made less.

The long hall at the Starfall. The big man, the Hitaian one, slipping his sword into the rushes that served as the roof. A temptation. A trap. He should have been the champion, not the woman with the spear. She knew it, the big man knew it. Her broken sword, her broken honor, all on that woman.

The big man.

The smell.

Just a taste on the air, long-gone now. Ridiculous to imagine it was him just because her mind swirled around to that memory, that one image from the worst day of her life. She thought of that day often, after all. And yet, she knew it with absolute conviction.

So. I never hoped for the chance to try him. Perhaps I will, yet.

And that meant she could not stand in the road. There was business to get done. If she was going to fight the big Hitaian before she went home, she would need her sword whole. That meant finding the forge.

Burial

Erlo stood over the corpse, hand over his eyes, trying to hold in the grief.

"Damned sorry," the man said. Erlo did not even know his name. One of the new ones, the ones who came after the battle. "He was your friend."

"I know what he was," Erlo said. His voice tasted like blood. "I could use a drink." But he said that out of habit. He had not touched the horn for twenty days now. The first of those he had shaken, teeth chattering, skin itching. He had stank and his eyes had hurt. After four days his lodge-mates had tossed him in the lake. By the fifth, he could eat again, and after ten the children had demanded he come back to teaching.

"Sorry," the newcomer said again, and backed away.

"It happens," Erlo said. He took the hand from his eyes and the tears flowed out as though that hand had been a dam. "It is not fair. He was a good man. The best of us, really. And I go on."

Mang lay on the path to the outhouse, curled up with his knees to his chest, dark skin graying in the morning light.

"He was sick for years, you know," Erlo said. There was nobody around to hear, he knew that, but he spoke anyway. "Chewed those leaves like we would not notice. Made the pain go away. Cost him all his teeth, which hurt more, so he just chewed more leaves. I had forgotten. Forgotten."

Morning. Too early, always too early. He hated to leave his bed, empty though it was now. The day was full of work. He loved the children, every one of them, but teaching them was the least of his labors. Each moment he did not scream was a victory, every day he did not strike out a battle won. And keeping the mead off his lips the greatest of challenges. But the newcomer had woken him first, Erlo of all people, Erlo the useless. The sot. The weakling.

"You should see. You should come. They will all look to you."

Erlo wished the man had shaken Ham awake instead. Ham had been here as long, knew Mang as well. No-one really knew Mang, in truth.

Well, nothing to do now.

He stooped, cradled the body in his arms, lifted. Mang came away from the gravel with hardly a fuss. Bits of rock dropped off his skin to patter back to the ground. He was stiff and cold, not changing position as Erlo lifted him, and light. Much too light.

Dying all the while. You lived, made us think you were living, but you were dying.

Erlo carried his friend into the long hall and laid him on the hearth, thinking the fire might start to unfreeze his bones, but he knew it was too warm for him to be frozen. This was a death thing, the hardening of the body as the spirit left it. A good spirit, a brave spirit.

Ham came in, fixing his clothes. "I heard about Mang. Is it true, then? This him?"

"Yes. Died in the night."

"They'll want us to bury him in the sheepfold, most likely."

"He was the first of us," Erlo said. "When I got here with Chess, do you remember? You were here, and the Xins. And we asked who was in charge. You all pointed to Mang."

"He had already built a hut by the lake," Ham said. "Didn't speak any Hitaian at first. None of us did. Had to work it all out from the start. And Mang was the one. Decided we were to be peaceful folk, to work together, to have one way of speech."

Erlo found tears in his eyes and his chest heavy. His arms felt like he'd swung Korina's hammers all night. "We'll not plant him in the pasture like a seed corn. Not Mang. The old way for him. The first way."

"These are not our people," Ham said. "They are no Sorubers."

"Neither are we, now, old friend. We are Starfallers, all together. And Mang was the first of us, the first to touch the water, to drink it, to ask what it wanted. If anything of the god still lives out there, let him have one more chance to touch it."

Ham put his hand on Erlo's shoulder. "Who is going to build his raft?"

The first of the children came out of a room to the side. Chara, a dark little girl from Hitai. Complicated blood in that one. She looked at Ham as she always did: with a hint of fear and a lot of curiosity. "Erlo. You woke up first."

"Yes, baby."

"I am not a baby. I have six years."

"Oh, so sorry. So sorry. Go and make your toilet, little one, and then bring me a bowl of water and some cloths. We have some work today."

"No lessons?" she said, pouting.

"Hm. Lessons, yes. Today we are going to learn how to wash the dead and dress them the best we can, how to build a raft to float them on and how to burn it. Today we are going to learn how to say goodbye to our friends."

The girl just stood there, tears filling up her eyes. She seemed to notice Mang then, lying on his side on the hearth like a thing, an object.

Erlo said, "I should say not to cry, Chara, really I should, but that is another thing to learn today: how to cry. Go on, now. We have much to do today."

***

His uncle sat on the throne and Jul glared at him from the step below.

A servant from the Preserves stood in the middle of the audience room, a black-dark woman whose clothes marked her as a warden. "Six red elephants this year," she said. "It seems the monster had strong blood, Great One. Every cow he touched calved a red son, and each of those three has calved a red son, and so far the lions and hyenas have gotten none of them."

"Of those?" Chans said – only he was called Ergol now. Jul had to remember that: Chans was Ergol.

"Of those?" the slave repeated. "Great One, is my speech improper?"

"No," he laughed. "Of the lions, how many? Of the hyenas?"

"Oh. Eighty-two lions, nineteen of those under a year of age. One hundred twenty-two hyenas."

"So few?"

"They range the preserves, Great One. Giant killers like them need much room to wander. Too many and they eat through the meat too quick."

Space, Jul thought. *Lions need space.* He fancied he was a lion and his uncle a hyena. No hyena was much of a match for a lion in his prime.

"My nephew is bored with all this," Ergol said. "If you say it is well out there, Hilga, I believe you. Talk to the engineers about that dam. I agree: building a small bywater will help the crocodiles continue their recovery."

"Yes, My King," the woman said, and bowed her way out.

Crocodiles, lions, hyenas. Dams and bywaters, by-blows of red elephants. And not so much as one drop of blood spilled. "Uncle, when will we see a criminal?"

"Bored, as I thought," Ergol said. "You have to be here for now, Jul. This is your seat – I only keep it warm for you. When you are of age you will build your own, in truth. You might not find your mother's seat a good fit."

"But I want-"

Ergol cut him off. "To torture some poor soul, yes, I know."

"Nobody interrupts a Prince of the Blood," Jul said, all but snarling.

"Wish that were true, boy." Ergol actually chuckled. "Bloodthirsty lot, our family, aren't we? We should go a-touring soon, see the tombs. The Gravetenders always insisted we could learn something about life from wandering around out there in the sand. Look, next petitioner is one of the Masters. Nasty lot. Slave-runners, they are. You handle him, all right? I'll be here to watch. Can't be too wicked to those people. They like to torture children."

Jul's cheeks flushed but he also smiled. *Does he know about the puppies?* And, *If they are bad, am I bad?*

Except the Masters would never be Kings.

The man came in. Not tall, wide without being imposing, rounded belly. He had the dark skin of The Blood but none of the rank, only a leather kilt. He was so low that he carried a full-sized lash. Barely more than an overseer, then.

"What is it?" Jul said, crossing his arms and taking a wide stance on the dais. "What brings my builders in from their work?"

"Ah, My Prince, ah, well..."

"If you enjoy the taste of your tongue in your mouth, best you use it to form words. Now." That felt good. Jul struggled to keep the smile off his face.

"It is the new Gravetender, My Prince," the man said. "Master Ramble sent me, quick as he could, you see. She, ah, the slaves, My Prince. She wishes to turn them all loose."

"So?"

"So? So? Ah, from what projects does My Prince think I have come? She orders no building. Draws no plans. Only raids the tombs for scraps of parchment and tells us to send the workers home to their mothers and fathers. With no children to cut the stone and no plans by which to cut it, why, there is no work to do."

Now Jul did smile. The new Gravetender was his old teacher, and he had some debts to settle with that one. "Very good, Master. This is excellent news."

"Is it? It is? My Prince?"

"Oh, yes," Jul said. "And you are to be rewarded. Only, bring her to me. Here. I will deal with this Gravetender."

"Yes, My Prince." The man all but ran from the room.

Jul turned to look at his uncle.

"That was well done," the older man said.

"I know it was," replied Jul, smiling.

***

Hilga, the warden from the preserves, waited outside the audience chamber while the Master went in. He clucked his tongue at her, perhaps in disapproval. She did not cluck back. That whip made her ill, though. She imagined she could smell the skin and blood that must be stuck to it.

But the man on the throne... A Prince, he called himself, although Hitai must have a king. Always had there been a King. The Blood ruled in this place and his was strong.

Hilga had good blood, also. Not so close to the ruling line as Ergol's or Jul's, but also far enough from that branch to be strong. A thing learned watching animals very closely: fresh blood was good for the family. And Ergol had looked at her the way a man looks at a woman. She had looked back just as frankly.

So now she waited outside in case he had a real interest. Hitai also had Queens.

She listened to the Master's speech out of boredom and because there was no way to not hear short of leaving. A few moments later, the wretched man all but ran out past her, still taking the time to disapprove of her once more with his eyes.

There were no more people waiting to see the Princes. Inside the chamber, those two argued a little then went silent. She stuck her head around the corner to find the room vacant.

Well, perhaps next time. Truthfully the inside of the palace was no good place for a ranger, a warden. The open sky called even now. Still, as long as she was here, she could go see the monster itself.

The last King, Ynn, had called a hunt and his daughter had brought in an elephant warped by the weird, slow magic of the Starfall. The trophy room was just below here, a big space for big things.

A few doors and some marble stairs and there it was. Light came in from above, windows around the edges of the ceiling on two sides, reflected by shiny brass plates. No torches or brassieres. By the yellow sunlight, Hilga could see she was not alone. Another woman sat on a stone bench next to a stuffed cheetah as though visiting it. The cheetah was posed sitting, tail curled around it, mouth shut.

There were lions and hyenas here, of course; a giant crocodile; two great apes. Those were all posed to show off gigantic teeth, bodies staged as if in mid-attack. And the elephant dominated the room.

He was the biggest living thing Hilga had ever seen. Or formerly living, she supposed was more accurate. He had long, wavy red hair over his whole body. Four tusks stretched over her head from his face. A terrifying animal. His progeny had mixed heritage; they had sparse red hair, just two tusks each, and some of his size. They were only pale copies.

"I was there," said the woman on the bench.

Hilga looked at her more closely. Her own age – old enough for a few gray hairs at her temples, young enough to still be comely. Her face was plain except for a few old scars that made her almost beautiful. "I am Hilga, come in from the Preserves. Thought I might look on the father of some of my charges."

"Xenia," the woman said. "And this is Ngali. She had the honor of the kill. Ynn liked that little. Smashed her with his scepter. But I had her brought back to life to watch over her queen. Her King. She's dead too, now, so Ngali sits here among the trophies. It turns out that a stuffed cat is not fit guard for a King. Do you like her?"

Disagreement seemed like a bad idea so Hilga shook her head yes. "Bloody work, out there in the wild. The animals work together sometimes to survive but, in the end, they win or die. By tooth or claw or horn, make meat of each other."

"Hardly better here."

"I should return to my wilderness."

"Not so wild," Xenia said. "The old people tamed the grasslands and the marshes long before we arrived here. You will see more blood spilled here if you have eyes to look."

"Just so," Hilga said. "Have you ever known a Gravetender to be executed? Neither have I. But they just sent out for the new one. The young Prince means to have her killed. Two Gravetenders put to death." She saw Xenia's interest and wondered if she had said too much.

"Truly? Dllyx sent the woman out there to protect her from her bloodthirsty son. Could not protect herself, though. Life here has become uncomfortable for me, as well. Perhaps I should talk to the new Prince. I thought he might have suggested a union, another step up in my rank. But I can draw, too, when we get around to it. The other... Too like Dllyx' fate."

Hilga could not scrape any meaning from those words and was really better at the politics of the field. The lion would kill all the cubs when he took over a pride. That was brutal, sickening even, but understandable. The politics of The Blood were rarely kinder or more comprehensible.

"As you say, Lady," Hilga offered, and retreated from the trophy room with one more backward glance at the cheetah. Her report had not included those. A few maned wolves left, a few foxes more by presumption than sightings, but no more cheetahs. All the cheetahs left in Hitai were those kept in the yard above.

The sadness that thought offered was a real thing she could know, a kind of balm from the odd menace of Xenia hiding in the trophy room from a ten year old boy. She accepted the sadness gratefully and cried much of the way home.

Forge

Zhang made a left turn onto the lane where people had told her the forge could be found. Not much of town lay beyond the forge. The building was low, hunched like a toad about to leap. Gray and black stone with ivy growing up one side. It smoked like a gateway to the underworld but there was no sound of hammers falling or bellows blowing.

As she reached for the door handle, two people came out.

Zhang knew them both instantly.

The small grayish woman, dark-haired and dark-eyed. The white woman with hair like spider silk, skin made of scars. Bright eyes behind a grimace enshrined on her face in deep lines.

Zhang reached for her sword but the only weapon she had kept was the broken iron trophy of her own disgrace. She had half a sword between them in a heartbeat. The two women noticed her then, shock washing over their faces.

"Stop!"

That voice came from behind. Hitaian laced with a village accent. It did not belong here.

"Come no closer," Chess shouted, not taking her eyes off of Zhang. And, to her, "We never meant you harm. Do you remember? I tried to save you, to take you in." She put one finger on the broken sword and levered it away from her neck an inch.

The other one had a sword, too. She raised it. The tip trembled. Zhang swatted it away, took Chess by the back of the head, pressed the sword back to her neck.

"You broke more than my sword," Zhang said. "You did worse than kill me."

From behind, closer: "And you did worse to me, Zhang. You gave me an obligation and I would pay it now."

Ah, the boy.

There were others with him. Muttering, whispering. Trying to hold him back.

Zhang pushed Chess away and stepped back into the lane. Stepped backwards until all the Starfallers were in her field of view. "Vengeance all around then, is it? What if I give you the life of this old woman and we say all debts are discharged?" She took one more step back. There was Chess, the small woman, Gareth, three friends with him. The small woman had a sword and, even with no knowledge what to do with it, she might be dangerous by accident. Chess was slow, hardly able to move. The young ones had a ragged assortment of weapons. Gareth's half-spear looked familiar – it just needed a red tassel to be the twin of her Captain's spear.

And one of the girls had Chess' spear.

The one that had broken Zhang's sword.

It was unmistakable. Red spear-tip like bloody copper, black wooden haft.

Zhang kept the rage off her face, and the glee. Plague at sea had been a blessing after all. Here was the woman who had ruined her, ruined everything – and that girl must be her daughter. There was the spear with the magic and the strength to break steel. A fortune, an eternal fortune. And all she needed do was take it.

Another day.

Gareth moved up, another of those magic weapons in his hand opposite the half-spear. It looked like a slab of jade, shaped like a giant knife. "Me first," he said. "You owe me."

"I thought it was you who owed," Zhang said, and stepped closer with one foot – then pivoted to run behind the forge, into the smoke. She ducked around the back wall. Someone hammered down the track behind her. When they cleared the wall, she punched them in the head. Not checking on the damage done, she pushed off and kept running, back towards the city where she could get lost in the crowd.

"Stop!"

"No, let her go."

"A trap, it's a trap."

"Guarl – is he badly hurt?"

All those voices behind her as she ran. She looked over her shoulder as she regained the lane two alleyways later and, looking backwards, smashed headlong into some low and solid thing. She tangled to the ground, crying out. On her back, breath coming fast and hot, she looked up into a set of inhuman eyes.

Animal eyes. Jade green like Gareth's little sword.

Its breath was hotter than hers. It stank of rot and blood. Black fur that seemed to have blacker spots over flanks that rippled with muscle. It was death. Her death.

The jaguar put one foot on her chest as she tried to rise, slamming her back to the ground.

Footsteps in the alley. Running hard.

"It's him! Moburu, he's here! He has her!"

Zhang did not take her eyes off the jaguar to see who shouted. But it seemed to forget about her, leaping away towards those voices. She scrambled back and up in time to see the animal crash through the space between Gareth and the other boy, sending both sprawling. Gareth tried to score it with the spear. Then it was gone.

Gareth righted himself, dragged the other boy to his feet. Glanced at Zhang on the ground. Swore under his breath, turned to chase the jaguar.

Moburu? The black man with golden hands? Is this what he became? But how?

She should keep running, Zhang knew that. Get away, regroup, hunt these people down one by one – become a jaguar herself. But the thing had had her. And it wanted someone else more. Or some*thing* else.

And she had to see.

So Zhang got her feet under her and followed Gareth and his friend, making sure to keep hidden as she went, pain radiating from the middle of her chest where Moburu had hit her. She set that aside for later, hoping nothing in her chest was broken, and looked around another corner.

In the lane, the two boys ran towards the two girls. Another hundred feet beyond them, the small woman stepped in front of Chess, sword up, as jaguar-Moburu charged. He ran like black lightning, a streak of darkness, hard to see even in the full light.

He closed to within a few feet and leaped up. The small woman swung at him. From her angle, Zhang could not see what happened. All three went to the ground and only the animal came up again, bounding away with the sword apparently between its teeth.

He jumped again, getting onto the roof of the forge and then thirty feet into a tree near where the city gave way to forest.

Chess' daughter was on her feet again now. She hurled the spear, grunting with the effort, taking two steps beyond the release. It whistled through the air in a high arc.

Moburu jumped again, aiming for the next tree. The spear crossed through his path, just touching him along the chest.

The jaguar that had started the leap was gone. A man fell from the air in its place, striking the ground in a plume of dirt.

Zhang was back at the Starfall in her mind. She was the champion, the greatest warrior, and her steel was strong. And then it was all over, her sword broken, some bumpkin woman with a spear smashing everything into pieces. Alive to see it, alive to know her life was a ruin, her honor dissipated, her future a wreckage.

When cats could be men and spears could break swords, when life made no sense, the wise limited their involvement.

Zhang gathered up the pieces of her wits and retreated. Let these people have their madness; she could find another ship off this accursed piece of land.

***

Whilla watched the spear curve up through the air, knowing she had missed: it was well to the right of the jaguar and moving fast. When he collided with it, she was so surprised she forgot to feel anything else.

Xin Ban punched her on the shoulder. "You did it! You ended it!"

"I..." Whilla had no other words, no other thoughts. And the surprise was confounded with uncertainty. A jaguar had streaked through the air but a man had landed in a jumble of limbs with a wet sound like a net full of fish plopping to the dock.

She and Xin Ban ran forwards, Gareth and Guarl right behind them. "Good throw," Gareth said.

But Whilla's eyes were on her mother.

She and Jeen still sprawled where the animal had left them. Jeen lay over Chess, back arched, arms and legs splayed. There was no blood. Whilla came close, skidded to a stop. Jeen's face was empty, mouth hanging open, eyes shut.

Chess' eyes were open. "Careful," she said. "Move her carefully. She is hurt."

"Mother?"

"I am well enough," Chess said.

Whilla knelt, slid Jeen off of her mother. Chess helped as she could. Jeen did not wake or stir. Whilla felt her for injuries, fearing blood, finding her arms and legs to be well, her stomach and neck intact. But her chest was ruined.

Jeen breathed but shallow and a wet sound came with each intake. Whilla split the woman's shirt up the middle to see the damage. The jaguar's strike had broken her sternum, leaving a deep dent. Her skin was puckered and stretched around bones pushed out of place.

"She will die," Chess said. "Such a wound. No person can last long through it. Perhaps she will speak soon, tell us her last wishes, but more likely she will only slip away."

"No," Whilla said.

"I am sorry, my daughter. We knew it was dangerous to come here. She knew. At the end, she was well. Coming away from that place helped her put some of the grief in its right place. She hardly cried at all."

"No."

Chess put arms around her, brought her close. Whilla's eyes were full of tears and she spoke once more through a raw throat, through a chest that seemed as heavy and broken as Jeen's.

"No. I can help."

"What can you do besides ease her way?" Her mother stepped back, turned her daughter to look into her eyes.

Whilla put a hand on Chess' chest and pushed her, gently, one more step away. "What I did for you. But now I will do it knowingly." Then she knelt again over Jeen's body, listening as her shallow breath came more faintly, as the gurgling sound overtook the noise of air moving. This wound had been taken willingly, lovingly. Jeen had stood in front of Chess knowing what would happen. A sacrifice.

I love you. I love your pain and the way you keep it fresh. I love the way you love.

Whilla put out a hand, held it over Jeen's chest.

Love and pain. I love you. I hurt to see you so hurt.

She concentrated not on the thought, but on the feeling. On the raw grief and on the love that lay under it. For Moburu she felt nothing, no grief at all; for this woman she felt deep and abiding pain, because love and grief were the same.

Blue light came out of her skin like sweat. Not from her hand but from all over. Droplets at first, lake-water untouched by anything in the world, then a flood, until she was a bright blue beacon in the midst of a gray day. She held onto that as she held onto the grief, and she put it into her friend, her teacher.

Love and pain are the same. Health and injury are not the same but they might be. Strength and sickness, fear and courage... These broken ribs could be stronger. This crushed chest a point of honor. On this side of life, possibility.

She did not know how long she sat under the lowering sky, grieving and loving and contemplating. When she was done, though, her mother cradled her in her arms, and Whilla held Jeen in her lap.

Jeen breathed well, eyes open, hands wrapped around Whilla's.

"Grief is love and I loved him well," Jeen said. "My heart is well. I could feel myself stretching out. Like painting varnish onto a plank, stretching it and stretching it, but nothing left in the bucket to wet the brush once more. Running out. And then, the brush was wet again. Thank you. Thank you for the chance to grieve a little longer."

"Are you tired now, my child?" Chess asked, planting a kiss on the back of her neck.

"No," said Whilla. "I feel strong. Now, let's go and see Moburu."

***

Gareth had no thoughts in his mind for Jeen or Chess. Half of him wanted to go after Zhang, who he knew had followed and watched. The other half wanted to rush after Moburu and make sure he was dead. That part won out.

He and his friends all rushed forwards. Whilla split off to see to Jeen and Chess. Gareth, Guarl and Xin Ban ran up on the fallen Moburu. He lay in a heap under a tree, a tall, dirty man with dark skin and tight, curly hair. He had a heavy beard shot with gray.

He seemed to be trying to get to his feet but like someone who had stayed too long at the drinking house. His face was part confusion and part rage. Moburu turned angry eyes on Gareth and opened his mouth to speak but only growled.

Xin Ban took up Whilla's spear, leaning on it more than brandishing it. Moburu must have seemed as little a danger to her as to Gareth.

"So easily knocked down," Gareth said. "We thought you were a great warrior. A god of sorts. You inspired so much fear. Yet here you are, unable even to move."

Moburu scrambled away a little, got to his hands and knees. Then at last he used the tree trunk to haul himself upright like a person, but hunched and cautious as a cornered cat. "What have you done?" he said with a voice like old nails after too many seasons in the fence: rusted.

The sword was behind him. Jeen's sword. It glimmered in grayish light dappling through the treetops.

"Yohn said you died," Gareth said. "Died a hero. You should have let that be. In going on and on, you became a monster."

"I was always a monster," Moburu said. "The thing in the lake. I asked it to make me something else, to let me be a part of a larger plan, but it could not change me. I only became more of who I was already. It called to me. Ah, words are so hard after so long..."

"Gareth." Guarl put a hand on his shoulder, pointed back towards Whilla. "It looks bad over there."

Xin Ban said, "What should we do with him? Seems the danger is over, if the cat is dead. Will it come back again? I'm worried for Jeen. She looks bad."

"There is still time for this to come out well," Moburu said, slurring like a drunkard. "The lake spirit called on me. Told me to take the sword. All this was about the sword. Jeen's sword. Let me take it and go."

"You're a murderer," Gareth said. "Much too dangerous to give you a sword and send you on your way."

Gareth felt a compulsion to look away, just as Moburu had said. It was too strong to deny. His eyes dragged away from the old man, through the trees, back to Whilla. He expected to see her kneeling over poor, dying Jeen, but the scene was all wrong. She was blue. Blue light shone from her skin, her clothes, her hair. She was so bright it hurt to look at her – but the light touched nothing else. Jeen in front of her, Chess behind, appeared in the same gray light as everything else, unpainted by Whilla's glow.

When Jeen sat up, Gareth knew what was happening. He could feel Whilla's choking grief, her deep love. He could feel her making those the same. And he understood.

That's what the god in the lake did, what it does. It makes things that were once different the same. It makes iron and bronze into metal; granite and quartz and limestone into rock; desert willow and elm into wood. It made Moburu and the jaguar into one being: a hunter, a killer. The five of us, one mind, one thing in the world.

He knew another thing: the god in the lake would not act against him, because he was it. Whilla was, and Guarl and Xin Ban, and Vault too. They had touched it, taken it into themselves just as Moburu had taken in the jaguar. Whatever its purpose in bringing him to this place, it was not to keep that sword away from him.

The light faded around Whilla and the pain faded from his chest. He wiped tears and snot off his face, only then realizing he had been devastated by her sobs even as he worked through the problems in his mind. Guarl and Xin Ban were equally affected. Guarl, red-eyed and chest heaving, kept a stern watch on Moburu. Xin Ban had hands over her face.

Then another thing struck Gareth; his encounter with Zhang. What she had done to him. His friends must have felt all of his emotions and shared some of his thoughts.

"What they did," said Xin Ban, "they did to all of us. They hurt you the worst, and you can try to keep that a secret, but if hurting you pulls you away from us, that hurts us. They did it to you, and what they did to you they did also to me."

He had thought she meant only their friendship, not the rest of it, and he flushed with shame – and a renewed resolution to extract revenge. Once Moburu was dealt with.

Gareth strode past Moburu and snatched up Jeen's sword. It had Korina's mark on it and everything about it screamed of her identity. Cold metal that had been folded and folded. Sharp, symmetrical, perfect. It balanced just behind the hilt, a plain bronze crossbar with black end caps.

But it was also wrong. Unfinished. He could not say how, and yet he still knew: the metals in it were alloyed, melted and mixed, but still separate. Like Moburu and the jaguar: their fusion was incomplete. The man could walk on his feet at some times but soon the animal would take over and he would be lost in it, suspended in it.

It was time for a final fusion.

"Moburu."

The man turned to look at him, confusion gone now, rage the only thing left to him – but his human body was too weak to enact his anger. "I did nothing to you. I saved all your lives. Leave me in peace."

"I can't," Gareth said. "You ever hurt so bad for so long that you forget you're suffering?"

"I never suffered this thing the god did to me. It never hurt me but perfected me."

"No, not perfected. And I mean the pain that started before you came to the Starfall. I can see it in you. I know about it. I can take that from you."

"I am," Moburu said. Gareth waited for more but there was nothing else. Just that.

"No, Moburu. You were."

Gareth held up the sword. Imperfect, flawed. Something his sister had made, something he could love. Shaped so carefully, slaved over. He could imagine her hunched over the anvil, shaping and reshaping the edge until it was flawless. Dipping it in the lake, hoping for the same miracle that had changed Chess' spear point, Vault's sword into something else – into *metal*.

But the spirit was no longer in the lake. It was in Gareth and his friends.

More:

Moburu. Flawed, imperfect. A man who had made himself into a monument: the perfect warrior. An indomitable hunter. Absent any human compassion, absent any fear. But he did fear. His fears of compassion had driven him to become this thing. Because compassion might mean pain. There was Whilla behind him, putting together grief and love; here was Moburu in front of him, unable to feel his grief and so driven mad by it.

Now that Gareth could see the pain he could feel it. It rattled up his arms into his chest, crushed at his heart.

"I love you, Moburu. Only someone who can feel such pain is worthy of love. But nobody could see how you hurt."

The man said, "Whatever you are going to do with that sword, just do. I know what I am. Save your love for someone who can endure it."

One hand held up the sword. The other fell on Moburu's shoulder.

Xin Ban said, "He is just like Whilla."

"We all are," Guarl said. "Even Vault, wherever he is."

"No, I mean, the light."

Gareth imagined light crawling out of his skin as it had for Whilla, but set that aside. For now, the love. The love. The pain. Flaws made perfect. Perfect alloy, perfect pain.

When it was done, he drove the sword into the ground and let it stand there. He thought he should feel exhausted but he did not. He felt strong, unsated. Awake.

"What did you do?" Xin Ban asked. "Are you a killer again?"

"No," Gareth said. "Moburu died a long time ago. The spirit did not bring him here to thwart us. It brought him to at last show him some mercy. To free him from suffering he did not know he had."

Guarl said, "But where is he?"

Gareth pointed to the sword. All of the metal was now utterly black. It reflected no light, had no shading, caught nothing of the dappled, diffuse sun. It was like a shadow.

"You did. You killed him." Xin Ban put her hands over her face again.

Gareth said, "No, I perfected him."

Rebirth

Wyrrn knew she had made a mistake. A crucial one.

The Masters profited from the practice of slaving. They kept money that would otherwise have gone to the workers, and they gained a kind of standing, the only kind they could out here.

Three of them stood in her workroom. They were high enough in the ranks to have short, useless lashes. These were women who expected to be obeyed, who would not honor their victims by hurting them personally. They all looked the same: medium height, wiry builds, hair concealed by headdresses that were on the same model as the Gravetender's. Bronze kilts completed the uniforms.

"You will come with us," one of them said. "You are to be accorded honor: arrested by the High Masters to be taken before the Prince of Hitai."

"Honor," Wyrrn said. "A kind of standing?"

"Indeed." The other two remained silent.

"There are two ways to gain standing. Do you know what they are?"

"I remember," the Master said. "They said you were a teacher. Well, teach as we walk. It is far to the palace. Best we leave now."

Wyrrn made no move to leave her work table. "One way is to be promoted. To get closer and closer to the highest rank, elevated above others. Sometimes by merit, perhaps more often by the pleasure of the ruler."

"You will come with us or we will have to beat you. See how we honor you? I will beat you myself."

"With that little whip? Do not be a fool," Wyrrn said, forcing a smile. "The other way to earn standing is simpler. Do you know what it is?" She did not wait for them to answer as it was plain they did not intend to engage in this conversation. "The other way is to make ranks lower than your own. Any worker could aspire to lead a team but few could achieve it. So they made slaves out of children. Now, with someone below their own standing, the felt their own standing was elevated."

"Your service to Hitai has earned you some patience but not so much as this."

"But think on this. I build a tall tower and climb to the top. I find I am not yet close enough to the sky for my tastes. So I descend to the ground and dig all around the tower. I dig a hole as deep as the tower is tall. Now when I climb back into the heights the ground is twice as far away as it was before. But I am no nearer the sky."

"Take her," the woman said, and the other two came around the table, one from each side.

Wyrrn had been waiting for just that, hoping for it. She was not a young woman, not really, and not strong or fast. But neither were these three. They never had to enforce their will with actual bodily strength; those little whips did all their work for them by marking them out as those with power.

Wyrrn waited until they were almost close enough to touch her. Then she stood suddenly and leaped over the table, skidding across its flat surface, sending parchments scattering and skittering to the floor. She bulled forwards, knocking the first woman down, and ran through the doorway.

Outside, every Master and overseer stood in a mass around her little workshop. A thousand of them, maybe more, all with lashes or full-sized whips. Nowhere to go.

The three highest Masters came out behind her, taking her by the arms. "You soil us by forcing us to lay hands on you," said the one who had spoken before. Again, the others said nothing.

"No, my rank is higher," Wyrrn said. "Until the King or whatever he calls himself knocks this silly hat off my head himself, I have more rank than all of you. I soil myself letting you touch me."

The two silent women let go of her arms and recoiled.

Wyrrn went on. "More, I have accorded you great honor by knocking you down with my own body."

Ramble was there in the crowd and he stood forward. "Tricks," he said. "She tries to trick us with her words."

"But her words are true," the first Master said. "The Prince did not send that she was to be hurt or stripped of rank, only brought to him."

"He may not dispose of me, either," Wyrrn said. Her heart hammered and she tried to keep her voice steady. *A lecture. Yes, a speech to an unruly student.* "The young Prince hates me and always has but the new one we know nothing of. He may decide to keep me here, to let those children go free. Who can say? And imagine a better solution, a surer solution."

"She wants us to kill her," Ramble said.

"None of us have the rank," the high one said.

"You do if I give you the rank," Wyrrn said. "Who will succeed me? Who can say? But there has been no Great Overseer here since Lud died. That is what the records show, is it not? Who would be the new Great Overseer? The Master of all Masters?"

The crowd muttered now and Wyrrn thought that the mutters of a thousand people could deafen a person. She wished never to hear such a thing again.

The high one whispered to her. "Why are you doing this? You cannot wish to die."

"My death is assured," she said. "Yours, too, in the end – but mine seems imminent. All I can choose is the manner of it. Jul is a monster. He will have me tortured to death. You saw how his mother dispatched my predecessor, did you not? He will make me wish for such a merciful end. No. Kill me here and now."

The woman stepped back as if these ideas were flames that might burn her. But she said, "Then make me the Great Overseer. I am already in all but name. And I will ensure a merciful ending for you. I will say you died fighting us and bring your corpse before the new Kings myself."

The noise died down, muttering done. The crowd had taken two steps closer and now Wyrrn could start to feel the heat given off by their bodies. So many bodies so close together. "Done," she said. And, louder, "This woman... What name have you?"

"I am Doggra."

"Doggra is your new Great Overseer, the highest of the high, a Great One now in truth. Trade in your bronze kilt for gold. From this day on, your blood is of The Blood, all your children and their children until the end of time."

"A great blessing," Doggra said.

A great curse, Wyrrn thought.

"Take her," Doggra repeated, and now Wyrrn allowed herself to be taken. The two women walked her through the crowd and out into the waiting desert. Masters tailed along in procession, sending a plume of dust high into the big, blue sky. From the front she hardly ate any of it but the last of them, the least of them must have choked on it.

They walked into the Tomblands, Wyrrn's feet and legs tiring. "Here is as good a place as any, is it not? Or just there, or any place. Do you mean me to die hot and tired?"

"In the shade," said the woman at her left – confirmation at last that she could speak. "For your comfort, Great One."

That sounded like a sneer. Wyrrn would have worried only that seemed redundant for someone on their way to die.

"Suddenly I find myself in no special hurry. Let us walk as long as you wish."

"No more time," said Doggra. "There is your final resting place."

They were among the old tombs now, the first tombs. Not so grandiose as those that had come later: hills of rock rather than mountains, suggestions of shape rather than elaborate sculptures. Doggra pointed down a flight of stairs that only continual work kept at all visible.

Doggra said, "We already thought of everything you said. You must think us very foolish. The young Prince would certainly kill you but the new one might do anything, anything at all. He has been long away and he watches after the interests of the priesthood. Those ones always wished the slaving to end. Willing work honors the gods. So we arranged for you to have an accident. Out visiting the tombs, before we heard the order. Sadly, you fell down some stairs and were trapped in one of the old places, lost to time. This one has painted walls. Perhaps you will have time to read them. But, sadly, no light."

A long speech. In all this time, Wyrrn might have struggled, fought, tried to run. But where was there to go? And the chances of death were too slim. All that would happen was worse suffering. So she pulled away from her guards and walked down the stairs herself to stone door. It opened easily towards her. Inside was a plinth with a coffin on it just as dried-out as the door. The remains of a second box sat next to it, fragments of painted wood visible in a pile of dust.

The door scraped shut behind her and Wyrrn felt a momentary hope. That door would not withstand any effort on her part. The counterweights were still good; it had opened easily. She could be free in moments if she chose. Just wait for everyone to go away. Then she heard the sound of sand sifting down. They started a work-song up there.

A wonder they did not bring slaves to do their burying for them.

But she understood. Everyone would throw at least a handful of sand so none of them could say they were innocent. *How do you keep a murder secret when a thousand people know of it? Make sure they all do the murder.*

As sand covered the door the thin light it admitted faded. Within the hour she knew the desert had swallowed this place completely. No sign would be visible above the sand. Her thoughts went to Dllyx in her own tomb, locked away to die of starvation or thirst or perhaps to suffocate. That would be the most merciful, yes.

Even that might take too long.

By memory, Wyrrn walked over to the intact coffin. Perhaps there was a bone or a bit of metal or stone inside that she could sharpen and use to open her veins. Better that than suffocating.

But when she pushed the lid off the box, she realized the darkness was not total. Something in there gave off a light. Dim, orange, barely visible – but light.

***

Three carts rolled along the horizon, each pulled by two oxen. The sun set slowly behind them throwing the sky into a confusion of colors, blue and gray, orange and red, with the carts and their animals and their riders black shapes blocking out that uncertain light.

Korina was ready to camp for the night and knew she probably should. The desert was two days behind her now and out here was rolling grass, wind, and open sky. She felt free but also afraid of so much space, so much possibility.

Am I lonely?

Of course she was lonely. She was often lonely. Alone in the forge with just metal and fire for company, just the sound of her own hammer to pass the time, she knew about loneliness. That was the wrong question.

The real question is, can I stand it?

She could keep walking until after dark and meet up with that collection of wagons. They would stop soon. Too dangerous to push on through the dark. Oxen could not see where to put their feet. Or she could sleep and meet them in the morning. It looked as though they were converging on a point in the distance and moving at roughly the same speed.

She sighed and switched her bag to the other hand. More walking.

As the sun finally fell below the edge of the world, Korina walked into a camp made by arranging the wagons in a triangle. She whistled as she came on, some old Xunian tune she had learned from Mang in exchange for a story years ago. Nobody was surprised to see her.

Four old woman and two young men, all with light skin, light eyes, light hair. They all glanced at her and away, back at the fire they had stoked in the center of their camp. Pots bubbled and steamed.

"Numina," one of the women said, then something Korina recognized but could not keep up with. Soruber speech, like Chess and Erlo spoke sometimes between themselves.

Jeen had insisted all the children learn all the languages they could even though Hitaian was their shared speech. Among the older children, Korina had fared the best. Even Kwin who was born to speak Soruber never managed to pick up much of it. "I speak that," she said, "but slower. I am Korina."

Numina spoke again, slower this time. "Heading for Deyklaveyn. Biggest of the forge-towns. Share our fire. Bring anything to drop in the stew?"

"Half a rabbit," Korina said. "Got lucky yesterday morning. Snare." She reached into her bag and retrieved the remains of the carcass. One of the other women showed her which pot to throw it in.

They waited quietly for food to be ready. Then the young men passed around wooden bowls. Mashed tubers, stew, dried fish fried in pig fat. Korina ate her share sitting in the grass with her back to a wagon wheel.

"I am also going to Deyklaveyn," she said. She had not been, had not heard of it before, but it sounded like just the right place. "Is the road safe?"

"For adults," Numina said. "Safe enough. Slavers come for children sometimes. You don't look like a slaver."

It took Korina a moment to puzzle through that bit of more casual speech. "No. Starfaller." She used the Hitaian word for that, the proper name for her home. The others seemed to understand it, nodding and muttering.

"Good," Numina said. "If you were a slaver, we would have to kill you. Waste of good stew."

Korina looked up sharply but the woman's smile was clear in the light of the campfire. "I need an apprentice for my forge. None of the village children have the strength." She meant aptitude but could not conjure the word for it.

"A thousand apprentices in Deyklaveyn," Numina said. "A thousand more with the strength. Good place to look. We broke a pin on our wheel. Just bronze, not strong enough."

"I can fix it." She knew without even looking. Bronze she could just hammer back together, make it good enough to get home on.

Numina looked her over. "In the morning. For now, you can sleep under that wagon if you like. These boys will not bother you. Opia might, the old crow." The named woman flushed and laughed.

"Thank you," Korina said. She helped clean up and bank the fire, then crawled under the wagon to rest. A canvas for a blanket and her tool bag for a pillow. Sleep came, seeming to radiate out from her full belly.

***

There was not only a glow but a smell.

Wyrrn had been at a birth once. Well, counting her own, twice, but she could hardly be counted on to remember the first. The second, though, she had a mind for. And that mind went back now.

A niece. Wyrrn had been teaching children from around her own home then, the ones old enough to learn but not old enough yet to work. Reading a little history to know where they came from. Her sister's child came in the middle of a lesson.

"Send them away, all these children," her sister had said.

"Good for them to learn about this," Wyrrn had replied. "Life, how it begins, how helpless all of us are."

That lesson had gone badly. The sister died squeezing out that child and the baby died, also, unable to suckle from the women they put her with. But the smell of birth: of new flesh, of blood, of the afterbirth – that lasted.

The glow, the smell. In the old coffin, something alive was taking on form. There was not enough light to see it but she thought it was a body, a human form – but clearly not a human. People grew in wombs, not coffins in old crypts under the desert.

The glow stopped.

Wyrrn missed it immediately even though it was unsettling, even though it brought nothing of help. She could not look at the wall paintings by it, could not examine the room she would die in by it. No comfort, no warmth. It certainly did not fill her belly.

Then, a shuffling, scraping sound.

"No fear," a voice said.

"I am not afraid," she lied. What good was fear? She had meant to die to avoid being tortured to death and now she was alive to have this new adventure. Every moment answered a hope buried so deep she had forgotten it until just now: the hope to go on living.

"Of all the tombs they could have buried you in, they picked mine."

"So you are one of the Old Hitaians. Which one? Jemi the Fox? He was said to have been buried underground."

The voice sounded weary, old. "Not really my tomb either, I suppose. They were too lazy to build one for either of us."

"Are you a person? Why do you glow in the dark?"

"Just an after-effect of being reborn."

"Who are you?" she said.

"Me? I am the Gravetender."

Wyrrn laughed. "I am also the Gravetender."

"That does not seem correct. There is only one Gravetender, and I sense I am he. Or possibly she; I have not yet seen my body. Oh, yes, there it is. He, then, this time."

Wyrrn wanted to back away but, really, there was nowhere to go. "You could try speaking sense."

"I could try. The nonsense is not in my words so much as in your lack of comprehension. Your people... which one are you? The Old Hitaian or the New? In either case, those people all mistook the Gravetenders for people, just like themselves, when we are in fact artifacts."

"Artifacts?"

"Objects, found things. This place is a machine and we are its architects, but we are also the machine."

"Madness," Wyrrn said.

"Undoubtedly. I arose from a block of clay left here by a child who was also me. He got the clay from his mother, who was me. Both of them arose from blocks just like it. All of us do. When one dies, we remember that we were that one as well as all the others that came before it. Before then we have lives, histories, like a person. Since there are no others, I am born, as it were, remembering all of it."

"I am afraid it is an especially useless time to be born, and an inauspicious place. We are sealed in down here, buried. No way out. In truth, I wonder if you exist at all or are just the rattling of a mind in its final extremity."

The being was silent for a time. The dark seemed to deepen. Wyrrn's mind began creating things for her to see, keeping her eyes busy while there was nothing real for them to do. Flashes of light at first, weird colors. Then that long-ago birthing, her sister turning blue as the blood leaked out of her.

"Did I say this is a machine?" the voice said.

"Yes, but I still do not understand. What does it do?"

"Of course, not many machines in your life. Wheels, pulleys, levers. This place is like a wheel. It allows for travel more quickly than walking."

"Indeed. And where would you go?"

"Oh, exactly here," he said, "only here somewhere else. Do check the door, will you?"

Wyrrn turned to do as asked and found the door had bright sunshine behind it. Night ought to have reigned above by now, unless she had lost all of her senses. And the sand... She stepped over there and pushed the door open. It was just as cool and smooth as she remembered, but the steps were clear. Well-maintained. "Huh. There is light."

"So there is," the being said. "There is more than one way out of these tombs, you see. Always by the door but the doors do not always open on the same place. Will take a moment to get back home. I should remember the way. Only two or three such doors."

Wyrrn found she did not want to go up there. But as long as there was light, she could look at the walls of the tomb.

"No time for that now," the Gravetender said. "I have a lot to show you." He stood up on the plinth and seemed to look for a way down.

"Maybe more than I want to see," Wyrrn said, pointing as his groin and looking away.

"Oh. We shall have to fix that, I suppose. While we are on the subject of clothing, perhaps you would be kind enough to give back my hat."

She handed it over gladly, then offered him a hand down. They went up the steps together, out into the bright sunshine. All around were tall grasses and flowers, fields and fields of them. None of the Tomblands monuments could be seen.

"Barrowlands, they call these. Keep their dead underground. We shall jog over to the next one. About half a mile this way, if memory serves. Then pop up back in another place, then another, and finally your own place."

"What if somebody sees us?"

"They will not. No people here in four or five centuries. Wiped out. Perhaps a spirit or two but they cannot hurt us much."

Wyrrn followed along, alert for ghosts or specters or anything, really, that was not waving grass. "If the people are all dead, who calls this the Barrowlands?"

"Good question. Just me now, I expect. I will be around here somewhere, keeping the tombs up, keeping things aligned just right."

"You are right here with me."

"Quite so," he said. They found the stairwell and descended into the shade. Wyrrn felt better out of sight even though there was no-one to see.

This new tomb had just one box. The wood was waxed, shiny and silver in the low light. The Gravetender lifted the lid and pulled out the corpse. It had on a gray gown with gold inlay around the collar.

"Would not ordinarily rob the dead but these are unusual times. I have hardly ever been murdered before. And she had my offices burned. This will have to do."

The dress should have looked feminine on him but it looked mundane, ordinary. The corpse did not seem shy. Wyrrn helped put it back in its box and they managed without damaging it too badly. Sometime in the handling, dark washed through the tomb.

"The next stop," the Gravetender said. "Though no hurry. Quite pointless to go up there before daybreak. Not to worry, though. I shall help you."

"Help me what?"

"Why, help you finish the work." The Gravetender lay down on the floor – she could hear him – and in a few moments breathed the shallow, soft breaths of the sleeping.

***

Fum's steps came easier. The soldiers climbed a steep rise up a path that seemed to be made of one long stone – impossibly long, unbroken, fitted exactly to the contours of the land. The road reminded him of the causeway along the western edge of Hitai's outer provinces, the place full of crocodiles. Good memories of that place threatened his concentration so he focused on his breathing.

The breaths came easier, too, and he had to admit that marching south with these people had been good for his fitness.

He reached the top of the rise, noted how the grass was shorter here than down below, sere. Then the view opened up before him.

A city stretched from west to east as far as he could see, nestled between this rise and an adamant chain of foothills to the south. The buildings were sandstone, granite, whitewashed; rooves were tiles of clay or slate. A massive ramp rose over the city, running down from those southern hills, its purpose unclear to him. Great round buildings in tan must have housed grain. How many people to occupy such a place? How many souls?

"There," his keeper said, pointing. "Emperor awaits you. We can make it before dark, although Ramia is beautiful under the night sky."

"Ramia? This place?" Fum followed the extended finger with his eyes to a structure of most impractical character. It seemed to have no walls, only a sea of fluted columns that supported a thick stone roof. Steps led up on one side and each step seemed half as tall as the surrounding houses.

"Ramia is the seat of the empire and that temple is the seat of the Emperor."

"A seat sounds just the thing," Fum said, remembering he was supposed to be footsore and tired. Probably too late to resume the ruse now – and what was the point? He was so far from home, from his son, and what good was running when every direction led through more city and then more empire?

The streets were paved with the same strange stone. Clean and flat, they seemed to run unbroken forever, a stone web. People hurried about on them. All descriptions applied: dark and light, hirsute and bald, small, large, rotund and athletic. Fum saw little of sickness, though, or of great age. People seemed remarkable for that: they were hale.

The path through the city obscured his view of the temple. From down in the streets the place was a warren, dark even in the day, and cool. He lost his way a dozen times, turning down orderly, right-angle streets in a way that seemed designed to confuse him. Way the place was laid out, it seemed a simple thing to walk in quite a straight line.

Then the thing emerged from behind a wall, sudden. Shocking. Immense.

What he had taken for stairs were risers as tall as himself. A single trail of human-scaled steps ran up the middle. The fluted columns might have scratched the sky but for the roof that capped them. Inside: darkness.

"This is the best way to encounter it," his keeper said. "Another approach and you watch it grow from small size to dominate your mind; from this approach it leaps out at you."

"That is why the strange path here? Not to confuse me?"

"That too, of course." The man laughed. "Up you go now."

"Alone?"

"In Ramia, you are never alone. Remember that. A hundred thousand people live here and half of them are soldiers."

A hundred thousand? Fum rolled the number over in his mind, trying to make sense of it. He licked his lips.

"Well? Go on, then."

Fum went, trying to keep his wits about him, trying not to be overawed. The stairs made him feel heavy. They were just a hint too steep for even a tall man. There was some form of writing graven into the risers but it was beyond him. His shadow preceded him, cutting off even the dim light of the city behind him.

Then he was in the dark of the doorway. A black immensity rose over him, pushed his sense of himself down into meagerness. Tiny, he scuttled inside, just a rice-bug on a river barge.

Light flared ahead: a pair of torches that showed he was in a wide passageway now. The floor was smooth and uniform under his feet but changed between those torches. There, it took the form of a picture made of tiny stones all in different colors, a painting made of rocks: a woman, bathed in blue light as if floating in the sky, back arched, face obscured. She seemed to be falling into pieces, six pieces: head, torso, two arms, two legs. Blue light shone from the wounds.

Fum stepped with care over the picture and worked his way deeper into the temple. His heart sped. Nothing was good about these circumstances. He was about to chide himself for needless worry when the torches went out behind him.

Trial

Gareth sat on the floor of their small room, feet splayed in front of him, staring at the black metal of the sword.

There were two beds. Wooden frames, mattresses stuffed with straw of indifferent cleanliness. Blankets. Jeen lay on one, Chess on the other, both sleeping. Xin Ban, Whilla and Guarl all slept under the beds, sprawling around much of the floor, all touching.

One job was done. He touched the blade with his fingers, verifying for hundredth or thousandth time that it was real. It felt smooth, more like the finest fabric he could imagine than metal. Cold despite being in the same air he was in. And it was alive.

He could feel it. It was hungry. Powerful, confident, and hungry.

But Moburu was gone; at peace. That left Zhang and Roach.

He touched the sword again: still cold. Tense. Coiled up to spring.

Nothing was being solved in here. Five people slept while Zhang got farther away, while Roach did whatever he was doing to secure his position. So Gareth wrapped up his new sword in a blanket, sort of an improvised scabbard. He tied that to his belt and checked the sword would move in it. He imagined it would come out easily enough and he could worry about putting it back if he survived.

Then he slipped out the door. Behind him, his three friends fretted in their sleep.

There was still an hour of light left. Cold, gray light through clouds that would lower in the night and become a thick fog. He knew the way by now to the marker Roach had erected to his lost lover. Absent any other inspiration, Gareth went there. He imagined he might meet his aunt again, or that Roach himself might be waiting in the shadows to challenge him to a duel.

When he arrived, though, he had the gloaming all to himself.

He found a doorway and sat in it, back against someone's front door. And he thought.

This part of town was quiet. There was a drinking house nearby but people mostly stayed home due to the cold and wet. When a person walked by one road away, visible as she passed between houses, Gareth watched as though she could be relevant.

Bored, he put his hand on the sword handle. Nothing happened, and he wondered why he had expected it to. In the growing dark, exhausted from a day of fear, surprises and violence, he drifted off to sleep.

In his chest, the blue thing stirred. It saw the stars all looking down. The sky was infinity. Timeless. Spaceless. Here, in this body in the dark, Gareth had no notion of those things and so it forgot sometimes.

But in infinity, the past and the present are the same thing.

Gareth dreamed. Uneasily, his mind drifted into that night long ago. He watched two young lovers sneak away from town. He watched his great aunt watch them. And he saw another person, a man. Someone jealous. Someone he knew.

***

Chess woke from a dream. She was on the path, the long hall behind her, spear in hand. And before her was a jaguar. Immense, unstoppable, smoking and dark. It charged and charged, never seeming to come any closer, always threatening. Its feet hammered on the ground.

Awake, she still heard the hammering.

The door. Someone beat on the door.

Chess rolled out of bed, stepping on Xin Ban's leg as she did. The girl squealed and then everyone was awake and moving. Chess opened the door. Outside, Roach stood in a light rain, in the dark.

"A complaint has been filed," he said.

"What does that mean?" Chess asked.

"It means I have to investigate a possible crime. A citizen has claimed your Gareth insulted her honor and stole her sword. She said it was very distinctive. Black, like soot on the wind. Easy enough to investigate. Where is the boy?"

Chess looked around, expecting him to be there. "Gone, it seems. Although, nobody here stole anything from anyone. In fact, we solved your murder problem for you."

"How is that?"

"A large cat was responsible. A jaguar, from the high country around our home. We slew the beast."

Xin Ban said, "Whilla did it. With a great toss of her spear."

"The citizen suggests you murdered a slaver, in fact. With her sword." Roach stepped into the room, uninvited. "Slavers are unwelcome here yet still are not subject to murder. Perhaps I could see your spear. Inspect it for blood."

Whilla handed it over. "Be careful. It's sharp."

He looked at her like she had just told him rain was wet. "This blade is red. Hard to see blood on such a thing. I will take it as evidence."

"You will not," Chess said.

"You all leave me little choice," Roach said. "I asked you to leave town once. I gave these children everything they asked for. They had no further reason to stay here. I even let Gareth have back his father's sword. Yet they stay, you stay, dueling in the streets, causing all manner of trouble. And tonight I discover the boy is seen slinking around the site of his father's infamy. I will take this spear as evidence. I will search the boy for this sword. When you return the sword to its owner, I will give back the spear and escort you to the edge of town. Then you will leave and never return." He backed from the room.

Chess considered some kind of protest but nothing seemed suitable. This man was the authority here. His house, his rules.

Once he was gone, Xin Ban said, "At least we know where Gareth is."

***

They came for him as the sun started to rise. His three friends, Jeen, Chess. Those two were slow, carrying the weight of sadness and injury.

Gareth stood when he saw them, wiped water from his face. He shivered. "I'm sorry," he said. "I hoped when I came here... I'm not sure what I hoped for. Something. Movement. Moburu happened so randomly, after all."

"He was my friend," Chess said. "I knew he might have to die but I wanted to speak with him, help him."

"I know." Gareth looked at the ground. "I know. And I did help him. You don't know how much he was suffering."

Jeen touched his arm. "I know," she said. "I knew."

Chess ran a hand over the scars on one arm.

"Damnation." Gareth drew a heavy breath. "No end to the pain. But there was an end for him. He wished to be perfected and I perfected him."

"Would you do it to me?" Jeen said. "Perfect me, erase me from the world, make a thing of me?"

"Of course not. You're my friend. My teacher."

Chess put an arm around his shoulders then and his friends all came closer. "That is how I feel about him. But now we have to go to the magister. Something did indeed happen when you came here."

"Tell me," he said. While they walked, Chess filled him in.

"Zhang. It has to be. I saw her run away, though."

"Could be she circled back around," Chess said.

"Must be."

It was an hour's walk to the magister through winding streets, a messy, tangled stew of lanes. When they arrived, there was a gibbet set up outside. Gareth went in without remarking on it. A clerk pointed him at the stairs. His friends filed in behind him and followed.

The room looked much as it had before. A wooden privacy screen walled part of the area by the hearth. Otherwise the table was the same, the chairs, the windows, the light. The overcast had moved out with the sun, leaving yellow light to rule the sky. And Roach stood at the end of the table, the far end, by that screen.

Whilla's spear lay across the table.

"No hints of blood on this," Roach said.

Whilla said, "We admit we killed a jaguar. And you will find no more half-eaten corpses. That will prove our story is true."

Roach said, "No blood does not prove or disprove your story. And there is a matter of the sword. Is that it?" He pointed to the makeshift scabbard on Gareth's hip.

"This is my sword. Jeen had it when she first arrived. You saw it with your own eyes. An unscabbarded sword draws attention, doesn't it? I used it to banish the evil in the jaguar. That turned it black."

Roach's eyebrows drew together. "Draw it out halfway."

Gareth obliged.

Roach said, "That is not the sword I saw before. This one is blackened. As if in a fire. No, no fire could do that. Put it on the table."

Gareth untied it from his belt and set it on the flat surface just as it was, half-drawn. Roach stepped away, behind the privacy screen. A low-voiced conversation ensued.

Guarl stepped up to the table, pulling a small, wrapped package from the bottom of his pack.

"What are you doing?" Gareth whispered.

"Tombshade," Guarl said, hardly audible. "From where we found the spear, remember? She will touch the handle and then she will die."

He crushed the package in his hand, opened the top with the tip of a knife, smeared black liquid over the black leather handle. "I have to find a safe place for this," he said, then left with the little package.

Roach came back around the screen. He bulled between Chess and Whilla, took up the sword, carried it back. More low conversation.

"Tombshade won't kill anyone," Gareth whispered to Xin Ban, who looked distressed. "It would need to be prepared, boiled down. But a little on the skin can result in a short bout of madness. If that's Zhang behind there, she deserves all the madness we can give her."

"I'm worried about us," Xin Ban hissed. "Guarl didn't know that. He thought she'd die. We're very ready to just kill our way out of trouble. Whilla didn't know that spear wouldn't kill Moburu. You killed him without asking anyone."

"Might not be done killing yet."

Xin Ban crossed her arms and spread her feet.

Roach came out again, hands empty. "All you have to do is leave," he said. "The witness will drop her claim and you can keep the sword. Only go from this place and never return."

"We should do what he wants," Xin Ban said.

"We were leaving already," Chess said. "There is nothing left here for us to do and I am eager to see my daughters at home, my husband. My new namesake." Jeen nodded.

"The woman behind that screen," Gareth said. "I want to see her. She's lying about the weapon. I want her to lie to my face."

Roach said, "She may remain hidden if she wishes."

Guarl came back into the room, hands wet. "Chess and Jeen should go home. We should stay until our work is done. Zhang owes us something. And this man does, too." He looked at Whilla. "What do you think?"

Whilla's eyes were wet. "I want to go home with my mother. But we can't do that, can we? They sent us away from there, and this Magister is sending us from here. But Zhang hurt us. I mean, hurt Gareth. If she's here, we stay. She's behind that screen, isn't she, Magister Roach?"

Roach said, "The witness has chosen to stay screened."

Gareth stepped past him. Roach tried to grab him but Gareth ducked away. He grabbed the edge of the screen and pulled it down.

A woman sat back there on a chair. It was not Zhang.

Whilla said, "We're sorry. We don't know this woman."

"Just some stranger," Guarl said. "Must have watched from a window, seen the sword."

But Gareth knew her. "My father's aunt. You warned me, didn't you? Warned me that you would not treat me as family."

She had the sword point-down between her knees, both hands on the grip. Her eyes darted around the room and she licked her lips with a shy tongue. "It's mine," she said. "No, they didn't steal it, Roach, they didn't. But Flax owed me money when he ran away. He owed me something. Owed."

Gareth glanced at Guarl. This was an unexpected effect. Then he looked to Roach, whose anger clenched his teeth and brows. "Roach? Magister? Flax didn't kill those people, did he?"

"He ran from the scene," Roach said. Sweat started to form on his forehead, his upper lip. He glanced at the sword between the woman's knees, at the spear on the table.

Guarl said, "Running doesn't mean he did anything wrong. Does it?"

Whilla joined in. "Maybe he took his family away because he was afraid of something else. You, could be."

Roach sweated heavily now. "What did you do to me? My head is full of noise and color. You slipped me some poison, I know it. I knew you would find a way to cause more trouble."

"Tell the truth," Gareth's aunt said. "Not so hard, is it? I saw how you bit your lip when you hung him. How you paced and fretted."

Roach reached for the spear. Whilla snatched it up. And Xin Ban touched Roach on one shoulder. He recoiled but she kept up the contact.

"I love you," she said. "Nobody should have to feel as you do. Easier to say it, to let go of the lie. Easier..." She may have had a tiny nimbus of blue light about her but Gareth was not sure. "Give up the guilt. Let me have it. You and me, we can look at it together. Decide what to do."

"Out!" Roach roared, thrashing Xin Ban back with one arm. "Get out! I'll hang the lot of you. No, no need for that, only get *out.*"

Gareth walked up to his aunt, took the sword away, careful to touch only the blanket. "You could have asked for help."

"You understand so little," she said. "I came here not for my own gain. I came here because he asked me to. A favor." She looked sickly, old, the scar on her face puckered and white.

Gareth shook his head, backed away. The others were already halfway down the stairs. Roach stood by the window, panting and shaking.

Outside, the day had turned sunny. Warm, yellow light touched the lane. It landed in Zhang's hair, caught on her broad shoulders. She had her broken sword in her hands. "Duel," she said. "The old woman. Send her forth. We fight with swords."

Chess held up her empty hands. "The spirit that moved me is gone, Zhang. I fight no longer."

"And your sword is broken," Gareth said.

Guarl stepped up. "We've been meaning to kill you. Why shouldn't we?"

"Fight me," she said. "Fight me and I will tell you a thing you wish to know."

Gareth took a step forward to stand by Guarl, but Xin Ban spoke first. "I'll do it."

"You can't," Gareth said.

"I will." Xin Ban walked past him to stand ten feet from Zhang. "Only, your sword is broken and I haven't got one."

"I'll beat you with the shards," she said.

But Guarl was there, in front of her, muttering under his breath. "Whilla brought health to Jeen. Gareth forged a sword from a man. Xin Ban brought truth to courage. I can fix your blade."

"With your hands?" Zhang said.

"I do it and you say your piece. Then we give you a one day lead before we come after you."

"Do it, then." Zhang laughed, held up the pieces.

Guarl concentrated. Raised his own hands, put them on the metal. Shut his eyes, frowned.

Gareth could feel it. He'd felt Whilla's love and sadness. He had felt Xin Ban's honest affection for Roach. And he felt Guarl's love for the broken thing. When his hands glowed blue it was no surprise at all. When he was done, the sword seemed newly forged.

Zhang swung it back and forth, smiling at the sound it made cutting through the air. "No accident I stand here now," she said. "He sent me." She pointed at the window above. "Coward. He killed his woman and her man. He told me it was true. He paid me to kill you one at a time. But this... This is a grand payment. Things are almost well between us."

Gareth nodded. "No, not well, not good. I still owe you something. We all do. But now you should go, if you're going. I'll come and find you wherever you run."

She laughed again. "I am not running, boy. I am walking home, easy at heart."

Roach came down from his rooms, face purple. "Where are you going? You said you could best them, each one. Come back and do your job!"

Xin Ban said, "She said what you did. You couldn't tell me, but you had to tell someone, didn't you? So you told her."

His eyes were veiled when he said, "Yes. But I am the Magister. I am the law here. Nobody will believe you."

"My name is Fuhl," said Gareth's aunt from the doorway. "And I believe them. Indeed, I heard you myself."

And from a doorway across the lane came a woman with a child in her arms, giving suck. "I heard, too. You shouted it loud enough. Roach. I am so ashamed for you."

Roach screamed at the sky. Then he calmed. "A trick. They put poison into me, a spell to make my mind sick. To make me lie."

"To make you say the truth," Xin Ban said.

"Duel!" Roach yelled, then bit his lip. "Duel. I'll fight you myself."

Guarl smiled, reached for a weapon. But Gareth stopped him with a hand. "No. No, let the people of this place decide what to do with him." He nodded at the woman across the lane, then to Fuhl. "I'm glad you came here. It is good to have your family to help you."

Xin Ban rushed over and hugged him. "No more killing? You won't fight him, or Zhang?"

"You were willing to fight for us. I am willing to not fight, for you. For you, Xin Ban. Our hands will be bloody enough, I know that, but today... You are right. We are all too willing to kill."

Roach fell to his knees, hands tangled in his hair. "I can save something. I can flee. Flax fled. He fled. He fled because he was guilty."

Gareth said, "No, Roach. He ran because he saw what you did and knew who you were. He knew you would accuse him to save yourself. He bought himself a few more years."

Xin Ban hugged him again. "That means he was innocent all the time. Your father was a good man. Not a killer, a good man."

Gareth nodded, wiped away tears. "I wish it were true, Xin Ban. He was still not a good man, though. He kept this secret. Ran away to save himself. Left this murderer here to gain power. He was a coward."

Chess put an arm around him. "We all have moments of cowardice and times when we are brave. He did one bad thing and spent his life trying to atone for it. In the end, he gave up his life to save someone else."

"Vault. We still have to find him."

The group walked away, leaving Roach sobbing in the street behind them.

Campfires

Korina stretched out with a wagon wheel at her back and a fire to her front. Her belly was full and if the night was edging into cold, she had her canvas and a wool blanket and good company. The men sat across the fire from her, keeping their own counsels, pretending not to listen to the women.

Numina tossed the last of her ale into the fire then wiped out her horn with a rag. "Sun flees the sky. Enter the moon: a time for spirits."

Opia cackled. Korina scanned the sky for the moon but found none present. A few clouds marred the celestial perfection and stars bore down between them. "The moon does not rise only at night," she said. "Only in children's stories."

"Just so," said Opia. "Just so. But you have heard none of our stories, have you?"

"Perhaps," Korina said. "Some of my neighbors are Northerners. Sorub, they say."

"Far," Numina offered. "Far north, where the days and nights lengthen and the gods battle in the night sky."

Korina said, "And where bears are gods that love mortal people, where sea creatures offer up their teeth as swords to heroes."

Opia said, "We will go not so far north as Sorub. That place is haunted, yes. Fewer night-dwellers around Deyklaveyn."

"Kilrovexen," Numina said in feigned fear.

Korina glanced at her, stretched. "A story to frighten children?"

Opia cackled again. "He climbs over the walls by night. The town's guards, they all know him now, and he always goes out, never in. They let him pass. They cry, "Vex, Vex! Vex, Vex!" at his passing. Kilrovexen, full of vexation."

Korina did not understand some of those words but got the general impression. "A spirit who always leaves and never returns? It is said the dead can only replay events from their lives and never meet the living." She thought of skeletons garbed in ancient bronze armor, of weeks spent repairing their greaves and breasts.

Opia went on, "Always by night, out over the wall. Into the bogs. Some towns have moats and some have cliffs but this one has bogs to trap the unwary, to snare the innocent."

"Innocent?" Korina repeated, wondering at the meaning.

Opia did not stop to explain. "Kilrovexen, he goes out at night, every night. Sometimes he takes a shovel or a spade or a trowel. Sometimes he goes out empty of hand. He listens, ear to the wet ground. He wanders. Weeps and calls out. And always he digs, digs. Tears into the bog, futile holes that collapse as fast as he can dig them. They say the bog is sustained by his weeping. That his tears freshen the marsh that defends Deyklaveyn."

"What does he say?" Korina wondered. "When he cries out, what does he say?"

Opia cupped her hands around her mouth and shouted into the night: "Helnedrexenon!"

"I do not know this word," Korina said.

Numina said, "His daughter. Lost in the bog. Two daughters lost but he hunts only the one. The other, she went beyond his reach."

Korina thought to ask about the name of the second daughter but let it go. There was no knowledge in such a thing, just another strange word absent of meaning. "Thank you for the tale. The company, the... fellowship." She said that last in the more familiar Hitaian, hoping they would understand: their association meant more than her limited language could express. "Tomorrow night I might tell you one of our own stories. About the Blind Master. For now, I am tired."

"We all are," Numina said, "though Opia will never admit to it – or those grinning boys. Rest well, all. More days of travel await us, and more and more."

***

"She will be angry," Chara said.

"Perhaps," Erlo replied. He bent to open the slot in the forge wall. Foggy soot wafted from the oven chamber. Greasy, dark. He thought briefly of sex, put that out of his mind. "She ought to have said she was going, and whether to expect her back. We will keep this place for her and hope. Clean it. Love it."

"I do not love it," Chara said. She was on her hands and knees. A brush made of wood and boar bristles ground water into the floor stones. She was not heavy enough to do much more than push it around.

"You are loving it," said Erlo. "Look how you labor. Your knees are dirty, and your dress. There is soot on your face. Scabs on your palms."

She looked at herself, at her knees and hands. "I am not dirty because I love this place. I am dirty because I love you. You said to come and help and I said yes. Mother says we love our elders through obedience."

Erlo rubbed his temples; now both he and the child had sooty faces. "What do you think love is, Chara?"

She thought. After a moment, she returned to scrubbing the floor. Then she said, "The way I feel for Mother and Father. The way I cried when Tabby was born. The way I cried when Mang's boat caught fire and started to sink."

Erlo took down Korina's broom from the wall and peered into the oven, wondering how she ever meant to get the clinkers out. "One way to see it, sure. One way. What if Tabby were hungry, and that made you feel badly but you did nothing to help her?"

"If she is hungry, Mother feeds her."

"Fine, then. What if Mother did not feed her?"

"She must hate her."

Erlo poked the broom-handle into the oven and tried to use the end to scrape out some coals. They fell to pieces, crumbled, rolled away. "Now we are getting somewhere."

"Where?" She looked around.

"Love and hate are things we do, girl. Maybe things we feel, too, but if you only feel love and do not do it, what good was it?"

"I could not say." She lowered her head again to scrub at the stones. The brush kicked up a brown froth.

"You feel no love for this place but you yet love it. You love it with your brush, with the strength of your muscles."

Chara sighed. "Is this how Chess loved us?"

Erlo was struck by sudden tears. He wanted to reply but could not force words through his throat. He swallowed a few times, blinked his eyes. "Yes, child."

"I think I understand now."

"Me too," he said. He thought of Neea, alone in her own bed a few steps from his while he slept away ten years with his wife. While he drank so he could stay asleep there with her. He loved her with his heart but hated her with his actions. Cared for her so deeply her wounds shattered him, her very heroism broke him but, in the end, he did nothing to care for her in the world.

He sat down on the cold ground, knowing the stones should be warm. Hot, even. "Nothing for it, Chara. I think the only way to clean up in there is going to be to go inside."

She laughed at him. "You are too big. That door is too small for you. I shall have to go."

He laughed, too, wiping away tears one more time. "You might be right. But I shall have to try."

"Why?"

"Because I love my wife just as she loves us."

"Oh." She moved her bucket to a new spot and resumed her scrubbing.

***

Jimina pulled down another row of wall thatch and carried it the few steps to the refuse pile. Later, those dried out fronds and leaves would be a bonfire, a bright, smoky shout in the night. For now, they looked withered and sad.

"Why do we have to pull it down?" Neea said, pulling on Jimina's skirts.

"A family might live here one day," she said. "But it will need new walls, a new roof. The floor must be cleaned, the posts washed. New bedding. This cot... we should burn it, too."

"He died," Neea said.

"Yes."

"Is it catching? Like the Cough?"

Jimina thought of the other village, the poor sick ones around the lake from here. *Starfallers too, just like us.* "He was sick a long time, sweet child. A long time. He pretended to be well. Always kind when he could be. But if he was catching, then we would all be sick by now."

"Oh."

They went back together and worked loose another line of thatch. Then another and another. Mang's hut slowly dissolved into just a pile of loose vegetation.

Like his body.

Fire had taken much of the corpse, the lake the rest. Her son would have said they were the same thing, fire and water – both aspects of chaos. And that fit. The body was born orderly: eyes here, lips there, legs and feet and toes, arms and hands and fingers. Now, everything was mixed up, scattered into the air, under the water. Taken off by birds and fish, worms, plants. Breathed up in the air.

Chaos.

The walls were gone now. Warm air crept through the remains of Mang's home and took away dust, stray hairs. The last worldly remains of her friend. His cot looked squalid. Too low, too rough for him. A threadbare blanket, some musty old straw.

"Neea, help me drag this to the pile. Neea?"

Jimina turned to look and found her standing by one post, her face in her hands.

"Oh, baby. I did not realize you were so sad."

"I wasn't, Mother-friend. I wasn't that sad." She sobbed, sniffed, kept her face covered. "Then I saw the trees through his walls. He couldn't see another house from here. In the middle of the village he built and he was so lonely."

Jimina's own grief washed up, too. Once, after Flax was gone, she had come here. Lonely, sad, wishing she could come back to life in this place that war had seemed to knock into fretful sleep. Mang was a good man. Strong. Not too big, not a heroic figure like Moburu but a good smile. Always patient. And she was so sad after Poli died, buried under her griefs.

But Mang had just smiled and turned her away. Politely, patiently, resolutely.

"You are lonely too, I know it. I have had my love. Flax was my life. My children... But we could keep each other warm."

"I wish I could say yes. I have known no love in so long I have almost forgotten when. But I made a promise. An age ago. A good promise. It has kept everyone safe and well."

That was that. They had never spoken of it again. Jimina blushed to think of it now, to think of him saying no, of her taking the risk. But the girl was right. Mang was lonely. Surrounded by people. Friends, would-be lovers, children. Work. And utterly lonely.

"You are a good girl to notice," Jimina said, and swept the child into a soft embrace. A soft body was one of the prizes won through aging and she shared it with the little girl.

"We should find all the lonely ones and hug them."

"Yes." Jimina let Neea go. "We should. For now, can you help me finish with this place? We need to drag out the bedding. Then we are almost done."

Neea came forward and took one corner. It came away easily. She dragged it to the pile, wiped her hands on her skirt. "He died here," she repeated.

"Yes."

"And it isn't catching. Death."

"Oh, sweet one. We all die. But his sickness, no."

"Will he haunt us?" Neea said then. She took up a broom to sweep the floor clear.

"No point in sweeping. With the wind, and no walls..."

"I want to," Neea said.

"I do not think he will. Haunt us." Jimina wiped her hands, rubbed them together. "Who can say about such things? Ghosts and spirits. If you want to know what I think..."

"Yes?"

"I think his death is the end of his haunting, not the beginning. He's been hardly more than a spirit these past years. All of us have. Some have awakened back into life. Chess. Erlo. And some have slipped off into deeper slumbers."

Neea started to cry again, and kept sweeping the floor.

***

The interior was as dark as the night sky. Darker. Fum listened to his own footfalls. He thought he sounded frightened. His breath came in mouse-wisps and his steps like a timid deer before the wolf. Hands outreached to either side, feeling for walls that were not there, he paced slowly into the middle of the temple.

The Emperor awaited him somewhere ahead.

Fum tripped over nothing. The floor was impeccably hard, smooth, solid, but one of his bare feet hung up on it nonetheless. His sandals, ruins of leather held together mostly by road grime, had been abandoned outside lest he profane this place.

He caught himself. Correcting his posture, he tried to walk with more confidence. What was an emperor, after all, but a kind of king? His father had been a king. No, a King, a God. Fum himself might have been one but for his disinclination to murder his siblings. He could handle this person.

A light ahead. Warm, yellow, and faint, it outlined a door. A few more steps brought him to it. As he felt for a handle, the door swung inwards and he saw that it was a single piece of quartz crystal as huge, smooth and perfect as the floor. Then, inside, the light illuminated a single chair as grand as Ynn's golden throne atop a carpet of woven rushes. Green walls glistened in flickering candlelight. And a person stirred in the seat, lost in its shadows, hidden in its immensity.

"Your soldiers said you wished an audience," Fum said. "I usually try not to see people with so little forewarning but in your case..."

"A coward," said the person. A female voice, low and enticing despite the opening insult. She stood and came out of the shadows and she was perfect. Like the woven rushes, the door, the floor, like the walls made of emeralds, she was perfect. She had dark brown skin and black, kinky hair, brown eyes with bright orange highlights. Her lips framed her words like they were made to say them.

Fum felt himself growing aroused and clamped down on that feeling. His heart hammered all the harder.

Nowhere to run.

She continued. "Yes, a rabbit. A toothy rabbit at times, yes, but a rabbit. You survive, yes? Fum? You survive and damn the costs."

"Yes," he said around a tongue gone dry. His upper lip sweated and he noticed how hot he felt. "I do. I survive."

"But there is a brave man in there somewhere. A convicted man. Mm."

The woman stepped closer. Into his body space. She was small, almost tiny. Robes concealed most of her body, golden and silver robes embroidered with flowers. Her hands looked strong and her neck was corded with sinew. She looked up into his face.

"Are you the Emperor's consort? Truth-speaker?"

She frowned up at him then and took one step back.

Fum looked around the room again and saw nobody else. "You are the Emperor?"

"Am I not mighty enough for you?" she said. A hint of humor flickered around the outside corners of her eyes. "Your father used you badly, Fum. And your brother, too. Taught you nothing of real leadership. Of power. It's in more than your fists."

Fum was about to fall into her eyes and drown, to be swept along by her sweet voice. Death was at the end of that stream. He knew it and wanted it, wanted an end to it.

But his son...

Fum summoned up all the hauteur he could manage, all the careful disdain Dllyx had shown him. He directed his eyes to this Emperor's crotch and said, "Where is your power, then?"

Her eyes went wide and then narrowed. "I underestimated you. Good. The brave man might be worth saving after all."

"Saving?"

"I want to make you perfect."

"Me?"

"You, me, the rocks and trees and clouds, humanity, everything."

"Humanity?" It was a word Fum did not know, could only guess at. And it occurred to him he spoke Hitaian to this woman but could not identify the language she spoke back despite understanding most of her meanings.

"You are many things, Fum. Too many. They conflict. The brave man fights the coward within you. You do not know what to do. So you run and fight at the same time. Ah, I see, I see so many of you – a lover, an adventurer, a trickster – that too! – a rider, a murderer.

"But I only want one of you: the brave one, the fighter."

Fum looked around, made a pantomime of it. Doing so, he took one step backwards towards that quartz door.

"Have no worry, brave Fum," she said. "This does not hurt. Not for long."

She did not seem to do anything, only stood facing him across the rug. Fum, though, saw her split into two. No, he saw her briefly, for a fraction of time, from two places at once. And he had a choice ever so briefly of which self to be: to continue as he was or be new, to go left or right, to fear or struggle no more.

My son. I have to return to my son.

Then his vision settled down and he was one man standing in a room before one woman in the light of a candle, far from home and full of pain from the road but standing.

Then his own voice sounded from a pace to the right of him. "This must be how Moburu feels all the time," he said.

Fum turned to face himself. There he was, tall and magnificent, sculpted like Moburu but with his own long face and long nose. One hand made a fist and both Fums stared at it. His twin looked up at him and sneered.

"Time to run, Rabbit."

This new man's voice seemed to echo the voice in his own, the same words with different inflections. And there was no conflict. None at all. He turned, dashed through the door, fled through the darkness of the temple and into the darkness of the night. He did not stop for his shoes but only kept on running. Behind him, dogging his steps, was the sound of his own laughter.

The new him sounded just like his brother.

The Name

"Old Milla One-Tooth." Gareth said it into her face, close, soft.

"Jarl sent you then," the woman said. "None else call me that."

Gareth glanced back at his friends, waiting around the doorway. The drinking house smelled of sick and rancid spirits. Fried food, sweat. Inside was hot and close, no real relief from the cool, gray day outside. "Jarl, Hobe too. I took it for your name."

"No matter," she said. "Call me what you like, only lay a coin on my plank."

He fished out a bit of silver. The Starfallers did not have many coins between them but they would be off soon, into places where money did not buy food. It made a hard noise on the bit of wood between them. "Both men said you knew everything."

She laughed, a nice sound. Pretty. "Know enough, sure."

"Our friend. Came through a long time ago. Ten years. Had a sister, smaller. A mother. She was running. Would have gone straight to the magister. Slaver-dark. A hard woman."

"I remember, yes. Had a name. Jack, they called her."

"Jac, yes," Gareth said, softening the end sound a little, making it cough in the Hitaian way. "Did they stay here?"

"Memory has a way of going fuzzy," she said, pushing back from the board. "Strangers with arms full of weapons, not interested in my fare."

"Give her another coin," Xin Ban said. "Give her all the coins. "Tonight we can eat what we catch with our own hands over a fire we make ourselves."

Gareth set a little cloth purse on the counter. It was unimpressive.

"Clinks," Milla said. "I'd bite one, but I've only the one tooth, you see."

"Vault. Jac."

"They came. Did their business with the Magister. Took a house in town for a season and then two men, slavers, came looking for her. They all left together. Out for the plantations. South-east. They'll stand out."

"Thanks to you," Gareth said.

"Thanks and clinks, if you please," Milla said, and scooped up the little purse. "Now take those weapons away from here. They make me nervous. Stink of age and blood, all of them."

"As you like," Gareth said. He and his friends slipped out the door.

Guarl said, "A direction. Out of town, south and east."

Whilla pointed a different way. "Zhang would have gone south and west. Looking for a ship. We might still catch her."

"And then what?" Xin Ban said, her voice tight. "Kill her? She's no tavern brawler. She's a killer. A real killer. A soldier, an honor-fighter. Are you Chess to break her sword? Will you magic her away with blue glow?"

Gareth stilled her with a hand on her shoulder. "You're right. We've become too casual about violence. Zhang drags death along her path. Let's go towards life. Our friend."

Whilla shrugged. "Fine. Sure." She breathed for a minute while they walked. Then: "You know, I am almost as afraid to see him as to fight with Zhang."

"Yeah," Guarl said. "After so much time, what will we say? How will we be?"

"No time," Xin Ban said. "He never was away from us. And there is plenty of time to think about it. We still have to find him. It isn't certain we can."

Gareth nodded, leading the pack. *More certain with each stride.*

***

The two women had their arms around one another's shoulders as though they were both drunk. Chess, the taller of them, felt strong and lively. Jeen leaned on her and breathed heavily, one hand on her chest.

"Is this what it felt like after the lake spirit left you? After the war?"

Chess smiled and did not know why. "I do not know how you feel, dear one. Thus I could not really say. I only wanted to sleep, to weep, and sometimes I wanted to die so that the pain would end."

"I am only tired," Jeen said. "And also strangely not."

"I think healing from so grievous a wound takes much energy."

The lane rolled past a big building that smelled like meat. Beyond that, fields planted with saplings. One of those stood out, a tree big enough for some ten years of age, bigger than most of the trees around it. A red line grew in the soil around it and the tree itself was an unusual mottled yellow and black, waving in the wind in a way the surrounding foliage did not.

"Too tired to look at a wonder?" Chess said, and pointed at the tree.

Jeen lifted her head. ""Now there's a thing. Does the Starfall stretch this far?"

"You're proof of that. I am, too."

"Let's go closer."

They did, picking their way across soft earth. The overcast sky wept on them as they went, plopping, fat raindrops as cold as fear.

"Mushrooms," Chess said as they closed. Red-and-white mushroom tops formed the ring around the tree, glistening in the new rain.

"And butterflies," Jeen said.

"How many?"

"More than I have words for in Hitaian."

They preened, slowly opening and closing their wings. Yellow with black spots, wings just an inch or so across, blanketing the tree like its own leaves. They were not disturbed by the early autumn rain.

"Why do they not fly off as we come closer?" Jeen said.

Chess touched on with her finger, tried to get it to come away on her hand. Then she pinched the wings together and tried to lift it away. The wings came off the body and then she saw that the insects had not landed on the tree at all: they were a part of it, bodies formed of the bark, legs either missing or deep in the wood. She gasped and backed away a step, dropping the wings she had pulled off, rubbing her hands on her clothing.

Jeen realized, too, what had happened. They both crushed some of the mushrooms in their haste to back away. "I thought it was beautiful but it is disgusting," Jeen said, one hand over her mouth.

"Shocking," Chess agreed. "And after the shock, there may still be beauty here. Let's not mar it any more by being so close to it."

Jeen shuddered. "Could be it will be beautiful again from a distance. Let us find out."

The lane came to an end at a wall of forest. Chess turned to look back at the tree from there, a few hundred steps away. Sun pierced through the clouds above, through the rain, and a rainbow seemed to hover over the strange glade. "Beautiful, and unexpected."

Jeen did not look back but waited for Chess to be ready. "Did we get what we came for?"

"No. I had no chance to talk with him, to see if he had any humanity left. That is why I came. The lake spirit, it uses us and tosses us aside with no care for our desires, our aims. But he is gone now, properly gone. Not just a rumored death, not a tortured life confined to abstraction, but really gone. Beyond suffering. Is that good?"

"Maybe good enough," Jeen said. Now she did turn, leaning again on her friend.

The tree fluttered on and from here the mushroom ring seemed unbroken. After another minute of silent reflection, the two moved off into the woods, towards home.

***

The forest closed in around them. Dark came with it. Sun dappled fallen leaves and black soil highlighted tiny saplings sprouting into shade from their giant parents. Within an hour of walking past the outermost building of Hong – a warehouse for grains – only the leafy lane before them gave any sign humans had ever been in this place. The city was lost in the trees behind them. Sight, sound, smell, everything.

Gareth kept his bow strung and ready in one hand. His other weapons hung from his belt. The sword had an improvised sheath, the blanket now sewn to retain its shape. The spear had a bit of twine reinforced with thread, one loop over the haft and one around the belt.

Xin Ban had made a sling and collected stones as they went. Whilla and Guarl both had new bows, rewards from Gareth's first duel.

"I miss my mother," Whilla said.

"Too many goodbyes," Guarl said. "Once at the Starfall. Once at Hong. And again when their adventure was over."

Xin Ban sighed. "I miss my family, too. The village."

"We are together," Gareth said. The words sounded sweet but tasted bitter. He had a thought that he would not let coalesce into words and it poisoned the comfort of togetherness.

To the right, birds burst out of a bush, fat ones whose wing-beats drove noise through their throats.

Gareth snapped off an arrow. Whilla and Guarl brought up their bows but the birds were gone by the time they had arrows loaded. Xin Ban dropped a pebble into her sling then took it out again, shaking her head.

"Have to make some birding arrows," Gareth said. He stomped off through the underbrush to retrieve his spent shaft. It was stuck in the bole of a maple, a tall and majestic tree unlike the split-trunked dwarf trees of the desert around home. Hanging from the arrow, impaled, was one of the fat birds. It dripped blood into the leaf litter, a bright color among the muted oranges and yellows in the woody dark.

"Good shot," Guarl said. "You found dinner."

"Let's make a fire and eat it," Gareth said. "I don't have the heart to walk much more today and the night comes suddenly out here."

"I can make the fire," Whilla said.

"And I can set snares," Xin Ban offered. "Maybe we'll get some breakfast, too."

The two boys dressed the bird. Feathers pointed the direction of the wind, flowing away from their forming camp in a steady stream. Soon the bird crackled over an open flame, skin crisping, fat dripping into the fire. The four ate quietly.

Gareth looked around at each. Whilla licked her fingers after each bite. She was uneasy. Her thoughts tended to her mother, to the long walk Chess would have to make back across the dangerous preserves. He could hear the thoughts in his head like they were his own. Xin Ban's conscience gnawed at her. She worried about confronting Zhang, that a peaceful resolution might mean trouble later, that thought mingled with worry over the man they had stabbed together in the preserves. Guarl chewed a bone, trying to get the last greasy goodness out of it. And he was afraid. He tried to look calm and confident, but he was afraid. Vault had been lost a long time. What if they were wrong about him? What sort of man was he becoming?

Gareth carefully kept his own counsel. He ate slowly. The bird had been as big as his two fists but that was still not much meat among four growing people. Xin Ban tossed the remains of her meal in the fire and he could tell she was still hungry. The fatty meat churned up acid in her stomach. He handed her the remains of his portion without comment. She raised her eyebrows, checking he was sure, and he nodded, and that was that.

When Gareth set up a log from which to keep first watch, nobody objected. They all lay down around the embers, bodies touching in one way or another, and quickly slept.

I have to leave them.

It was a loving thought. The closer they became, the more they knew what was inside of him as he knew their thoughts and feelings. He would spare them the shame, the pain of his moral wound.

What Zhang did...

Xin Ban moaned in her sleep as he remembered. She rolled over, nearing wakefulness. In the woods some creature called out.

Ships at anchor. Rocking, rocking, swaying. I've never seen a ship with my own eyes. What a thing to see. Cats on the rooves of Hitaian hovels, watching us pass.

Xin Ban settled down again. Whilla moved closer to her. Guarl snored, a heavy sound for a quite spare young man.

Gareth knew. He knew he must leave his friends. They would suffer for him. They would do it willingly, as willingly as he had suffered for the chance to save Neea, and that was why he had to leave. He loved them. While he watched, though, he kept those thoughts low in his mind, buried under a stream of recollections. Good times, pleasant feelings to help his friends rest.

Underground

Jul stared down at the Master, rage on his face. "She died?"

The Master looked away. "Yes, My Prince. Tragic accident. Fell down a flight of stairs. Hit her head. We buried her where she lay."

"Accident." He looked down the steps at the man with the little lash in his hands. Jul straightened his kilt, looked up one step to where his uncle sat on the throne, back down at the Master. "I think I had best come and see for myself. And find out who is responsible. My mother promised her she would be safe out there and I mean to make my mother a liar."

"Indeed, My Prince," said the Master. "I shall ride ahead and announce you."

"Not necessary," the young Prince told him, walking down the steps and past him. "Follow me." He expected Ergol to follow or at least to call out some objection but Ergol just let him go. He went down to the trophy room where Xenia had been moping since her Queen had been interred.

There she was, sitting next to that smelly stuffed cheetah. Dreaming, no doubt, of the glory days. Well, those days were over.

"Jul," she said, standing. "My Prince. How may I serve?"

She did not look like she wanted to serve. She looked like she wanted to leave. "Get together a brace of guards. Pikes and shields. Chariots. Treason in the Tomblands. We ride."

"As you say, My Prince. No treason may withstand the future King of Hitai." She made to hurry out, ducking under the elephant's tusks.

"Return here when all is ready."

"Yes, My Prince."

The Master stared at the giant red elephant, nose wrinkled. Other monsters rested on their pedestals all around. The stink overpowered even the smell of flint from the messenger from the Tomblands.

"They all stink," Jul said. "Do the dead in the monuments smell so bad?"

"I rarely go so close to them, My Prince. But mostly they smell of salt and spices and flint. Dried out. These, though. They are grand trophies."

"Tell me your name, man."

"Ramble, My King."

Jul paced from one monster to another. "Glory days," he said. "This armor. Moburu took it from some hapless soldier he found in the marshes. Look at this, now. A salamander stretched over a lion's form. A giant spider. Trophies from a dead time."

"Yes, My Prince."

"You are a liar, Ramble. A bad liar. They sent you here to die."

"Please, My Prince, do not say such things. I am your truthful servant."

Jul turned around to face him, looking up into a face curiously absent any fear. "I shall have a trophy of my own. The taxidermist has had little work from the palace since Moburu was exiled. We have grown too civilized for hunting. But I will give them a skin, yes."

"I can show you her body," Ramble said.

He should have wrung his hands, or looked away, or sweated. This place was hot enough for sweating twenty hours of the day. Jul found himself hating him. "Your skin, some other Master's skin, what do I care? Only someone will have to pay for the loss of my servant. My Gravetender. I was looking forward to killing her inch by inch. What would her hands be like? Like a jackal's hands?"

"My Prince? Her hands seemed ordinary enough. She is dead in an old tomb, under the sand. We will go there. You will see."

Jul felt uneasy. He glanced at Ramble's hands. One held the little lash of his office, the other was empty. He wore the crossed leather straps of a Master, the leather kilt of a low-ranking servant. No belt, no weapons. His hands were flabby, his shoulders rounded with fat rather than muscle. Still, Jul thought it might have been a mistake to bring him here alone.

"Wait outside," Jul said, snapping the words off.

"As you like, My Prince." Ramble turned to go.

Damn. I want to get him out of my sight, but I cannot let him get a message ahead of us.

Xenia saved him. Efficient, competent despite having been raised above her station. "We will be ready to leave in a few moments, My Prince. Shall we climb to the front yard?"

"Yes," he said. "And take this man in hand. He is not to speak to anyone but palace guards at any time. And he must be ten feet from my person."

Xenia had weapons: two bronze swords, a dagger, a dirk in her boot. She had boiled leather armor and a bronze kilt. Boots rather than sandals. The pudgy slave wrangler at last realized his position as she poked him with one finger, pressing him ahead of the young prince, up the stairs towards the yard. Jul could not see his face but his posture had improved. No longer haughty but hunched and fearful.

This should be fun.

***

Wyrrn never thought to see the city of Hitai again and yet here she was. On the outskirts, to be sure, but in the city. From here the temple of prostitutes was just a vague bump on the horizon. The Gravetender slowed his pace beside her. He had the appearance of a middle-aged man approaching his wizening, but was a demon for walking.

All around, people hawked wares from wooden stalls. A few guards held their spears vertically and stood as straight as their weapons. They looked at the thronging crowds with narrowed eyes from pockets of space.

Tense.

History told her peace in the city was always fragile. A careful balance, the old invaders barely tolerated, revolution or the attempt never more than a spark away from wildfire.

She was grateful when the market bazaar was behind them. "Did you notice..." But the Gravetender was not listening.

"Here's the place," he said.

"This house? With the curtains drawn?" The place looked old. Clay walls had chipped and cracked, revealing some of the rotted wood skeleton underneath. Formerly bright paint on the outside had faded until the design was beyond recognition. But the doorframe was splashed with paint the color of blood. A red 'X'. "Who lived here?"

"A man they called Grandfather. He was scarcely so old as everyone thought, and many men live to be grandfathers. But it was a joke."

Wyrrn tried the door. It was shut up tight. She felt around with her hands, found nails holding the door in the frame. "Not going in this way."

"The Gravetenders are all architects. If one understands how things are made, well, it is simple enough to unmake them." He put a hand against the wood. Moved it, shifted, slid. Then he pushed hard. The frame came away from the wall around it and the whole construction dropped noisily to the floor inside the house.

Wyrrn heard the sounds of scampering feet inside, some wild things that had found solace in the shade. "You first."

The Gravetender laughed. "Just rats. Hiding from the cats. This city is full of those." He went in, slowed as the shade covered him. "Over here."

Wyrrn's eyes adjusted slowly to the dark. The curtains moved in a breeze, shifting broken glass in the window frames. Good glass was costly. This place was not the hovel it appeared to be. The floor was made of good planks, fit tightly and smoothed. They were covered in rat droppings and dust and dirt, splashes of old blood. A pair of arrows stood out from the far wall, clay cracked all around.

The Gravetender lifted a trap in the floor. "The lock is broken but the cellar will still do its job."

"What job is that?"

"To keep us hidden. They stopped patrolling this place years ago. Old and useless. Nobody would plot from a place known for its plotters."

"What are we plotting?" Wyrrn said. "You said we would get away from the desert and get to the work. I thought the work was building tombs."

"Oh, it is," he said. "Most surely, building tombs is the work. These people, these self-styled Kings of Hitai... In their quest to be Gods, they have come between us and the work. It has been a long, long time since a Gravetender has been murdered."

"Dllyx never believed your claims of political neutrality."

"They were true."

"They were?" Wyrrn followed him down the creaky steps into true darkness. "You stood aside?"

"We did. When Dllyx had me murdered, however, she broke an old compact. The machine will be built. It will roll over mortal people, even over the Gravetenders. We no longer stand aside."

"This place seems somewhat aside. Under the ground, in the dark. Much like the tombs we just left, as it happens. Can you make light or are you limited to knocking down walls?"

He chuckled in the dark. "Anyone may make fire if they have sparks and fuel." He fumbled around for a minute. Then sparks lit the room in brief flashes before taking on a wick.

"Candles."

"Indeed."

The cellar looked better than the space upstairs. It clearly had been raided but the walls were undamaged, the floors clear of debris. The Gravetender led her around plain, unfurnished rooms. They smelled clean and held cool against the day upstairs.

"So," Wyrrn said. "What do we do now, architect? Build some grand scheme?"

"Oh, the scheme is in motion, has been for a generation. We await a few bits of material for the next stage of construction."

"Sounds dull."

"I have to educate you. That will pass the time. The last King declared you a Gravetender and we might as well make an architect of you."

"Wonderful," Wyrrn said. "Well, so long as I'm going from teacher to student and I must endure your mystifications down here in this grave, do you have a name I can call you? 'Gravetender' is so unwieldy."

"Most of us forget our names. I never had the chance to have one. Call me what you will."

"Oh, I can think of some things to make you regret that invitation."

He laughed again and the sound warmed the cool space.

***

Slaves hauled away sand in buckets.

A small girl carried a wooden bucket into the hole. It was deep now, twenty feet, with some of the stone steps growing visible. She joined other children down there in scraping sand into the containers.

Jul watched from a makeshift shade. Silk hung from banners, keeping off the worst of the sun. Xenia stood beside him, a ring of guards around the shade. High-ranking Masters waved him with palm fronds. The one calling herself the Great Overseer held one of the fronds. Jul stilled a smile at the hard set of her face. She must feel awful: the most powerful person in her universe suddenly reduced to fanning a Prince.

Of course, she should feel great honor at such a thing. But Jul had found they rarely did.

The girl came back with her bucket half-full. She was followed by several other children, with buckets progressively emptier.

"Must be ready to open," Jul said. "Just another thing to do."

"Name it," Doggra said, but her tone did not match her invitation.

"Sweep the steps free of dust. I will mount clean stairs. Sand in my sandals might make me moody, and moody Princes act rashly."

"I will have it done," she said.

"See to it yourself. I trust no others." She stalked off. Now Jul did smile. "You there. With the short lash. Pick up her fan."

"Yes, My Prince."

Doggra came back a little later. "The way is clear, My Prince."

"Lead on, Captain," he told Xenia.

She rattled her swords in their scabbards and headed across the short span of sand towards the buried tomb. "Get those slaves out of the way," she said.

Masters herded kneeling children back with their lashes. Jul scowled at them. The children belonged to him; it was his right to hurt them.

Inside the tomb, sand spilled across the floor like seed scattered for hens. He remembered feeding hens at the palace. He had been much younger, five years old, and his mother had held his hand. The hens smelled of their own feces.

The memory-smell clashed with the thick odor of sand in the present. Flint and something else, metallic, harsh. Down here, the spicy smell of corruption was long gone. He slipped a little in the sand and thought of having the Grand Overseer beaten. But he had told them not to unseal the door without him, and he had not said to sweep the floor, only the stairs.

"A ruler must be fair," he muttered, remembering something Ergol had said.

"A ruler does as he wishes," Xenia said softly. "A King is a God. Fair is as he says it is, My Prince."

He nodded, taking a long look at her in the shadows. Taller than him by a foot or so with long, lean limbs. Well-scarred. Deep claw-marks had been graven on her forearms. He would need a queen one day. Perhaps soon, to secure his lineage. If he married before Ergol it would help his case.

She was low-born but, as she said, a King could do as he pleased.

The coffins in front of him had been disturbed. One was little more than dust and scraps. The other had been dumped out. One of the sides hung loose and, even from here, he could see that it was empty.

"Where is she?" he said, not raising his voice.

The Great Overseer came in behind him. She glanced around the place, her breathing growing fast and light. "This is the right place," she said. "I know it." She looked behind the plinth. Around the walls as though she might be found in one of the old, faded murals. "She was here!"

Jul crossed his arms. He had expected betrayal. "Bring me Ramble."

Noise from the stairs indicated people rushing to obey. In a moment, the haughty man stepped into the shade, eyes wide. "My Prince?"

"I am missing a Gravetender," Jul said. "I had plans for her. Seems I have to promote someone."

"Promote, My Prince? Not this one. Such a station is too high for one such as me. Let me serve humbly."

"Well spoken," Jul said. "This Great Overseer. Who declared that one would replace Lud?"

She turned from her frantic examination of the walls. "The Gravetender herself."

"And you enjoy rising in rank, yes?"

"All people serve as best they can," she said. "I climbed high on great ability."

"If you like," Jul said. "Serve me as my Gravetender, then."

Her face sagged, surprise in her eyes. A slow grin twitched the corners of her mouth. "As My Prince declares."

"This one can take Lud's position. Ramble, oversee my Tomblands. I want all the old tombs torn down. No sense anyone else becoming lost out here. Rip them down and bury them. Use all the slaves, not only the breakers."

"Yes, My Prince."

"What shall I build for My Prince?" Doggra said. "How will I build it with all the slaves set to breaking?"

"Nothing," Jul said. "My plan for my Gravetender was to torture her to death. As you have robbed me of her and accepted her position, you will have to do. Xenia, bring her."

He turned and climbed the stairs. Behind him, Doggra gasped. She struggled, a scuffle with Xenia told in scraping noises, and then started to scream. At the top of the stairs, he picked out one of the children – a boy of four or five years. It was hard to tell among the poor. He tapped a guard on the shoulder. "Man, bring me that boy. Put him in the shed with the jackals behind the palace."

Smiling, he mounted his chariot and waited for his people to form up.

***

Ergol walked up the stairs again, feeling exposed. He was alone and this time his identity was known. The Chans disguise was done with. Behind him was a whole city of people who could see a Prince of the Blood, a Regent of Hitai, climbing the stairs into the Temple of Caiph. The Temple of Whores.

Myrsa herself greeted him at the top. She offered him a seat next to her on the padded couch. A silver platter held bites of melon and berries and a ewer dripped dew onto the table. "Wine?"

"Water," he said. "I am a fat old man and there are many stairs to climb."

"Of course," she said.

There was silence between them. Ergol ate some of the melon. It was sweet and cool but no balm for the quiet. Myrsa just looked at him, no expression on her face. Ergol felt a flush working up from his chest to his neck.

"Well?" he said. "What do you want me to say?" He kept from shouting by an act of will.

"There is nothing to say. Just rise when you are ready. A boy will show you down to your duty."

He wanted to stand up right then but his legs were still a bit wobbly from the climb. And a certain performance was required of him. His stomach clenched. The idea of what she wanted was not pleasant, not at all pleasant.

Myrsa smiled. "You sold them as slaves. Captured innocents and took coin for them. Not all of them ended up working stones for tombs and not all of them ended up in nice houses with little old women. In a way, you make much of this possible."

"You are not helping."

"That feeling in your loins now. You want what we offer. Is it such a difficult duty? You will do much worse than this as Regent, you know."

"I know," he said. He picked up another bite of melon then set it back down. "Ynn tried to tell me."

"Yes?"

"How much he hated this particular duty. I was a child then, and a spoiled one despite it all. Too young to listen." He stood up. "I grow no younger and no more enthralled with this idea. May the gods find mercy on me. I should turn and go but we made a deal."

Myrsa took a small chime from under her seat and rang it. "Gods there are," she said. "And we serve more than the gods. We serve your people. We serve The Blood."

"How?"

Myrsa only smiled again. "The boy is here to take you downstairs."

"Why come up all those cursed stairs only to climb down again? Why not make a door..." His words dried up as the boy came through the opening to the stairs down.

He was around twelve years of age, one or two years from his first facial hair. Short and wide, he might have been a twin brother of Ynn's but for the fifty years making that impossible.

We serve The Blood", indeed. But to what ends?

Myrsa spoke again. "At the end, Ynn sent us a proxy. A guard. We tolerated this because we already had what we needed from him. Not good for a King to have such a soft heart, I think, but you are only a Regent, yes?"

"The things we do," Ergol said, and followed his brother's ghost into the dark.

***

A girl sobbed quietly in the dark.

Myrsa sat in a cool cell, deep under the temple. Down here the air never warmed and never chilled but stayed just as it was: cool, dry and perfect. A torch in the hallway barely touched the darkness in the cell. The sobbing came from two cells down.

"He has much of his brother's blood," said a voice. The cell had a chair and a bed. The chair, plain and ordinary, had only what was needed to serve its function. The bed, though, was wide, soft, and clean. And it held a treasure.

"This is known," Myrsa said. "Ynn worked it all out."

Down the hall, the sobbing quieted, ceased.

"How much did he know?"

"Too much." Myrsa could not see the figure on the bed, had never seen her. The voice was smooth and low, giving few hints or clues to the speaker's age or background. "Why work so hard to save his line when he worked so hard to spoil it?"

"The son, that incestuous monster. We had only two successes from Ynn and both were females. Good breeders yet only half the line. We need Jul to preserve The Blood."

"Yes, but you have never told me why. Why save it? What is the significance?"

"It may be you never know, girl. If you are fortunate, you will die before such knowledge is needed. If not..."

"What?"

Down the hall, the girl began to cry again.

The voice said, "Go and see to Kadarin. Their first time can be hard."

Myrsa restrained a sigh. "Yes, Mistress."

Kadarin sat on the bed with her knees drawn up close to her chest. Her face was bedecked with tears like streamers from a festival boat. Dark hair and dark eyes, black skin and golden palms all told her heritage in the light from the hallway.

"Did he hurt you?" Myrsa said, her voice solicitous.

"Not on purpose," the girl said. "I did my duty."

"Duty. Yes. Tell me what you feel like."

"Not holy. The Mistress whispered that this was a holy act but I never knew that. Only unclean. I wish I could kill him."

Myrsa let the sigh out now. She sat on the bed next to Kadarin and put an arm around her shoulders. "We all go through this."

"All?"

"Yes. Wondering if we serve our faith well or if this life is only torment to no end. Trapped between the holy and the profane. Some girls come to believe it, to have faith. Their way is easier. If only I could give you that faith. But your test has only begun."

"I did my duty," the girl said, sobbing again.

"No, child, only the start of it. In a few days we will know if the real trial is under way."

When the girl was settled, her tears dried and her body warm under silk and wool, Myrsa went back to the cell where Mistress had been. She sat in the chair and rubbed her own temples. So much doubt. She wished Mistress were there to soothe her fears as she had soothed Kadarin's, but she did not need light to know the other woman had gone.

Blur

Gareth touched Xin Ban's shoulder. She rolled away but stayed asleep, so he touched her back, her hair. "Your watch," he whispered.

"I'm awake."

But she wasn't. He held her hand until he was sure she was with him. She sat up, only a blur of shade in the last orange light of a burned-out fire.

"You're leaving," she whispered.

"I'd thought I'd kept that secret better."

"Yeah. But I can hear all the things you're thinking to not think about leaving. They're like silence. Like not talking about something. I know you. I practically am you."

"Damn," he said, and scrubbed a hand over his face. The very first tracings of beard stubble scraped under his hand. "Damn, I'm sorry."

"Should have left while I was still sleeping. I was dreaming of silence. Of a man with his lips sewn shut."

"That's why I have to go," Gareth said.

"What makes you think distance will stop us from hearing your thoughts, or you hearing ours?" She was on her feet now, dragging some light logs towards the campfire.

"We haven't heard anything from Vault. We know he's out here but haven't touched him since the lake, around the god. If I get far enough away, I can spare you my pain."

"Yeah," Xin Ban said. She blew on the embers to produce a brief flame. That caught on some dry leaves on one of the logs and soon there was a cheerful fire again.

"You aren't going to try to stop me."

"No point. I am you, remember? Besides..."

"The killing," Gareth said.

"Yeah."

"Sometimes it has to be done. That man was dying anyway. The tall man in the drinking house, he was a menace."

Xin Ban sat on Gareth's log. "It needed doing, sure. And so long as you're around, killing is always going to be what needs to be done. I love you, Gareth, and I can't stand it. I can't bear to be a killer."

Gareth pinched off tears, spoke through a tight throat. "I am afraid. Afraid you're right. It's for the best."

"No, it's not. I don't think our lives are going to have much to do with what's for the best, not for a long time. Maybe never."

"Tell Whilla... Tell Guarl..."

"I'm awake," Whilla said. "Tell me yourself."

"That I love them," Gareth said. "I'm going for love. I don't know what else to do."

"Come with us," Guarl said. "Vault is waiting. We should see him together. Maybe he knows something. We can decide then."

Whilla sat up and wiped at her face. "No. He's not coming. I see. If you get close to Vault, if you get near him and he's innocent yet, then you'll make him a killer, too. You'd spare him that guilt. And the shame. Of what she did to you."

"That's not right," Guarl said. "Any of it."

"It is," Xin Ban said.

"It's worse," Gareth said. "Worse than all of that. See, I don't just want to spare you what I've done or what Zhang did. I want to spare you what I'm going to do."

"What's that?" Whilla said.

"I'm going to catch up with her. No matter how long it takes, I'm going to find her. And I'm going to make sure she meets Moburu."

That was the end of the argument. They ate together one last time – a pair of stout rats from Xin Ban's snares. Then Gareth packed up his few possessions. When he came to the green sword, he stared at it for a few moments. "This isn't mine," he said. "Give it to him. It was always meant for his hands." He passed it to Whilla tenderly, a last act of love, and strode away the way they had come, into a forest slowly growing light as dawn crept past the horizon.

***

"In the next village."

The little brown man pointed east, bent back to his weaving.

"Always one more village," Whilla said, leaning on her spear.

"And then one more after that," Guarl said. "We must be halfway to Lurk by now."

"It's only been four days," Xin Ban said. "And the living is good. Gareth was right about birding arrows. I think I might be getting fat."

Whilla laughed at her. Xin Ban was made of gristle, long and lean and tall. "We shall have to find you a husband, then. Fatten you up for a wedding."

Xin Ban went quiet. Guarl started walking again, head down.

Did I say something wrong? Whilla wondered. Guarl's discomfort was obvious. Xin Ban's mind had gone blank. *Wait – those two? I suppose it's natural.*

"No," Xin Ban said. "Not that." She glanced at Guarl, who blushed. "I had just never considered it. Not since we left the Starfall. I never imagined we might somehow find normal lives. Weddings and houses and chasing babies don't seem a part of our future. Have you thought of it?"

"Not until now," Whilla said. "I just joked out of habit, but maybe you're right. All of that seems unlikely now."

"We have each other," Guarl said, still blushing.

Whilla knew he had a whole range of possibilities in his mind. Comfort, companionship, rutting, growing old together. She did not want to think about it. "We have each other, yes. And some of those possibilities would make us... complicated."

"Yeah," Guarl said.

Xin Ban took one of his hands and held it as they walked. Whilla could feel her affection for him, for Whilla, for Xin Ban herself. Uncomplicated, true. Whilla took his other hand, shifting the spear to her right.

Stick huts faded behind them. These lands were clear of trees. Black soil hosted rows of maize just coming into season. The fields went on for two thousand steps and then the three plunged back into woody dark, a relief from sunshine that had been growing oppressive.

They are close now.

That was a clear thought. But it was not Whilla's. She looked to Xin Ban and Guarl. Both looked a little surprised. Xin Ban looked back, shook her head sharply, once. *Not me.*

It has been lonely here. Lonelier since the dream of the lake, since learning what kind of closeness was possible. I hope to see them soon. More dreams last night, dreams of my friends. I'm afraid, afraid too much time has gone by.

"Vault?" Whilla said out loud. "Are we hearing him? We must be close now."

Guarl shouted in surprise and dodged to one side, knocking Whilla sideways and pulling in Ming down. Something loud passed through the space where he had stood. Whilla got her feet under her and brought up her spear. Xin Ban rolled onto her feet with bow in hand, searching for game.

But the thing was no bird.

A dragonfly as long as Whilla's arm came to rest on the bole of a nearby tree. Its wings caught light and threw back rainbows. The body was red and gold.

She said, "I haven't seen something like that since..."

"The Starfall," Guarl finished for her.

"Can we eat it?" Xin Ban said.

"Who knows?" Whilla said. "It might be mixed with anything. Mango fruits or venomous snakes or poison ivy. Or it might be only an earlier form. Dangerous to eat, I think."

Xin Ban lowered her bow. "It has eyes."

"All dragonflies have eyes," Guarl said. But he looked closer.

Whilla did the same, taking two steps towards the thing. "Ugh. Eyes like a person."

The insect buzzed its wings, lifted again into the air. It rose up through the trees to disappear in the branches somewhere overhead.

"What does this mean?" Whilla said.

"Same as the thoughts," Guarl said. "It means we're close."

Another mile, and the trees began to thin out in advance of another village. The boles were orderly, spaced evenly in rows. Mango, orange, pear. Xin Ban pointed out each variety as they passed.

"But what is this one?" she said, touching a tree with mossy green bark. It twisted up over her head, limbs laden with golden leaves and heavy fruits like giant, leathery eggs.

"Best to leave it alone," Whilla said. "More of the change, I think."

Bees hummed around the orchard. Some of them had wings like butterflies. From another tree, mushrooms hung in place of pears.

"I understand," Xin Ban said. "I understand what the god wants, now."

"Gareth was right," Whilla said. "Right after all. But I do not want to leave you, to go out alone. Who cares what the god wants? It never asked if it could use us."

They all three stopped. Ahead, some local people spotted them and set down the tools they had been using to excise a blighted tree from their orchard. Orderly piles of branches lay around them, children stripping the limbs.

"It knew the lake was a mistake," Guarl said. "The change came slowly there and moved out but could only reach so far. And people came for it, tried to carry it off. Turn it to their own purposes."

"We're dandelion seeds," Xin Ban said.

And I've taken root, Vault intoned in their heads.

The villagers advanced. They were a group of four, dressed in doe-skin that covered most of their bodies. Their clothing was sticky with sap, stained with plant juices. One, a smallish woman of middle years, held up one hand. "Slavers," she said.

The accent was strange, not like the Greenlander speech of Hong. Whilla had noticed each village drifting away from the speech she knew as they got farther from the city. "Not slavers. Only travelers. We're looking for a friend of ours."

"Slaver-friend-la. Works far side, by river-la. Does less damage away from fruits. You bring trade-la? News?"

Guarl said, "Last village over is ready to harvest their maize. Two villages back, the sugar cane caught a blight. They won't have much for trade this season."

"Ah," the woman said, then turned to chatter with her companions. The four drifted back to their work, axes and wedges slowly dismantling their tree.

"Keep going?" Xin Ban said.

They did.

Past the orchards, some houses were built into elm trees. At ground level, one used four trees as corner-posts, vines and boards woven around them to create walls. Higher up, planks and boards made tree-houses, ropes and ladders dangling down like air-breathing roots. Whilla gaped at these wonders as they passed under and through.

"More of Vault's power? Trees that are also houses?"

"No," said Guarl. "I'd say they were made this way. Look old. See how the moss grows on one side of this house."

"Oh."

The sound of running water grew into her senses. Once the houses were behind them, she could see a break in the trees ahead. Light glanced off a creek. Dark, earthy banks rose to either side and a few people managed nets. Hitaians.

"Vault?" Whilla cried out. That was him, it had to be: the young man of about her age, wispy hair on his upper lip, short and square body. Tight cap of curly black hair, eyes like kohl.

"Whilla?" He stood from his net, remembered it, dragged it out of the water. Something silver and lively thrashed in it on the shore. "Guarl? Xin Ban! But where is Gareth?" He spoke Hitaian. Whilla needed a moment to adjust, having used Greenlander for so long.

"He..." Whilla put her things down, swallowed acrid grief. "He said to tell you how much he loves you."

Vault sloshed through the creek and came up the bank to meet them. The other people watched, caution on their faces. "I wanted to come to you but they said it was dangerous. Too dangerous."

Guarl hugged him, punched him on the shoulder. Xin Ban grabbed him next.

"I haven't missed you," she said. "I've felt like you were always with me. It is good to be right again, though, to see you with my eyes as well as my heart."

"I know it," Vault said. "You have come at a good time and a bad one. The change centers on me. You must know it by now. It is time for me to move on from this place. The villagers, our friends, have been patient to now but the change grows more threatening."

"Good and bad," Whilla said. "No home here, but we can travel together."

"Yes," he said.

One of the women stood up from her nets, shook water from her hands. "I knew this day would come. I am glad to see these are friends and not murderers from Ynn's court. And yet my heart still fears. Vault, you have a destiny. Let us go home and speak of it."

"No need," said Whilla. "I brought it with me." She reached into the sack over her shoulder and brought out the green sword, Flax' sword taken from Hong.

Jac sighed. "My son, my son. And still we must speak of this."

"Yes, Mother," he said, and took the sword in steady hands. "But change is here for all your work to keep it away."

***

Alone.

Gareth stood on a stump and surveyed his solitude. A few apes lounged under a tree nearby, alert to his presence but not apparently disturbed by it. Their orange fur ruffled under a light breeze, accompanied by the shisshing sound of leaves rubbing together. Trees all around. No track, no sign of people.

Fungi grew in clumps. Some on the ground, rings of little white heads poking up from the leaf-litter, thumb-sized beetles trundling around as though managing a fungal farm. Some of the mushrooms grew from the boles of trees, half-circles climbing around the trunks like steps.

Dust and pollen drifted across his field of view. Sunlight cut through shadows in shafts like bits of bright metal, like the glass he had seen once in a window in Hitai.

And his mind was quiet.

The thoughts and feelings, dreams and impulses of his friends were gone.

That was a lonely relief.

Xin Ban's love/desire/contempt had been hardest of all to bear. She was a woman now, not a girl to have innocent friendships with any longer but someone with adult feelings to consider. He had his own growing feelings, too: the warmth in his groin at night when they slept close together, the way his eyes crept to his friends' hips. Whilla and Xin Ban knew he was looking, knew he knew they knew, knew he was ashamed and did not want to stop.

So much simpler, quieter, out here alone. So much better to not pollute his friends with his pain, his shame.

But that was heavy.

In the quiet, he bore it alone.

He stepped down off his stump into moist grass. Trudged through the beetles' little farms. In the hazy, dusty morning, he carried his shame west.

Zhang was out there somewhere. If there was an answer to his growing pain, she had it.

Moburu rested on Gareth's left hip. He had improved the scabbard a little each night using needles made from bones and sinew drawn from the birds and rabbits he caught. It was more sinew now than wool, looking skeletal. Moburu might have liked that but he was silent on the topic. Moburu would want revenge, too.

He passed a village, then another, making fast time the way frustrated young men can. He forgot to hunt. When a covey of plovers scattered from the undergrowth to one side, he did not think to shoot one. His mind was on time and distance. How fast would Zhang be moving? Would she be alert for pursuit? Would she still be in these lands at all after so much time?

He tripped, stumbled, sprawled in musty detritus. It was dusk now, the sparkling, lonely morning long past and hunger in his stomach. He thought he heard laughter. When he made to stand, something snugged around his ankle. He shook his leg to clear it but the ankle remained tightly held.

"Brave lad to travel alone through these woods."

Three men came out of the trees, dropping down like monkeys. In the dusk they were hardly more than shapes. One held a thin rope.

"Who are you?" Gareth said, but he knew. They spoke Hitaian, he responded automatically in the same language. "Slavers."

"Right you are, boy," one of them said. "You may be too old for the rock markets. Too old to sell north. The pleasure houses like their boys young enough to train."

"New kingdom south, Worlin," said another. "Like to make fighters of them. He has him a sword."

"Gladiators, they call them," Worlin said. "Hand over the sticker, boy, and let's discuss your future."

Gareth rolled onto his back. His heart hammered hard, blood rushing through his ears so loud he could barely hear the slavers. His palms were slick with indecision.

"Get that spear first, Orbo," Worlin said.

The third man, the one with the rope, kept it tight as he came forward. He reached for the spear to Gareth's side. It had fallen off his belt when he tumbled, lay just near his right hand. Gareth snatched it up, jabbed it at Orbo's reaching hand.

"Easy now, boy," Worlin warned. "Hate to have to kill you. Could just wound you, but no profit in that."

"Haunted," Gareth blurted.

All three men took a step back. The rope tugged at Gareth's ankle, dragging him a step.

"The spear. Took it off a ghost on the old causeway. Starfaller magic all over it. Just trying to protect you."

"Ghosts," Warlin laughed – but he kept his distance.

"Sword, too," Gareth said. "Trapped a jaguar in it. Evil spirit. What gods do you keep?"

"Looks like just a sword to me. Nice work on the sheath, though. Get a few gold coins for that one. Orbo, string him up."

Gareth panicked, tried again to stand, but Orbo dragged him back off his feet and tossed the end of his rope to the unnamed man, who threw it over a thick tree limb and tugged. Together, they hung Gareth by his ankle. His hair, long and unruly, brushed the ground. The rope bit at his ankle and blood suffused his face.

Orbo snatched the spear away. Gareth watched him, upside-down, pass the weapon to the Warlin.

"Looks dark enough," Warlin said. "Bloody black haft. Blade is corroded, notched. Seen some action. No value here." He tossed it into the woods.

"The sword?" Orbo said.

"Ah, let the boy tire there. Make a fire. Good enough place for camping the night. Let's have a drink, celebrate some. Our first catch of the run. Boy will give up the sword once the hanging has worked on him long enough."

The three men all laughed again. Warlin watched Gareth while the other two set up a fire and pulled supplies from their packs. Fire meant light, and Gareth could now see his captors.

Warlin was tall and slender. He had whip-thin arms and a face to match. Tall, narrow teeth in a long face, receding hairline. Mismatched clothing of leather, wool, undyed cotton. Leather bracers over his forearms, good boots.

Orbo looked stronger. His jaw was square. Gray skin and black hair marked him as one of the Old Hitaians. One of Jeen's people. He wore a steel ring on one finger.

The other man had a shifting gaze, a way of glancing around the area. He was smaller than the other two without being stocky. Younger. His face bore a scar from the right cheek, through his lips near the middle, to the center of his chin.

Gareth's vision, already going pink as the blood filled his head, seemed orange in the firelight. His hands rested in moist soil over/under his head. He tried to push against the ground to rest his ankle, which burned painfully; tried to get the loose leg in a comfortable situation. It was no good. He couldn't keep it against the tied leg because his muscles were quickly tiring, and he couldn't relax it because it pulled at his groin and made his whole body hang at a weird angle.

Warlin glanced over at him. "Be more comfortable if you let that bow drop off your shoulder. Trying to hang in your face."

It was. The arrows had already rained down out of his quiver, and the sword dragged his belt up his body, rubbing on his ribs.

"You should let me go before this gets bad," Gareth said, teeth clenched.

"He's trying to be brave," Orbo muttered. "Too old. Told you he was too old. Should just gut him and take his things. Sword could be worth something. Haven't seen the blade. Bow is good. Black wood, unusual."

"What is it then, boy?" Warlin said. "How long do I have to be patient with you? Time is not your friend."

Gareth reached up to his waist, put his hand on the hilt of the sword. He drew it out quickly. The weight dragged his tired arm down.

Orbo stepped in and kicked his hand. Orbo had boots, too, like Warlin. Gareth felt one of his fingers break and the sword dropped into the leaf litter a few feet away. "There," Orbo said. "I feel better already."

Gareth shouted in pain, grabbed his damaged hand with his healthy one. He wanted to curse, to demand, but sudden helplessness rushed through his mind. And, with that, rage.

It was a ball inside of his chest. Hate, anger and despair all swirled up together with nowhere to go. He could not fight, could hardly move. The futility angered him more, fed the helpless rage.

Zhang had told her men to hurt him in the most shameful way possible and they had. They had seemed to enjoy it. He could smell their dirty bodies again, feel their heat, their laughter.

A growl started in his throat and became a cry, a war-cry, pure rage. It ripped his throat up, burned with hot tears.

"Shut him up," Warlin said.

The little man stepped in and punched Gareth in the gut, then again right under his ribs, taking his air away. Then again and again until Gareth felt nothing more.

Homecoming

Chess and Jeen stood in the long hall. Both had their mouths open, half-smiling and half-dumbstruck.

What happened here? Chess thought.

Children huddled around the floor, each with their sand tray. Erlo smiled and waved to his wife but stayed with the lesson. He bent and helped little Frans with one of his letters, stood and moved to the next child.

"Good, Vil. Neea, those loops are too grandiose. Remember that Old Hitaian is a practical language, not like Greenlander."

Can it be true? Can he be back from the dead?

Her husband was awake and aware, looking a little more haggard for time but trim and lucid. His hair was tied back in a braid, out of his face, showing off a pink scalp that looked freshly washed. His clothes were clean, eyes bright and smiling.

One of the children looked up from her tray. "Jeen! Aunt Jeen is home!" She started to stand.

Erlo corrected her quickly. "We will have reunions after lessons. Lessons are time for lessons. Concentrate, Chara."

"Yes, Erlo."

"Good girl." He smiled again at Chess and Jeen and offered a playful wave.

Chess went to the family stall and set down her things. A pack, a walking stick, gourds. She took off her shoes, changed clothes. She had to look around to find something new to wear. The space was clean, fresh-smelling, and organized, nothing where she had left it. Overhead, all the thatching was gone from the roof. Now there were boards, the tiling project complete.

Jeen came in. "Home is not as we left it."

"No."

"Neither do we see it with our old eyes."

Chess nodded. "This is as I wished and beyond what I could have hoped. I slept in my pain and you slumbered in your grief and all around us the people watched. Their two village heroes..."

"No, not me," Jeen said.

"Yes, you. Two village heroes who were killed in the war but never died. They looked to us to be leaders to them and we could not. We led them into sleep. Leaving was the slap they needed."

Erlo came in behind Jeen. "A cruel lesson, my love."

"I will be going," Jeen said. "See if they scrubbed my stall so clean they forgot I lived there and gave it away." She backed out, grinning tightly.

"I did not mean to hurt you," Chess told Erlo, stepping closer.

"I know. And you did not. I was hurting already. You just had to let me hurt. Feel it. You fought for us, for all of us."

"I know. I had to, and I was glad to."

"Hush, woman. You fought for us and kept us from fighting for ourselves. I watched the children while those dirty Xunians murdered you. Do you understand?" He gripped her arms at the biceps. Tight, too tight. "We all did. We let them kill you, let you fight for us. You saved us, but made me a coward. That's all right – I always was a coward, truly. Then, when you went, I had to face that again."

Chess stepped even closer, embraced him. "No, no coward. You never were."

"I was. A man of character would have come after you. And when I faced it, when I knew it was true, well, then I had a decision. Let Neea grow of age with no father or shake it off and stand up."

"I am proud of you, husband. Very proud. You are the man I married. You are the teacher they need. You seemed to resent that I was the warrior, the champion, and not you, but you had your own battle to fight. Now you are the teacher."

"Hah. I teach nothing. They showed me how to make all the letters. I just repeat back what they taught me."

"I do not mean letters, my love." She kissed him then. Their first passionate kiss in years. When she let him go, they were both breathing hard.

"I am glad to be worthy of you again. I hope to be. Of you and Neea, Kwin and little-Chess. What I have done, though, was not really for you. It is all selfish. I want to be a man I can respect."

Chess pulled him towards the bed. "I would hate if you lived only for me or only for Neea. Be with me now, though."

***

Deyklaveyn.

Korina shivered, a feeling that had lost its novelty. She was alone now, the caravan having turned aside a few days ago for village stops. There was frost under her feet, tall grass made stiff with cold and dried brown by the wind. Ahead, against a blue sky so pale it was nearly white, sooty pillars of smoke rose into the air to flatten out and mingle into a black haze. The forge town wall was of fitted local stone, gray and imposing, the biggest thing Korina had ever seen built by human hands.

It was another hour over half-frozen marshes to the gate. Every step, she remembered the story her new friends had told of Kilrovexen, out digging in the bogs, searching for a lost daughter. *What a miserable time that must be, with this cold, with ground made of slushy ice.*

The gate was guarded. Two women in steel armor. Korina's jaw hung a little loose at the sight of that – so much wealth to fashion whole sets of armor from steel. Even the cost of a sword or a knife was a fortune in Hitai. The women watched her come on and did not open the gate, but neither did they reach for weapons.

"State your business," one said. She had yellow hair under her conical helmet and a little wisp of mustache.

"I have come to find an apprentice. I am a forge master from the south."

"Look a mite young to be a master," the second guard said, eyes on the horizon. "And a bit old to be an apprentice yourself."

"Different ways for different people," Korina said. "Truth: I am the most able smith within a hundred miles of my home because there is only one other and I taught him everything he knows."

Both guards laughed, a raucous sound. The first said, "Pass within, then, sister. But choose your words carefully in Deyklaveyn. The masters, the real masters, are jealous of their titles. Say you are a hedge-smith. They will know what to do with you."

"Hedge smith?"

"Untrained, a little uncouth, but due some measure of respect. You have been through your own sort of crucible and done some service to your people."

"Ah. My thanks to you then. The gate?"

"Postern," said the second woman, and pointed to a door set in the gate.

Korina noted even the thick beams of the gate were banded in steel. No plain iron here, no brass or bronze. This place was built on steel and that wealth was not hidden away.

She passed through the small door set into the big doors. She felt small next to the wall, next to this huge town. Insignificant. And, inside, people were everywhere. Hundreds, maybe thousands. More people in each single glance than in all of the Starfall village.

They carried packages, walked with children, sat in groups under awnings. Sold one another sundry goods or a few luxuries. Chatted together.

None seemed to notice Korina pass by. She was just a strange face in a host of strange faces, in a place so large strangers were commonplace.

Now she felt both small and somewhat nervous. The forge was home. It had a close stone ceiling in place of the sky and four walls in place of far horizons and, most importantly, she was nearly always the only person in it. She itched to turn back through the postern door and hike straight home without ever looking back. But that would not do.

Easy to decide to do a thing. But to enact the decision meant to keep deciding it. Every day for two months she had decided to keep walking north to this place and, now she was here, she decided to stay.

Korina made her way through the moving masses of people. Farther into the town, things grew somewhat more sedate if no quieter. The forges were mostly against a low mountain range that served as a rear wall for the town. The sounds of bellows and hammers began to fill her ears, a rush of noise that calmed her tripping heart. Home might be uncounted miles behind her but it was also ahead, in each of these places.

She picked one at random, a squat building made of local red stone. The windows had real glass, smoky and impure, with wrought iron reinforcements. The door was plain wood with an iron handle. The place looked stout and well-built but not ostentatious, not for show.

Inside, a low counter kept visitors about twenty feet from the oven. Two women worked back there, one pumping a bellows made of leather, the other turning a bit of metal over and over the coals. It glowed pale orange, then yellow, then nearly white.

"Good enough," said the one with the tongs. She had white hair mostly tamed under a black head scarf, a face seamed with lines and sooty with work. Her skin was red in the glow of the fires. "Customer."

The woman at the bellows seemed younger if not cleaner. Her hair was yellow. Some of it poked out from under a leather cap. She had on an apron and long gloves. "Kass," she said, coming to the counter. "Help you?"

Korina's tongue betrayed her. Now the moment was here, it locked up behind her teeth and she just stood there staring.

"New to Deyklaveyn? Here we do business, girl. Business means saying what you need and how you shall pay for it."

Korina stared a moment longer, trying to force out some word. To remember what she meant to say. *I could just go, try someplace else.*

"Mute? Slavers take your tongue? Look like a slaver yourself. Is that it?"

She took a deep breath, shut her eyes. Then the words finally came. "I am looking for an apprentice." She sounded inane to herself, clumsy in the northern tongue, hopelessly naive.

Kass scoffed. "Have you lost one? A runaway? Slavers take apprentices? Thought you only took slaves. Apprentice slaver?"

"You talk too much," Korina said, immediately regretting it.

"My place. Mine and hers. Talk as much as I want to. So? What are you doing here looking for an apprentice?"

She was baffled by the question. What she was doing here *was* looking for an apprentice. "New to town, as you say. Not a slaver. I have my own forge at the Starfall. You know of the Starfall? No matter. Only me there. I need to find someone to take over the work, to grow into it. No good students in my own village."

The older woman finished up what she was doing. The bit of metal hissed in a vat of some liquid that did not smell like water, then she set it on the anvil. "What's she want, Kass? Wasting time."

"An apprentice," Kass said, laughing.

"She is one?"

"No, she says she needs one."

The woman came over to the counter, too. "You have no look of age about you. Twenty-four years at most."

"About that. My name is Korina."

"Whestle. Kass you know. Smart mouth on that one, no mistake, but a strong back. She has twice your years and will be ready for her first apprentice soon. Come back here."

Korina moved around the end of the counter. Whestle handed her an apron and some long gloves and she put them on.

"Tie back that hair. Good. Making a sword. Slavers love them. Get a fortune for it. Steel sword. Pick it up. Feel it. Good. Now, Master Korina, this bar has been heated and quenched, beaten flat and quenched again. Once in water, once in oil."

"Oil?"

"Ears work, that is a start. Next step, please."

"It was white hot," Korina said. "Not something I can do in my forge. I am only a hedge-smith. Never claimed to be a master. Uh, well, if I could get metal that hot, next I would heat it half as hot and shape it, let it cool slow. Then heat it so hot again and cool it fast. What is oil?"

Kass laughed.

Whestle said, "Take off the apron. You have not earned the right to touch a tool yet. *What is oil*. The smallest child knows what to do next. Leave you to it and you will be trying to beat out the impurities with a hammer."

"Yes."

"This is hot-smelted iron, girl. It has no base impurities."

"Amazing. How do you keep your oven rocks from splitting in the heat? What tools-"

Whestle stopped her with a gesture. "Would-be apprentices line up outside the gates on choosing day, twice a year, for the chance to be selected. They study. They work like mules to be the best. The ones not chosen, they go to work hauling ore or stoking fires just for a second chance later, or just to be able to sleep near the forge. You... I would never send a young hopeful home with you."

I have so much to learn. She is brutal and not wrong.

"Whestle. Master Whestle. I humbly submit to your judgment." She had to fish around a bit for some of those words and felt clumsier every moment. "My forge produces mostly bronze and some crude iron. I built it myself, with my father. I have worked it for ten years, mostly alone, and I meet the needs of my people. But you are right. I have found my apprentice, Master Whestle. She is me. I am the apprentice that I need.

"Those children who wait around outside hoping for this chance, I hope they can forgive me. Take me on. Today, now."

Whestle took a step back and looked Korina up and down. "I can see by your shoulders you work hard every day. Stronger than Kass, maybe. Good hands, good forearms.

Respectful, not afraid to hear criticism. Ready to learn. That anvil. Yes, the small one. Lift it over your head."

Korina set aside the apron on its hook. Then she took the anvil in her hands and hoisted it to her chest, pressed it over her head, set it gently back down. It was heavy but she did the task in silence.

"I will not take you," Whestle said.

Korina's eyes dropped to the floor. Too much to hope for. While it had been a whim, she still felt dashed apart.

"She will," Whestle said, pointing at Kass.

"I will?" said Kass.

"Yes. You have as much to learn about being a master as she has to learn about steel. You will be a good match for one another. You will teach her, and I will teach you how to teach her."

Korina smiled.

Kass did not. "You are going to work harder than you ever have before. You know that."

"I know it," Korina said. "I am accustomed to hard work. Truthfully, I have missed it – walking across the world has been restful. My arm yearns to swing a hammer."

"That one, then. The pound and half. The small anvil. Here. An ingot of raw iron. Tell me what you see."

Korina took the ingot. It was four inches by two by one. Dark, heavy. Rough and dry-feeling. She smelled it. Closed her eyes and just felt its weight. "Excellent purity," she said. "The slightest hint of tin, I think. This bar wants to be worked right away or else it will begin to rust."

"That is what we will do. But one can coat iron in oil to prevent rusting."

"Oil again. This is what?" Korina said.

"Fat rendered from animals. Sometimes the foul-smelling secretions of tar sands. The hammer. Show me how you flatten out that bar and fold it."

Korina started. She knew how to flatten out bars, easy enough, but had never worked with such high quality iron. It began to split almost right away. She tried to save it and failed.

"Too hard," Kass said. "You beat the metal like a farmer beats a mule. Gently."

"I thought I was being gentle," Korina laughed.

Whestle picked up her own hammer and set to her work. "Listen to your own advice, Kass. This one is no raw child full of impurities. This is high-grade iron that needs to be tempered, not beaten."

"Yes, Master Whestle. Here. Let me show you." Kass put one hand over Korina's. She lifted the hammer, let it fall with hardly any force imparted. Again, again. "Like this."

Korina smiled again. "I made all these muscles for nothing, it seems."

"Oh no, you will need your strength. I am just seducing you with the iron now. Tomorrow you pump bellows and haul ore and mind fires. And the next day, if you do well I will let you touch the metal."

"I hardly mind," Korina said. "The fires are my favorite."

***

Jeen sat in the doorway of Yohn's hut. It faced the lake. The sun was high but cool, the fish quiet. The water rose, fell, lapped around the pilings of the dock. It seemed to match her mood, her thoughts. Behind her, Kwin and the baby slept.

By the shore, Chess led a series of movements. Staves and spears. Women and men.

Moburu was gone, truly gone. The war was ten years ago. Even Jeen's grief had started to find its rightful place, dissolving into weed-choked wilderness like the bodies and artifacts they had found all along the causeway.

My grief was locked in time. Theirs only begins.

Spears and staves. Things of war among a people at peace. All of the traumas, the losses, the hurts, each handled them in their own way. Korina by immersing herself in her fires and metals and smokes. Erlo by sinking them into strong drink and himself into sleep. Chess' followers by practicing for the next war, by making idols of heroes.

Moburu had been a hero in his way. Jeen knew what he was: not a god, not a God; nor only a plain man. Something complex that suffered, that strove but also tormented. But he had fallen easily enough. Not a monument, then, only a thing of flesh.

Out by the lake, Chess led her students through a series of sweeping attacks. They followed with smooth proficiency.

You said you were done with all that.

That was Jeen's fear now, of course: that the past would emerge again into the future, all the lessons forgotten, all the horror reborn as Moburu had been reborn. They thought they prepared for war to keep it at bay, as a necessity.

When Jeen cried, it was not the wailing, disconsolate grief of the past, of the fresh loss of her love. These were hopeful tears: pain in the knowledge that things could be better.

After a while, as the fighters began to tire, Jeen got up from the doorway and strolled towards the long house. It had been long since she had taught children and Erlo was doing a fine enough job of it now. Today's lesson was about food: how to tell pure things from those mixed up by the change.

She sat and listened to him, smiled for the children, smiled for love.

We need these lessons. We all need them. The long hall was meant to bring us together, keep us one people. But we need more.

Erlo's lessons were nearly done. "Now a bit of real work for you, children. I am minding the cook pot tonight and we will have a stew. Each of you are to go out around the village and bring back one thing to throw in the pot. Remember your lessons."

When the children were gone, Erlo sat on the hearth, a smile behind his eyes. Jeen went to him, sat beside him.

"Jeen. You look lovelier each day. Come to take back your children?"

"Not a bit of that," she said. She took his hand. "I... Mang died. He was a good man. Was he not?"

"Oh, yes, a good man. A friend. A leader, even, in his way."

"You know that Yohn worried about that. About how to be a good person. He..."

"He loved you," Erlo said. "A blind goat could see that. That is what tormented him so. How to love."

"Being good is about loving, of course. But they no longer worry."

"Who?"

She leaned in a little closer, lowered her voice. "The people who live here. Half of them are strangers, newcomers since the war. And they do not worry about what it means to be a good person. They think they will fight for the village but what is that? What is it now that the god has left us? We are awakening after a long sleep to find the world changed around us, and none worry."

"Yohn was the philosopher," Erlo said. "I can throw an axe and roll a log with my feet. I make a decent enough stew. Anything else you should tell me plain. In small words."

She smiled for him. "A fool to think yourself a fool. Tonight, after we eat, I want to speak with everyone. A gathering."

"We used to do this. In the old days, when things were fresh. The whole village, all together, all voices equal."

"Our leaders have all died. Some of us have crept forth from our graves and it is time we stood again. Will you help me?"

"However I can," Erlo said. "For now, I have to chop this mutton."

Bindings

Gareth vomited.

He struggled to his knees, stomach empty and uncertain, the stink of it making him want to do it again. The world seemed to turn slowly about his head and the daylight was too bright. His hands were tied behind his back. Tight, too tight. Fingers cold, hands numb, muscles rigid with icy pain. His right hand throbbed but that pain was far away, buried under an urgent message from his arms, his hands:

Tight, too tight.

Thin cord held his wrists together. It wrapped his forearms and cramped his elbows so close behind his back that they almost touched. The cord bit deep into his skin, his muscles, and it felt like it had been there hours already.

Someone dragged him up to his feet and he found his balance. A dead campfire cooled under a new day. Trees rustled indifferently all around. And three men watched him from under half-lidded eyes.

"Orbo did not kill him after all. Looks like I owe you a copper coin, Lidk."

"Almost a shame, Warlin. This one is going to be more trouble than he is worth. Look at him. Already planning again in his head."

"You planning, boy?" Orbo said.

Gareth was having trouble remembering who these people were. His body hurt and his head was starting to sing and ring. It felt like he had been kicked in the temple. He tried to speak, to ask for water, but all that came out was gibberish.

"Not in good shape for rebellion, I would say," Orbo said. "Put a rope around his neck. He will keep up and keeping up will keep his head out of trouble."

Before he could think to mount any resistance, Gareth found a thin noose slipped over his head. It made him think of the lasso he'd been caught in, of the failed rescue.

Not failed. Neea went home in one piece. It was me that was broken.

Then he was dragged along by the neck. The men set an indifferent pace but Gareth could not easily match it, not with his hands tied, his body aching, his balance thrown out. Once he stopped to vomit again and Orbo dragged him by the neck until he lodged against a tree root.

Warlin stepped in and hit Orbo in the chest. Gareth heard it, saw part of it as he got to his knees, back to his feet, spitting bile that tasted bloody. "If he dies, this whole venture is empty," Warlin said. "How will I pay my gambling debts to Lidk on an empty venture?"

Orbo rubbed his chest and frowned at Warlin. He said nothing. Gareth strained to hear the man's thoughts. Silence, nothing. Futility. Then he remembered he was not the same as Orbo. He was mixed up with some other people. Friends. He had friends, and they were him, and he was them.

These people were not his friends. They were slavers.

Orbo had Gareth's sword slung over his back. Lidk had his bow. It was unstrung, and Lidk walked with it like a staff. Warlin had the half-spear tucked into his belt. Gareth thought he remembered that being pitched away as trash. What did it mean that Warlin had recovered it?

Desperation.

Gareth spat, coughed, lurched back into movement as Orbo tugged on the rope. "The spear..."

"Quiet," Warlin said. "Slaves talk when their words are required of them. Otherwise, they tend to be noticed by the Great Ones and that notice seldom brings joy."

"A warning. Danger. Great One." The honorific tasted like the bloody bile in his mouth but he tried for sincerity. "A good choice. Let the hirelings have the other things but always keep the spear yourself. These small people couldn't control it."

"Stop." Warlin turned around and walked the three paces back to Gareth. "I am no Great One. Not a King or a God. But you will learn to heed my words. Remember being hung by your ankle last night? How did that feel?" Gareth did not remember but Warlin gave him no chance to answer. "One word from me and this rope could go back over a branch again. Want to find out if hanging from your neck is any better?"

Silence seemed the prudent option, so Gareth chose it. The tingling feeling in his hands gentled and he wasn't sure that was preferable.

"Better. March on. It is a long way to the new frontier and we will have to take ship to get there. The frontier is too risky."

"A ship?" Lidk said. "Never been on a ship, me. How we going to pay for that?"

"That sword is worth a goodly sum. See how I trust Orbo to carry it? The bow, too, if you do not ruin it using it as a walking stick. Black wood. Not ebony. I have never seen the like."

"Starfall wood," Gareth choked out. "Magic. Just wood, not any kind. Shoot through bronze armor with it, or kill a deer from half a mile away."

Warlin stepped back again. This time he put a fist into Gareth's ribs. Something snapped. Gareth fell to the ground, a scream jerked from his mouth. Warlin kicked him in the back.

"Wait," Lidk said. "Magic? Make him tell us." He flexed the bow, unable to get much bend into it.

"Magic is for children. Flesh is for sale." Warlin used a foot to push Gareth over onto his back. "Now you have made me hurt you. Broke a rib, I fear. We will have to rest here a while until we see if you are going to bleed inside and die or if you can go on."

Gareth groaned, said nothing. The pain drove reason back out of his head. There seemed nothing to say, no reason for speech.

Lidk pulled the bowstring out of a pocket. He tried to restring the bow but could not bend it far enough. "Magic, he said. And I am not strong enough to string it. Could be he is the only one who can."

"Give it to me," Orbo said, dropping the end of the rope. "Weak-Blooded fool. He is just trying to distract us with tricks. Let me do it." He set one end against the ground and leaned on it. He put a foot on the stave about a third of the way up, pulled the other way with his body weight. He came closer than Lidk but still could not string the bow.

"Together," Warlin said. "I find myself suddenly interested in this piece of wood. A better bow means more money. Perhaps enough we do not need the boy at all."

The two men grunted and strained and finally slipped both loops of the bowstring over the ends.

Lidk had Gareth's quiver, too. He pulled out a light arrow with a splayed tip, set it on the string.

"Not that one," Gareth hissed out between his teeth. "Birding arrow. Light, slow. Flint tip, you want a flint tip." He expected Warlin would beat him some more but the other man went to Lidk instead.

"This one, idiot. Look, the boy makes his own arrows. Could be useful. Maybe more useful as a maker of things than as a slave. Though the merchant's life does not call me. Look. That tree. Only clear line through the woods. Need open space to range-test a bow but if you can hit that tree..."

"The one with white leaves? What sort of tree is that?"

"Never mind now. Just aim at it."

Lidk took a stance. The bow, strung, was a few inches taller than him. When he angled it up, the lower tip came off the forest floor. The bow bent back and back, creaking as it came, until the point of the arrow sat against the bow. When he loosed it, it made a whooshing sound like a pile of linen dropping to the ground. The arrow moved too quickly to follow. All four men searched for it against the sky.

"Good shot," Gareth said. He tried to roll up off his arms but that put his chest against the ground, which was even less comfortable.

"You hit it," Warlin said. "The bow must be magic after all if a clod like you can make that shot. How far is it? Three hundred yards?"

"At least," Orbo said. "More, even. Let me try."

"It is mine," Lidk said. "My share. Warlin said so."

"We need to think this through once more," Warlin said. "Let him try. Listen, we did not know what we had."

Orbo took the bow, tugged it away from Lidk with a look. Lidk's eyes drooped and his teeth flashed, just briefly.

"He did not lie about the bow," Lidk said. "What if he did not lie about the spear?"

"Curses?" Warlin said. He spat the word but his eyes flickered to the sword, to Gareth. "What does it do, boy? The spear. What is the curse?"

"I can hardly breathe down here. Help me stand, someone, so I can talk." He panted, spat a little blood. "With my hands tied. Like this. Hard to breathe. Too tight."

"Get him up, Lidk. No good if he drowns in his own blood."

Lidk helped him ungently to his feet.

"The spear. Haunted. Giant from... Xun. Seven feet tall." *Eight with the hat, he thought.* "My brother... broke his leg... with that very bow. Cracked... his thighbone right... open." He spat again. Less blood this time, pinkish foam. "Giant died with that spear in his hands. Found his body as I walked down from my village. Ten years old, covered in mushrooms. Tombshade. He stood up, the dead giant, and put that spear in my hands."

"He never did," Orbo said. He had not fired the bow yet.

"Wait," Warlin said. "The village. Was it the Starfall?"

"Yes."

"They say the dead walk around the Starfall. That cats are sometimes men, that things fuse together with other things. Monsters." Warlin drew the spear out from his belt and stared at it.

"All true," Gareth said. "Magic, evil magic. A person who knows the ways of it can work wonders. He gave me the spear and bade me keep it, keep people safe from it. But you are greater than me, it seems. You will have to do it. Keep the world free from the plague."

"Plague?" All three men said it, and all three turned to look at him.

"The plague my brother used to save the Starfall when arrows did not turn the fight. Infected a thousand soldiers, killed them in three days. Every last one. That's the curse. The spear, the ghost-giant, the tombshade fungus. You have touched it now. It is yours."

The two henchmen backed away. Lidk put a hand over his mouth. Orbo had an arrow on the bow, had it pointed at Gareth. It was a birding arrow but from this range it would do the job, go right into a lung and lodge there.

"No good to kill me," Gareth said. "Not my words that make it true. Ah, it hurts." He remembered the man he had stabbed, made all his friends stab together. Remembered him pleading for death before the hyenas could eat him from the inside out. He had saved the man from that but here Gareth was, being pulled apart by hyenas. "May be good to kill me, after all. End my suffering. May be that you have killed me already."

"A fortune in this bow," Orbo said. "Another in that spear, if it is what he says. Power. And the sword..."

"A fire," Warlin said. "Lidk, Orbo, build a fire. We can burn the spear to be sure. Kill the boy just in case. Orbo, what are you doing?"

The birding arrow stood out from Warlin's eye, the splayed tip caught up in his brain. The man dropped to the ground, strings cut, dead without a further thought.

"Burn it? Fool. Use it. Sell it. Profit from it. Tired of him. Hit me for the last time, Half-Blooded driver of donkeys. Never trust those who claim The Blood, Lidk. You are lowborn, old stock, and I am just as low if not of that race. We will be better off without him."

"You killed him," Lidk said. "Killed Warlin."

"Told you, he was going to foul the whole deal. One less fool to share with."

Lidk spat, crossed his arms. "How do I know you are not going to kill me, too? When I am asleep or when I have carried this boy to town or whenever you are done with me? When it is time to divide up the spoils? You want the bow and the spear, good by me. Give me the sword. I will take that as my share and you can have the rest, including these corpses."

"Partners, we are. Have been for months. Think on it, Lidk. Who takes care of you?"

Gareth swooned, tried to lean on Lidk but found him gone, moved. He fell to the ground. When he looked up, Orbo had pulled another arrow from the quiver.

"You do mean to kill me," Lidk said. "Have it your way. Keep everything. I will be happy to leave just with my skin on. I knew this was trouble. Slaving, as if I were better than a slave myself." He turned to walk away, took three steps. But, as he neared Warlin's corpse, he dropped into a crouch and came up with the spear in his left hand. He spun and threw it, underhand.

Orbo shot him in the neck. The spear fell short, a clumsy, desperate toss that accomplished nothing.

"Well, boy," Orbo said. "Looks like just you and me. You and me. Suppose I ought to keep you alive. We still have the sword to talk on."

Gareth lay where he was, trying to wiggle his fingers to work some blood into them, some feeling. His hands no longer tingled, no longer felt cold. They felt like nothing at all.

***

Vault rolled from his hammock. The ground was cool and rough under his feet, the sky still dark. He took a step towards the door of his little hut and his foot brushed Xin Ban's leg.

"Surprised you slept," she said.

"Surprised you slept on the ground."

"We always do."

He nodded, knowing nobody would see him and she would know it, anyway. They had told him about the thought-sharing and a few hours together was enough to prove it. He had known anyway. The doorway waited.

Outside, Fum waited for him, leaning against a tree. Yesterday the tree had been an elm. Now, in the light of the stars and a weak moon, it seemed strange, changed. Fum seemed just the same. Thirty years old, slender, dressed in bits and pieces of clothing from the many places he had been. Hair kept short, face shaved clean.

"We have to go," Fum said.

"This again, Uncle? At least let me pee before you start in on me again."

"Your mother-"

"Did not steal me away from the Starfall so you could drag me back to Hitai to be murdered. Like Oona." He stalked off to the water to make his contribution. When he came back, clean and refreshed, Fum was still there.

"This is not your place. Not your sister's place. She is happy there. She has a good life, a temple life. I want to show you Hitai. The city. The lands. Places where they speak our language. Food. The women."

"I have no interest in any of those things, Uncle. Please. My brothers and sisters have only just come. Let us rest and talk a few days."

"They are right behind me," Fum said. "In a few weeks or a few days, this place will be full of soldiers with bright spears and dull minds, looking to grind away..."

"What?" Vault said.

"I do not remember," said Fum. "Something important. We have to run!"

"Leave the boy be," Ghurub said from the doorway. "You have woken everybody, and the sun still sleeping."

"He means well, Father," Vault said.

"Princes. They mean as they mean and the rest of us, we muddle through it." Ghurub went back inside.

Fum chuckled, fear momentarily forgotten. He had been this way since he returned from hunting a few days ago: desperate in one moment, sly the next, then full of strange good humor. "How many people do you have in there? Three Starfallers, your mother, Ghurub, you. Never lived this way at the palace. Still, I have never regretted leaving."

"Then why do you want to drag me back? Never mind. I am going back to sleep."

Inside, his mother had her feet hanging over the edge of her hammock, her back braced against a wall. "That man is trouble and always was."

"You should never have become involved with him," Vault said.

Jac covered her mouth, expression lost in the dark. "You owe that man your life."

"And he is interesting company," Vault said. He got back into his hammock.

"What is he nervous about?" Guarl said from the pile on the floor. "He seems eager to take you away from here."

Not away. Towards. Towards some destiny.

Vault could not tell whose thoughts those were. They seemed to be from more than one person at once; maybe partially his.

Destiny. They have always tried to infect us with destiny. With names, with omens and portents, with the way they trained us to fight as children. With that trip to Hitai. Do you remember? No, that was Gareth's memory, and he's gone now.

"Maybe Fum is right, after all," Vault said. "It does not seem any more sleep is due us this night."

They lay awake in the dark, listening to the night and to one another's thoughts, to Ghurub and Jac breathing back towards sleep.

Vault thought he heard Fum pacing outside, muttering and mumbling to himself.

***

Zhang hated the forest. It stank of decaying leaves or pine needles. Insects tried to drink her dry of blood. There was no way to keep track of where you were going. And, worst of all, the forest was not a ship bound for home.

But the harbor remained blocked and the way south was full of soldiers. Not fighters for hire like Zhang but orderly, disciplined soldiers with hard faces and slab shoulders. Thousands of them, all dressed alike, all armed alike.

So Zhang slogged through the forest, thinking of the next place she might try to go. She had seen a map once that suggested the world was a sphere. With east and south blocked, she could try west through the lands of Lurk, hope to get to Xun the long way around. It might take five years, but it was possible.

"And I'm never getting back going this way," she said into the gloaming. Her voice was rusty, raspy. When had she last said a word to another person? Days and days.

Her stomach reminded her that she was mortal and a flitting bat that the hour was late. Time to settle in for the night. Walking around the woods in the dark was a recipe for hurt and futility. So Zhang set a few snares with threads from her new clothing and a few crumbs from a bit of moldy bread in the bottom of her pack. A nice fire would keep the animals away and the smoke would keep the biters off. A bed would be nicer – and a berth on a big boat nicer still – but she remained a free woman with a pocket full of money.

Zhang stood her sword against a tree next to the fire, within an easy reach in case of trouble. But there would be no trouble. These woods were empty of people. Yesterday she had walked through a village, an orchard. No people stirred there. Just moldering bones and an old smell, a familiar smell. The fruits had run riot on the trees, unpicked and untended, and rotted in the soil. Quick disorder already blurred the neat rows. Bats and birds fought raucous battles over the spoils with crows the day's main victor and the hum of burgeoning insect life settled over the whole scene. And, in the sky, hawks had circled, waiting to pick off the crows.

No, there would be no trouble. Moburu had been here before her. The man-cat, the night-cat. He had cleared all the trouble out of this place, leaving behind nothing but ghosts.

"If a ghost comes, I will cut him." She touched the sword again, checking the reach. Since the boy had repaired it, it seemed sharp enough to cut a ghost. What a waste to let those children stride about the world unchecked. They could be very useful to a soldier-for-hire. Making swords, fixing armor.

Sleep pushed against her eyes. The fire crackled and popped into the night, sending unseen embers into the sky, and Zhang's mind started to follow – out of the world, into the smoke.

She woke in the morning, sore and irritable. The sword was where she had left it but the fire had burned itself out and a damp chill had found its way into her bones. She restarted the fire – one thing to be said for the forest was that there was always plenty of wood – and then set out to check her snares.

A footprint stood out between broken ferns. A boot, man-sized. Someone had come up in the night, right to the edge of her fire-light. More tracks. Two people. Watchers. Not the people who lived here – they were small, light, bare-footed folks.

Zhang chewed her teeth. She worried the problem for a few seconds, then went about checking her snares. Luck was in: a little black squirrel struggled in one of the loops, caught by a foot. She broke its back and tossed it in the fire to get rid of the fleas and ticks.

Watchers. And none too careful. Well.

Who and why? She dismissed the questions as they came to her. If she saw someone, she would decide what to do. Until then, they hardly mattered.

Ruling

Jul stalked through the halls of the residential quarter. His bare feet slapped on the stones and echoed back and the sound reminded him of his mother's guards punching him, punching, careful to avoid bones and inflict more pain than damage.

His feet felt nothing. Not the texture of the stone, smooth and polished; not the cold. Thrashed and burned, they had no feeling left.

All this only made him angrier.

He arrived at Ergol's rooms. He had taken Old Grandfather's space, a gigantic chamber with huge brass doors. Two women stood guard outside. Comely ones, with wide hips and kinky hair and grins to match. Smooth, dark skin, black eyes.

"Good morning, My Prince," one of them said, crouching down as though to speak to a child.

"Open the doors."

"He wishes not to be disturbed, Oh Future King," she replied. The other one blushed.

"Does he?" Jul said. His mouth tasted like venom. "The man who used these rooms before was named Bassa. My teacher told me that. His name was Bassa, not Old Grandfather, and he was my mother's father's father. Now open the doors."

"If you wish it," the blushing guard said. "We did warn you, My Prince. You may see something you do not wish to see."

"Hurry up." He clenched his fists, his jaw. The two women had the door open barely a crack before he was through it, rage carrying him forward faster than his eyes could take in the scene.

Is that Xenia?

Why is she unclothed?

Why is he underneath her that way?

He knew of rutting, of course he knew. It was impossible to loiter around the animals of the royal menagerie for very long and not come about that kind of education. But to see his uncle and this low-caste woman doing this animal thing fanned his rage with shock.

"You are supposed to be immortal," Jul said.

Xenia got down off of Ergol and covered her nakedness with a sheet. Her face was impassive as she eyed the boy.

Ergol was worse. He covered his crotch slowly, casually, and smiled a slow smile. "Ah, a visit from the future King of Hitai." The bed was thirty paces away across a dim open space, only the tableau lighted with tallow candles.

"Your behavior is shameful."

"You would do well to emulate it, little prince. You know lines are secured thusly. Or have your teachers been remiss in your education about certain matters?"

"You care nothing for my line," Jul said, on the verge of shouting. Hot tears welled behind his eyes and he shoved that feeling away. Crying was for children and he could afford no more childhood.

"What disturbs you?" Ergol said, sitting up, getting comfortable.

Jul came closer. "The slave boy I took from the Tomblands. Who untied him?"

"Oh, was there a careless accident?"

Jul's eyes narrowed. "Never mind that. You tried to have me murdered."

"Only a little," Ergol said, eyes dancing.

"What does that mean?"

"Were you hurt? Threatened by a slave boy half your size?"

"No," he said. He had a scratch under his eye, half-forgotten. Mostly he was angry because he had pushed the child against the hyena pens and, when they were done with him, he was not able to have his fun. If the child had had any sense, he might have let the dogs out himself, and then where would Jul be? "His sense of self-preservation was stronger than yours."

"You are too bloodthirsty," Ergol said. "Xenia, sweet woman, perhaps you should return to your other duties."

She climbed from the bed and picked up her kilt from the floor, dressing slowly. Jul watched her, a feeling creeping into his loins.

Ergol went on. "Your mother was right about you, at least somewhat. You have grown nearly to manhood here with few threats on your life. Some siblings would have made you more cautious, more... circumspect. Siblings try to kill you and thus teach you how not to be killed. I merely add some spice to your bland life. And you will do the same for me. In the end, you will have to replace me. How will you do this if you never learn to plot and to avoid plots?"

"I will kill you."

"I hope this is true," Ergol said. "It is the wish of every father to be murdered by his children. Well, at least when the father is the King."

"You are no father of mine." He stepped closer still.

Xenia, dressed now, walked past him with a wiggle in her step Jul had not observed in her before. "Are you going to fight him?" she said. "I hope you do not fight him. Poison, perhaps. Look how he grows fat. The threat of poison would keep him lean and trim." Then she was past him, her hip-swaying walk taking her to the door.

It was only when she went outside into the brightness of the hallway that Jul realized he was staring at her, the feeling in his groin intensified.

"Siblings," Ergol said. "They find what you love and use it to kill you. You love to torture the innocent. Puppies, children. Maybe babies if I let you. Old women who cannot fight you. A vice. A weakness."

Jul found his anger still hot but now tempered with this new feeling, this visceral reaction, this turgidity in his loins. "I know what you love too, Uncle. Remember that." He turned to go and made it almost to the door before Ergol replied.

"Good." And the big man laughed.

But Ergol had not won. Not completely. Jul still had his new Gravetender to play with.

***

Xenia slipped back into the bedchamber. Ergol sat on the edge of the bed with the sheet wrapped around him. Half his chest was exposed: one black nipple with a crown of hairs; thick muscle running to fat; a scar from some long-ago conflict. She glanced at his feet and away, feeling ashamed.

"Have you come for more bed-play?" he said.

"He ordered the Masters to tear down everything in the Tomblands. He grows reckless."

"He tests the limits of his power. I told the obsequious one... Ramble? I told him to check with me before instituting any orders of Jul's. The tombs, they are us. To be so aggressive towards them speaks of a powerful self-hate. I will stand between him and his symbolic suicide."

She stood in front of him and put her hands on her hips. "You bait him."

"Yes."

"Dangerous."

"I hope so."

"Do you want to die?" She stared down at him, surprised at the feeling in her chest, the volume of her voice. *And why should I care?*

He sighed. "You know this place as well as I do. This city and her people and her customs. More than my life is at stake. The only way to save the boy is to be murdered by him. The only way to die a King..."

"You came all the way here just to die. What good is it to rule a place if you cannot make any choices? Damn the priests and the priesthood. Damn the temples. Jul is right – we should till them under the soil and plant crops, bury the whole mess."

Ergol stood, pulling the sheet closer around himself. His eyes glanced around the floor until they found his trousers. "Be less quick to hate that place."

"What?" Xenia stepped back.

"There will be no destruction of the tombs. There will be more great projects. You will oversee them." He let go the sheet and found his tunic. "You will be the next Gravetender."

"Out there in the sand? For what?"

"For the Kingdom."

"I thought..." Her eyes found the rug and stayed there. She blushed, hated herself, and blushed more.

"I know what you thought." Ergol put a hand on her shoulder, let it linger. "And that can yet be. For now, though, safer for you in the desert."

She shook off his hand and strode for the door. *That's what Wyrrn thought.*

***

Another visitor.

Ergol finished dressing himself and ran fingers over the remains of his hair. *So much scalp under my touch now. What does this signify?* Then he opened the door with his own hand.

"Myrsa?"

"Yes, Great One. May I enter?"

Ergol stepped back and used one arm to invite her in. "Do you regularly visit this place?"

"I have come to the palace exactly twice now." She found a chair in a corner, dragged it out and sat.

Ergol glanced around for another seat. There were none, only the bed. That still being damp from his exertions, he chose to stand. "What do you want?"

"You know what I want."

"Do I? Then imagine I just want to hear you say it."

"The boy. The young Prince. He needs to come to us. He has a duty to the gods."

Ergol nodded. Then he shook his head, brows pulling down. "Gods, you say. What sort of gods would tolerate your temple of whores?" But that word tasted wrong now. Whores were willing. Something else was going on there. "And him just a boy yet. Let him ripen before you try to pluck his fruits."

"We had an agreement."

"Yes, and I will keep it. But not today. He is not ready."

Myrsa looked Ergol in the eye. "A rich one like him, so tall and well fed... The change is known to come on early for ones like him. And there are things we can do to speed the change. A little oil in his oats..."

"He will think it poison, and I shall not disagree."

"Then at least let us tempt him. Test him. A nubile companion, a playmate."

Ergol sighed. He enjoyed sparring this way and enjoyed Myrsa's direct looks. He wondered suddenly if the room smelled like sex and put that thought aside. "As you will. Have Xenia examine her background before you introduce her. Jul's life is precious to me. And another thing."

Myrsa was in the process of standing, rubbing her hands together. "Hm?"

"He is not fledged, but he already has appetites. This is a cruel place and requires a cruel hand. His mother taught him well, the monster."

"We accommodate many... appetites," Myrsa said, now looking at Ergol sidelong.

"Yes, well. He likes to torture animals and, if I let him, children. I lack the stomach to let him take that so far as he would but it is probably good for him. That was Ynn's problem, you know."

Myrsa nodded and turned to go. "A soft heart, yes. A weakness in his offspring. The mother must have had a hard heart indeed."

Ergol walked to the door and watched Myrsa drift away down the hall. The guards outside the door looked a question at him and he shook his head.

My dear dead brother. I have finally usurped you and I find I begin to understand your nature. Must I become you, in the end, as I became Chans?

***

From a shadow, the seer watched a Tomblands guard.

The guard lingered outside Grandfather's house. The damage to the door frame was obvious. Any person with sight could see it. And any fool could see it had been repaired with haste, the frame stood back in its place in the wall.

The guard scratched his head and glanced around. He ought to have been with a partner but his mate seemed to be indisposed. At a brothel or a drinking house or maybe just making a toilet, the seer could not see. She only knew God had prompted her to be here at this place, at this time.

Finally the guard stepped to the door and, absurdly, knocked. There was no answer. A cat scuttled across the roof and she saw it hunting mice, birthing kittens, eventually dying in a snare meant for a desert hare, her own shadow across its back as it was over this house, this guard – but not over the missing man.

What do you want me to do? I never touch this world, not heavily. Shall I get real blood on my hands? Have I not enough guilt to carry?

She knew the answers to such questions, though. God never spoke of them, but they had made a deal, a compact. Years ago, an age ago. She accepted the guilt because to deny it was to place it on the shoulders of another. She had tried to spare Helnedrexenon and failed an age ago, making this burden so much the heavier.

She had a knife. It was blunt, almost stubby, a thing used for slicing her meager rations. She thought of tossing it at the soldier. Of sneaking up and cutting his throat. *So bloody, and me so weak*. But the future was in Grandfather's run-down house. Everything that mattered revolved around this moment.

Mithodroxes crept out of her shadow and away from the house. A few streets away, through dusty streets lined with cats, was a bazaar. Vendors sold food and wares from wooden carts and stalls. Smells collided and clashed and noise rattled through the open space. Here a woman cried out that her brass pots would never rust and here a man held up a fistful of dates. Children scampered about like rats without cats big enough to hunt them.

That was what she wanted: one of the children. She snatched at one as he went by, a boy of four or five years. The child pulled away and looked reproach at her.

"Summer greens," she told him, and put the knife in his hand. "Tell your mother. Summer greens."

The boy ran off, no understanding in his face. Mithodroxes glanced forward into the next moments, the next hours.

Better to have just stabbed that poor guard. So much bloodshed. If only I were stronger.

Leaving the Greenlands

Guarl rubbed his face with one hand. The sun was in his eyes, the cabin to his back. His fingers found wispy stubble on his chin. "We have to go."

Vault stood beside him, Whilla and Xin Ban in front of the two boys with their backs to the sun. Their thoughts churned around, mingling, unspoken.

south into new lands Lurk to the east dark mysterious Lurk family home the lake the dead lake home Hong with its walls Fum brought a warning north into safety

"North, then," Guarl said. He spoke for all of them. "If there is danger to the south, we will go away from it."

"I feel like a coward," Xin Ban said. "To be afraid of danger."

"Killing danger," Whilla whispered, or maybe did not say at all.

"Yes." Xin Ban rubbed her own chin as Guarl rubbed his.

All around, under the trees and along the muddy banks of the river, green grass turned slowly blue. A butterfly floated between them and it dragged a wasp's stinger behind it. Birds in the tree chattered like squirrels.

"We cannot go home," Guarl said. "Not like this. There *is* danger in the south, and it is us. What might happen to our families?"

Vault thought of his own family. *take them leave them abandon them run from them miss them take them save them*

The door to the cabin swung open and Ghurub stepped out. "Why not stay?" he said. "We hear you speaking."

"You know why," Vault told him. "Mother knows why. The change will go on and on and everything will be affected. It goes stronger with time. What might you be tomorrow if I stay with you?"

"I will come with you."

Guarl said, "No. I love you too much to risk you." Then he realized he had said Vault's words as his own. *What will Ghurub become? What will we become? Just one person in four bodies?*

"He is right," Vault said. "You and mother must remain. I will come back for you when we have found a way to control the change or to stop it. For now..."

A cry cut him off. From the south, a voice called high and frightened. "Run! They come now!"

"Hitaian," Ghurub said.

"Fum," the four Starfallers said at once. Then they took up their few possessions – weapons, mostly – and began to run.

South. Toward Fum's call.

They jumped over the creek like gazelle evading a lion and swarmed into the trees. Mangos and banyans and stranger things confused the view. Guarl saw a few villagers running the other way with baskets half-full of fruit or tools in hand. Fum called the warning again and they turned slightly to keep going towards him.

There he was, running right at them through the trees, ferns slashing at his shins, all knees and elbows as he sprinted. His eyes widened as he saw Guarl and his friends. "Away!" he said. "Soldiers. Run!"

Guarl and Xin Ban moved a little apart so Fum could pass between them. The four came to a stop, staring south.

Arrows fell around them as if from the sky. Just a few, six or ten, short and evenly fletched. Then a soldier appeared through the underbrush. He had bronze armor, greaves, a helmet that covered half his face. Weapons hung from his belt and a short bow stood up from his hand. The other hand held an arrow. He nocked and drew.

Guarl saw the head of the arrow point at his face so that he looked straight down the shaft over a few dozen feet. He knew he was dead. All four of them knew they were dead because they were all one person, all Guarl. They knew, too, that the bow and the arrow were not two things, they were one thing, one weapon; the soldier was a weapon not separate from the bow.

Guarl's vision went blue. *Is this what it's like to die?*

Someone screamed and Guarl thought it must be himself, dying, though he could not feel any wounds. Then his friends grabbed him and pulled him away, back to the north.

"We killed him," Xin Ban said or perhaps thought. "We used our power to kill that man."

Whilla said, "No, we only punished him. Made his hands part of his bow. We protected ourselves."

"Did what needed doing," Xin Ban said, and Guarl heard Gareth in her voice, heard her hating Gareth.

Never mind that now. Run.

Their collective mind had decided and they obeyed. Guarl's vision cleared. He caught up with Fum, took him by the elbow. At the cabin, Jac and Ghurub had cloth bags full of food and gourds of water. Wordlessly, they all divided up the supplies and jogged north out of the village.

***

Gareth stumbled. His flesh remembered where Orbo had pushed him and he promised himself retribution for that as well as all the other pushes, punches, kicks, for the ropes and the hangings.

Three days since Orbo had killed his companions and Orbo had grown no more pleasant a travel-mate.

Gareth stood as Orbo reached for him, shook off the hand. He marched ahead as gamely as he could with his hands bound behind him, rope to the elbows. "I can walk."

Orbo scoffed, his voice a mix of humor and malice. "Walk, then. And tell me again about the sword."

Gareth restrained a sigh. "A smith made it at the Starfall. Dipped it in god-water. I stabbed a monster with it and now the monster is inside it."

"Stabbed?"

Gareth instantly regretted the embellishment. "In a way. Not with the sword itself but with the intention of it."

"Intention? Speak sense."

"I can't. It doesn't really make any sense. But you saw what the sword can do."

Yesterday, Orbo had used the blade to slice through trees like they were plump melons. He had tried to bend it with his foot, to snap it by bracing it against a tree stump and pulling on the handle. The sword remained unchanged: black, smoky, menacing.

"Magic." Orbo spat.

"You don't believe in magic." Gareth tripped on a tree root but kept from falling. His whole body hurt as if it were made of bruises and his head was filled with gray wool. His mouth was dead dry. "Doesn't matter. Magic, no magic. I put a man in that sword, a man who was also a jaguar. They're both in there. You don't have to believe that. You only have to believe the bow helps you shoot straight and the sword can cut almost anything and keep its edge and the spear is cursed."

"Why can I not just leave it in the woods?"

"For some poor stranger to find? Cursed things have a way of finding their way into the worst hands." Every night at the longhall had been stories, the myths and legends and histories of a dozen peoples. The lies came easily. "We have to keep it. Protect it. You have the sword and the bow. You can control it. If you are strong."

"I am strong." He paused, though, just for a second between steps. "What if you carry it?"

"Me?" Gareth forced a laugh he did not feel. "I would need hands for that. Even if you untied me now it would be hours before I could grip a spear. And if you don't untie me soon my hands will just fall off. It has been hours since they stopped hurting. Ever tie up a sheep's tail?"

"Sheep?"

"If you let them keep their tails, they shit in them. So you have to dock them when they're still lambs. You take a length of hemp and tie it tightly around the tail, just two fingers from the base. Make it tight. The lamb can't get it off. Two or three days, the tail just drops off. No blood, no nothing. A little longer with my hands tied like this..."

"This is a trick."

"I wish it were," Gareth said. "I like my hands. And I'm going to be hard to sell when they drop off like a lamb's docked tail."

They marched on a while. Gareth worked hard for his balance, for his wind. The gray wool seemed to rise through his vision until he wanted to beg for water, for rest. His footfalls seemed to echo in his head as if the woods were full of people rather than just him and his captor.

"Stop."

Gareth's feet halted in place as if he had been waiting for the command. In a way, he had. Orbo unsheathed the sword. Gareth heard it. It sounded like a snake on dry leaves. He felt a tug on his arms at the shoulders.

"There," Orbo said.

"What?"

"Your arms are free."

"They are?" He looked, saw his arms dangling at his side. He did not feel any different. His hands were blue-black. They might have been bits of charred wood for all he knew of them. Deep marks from the ropes made red rings around his wrists and elbows. Looking made him queasy.

"Here. Take it." Orbo pushed the spear at him.

Gareth tried to reach up to take it but his hands just hung there, inert. The spear pushed against his chest and he fell down on his backside. His teeth clicked. The spear came with him, ending up across his knees.

"Take it. Stand up."

"I can't." The world finally swam off into the gray fog in his head. The sound of footfalls continued all around.

***

Running.

Whilla's breath came short and sharp. Her stomach ached, a sore spot right up under her ribcage. Fum had fallen behind; Guarl, Vault and Xin Ban ran abreast of her, spread out in a line. Together they plunged into the prairie grass like a comb through tangled hair.

No more arrows fell between them. No more shouts followed from behind.

stop rest tired exhausted
danger run death murder

Whilla could not say if she and her friends were more afraid of being killed or of killing again. Even the idea of taking a rabbit for dinner made her stomach turn. In any event, there was no more energy left in her body for running. All guided by the same mind, the four friends dropped from a sprint to a jog to a walk. Panting and sweating, Whilla dropped to her knees and retched. Nothing came up but sour spit.

my parents

Not her parents. Vault's father and mother. A few miles back the soldiers had come close to grazing Whilla with arrows. Jac and Ghurub, leading the way then, had looked at one another. From a few yards back Whilla could sense their connection, their energy. A mutual decision passed between them. They had stopped running in much the same way as Whilla and Xin Ban and Vault and Guarl: without discussion, as one person. They had dropped their packs, drawn weapons, and turned into the pursuit.

A mental battle had erupted over a decision with unclear consequences. Values mixed and clashed, thoughts of courage and cowardice at their head. Fum had pounded past them, still fresh then, hurling himself away from the attackers like a rabbit before wolves. Whilla had followed. They all had.

I would know if they were dead
no they are not like us
let me believe it

It seemed clear enough to Whilla that Jac and Ghurub had given their lives for their son. Jac had grown to fierceness in the halls of the royal palace of Hitai, a place where murder was the only way to survive. And Ghurub... Long ago, he had risked her wrath to bargain for Vault's life. The two of them were all teeth and claws.

let me believe

"Yes," Whilla said. "Believe it. Those two are as much gods as Chess and Moburu."

She felt a wave of gratitude and also of acceptance – painful acceptance. Hearing the generous lie, Vault heard the truth behind it.

Fum caught up. He staggered into the circle they were forming. His skin gave off an awful heat and he stank of his exertions. "Keep." A breath. "Running." "Must."

"Nothing left," Whilla said, surprised at how fast her own breath had returned. "Best to go to ground now. Cover our tracks and hide. We are on the Preserves, at least the edges of them. Dangerous to hurry through them as to dawdle."

"Run," Fum repeated. His sides bellowed in and out. He staggered a few steps then fell to his hands and knees.

Vault stared at him, something in his eyes that Whilla could not quite fathom. Except she could fathom it. It was... contempt. "Ghurub was not the brave one," he said. "It was always Fum leading him into trouble. Their stories at night... Fum was the adventurer, the troublemaker. I've never known him to be so frightened. He did not turn to stand with his friend."

"None of us did," Whilla said.

Vault grimaced. "That might be my nightmare. Like Gareth and what they did to him, I will dream every night of that failure. Maybe we should go back."

Xin Ban put a hand his shoulder. "Not yet. Not like this. What could we do? The dream isn't useless. Remember what they did to Gareth. He is all of us. We ran in there like children, too eager to be heroes. And they..."

"We're stronger now," Vault protested, but weakly. Then: "No, you're right. A whole army and just four of us. Four children and him." He waved his chin at Fum.

"Hitai," Fum said. "Come home with me. We have to warn them. Be a hero by warning our people."

Wind rustled the grasses all around. Whilla glanced back the way they had come, at a line of tall trees that formed a wall, a border. Beyond that was darkness. "Dllyx will kill us all, starting with you and Vault."

"So we hide," Fum said. "Hide in the city. Send a message and run for Lurk or Sorub."

Vault rubbed his temples. "He's right. Not about running. About going to Hitai. My mother told me about it." One hand dropped to his belt, to the sword he had hung there. A thing of green metal bearing Flax' mark. "I have a destiny waiting for me. That's why she turned around. To buy me time to meet it. I have to run into Hitai the way they ran into those soldiers."

Peregrination

Sand stung Ergol's face. The Sun Gate was far behind him and tombs loomed ahead. Dllyx' snake, already wind-blasted and forlorn, showed stone through its paint. The Old Man. A column kept straight by unknown supports under the sand.

Ergol rode an ox. It strained under his weight, the weight of a dozen skins of water. Xenia walked beside him, untroubled by her bronze armor. Behind came a baggage train and a string of guards, all Xenia's hand-picked loyalists. There was a trouble: loyal to Xenia.

I could have stayed a slaver. It was a good life.

The thought was a true one, and also false. A lie he told himself. The slaving life was one of pleasure and sometimes of ease, of relative safety in being faceless. The Chans disguise had some appeals.

But his destiny was here. Beating his brother at last after so many years of exile. The throne. Children of his own, perhaps. A lineage.

His own tomb was out here somewhere. Just as shoddy now as any other after decades in the same sand that scoured his cheeks.

He glanced at Xenia. Haughty Xenia, tall and proud. There was no wiggle in her step now, just the sure strides of a leader. "My tomb is in need of repairs," he said.

"Hm?"

No honorifics. Ergol noticed and was neither surprised nor displeased. "I always hated my father. Old Grandfather. Ynn did too, of course, we both did. But Ynn wished to honor him."

Xenia glanced back at him and kept her pace even.

"Ynn killed the old man. Beat him at the contest of his own choosing. Ynn killed his own best friend to get a chance at him. A bloody mess, by all accounts. Now he is guarded in the afterlife by the man he blinded and murdered so that he could kill his own father."

Xenia maintained her silence and her untroubled look.

Well. We live in the same palace, after all. "When it is my time to die, I want to outdo Ynn, who came home from war mangled and bloody. I want to outdo Bassa, who went into the ground a sad old man, torn to pieces by a jackal, eighty years old. My tomb is in need of repairs and such will be your first job out here."

"Are you the King?" Xenia said.

"What is this, now?"

"The Gravetender might be queried by the King and by none other. And she takes no orders."

"Aha." Ergol suppressed a laugh. "Those fools are gone now. Dllyx killed them all. Good or ill, no more Gravetenders. Not real ones. But you will take the office and do as I ask."

"Why will I?"

Why will she, indeed? I am no King. Barely a regent. A grain of sand slipped past his lashes and into his eye, forcing him to squint and blink. *No good to rub that – only make things worse.*

Xenia surprised him by talking again. "It is said that in the south there are women who follow commands from their husbands."

"Oh?"

"The south is a strange place, of course. They live in houses in the woods, brick houses with slate roofs. They keep dogs and grow fruit in orchards. They bury their dead, all of them, as though people not of The Blood had honor. And sometimes, their women obey their men."

"An interesting thought," he said, blinking. The sand seemed to be gone but his eye still felt the insult. Sunlight blurred through his tears. "No Gravetender ever took a husband."

"As you say, I am not one of those fools with their gray skin and strange dress and obscure manners. I am a woman of Hitai."

"And of no Blood," Ergol retorted.

"Why else make me wear their silly hat than to bestow rank upon me?"

Too clever. Much too clever. "I never asked how many years you have known."

"Thirty and three."

"Too old to bear children."

"Hardly that old. Do you wish them borne?"

He thought of certain favors he had done at the temple and a flush found his neck. Dllyx, thankfully, was not looking. "They would be an inconvenience. An announcement that I might not step down if Jul comes of age."

"Interesting time to leave the city," Dllyx said.

"Your mind is like an antelope: so agile an old lion like me cannot keep up with it."

She eyed him again, perhaps to see if he was teasing. "With disorder in the streets. Dangerous times for an unblooded Prince."

"Unblooded but of The Blood. He will learn quickly. Or else he will not."

"I see," Dllyx said. "When I am installed as Gravetender, I think I know my first project. An old tomb that needs renovation."

***

Is this what Father felt like?

Jul rarely thought of his father. Most of his life, he had been preoccupied with his mother's attempts to murder or humiliate him. The thought felt good, so he dwelt on it a moment.

Two guards flanked him. A big man on his left swung a short sword the way a butcher hefts a cleaver. A bigger woman on his right had more grace, fighting with two short spears at once. Jul mostly tried to stay out of the way. Blood on his chest showed his successes were limited. Silk from Lurk was costly and easily ruined by blood.

The blood of my enemies.

The streets were full of rioters. They had pulled down some of the local buildings so that bits of stone and wood complicated the way forward. Men and women bore improvised weapons: slings and butcher knives tied to sticks and fishing gigs made into spears. One had a leather loop at the end of a pole. He waited for a guard to be distracted by a knife from a nearer assailant then slipped the loop over his neck and pulled him down.

Ten, twenty, maybe more. Counting was not something Jul excelled at. But he had a blase of his own. It was steel, gray and sharp, pointed. The gift Ergol had given him when he was still Chans. Morda, the woman at his right, blocked a charging woman with her body. When he spilled into Jul's path, Jul knelt on his chest and stabbed him in the neck.

Better than counting. Better than dirty scrolls made of ancient animal skins. Better than trying to plan an ambush for his uncle.

Maybe I am my father's son. Maybe I am meant for war and conquering.

Ahead, three women pulled down a soldier. They knocked her on her face then stabbed her in the back with spears, right between the straps of her breastplate. One of them looked up and saw Jul, caught his eyes with hers.

"The Prince!" she said. "Summer Greens indeed! It is Jul himself, all ready for justice!"

The other two women stood up straight. Morda and Waith, his other guard, narrowed the space between them, putting him a little at their backs. One of the women threw her spear. Morda knocked it aside with her own. It bounced and skittered between Waith's feet, bloodying one leg. Waith and Morda crouched low, ready for dirty work.

A rock hit Jul in the cheek. Pain burst out from his face, blinded him, knocked him down.

"Got him!"

Ambush. A trap.

Is this how Father felt?

He heard more stones go by him. He ought to have panicked, he knew that. He had seen enough slaves panic when the cheetah was released from her cage. They went weak, their minds blank, and they ran like frightened hares. But his own mind cleared. The world made sense. It slowed down. His heart eased. The pain in his face seemed both intense and far away.

Jul let himself sink to the ground as though he were dead or dying. He could hear Morda and Waith knocking back the three women with spears, could almost see them with his ears: block, parry, shuffle-step, brace, push, stab, stab. The women disengaged.

And someone else came close.

His guards had not noticed the ambush. Just one man, a small man, hardly bigger than Jul. He dashed in, right into Morda's shadow. His hands found Jul's clothes. Felt up his chest, finding armor under the silk. Jul felt a knife press at his neck. But that was armored, too, with a thick bit of bronze that reached up to his ears. And now the man was on top of him, his own belly exposed.

Jull stuck him with the knife. It slid up under the lowest rib. A lung collapsed and Jul could imagine it in his mind. He had cut the lungs out of many a young jackal, watched them recoil from the knife like they had their own minds. From there it was a short shove to get the blade into the heart.

The assailant shuddered, spasmed, died.

Now Jul was covered in blood. Lurkian silk was costly, of course, but he decided to hang this bit of cloth in the trophy room.

Morda and Waith finished their fight. They were scratched up but hardly hurt.

"Withdraw," Jul said. "This is a fool's fight. It is their city. Let them burn it if they want to. When the rebels have no walls left, we will still have the palace."

***

Ergol called a halt. Behind him, his train of guards and porters clattered to a disorganized stop.

Ahead, half-hidden in heat-shimmer, a band of people stood in Chans' path. Sixty or so of them, he guessed. No more than one mile ahead.

"Sweet Gravetender, tell me what you see out there."

Dllyx squinted into the heat. "Ambushers, maybe. Or workers. Or an embassy of Masters."

"An embassy of fools."

"No way to tell from here. We have twenty competent fighters and a gang of dead weight."

Twenty-one if Ergol could count on his ox to fight.

Bad odds.

"We will skirt around to the west and see what they do." He led the way. An uneasy feeling crept through his guts, like the time Ynn had convinced him to eat a handful of live spiders. They had squirmed and died in his stomach, unable to bite him through the bile and acid but able to wriggle. And the fever he had had later... "Here's hoping I do not soil my trousers. I like these trousers."

"What?" Dllyx said, not looking at him. She had eyes only for the band of people in their way.

"Nothing. It looks like they are following us, moving to stay in our way. What does that tell us?"

"Precious little. An embassy would do the same."

Ergol raised his voice. "Weapons." Behind him, guards rattled themselves into soldiers. To Dllyx, he said, "Send a scout ahead to find out who they are and what they want."

"Yes, Great One. Bobe. Run ahead. Get close enough to see. If they are armed for war, ride back directly. If they appear as Masters, ask what they want."

The soldier detached from the group and trotted forward into the sand between the two groups. He was tall and lanky, dressed in bronze plate that covered his chest and shins and head. A short red cape swayed behind him as he ran. Soon he was all but lost in a fog of choking dust that rose up and clung to the air as if it might never settle.

Ergol waited. The ox snorted and shuffled his feet. The day was too hot even for biting flies but the beast was still anxious.

"An ox is no horse," Dllyx said.

Ergol glanced down at her. When he looked back at the dust, Bobe was truly lost to sight. "Ynn bred these ones to be like horses, to pull chariots. Very interested in husbandry, he was." That thought led directly to Ergol's deformed foot; a twinge of pain reminded him why he tried not to think about it too much.

"How old is that thing?"

"Not so old. The keepers followed his plan, advanced the stock after he was gone."

"There is too much dust, as if Bobe raised a storm with his heels."

Ergol agreed. Now he could see nothing of his scout and nothing at all of the party waiting ahead. It was as if a dust storm had arisen between them but nowhere else.

The ox snorted again.

He's as uneasy as I am.

A shadow moved in the dust cloud, a shape. Ergol strained to see, leaned forward on his mount, causing the ox to shamble forward two paces. The shape was a man, a man coming closer. "Bobe? What did you see?"

The man said nothing. He seemed to have his helmet in one hand, and to be limping, almost lurching. He stepped into clear air and dropped to his knees.

Bobe looked up at Dllyx. He opened his mouth to speak and blood ran over his lips. He gurgled one word: "Ambush." Then he fell on his face. An arrow stood up from his back.

Soldiers stepped out of the whirling sand. Household guards armed with spears and short bronze swords. Behind them, someone else lurked in the wind-driven dust.

Ergol had no time to consider whom. He raised the javelin he had not even been aware of drawing out, and shouted, "Fight!"

Hands

The pain was immense and immeasurable. Gareth lay on his back under a sky heavy with stars. A small clearing in the woods allowed for a little breeze to cool his fever. The fever made him sweat and the breeze made him shiver. But the pain came from his arms, just above the elbows.

Below them, he could still feel nothing at all.

He tried again to flex his fingers. He might as well have tried to flex the stars in the sky. They were dead.

Gareth laughed. Somewhere in his head, he knew the laughter was no good, that it was a step towards madness. But madness might be a relief from the pain, the fever, the knowledge that he would live briefly as a man with no hands and then die of the rot.

Orbo slept nearby. He had no fire, no blankets, but just lay in tall grass with his arms around his collection of stolen weapons. Before laying down, he had propped the short spear point-up in the ground, braced with rocks.

"Looks like you're dead, boy," he had said. "Maybe your spear is cursed after all. Killing you slow." Then he had nodded at the thing, at the dark metal and the gaudy tassels.

Gareth knew what he meant. Slow or quick. But the spear was not killing him; Orbo had done that by binding his hands so tightly for so long. The idea amused him: Orbo had left him a perfect weapon to exact revenge but no hands to wield it.

I wish I had a fire.

A fire was no good, though. It would only make him sweat more and therefore lose more heat to the breeze.

In the darkness, something moved.

These were the great woods, the nearly impenetrable barrier between the Greenlands and Hitai, a great, thorny peacekeeper. Something was always moving out here, even at night. Owls, bats, little fruit eaters with giant eyes. Bugs.

But this was something else. Something deliberate. Slow, stealthy. Trying to be unheard but failing, rustling through a pile of broken twigs.

Gareth thought about calling out. *Who are you? What do you want?* But the questions lacked meaning. Gareth was dead; the names and intentions of the living inspired no special feelings in him. Another spasm of shivering twisted his spine and he groaned.

"Shut up," Orbo said, his voice blurry with sleep. Then he sat up. He rubbed his eyes, just a shadow in the starlight. "Did you hear that?"

"No," Gareth said. He gritted his teeth and tried not to moan again. Orbo was not a good man and yet he was alive while Gareth was dead; no reason to bother his rest. "Go back to sleep."

A twig snapped from the edge of the clearing to the north. Orbo got to his feet and swished the sword back and forth in front of him, low and menacing.

Moburu.

Something clattered to the west. Orbo turned his head that way, then his body. "Circling," he said. When he glanced south, a shape came from the direction of the first sound – north – quiet as a whisper in the dark. Steel flashed. Orbo died quietly, spilling into the grass.

Gareth giggled and wished he could stifle the noise by stuffing his hands into his mouth, but nothing worked below his shoulders. The shadow came closer. It stood over him, blocking out the stars.

"You."

He knew the voice. The one word was enough. He had sworn never to forget her, to forget what she had done to him. "I wanted to kill you," he said. "Ever since I met you."

"Many men have said so," Zhang muttered. "With good enough reasons. Now you are free, what will you do? Take up that spear. Stab me if you can." She laughed. "I have watched you and this oaf who would be a slaver. Nothing offends me like slaves."

"Kill me then. I've been dying ever since you..."

"Do not say it. You will wish I was raping you again when I am done saving your life. That I promise." She backed away.

Gareth faded out for a while. He woke up to the smell of smoke. Zhang had made a fire. It crackled cheerily, sending white smoke up into the night.

Now Zhang turned back to the fallen Orbo and stripped off his leather belt. Her steel sword cut it well enough into the shape she wanted. Gareth fought when she stuffed it into his mouth but he had little left to oppose her with. "Bite that or lose your tongue along with your hands." Then she tied strips of leather around Gareth's arms at the biceps. Tight. Too tight. They bit hard.

He tried to protest but his head filled up with gray smoke again.

My hands. Don't take my hands. My arms.

Even Ham back at the Starfall had one arm to work with. One good hand to haul on nets and wipe his backside.

She's going to take my hands.

The gray finally swept his thoughts aside. A mercy. He did not feel what came next.

***

Whilla stumbled. Insects buzzed around her; locusts leaped from her path into the tall grass on either side.

"You well?" Xin Ban said.

Whilla heard the echo of the words in her thoughts, a reverberation through the other minds around her. More, she felt the thoughts: a concern, a worry, a hint of annoyance.

"Only tired," Whilla said. "Seems we've been walking all my life now. From Starfall to Hong to that little village, hardly a moment in each place." She did not mention that their water was running low but they all knew.

"No time for rest now," Fum said. He had lost weight in the last few days. His ribs showed through tight skin going sallow. His eyes roamed around the scenery, suddenly darting towards this sound or that. "They will kill us if they catch us."

They pressed on, Fum in front where he broke a trail for his smaller companions, Guarl behind, then Whilla and Xin Ban. Vault plodded along behind, a sullen rear-guard.

He doesn't want to go.

Why should he? His parents are behind us.
Dead.
Dead.
We never saw their bodies.
Hope is dangerous.

Again, the thoughts echoed and mixed and reverberated, becoming a feeling – a shared, sullen anxiety. Each thought had no source and not target. It just floated up between them.

Vault had the green sword in his hands. It wanted for a good sheath but such things took time and resources. It would have to wait. Whilla could hear him thinking on the function of swords: how strong was its edge? What could it cut? Could he win through to his parents with it?

She kept on marching, her own weapon reduced to the status of walking stave for now. Vault had not been with them when she and Xin Ban and Guarl and Gareth had used it to kill the raider, not far from here. He had not been with them as their guilt grew and compounded, as Gareth learned how his killing made killers of them all.

Could I swing this spear in anger?

That thought met with little response. It only hung there, as weighty as the spear itself.

"Maybe they deserve to be conquered," Guarl said. "Hitai. A nation that holds people in slavery. To be a child there, and not have royal blood... what a life."

Fum spoke from the front, his voice trembling. "Vault has The Blood."

"Weakly, through Jac," Xin Ban said. "Which does nothing for all the slaves."

Fum said, "You could end those practices. Make Hitai worthy of saving."

"How?" Vault said. "One frightened man and four people hardly out of childhood, not a cup of The Blood between them?"

"You have it," Fum said. "More than your mother has it. Vault, Ghurub was my friend. He agreed to act as your father, to marry your mother. We all agreed on it. To save you from what we now run towards."

Vault stopped where he was. "Ghurub was my father."

"Yes," Fum said, not stopping. "Come on, no time for delay, if you like your skins. These people are ruthless. Their leader is a God, a real one, with magic to cut her enemies apart."

Vault stood where he was and the others halted, too.

Whilla tried to focus on Fum but the thoughts rolling around their collective mind were too much, too distracting. Chaos, a mix of feelings and ideas and images. She covered her ears and of course that did not help because the noise was inside.

"You are my son," Fum said. "I sent you to the Starfall to protect you. You cannot know what it was like to live in that place, that palace – Moburu would have murdered you, in fact tried to but hit the wrong target. My baby brother, your uncle... he skinned the boy and a servant Mo took to be Bumbu's mother. Presented them to Father."

"What are you saying?" Vault muttered. His words were soft and quiet but Whilla felt the rage.

"Nothing more," Fum continued. "You have heard it all now. In the desert is a tomb with my brother's skin, a tomb built for you should you ascend to the throne of Hitai. It is still there, meaning the Gravetenders have not acknowledged your loss. They know you will come back one day. And I am taking you back there." He looked at the ground through the whole speech and, when it was done, turned to push through the tall grass again. He left little trails of blood on the stalks from a thousand tiny cuts, the consequences of a headlong flight.

Their thoughts trembled like Fum's voice. Whilla had known none of this, not a word of it. None of them had. She and Xin Ban and Guarl all turned their eyes to Vault. Their thoughts slowly converged. All four thought the same thing: *Prince of The Blood.*

***

The smell of blood and smoke soaked the night. Zhang, not ordinarily prone to flights of queasiness, took a few steps away from the rough camp and threw up into the underbrush. Food had been scarce enough that her stomach was nearly empty anyway.

The boy...no, the young man. Why did I save him? Why not let him die, let the slaver decide whether to bury him?

What she had said was true. Zhang hated slavery and hated slavers more.

***

Her war was over. The Hitaians had taken her trophy, the great steel sword that the big black man had stashed in the rafters. They had talked with one another for a while. Zhang had known she was the topic of conversation but could follow none of their speech, not then.

After a night on a cold, hard bench underground, she woke up to a prod. One of the guards had the shaft of his spear in Zhang's ribs. On another day she might have torn it from the man's hands and stuck it into the hole between his buttocks but this day she hardly had the energy to grumble. He poked her again and she stood, sullen as a wet cat.

There were three of them, all dressed in the neat bronze breasts and greaves and helmets of the Tomblands Guard. A man and two women, none as big as Zhang but all with armor and weapons. In her despair, it never occurred to her that she might make them kill her the way the Starfallers should have.

They talked at her in their barbaric Hitaian speech but the gestures she understood: up the stairs, back out into the punishing sunlight.

Up there, they stripped off her ragged clothing. Slaves came and threw buckets of sand over her. *As if I need to be dirtier.* The slaves were women with grayish skin dressed in cloth more suitable for grain than people. Downcast eyes told her their position. They pointed and chattered at her, too, but she understood nothing of what was happening.

Then they swept her down with brushes, course at first then soft and fine. Finally, she was allowed to dress in a gown of that sack cloth. It was too small, concealing little while at the same time binding at her shoulders. Again, despair did not allow the thought of fighting, not yet, so she put on the garment and let herself be herded into a group of passing slaves.

They marched into the heat until they came to a particular tomb. A foreman handed out bronze bars and heavy mallets. She stuck one in Zhang's hands. Zhang let it drop from her hands into the dust at her feet. Around her, silence fell.

The foreman pointed at the hammer and jabbered. Zhang, wishing she were dead, just ignored her. The foreman raised a little leather whip, suitable for goading one of the tiny horses that lived around the Starfall. She raised her voice and the slaves around Zhang started to edge away.

Then an enforcer came out of the sand. He had a longer whip, a real one made of bull hide. He backhanded her in the face with it, with the mass near the handle. That hurt enough to get her attention and Zhang snatched at the whip.

Then, sudden as a sea storm, she was surrounded by enforcers. They held her still while the first man lashed her back with the whip. That pain was a revelation, an awakening. When they were done, she lay in the sand panting and moaning like a first year recruit after her first battle wound.

The foreman came back prodded her with one foot until Zhang stood up. She put the hammer into her hands again and this time Zhang took it. Then the foreman pointed to a stretch of wall where other slaves worked. Some broke up the surface with the overlarge hammers while others dug into the new cracks with the bars to pull away the facing.

That night she slept on a wool blanket barely big enough for the local slaves that at least kept her face and chest out of the sand. She slept face down because the wounds to her back allowed nothing else.

If only I could cry.

She knew there was something under that thought, something about having a future. But she turned away from it.

A slave came around with balm in a clay pot. Zhang let her apply it to her cuts, wincing like a child whenever the cool hands touched her. The slave's words were alien but her tone was understandable: comfort and peace. Things Zhang had never known, not since she was a child.

Morning came cold and dewy. The crew went back to work demolishing the tomb. They were fanciful things, but Zhang did not notice. A slave brought water and she drank. Another brought mealy suet and she ate. These were things she knew: work, eat, drink.

There was another thing she knew, though. Until the woman with the red spear had cut her sword into pieces like a fishwife slices bread, until that day Zhang had been the foremost warrior in the world. Unbeaten and unbeatable.

The wall came down. They marched to another wall and broke it. They marched to a quarry to load stones onto wagons. Her wounds healed. She earned more wounds and those healed, too.

Every wall she levered down, something broken inside her mended a little. Masters and slaves had built these things she broke. The Starfaller had broken the thing she had built... but she mended it. These tombs were memories and she wrecked them all. Memories of gods and kings. Memories of her own smarting defeat.

But she wasn't defeated. She had strong hands, skin made for this sun, arms made to wield weapons.

Then, one morning weeks later, the overseer put that hammer into Zhang's hands. "Work there," she said. Zhang understood them now, if they spoke slowly and simply.

Zhang dropped the hammer into the dust between them. "Not today."

The overseer touched the absurd little whip at her belt. "I will call the underseers."

Zhang started walking. One way was as good as another out here, no good choices between directions except this one: away from here. Behind her, the Overseer started shouting. Zhang smiled at the woman's loss of composure.

One of the underseers came running from around the tomb they were meant to demolish. He rushed for Zhang like she was just another slave. But she was not a slave and never had been. She was the greatest living warrior not aided by a god. When the man ran at her she stepped to one side and tripped him and just kept walking.

Two more ran at her from behind. She stopped suddenly, took a step backwards and was behind them. She dragged them together, bounced them off one another, and let them fall to the ground. One of their whips became a trophy.

Zhang thought of her garb and the desert all around and wondered if one of the men's clothes might fit her. In that time, she was surrounded by Underseers. They always appeared out of the desert like magical things from children's stories. There were enough to compel her back to work.

"This time we are going to kill you," one said.

But Zhang did not care. All she knew then was that she was a warrior and warriors are not for labor. They are for killing. Live or die, she would be who she was.

Then one of the slaves tossed her a hammer. The wrecking hammers had heavy bronze heads like two fists pushed together and shafts longer than her arm. She caught it from the air with a brief thought that the slave throwing it was in for a serious beating.

All of the underseers stepped away. Zhang held the hammer like a fighter, not like a slave.

When she was done, there was nobody left to hurt the slave who had helped her. He was Zhang's first recruit.

***

Remembered hate filled Zhang with a warm glow the fire just could not provide. The glade stank of what she had needed to do to Gareth: the amputation, the cauterization; it stank of cooking flesh as the rotten parts of him turned to ashes in the bonfire alongside the Slaver who had nearly killed him. It stank of a life saved for the sake of hate.

All these smells she had endured before. She had done worse and for worse reasons. A hundred battlefields lay behind her and all their consequences. And there, on a pile of pine needles, mercifully unconscious, was the young man himself. He was naked under Zhang's own thin, gray blanket. He looked sad and weak, sallow, sickly.

If he woke, and sometimes they didn't wake when bits were cut off them, if he woke he might not thank Zhang for saving him. She had not thanked Chess for not killing her. In her heart, Zhang still wanted a chance to kill her in single combat.

Let him hate me. Only the living can hate.

She untied the mallet from her belt and stared at it for a time before finally tossing it into the fire to burn away.

Lineage

Chans laughed. That action hurt his ribs which should have made him stop but he only laughed harder and hurt more.

Broke my chest.

His right side was bloody. A bit of bronze stood out from between two ribs, a snapped-off spear blade. Those bones were almost certainly broken. Chans' breaths were short and shallow and his vision misty red.

We've won.

Corpses lay in the sand. Dust settled slowly on the bodies, sticking in bloody wounds, resting in hair spread out on the ground, blotting the scene as though a clumsy scribe had been here rather than a hundred screaming fighters.

I beat him again. I am alive.

That thought made no sense: Ynn was long in his grave, gone to dust like this desert. Chans looked about to see who was with him on this side of death. Ten guards with bloody spears and bloody faces. Servants from the supply chain who had caught up and wished they had not. An animal handler.

Xenia was not among those milling about between the bodies. Not among the walking wounded.

He looked at the ground, at each of the corpses. Armed as Tomblands Guards, these attackers were clearly something else – people of mixed races, half-Bloods, tradespeople with hard hands but little training. And there, in the back, a scrawny man wearing a silver kilt. Chans stood over him. With one foot, he flipped the man over to see his face.

The priest. Rept.

They have what they need from me and now they try to remove me – with open warfare.

That seemed too simple. The priests had never risked confrontation. But then, Dllyx had murdered the Gravetenders and threatened the Priesthood with death and dissolution. Equally unprecedented. A peace was needed but Chans could not see a way towards it.

A hand touched his shoulder and he sprang away, raising a broken spear he had forgotten he was holding. Grinning, he spun to see who had touched him.

"They will pay for this," Xenia said.

Chans dropped the spear and the grin. He grabbed Xenia with the arm on his good side and dragged her close. "I thought I had lost you."

"You had. I got cut off in the dust. My battle moved away west. But these were poor soldiers. Just dressed-up slaves."

"Are you hurt?"

"A little."

Chans held her at arms' length and scanned her for injuries. There was a cut on her face that would make another fine scar and her knees were marred by sandy scabs. Her knuckles were bloody. As he watched, a blowfly landed on one finger and sent out its little tongue. She shook it off absently, causing more blood to flow.

"They will pay," Xenia repeated.

"They already have," Chans said.

"I heard you laughing."

"Laughing?"

"And when I came upon you, you smiled like an efreet. I thought you would kill me. Dance away with my bones in your mouth."

"Smiled?"

"Your brother. They said the battle-madness came over him. He and Shimb would tell stories together when they thought none could hear them. About old conquests, battles with the Greenlanders and the Lurkians. He always hated ruling. Preferred braining men with his scepter."

Chans let his eyes crawl over the dead once more; like flies, they lit on this corpse and then that one, tasting each. *Like Ynn. Like Ynn after all.* Ynn had not believed in burying the dead. Out here, away from the city's water, in the dry of the desert, they would turn slowly into sand, bits and pieces carried away by the things that lived under this sun.

Guards, their pockets full of the trinkets of the dead, started to pull the bodies together for a bonfire. Ynn would burn neither his enemies nor his friends.

"Chans?"

He glanced at Xenia, saw her staring at him with a worried look in her eye. "He was a monster. Killer, tyrant, ruthless seeker after power. In the end he even raped his own daughter."

She reached out to touch the puckered flesh where the spear had taken him. He winced but did not flinch away. Xenia took the metal between her fingers and pulled. It came away with a wet, sucking sound; blood flowed freely now from the wound to patter in the sand next to the dead priest. "He was strong," she said. Then she put the broken shard of blade into his hand.

"No fires," Chans called. "Send a runner for more guards but say nothing of this. The woman or man who speaks of it will lose her eyes and her jaw. When we are at strength, make this whole scene disappear."

"Chans?" Xenia said. "Disappear?"

"Bind your wounds. Bind mine. Then pretend they never happened. There is more here than can be seen – a plot within a plot, a clumsy attack hiding something more."

***

Jul walked to the throne room with two guards in attendance. Wilp and Messa were young, as guards went. Finding people who had not served his mother and who had never beaten him or seen him beaten had meant going deep into the rosters, into new recruits.

There were already people in the room. Jul had ordered no petitions today, preferring to focus on issues of justice. He mounted the steps up to the throne and settled himself, his guards behind and to either side, then focused on his visitors.

The first piece of business was a report from a city guard. He was a small man with tight skin, his silver kilt banded with gold. Almost enough rank to live in the residences.

"Marshall of the Watch?" Jul said, inviting comment.

"My, uh, Prince. The last report I gave was to your father. Your mother did not hear my words."

"The slave she elevated has left the palace, marshal. When I kill my uncle, you will be restored to full command of our forces. If the news is good, that is."

"As to that..." The man squinted and looked sideways, a sour gesture. "Someone ordered a full withdrawal. Not what I would have wanted. Still... rioting went on overnight and part of the morning. Some of the newer temples were pulled apart." By newer, he meant places The Blood might frequent. "Then the usual uneasy peace settled in. You were rumored dead, young Prince, caught by an assassin."

"Still alive," Jul said. "So the retreat worked out well."

"Perhaps. I should like words with the captain that started it. Makes us look weak."

Jul held his tongue. The Master he had taken from the Tomblands still awaited more of his ministrations. That thought and the memories of the last session gave him a sense of peace and calm. "I hope you get your chance," was all he said.

The marshal left and two more supplicants came in. One was the priest. He forgot her name but she was from the temple of whores. A young girl stood by her side, pressed against her leg like a baby but more likely eleven or twelve years of age. She had gray skin and hazel eyes, dark hair that hung down to her shoulders in tight, kinky ringlets.

"What is this?" Jul said, eyes creeping over the girl's body. She had on a cotton shift that left her arms and legs mostly bare. Her skin was smooth and unblemished. A temptation.

"Great One," Myrsa said, hiding a faint smile when Jul switched his attention to her. "This is Warro. My keeper asked me to introduce her to you and to commend her to your service."

"Service?"

"Yes, Great One. Warro?"

The child spoke. "Great One, if it pleases you, The Mistress of the Temple has noted you have particular habits."

"Habits?" Jul clicked his jaw shut, reflecting that his vocabulary seemed to have shrunken to repeating the last word he had heard. This was no way to rule a kingdom. But there was drool gathering in the corner of his mouth. "Guards, wait outside." Once they were gone, he nodded to the girl. "Now you can speak freely."

"As you wish," she said. "Everyone of importance in Hitai knows you enjoy inflicting pain on animals, and they suspect you wish the same for children. The Mistress calls this sadism. She understands that a measure of cruelty is necessary for a King, especially for one not yet come into his crown."

Jul struggled for words, and came up with, "Is that what she says?"

"Yes, Great One. And even more: that she wishes to help you nurture this gift of cruelty but to learn discretion – another necessary trait for a ruler. To that end, she sends Myrsa with me as a gift for you."

Lessons. Mother taught lessons. So did Wyrrn. "What is the nature of this gift? How would you serve me?"

"I would be your companion, Great One. An innocent. You can do whatever you wish with me. To me. Whatever, whenever."

The bead of spit snuck out of the corner of Jul's mouth and slid down his chin. He wiped it away with a trembling hand. "My uncle... he thwarts such play when it goes beyond dogs."

Myrsa smiled again, openly this time. "Great One, let us worry about Chans or Ergol or whatever he calls himself now. It was convenient to use him to bring this to pass: you upon the throne as you belong. And for some other purposes. Now I am sad to say he has gone into the sand and if he returns from the desert, it will be as a changed man."

Jul sat forward now, his heart tripping. "Have you caused him to come to harm?"

"Of course not, Great One. However, your mother changed the rules. When she murdered the Gravetenders and threatened the Priesthood, she upset a delicate balance that we would restore – starting with having the right Blood on the throne. And starting with this offering."

"The girl."

"Yes."

"There is a price," Jul said, his eyes back on Warro. "That is how you work, yes?"

Myrsa laughed. "Yes, a price. A small one. You will come to visit my temple, to meet my Mistress."

"I know what happens in that place. I will not go."

"You will, when the time is right for what happens there. But for now, only to meet the Keeper, Mistress."

"Let me think on it," Jul said, but it was a bluff. Sweat stood out on his forehead. His hands gripped the armrests on his throne to still their trembling. That skin, smooth and unblemished, ripe for something sharp. For something hot. That honeyed voice – oh, to hear her cry out...

"Very well."

Jul was not sure if Warro or Myrsa had spoken and he did not care. The two turned and walked to the doors. He watched her and lusted.

"Wait!" he called.

The two stopped just outside the doorway, not turning around.

Jul took a moment to compose himself, to even out his voice, to find words once more. "Leave her. Warro, come stand beside me. You can listen as I mete out justice today."

Warro reached up to squeeze Myrsa's hand, then walked back into the room. Her step was light, happy, almost a skip. "Great One," she said with a nod, and took her place.

***

"They did not succeed."

That voice in the dark. Myrsa shuddered. Usually, Mistress spoke like a person, a woman of old age but good health. Sometimes, though, there was something else in the sound of her. Something dry and rasping like dead leaves scraping together. "No, Mistress. Chans went on to the Masters' camp. Our man says he was at full strength. He says Chans seemed to be wounded but he could not be certain. His woman kept her face covered, said it was for a devotional purpose."

"Rept?"

"Killed in the attempt."

"That, at least, is according to plan." Her voice was more normal again. Just a woman in the shadows, this time in a stairwell that led down into a basement. The smell of old grain came up from there, fruity and sharp.

Myrsa considered moving one step down, closer to Mistress. Perhaps she smelled of something, or perhaps she could see something of her outline. But she resisted the temptation. None could say they had ever seen Mistress' face, not even the eldest. "Perhaps it is for the best, after all. We still have not made certain of the boy."

"We have all the offerings we need from Chans. The girl is quick."

"Yes, Mistress. Accidents happen, even so, and it is only the one offering. Were she to sicken, or the child..."

"Unlikely."

"Yes." Myrsa listened closely for some further cue, some clue. For the sound of a breath or a rustle of fabric. She heard nothing. Soon, Myrsa began to wonder whether she was not alone in the stairwell.

Then Mistress spoke again. "Hubris."

"Mistress?"

"You are quite right. We must breed him as much as we can. The Blood grows scarce. We know Ynn had enough of it; he was the King, after all. Chans was cut from the same bolt of fabric but his deformity says he is too concentrated. And still, we must save what we can of this line."

"Yes, Mistress."

"Bring him to me."

Myrsa's eyes widened and her mouth opened. Then she realized she had lost her composure and collected it. "As a prisoner or a guest?"

"Oh, the latter, for now. I will find you again in a few days."

"Yes, Mistress." Myrsa climbed the two steps to the top and into the hallway. A torch burned twenty feet away. A black mark on the wall showed it had been burning for many years: soot piled on soot until the mark bulged out. She moved just slightly farther into the hallway and then stopped.

Curiosity is not a good trait for high priests.

Mistress had never been known to change her mind on a thing. And the girl, the temptation, was unprecedented. Myrsa remembered how she had been delivered, up this very stairwell.

A man, just a merchant, had sat sipping wine. His donations were steel coins and steel coins bought a lot of food; while his blood was weak, there were women of equally unlikely birth to give him what he wanted. Myrsa had asked after his interests.

"Young," he had said. "And plump. I care little for how ugly she is so long as her belly is round."

"Round bellies are hard to come by in troubled times."

He had dropped a handful of coins on the ground next to his seat. One of them spun there, making a delicious noise. "Most places. Not here. Good larder here, yes?"

"Oh yes."

Then an attendant had come up from the stairs in back. "Mother."

"What is it?"

The woman had come close, put her mouth to Myrsa's ear. "Smoke, Mother. From the deep chambers."

"Fire?"

"You should see."

"Excuse me," she had told the merchant, and stepped quickly away. She instructed the attendant and then trotted down stairs, along a hallway, down more stairs. Again and again through a maze both horizontal and vertical. To this place.

Smoke.

But it had not been smoke, not from a fire. What sort of fire left glowing mist behind it? And what sort of fire could burn down there in the places where the air grew old? The air shimmered with green and red light, sparkling and diffuse, dimming. And a shape moved in it, setting the light to swirling. A person. A child.

She came up the stairs. Naked and hairless, lacking eyebrows, features indistinct, she seemed something other than human. The child seemed to change as she closed, growing a little older, a little more substantial. Long, hooked fingers shrank into less disturbing dimensions; hair graced her scalp; her face flattened out and took on definite proportions.

"Mistress sent me," the girl had said. "To help you."

The voice... it had that strange, far-away quality Mistress took on when she was angry. "What are you?"

The child had smiled. It was a winning smile, practiced and fluid, and Myrsa smiled back. "Just a girl. Mistress said you knew what to do with me. I am to be playmate to a Prince."

The lights had all but dispersed by then and the girl looked quite ordinary in the dim torchlight. Just a little detail, a small thing really: the air was cool and the child was naked, but there was no hint of gooseflesh.

Now, those memories flashing through her mind, Myrsa thought about taking a step or two back to the stairwell. Perhaps to listen and perhaps to follow Mistress down, into the deepest parts, beyond even where the grain was stored.

What wonders must be down there? And what horrors? Tombshade-dreams and magics...

But she knew what was down there, after all: only things that mortal people were not meant to see. Myrsa sighed, set her feet to motion, and began the long climb back up through the temple. She had another errant Prince to manage.

To Ground

The city took shape on the horizon: a brown smudge with vertical and horizontal straight lines marking it out from the natural environment. Guarl's feet were filthy with mud from the riverbank.

For its part, the water sloshed and burbled along as though nothing were wrong with the world this morning. Fifty feet wide, slow-moving and silty, the water moving out into the Preserves made Guarl feel as though he were walking twice as fast in the other direction.

Thoughts whirled and swirled around in his head. The river hung up on a rotten log and spun out away from it in a weird eddy that made terrain on the flat plane a swirl described in bubbles, and that was the state of Guarl's mind – or the mind he shared with all his companions but Fum.

"If we stay near the river, we will come to a gate," Fum said. "Best not to talk to any soldiers. Not yet."

Xin Ban answered him but her mouth formed words for all of them. "I thought we were going to warn Hitai. Why not start with the soldiers? They will tell the rulers and we can just keep on moving."

Fum looked defeated. As usual, he was somewhat ahead of the group. His feet showed his nerves with short, rapid steps, and now his shoulders slumped. His back rounded as his head sank. "We should just push through the city and go on north. We will be safe there."

"For a time," Xin Ban said.

For a time.

Because whoever the invader was might not stop with Hitai. They did not seem to have stopped with the Greenlands. No place would be safe, not forever.

Guarl said, "What good is safety?" The vortex in his mind twisted around that idea, spun out from it like the water from the log in the river.

Xin Ban wanted safety not to void danger but to avoid the most basic response to danger: killing. Whilla wanted to protect her friends. She wasn't afraid of danger for her own part but for the harm that might befall Xin Ban or Guarl or Vault, and especially of making them more guilty by sharing her aggression with them. Vault wanted a confrontation. He had not shared in stabbing that man on the plains, had not shared in Gareth's suffering.

Guarl could not tell what he wanted for himself. It was all so mixed up, blended together, he could not tell if he were a person any longer.

"Safety is its own good," Fum said.

Guarl felt Vault's anger. It was hot and cold at once, clear and bright.

Vault said, "When did you become such a coward?"

Fum stopped where he was. He turned around like a deer startled by a sudden noise. "What did you say?"

"I said, you have become a coward."

"I always was," Fum said. "That is how you survive the palace. That is how you survive being born with The Blood."

"I remember a different man," Vault said. He stepped close to Fum, who flinched away. "I remember a man who taught me to hunt. Who stood for us when we moved out to that village. Thirty villagers with poles and knives and you faced them down. They called us slavers. You showed them we were peaceful people. That man is gone now. This new man... I don't know who you are."

Fum shook his head. "I do not remember that day. No – a lie. I remember it differently. I recall fear. Only fear. They had machetes. They stood in a line, facing us down. And I... I..."

Guarl had not been there, but he remembered now through Vault's mind. There was Fum, tall and proud in the dappled sunlight, full of arrogance but also something else: a sardonic humor, a diffusing smile. *Thanks to you for the welcome,* he'd said. *We are honored by it. But truly, we hardly deserve such attention. Let us earn it with our skills at fishing and farming.*

A brave stand in the face of fear.

So who was this man who always led the way as if he could not get away from the south fast enough?

"I lost something," Fum said. "Back there. Where we came from. I left something behind."

"What?" Vault said. Xin Ban and Whilla both adopted his posture: leaning forward, frowning, fists on hips. Guarl checked his own body and found he had done the same without thinking it. "You said something about a god, a real one."

"I cannot say," Fum mumbled. "I have forgotten again. I only know we have to get away from there. We have to escape."

"Then lead us," Xin Ban said. "Lead us somewhere safe, safe for the moment, and then we'll talk about what comes next.

Fum turned and started to walk again. His steps were still short and rapid but now less mincing. Some element of confidence returned. "This way. We can go around the Sun Gate, straight into the city."

"How will we climb the wall?" Whilla said.

"No wall. Only a gate."

All four friends were confused. "A gate with no wall? Like a door into no building?" Guarl couldn't tell who had said the words aloud. Him, another, what was the difference?

"It stands free," Fum said. "A ceremonial thing, hardly functional. Conquerors ride through it. We would go that way to visit the Tomblands. Delegations to the dead. The Sun Gate purifies all who pass beneath. But we will remain unclean."

Guarl thought of his dirty feet. "There are other ways to wash your body."

Fum turned again. "It is not our bodies that need cleansing."

***

Zhang crouched next to the young man's body. The fire had burned down for the third time. She was sure there was nothing in there now but ash. The last time she had built up the fire she had made it a pyre of absurd proportions. It had burned thirty feet high.

Now she stank of wood smoke. It was in her hair, on her skin. She could see it, a waxy, dark soot. *But at least the insects have fled the area.*

A smaller fire still burned, well away from the dead pyre. Squirrel meat boiled in a cup of water. The boy was thin. What was left of him was eating itself. He had not opened his eyes in six days and Zhang feared she had killed him. Each day that fear came and went. After all, what was the boy to her? Just some stranger, a person who had stood between her and her goals and was now surplus to any need.

Even so, some feeling nagged at her.

"He's one of us."

That was a long ago voice.

She had taken ship from Orpha, just a young woman with dreams of gold and glory. She was going to wrest some fortune from the world at the point of a bronze sword. That was what the Captain had told her.

Different time, different Captain. This had been a slight man with a voice much bigger than his body, a verbal tyrant who could flay with his tongue while laughing.

The ship was a fat-bottomed thing with one giant sail. Not a lot of rigging, not like one of the newer ships that could get away from the coastline. And still, a young soldier, young as Zhang, had managed to tangle himself in a line at the wrong time. It had zipped along the deck as the sail went up and half his leg had snicked off as if slashed with a sword.

He lay there on the deck in a pool of his own blood, gargling and dying.

"Throw him overboard. Here, let me do it." Zhang had been strong even then – strong and merciless.

"He's one of us." That was the Captain. "Sew up the veins and bathe the wound in wine."

"He will suffer," Zhang said, "and die anyway."

"So will we all," Captain said. "Life is suffering and none more than the soldier's life. Don't waste any more time now. Sew him."

Zhang spat on the deck. Wind swept through her hair and relieved some of the sweat from her skin, made it sticky with ocean salt. Over head, a blue sky indifferent to living or dying.

"Do not let me die." The young soldier on the deck. "I never even got to fight."

Zhang knelt. Someone tossed her a bone needle and some cotton thread. She set to sewing.

Now, crouching over a pot of squirrel meat, she could not quite remember the name of the young man. Captain had been there, the one she knew as Captain – seven feet tall and a jolly killer. He had still owned a name then and she could not remember that, either. But the boy had survived his wound. They had made a peg for him to fasten to his stump and he had limped into battle with them in Lurk.

Two years more, he had lived. Two years of raping and killing. He had died with something to his name: victories, a small handful of copper coins, a helmet made of a metal none could identify.

Gareth moaned, breaking her reverie. A glance showed he was no closer to life than a moment ago. His skin had gone from sweating to puckering with cold. Not much to do about that: the clearing was as hot as a rock in the sun. Her eyes flicked over the stump nearest her. Shoddy sewing work there, but holding. He did not move around much, which helped. The healing went slow. And in the end, what would he be?

Would he die one day in the future with something to his name? Or would he die in this clearing, with only her as witness, as indifferent as the sky over that ship, over that nameless boy long ago?

I should take his treasures and go. This is bootless.

Certainly she could not care for him for the rest of her life. It was hard even to remember why she had intervened so far. He was no business of hers. No concern.

The soup was ready. She sipped it. Thought. Eventually, half the soup was gone and the remainder was cooling. And the boy had to eat or else to die.

The choice again. Save him from his captor or let him die; cut off his infected limbs or let him die; feed him or let him die.

Life and death are not decisions for soldiers. These are decisions for commanders. They say where to kill and we go there and kill.

But here she was, deciding. She dribbled some soup into the boy's mouth. He coughed and spluttered. She raised his head up to help him swallow. Then Zhang dribbled in a little more broth, and a little more. Soon he rested more peacefully, his breathing a little more even. That skin-pucker had faded: the fire of his life had something to burn again.

Life and death are not decisions for soldiers. So what am I now?

The sun was near to setting, bringing early dark to this clearing. One thing she knew was that she had to move on in the morning. More soldiers had stalked around this camp. She had seen their footprints, the bent branches left behind to mark their passage. Leaving was prudent. Perhaps she could swim the passage back home to Xun. Better than waiting for these strange people to decide what to do about her.

And she had to do something about the boy. It seemed she had decided to keep him alive. And that decision came with some responsibility. But an idea was forming.

Roach owed her something. Roach or whomever they had put in his place in Hong. He had family there of sorts. He looked just like them but for his eyes. They would care for him.

All around were the materials needed to build a travois. She could drag the boy home, see that he was safe, and then go on about her life. That seemed a fit idea. Zhang, calmed by a course of action, stalked away from the camp to look for poles to cut. She took the black sword, not wanting to waste her own on sappy wood. She had burned so much wood disposing of bodies and body parts that it was a fair bit of walking to find something suitable.

The sword made the work short and Zhang reassessed which sword to keep. Soon she had two long poles and enough long strips of bark to start working with in the morning, when the light was good again. Striding back to camp, Zhang felt good again, confident. Ready.

The light was nearly gone by the time she got back. She stepped into the clearing and glanced at the fire to see if there were any coals left. It seemed dark. Her eyes took a moment to register why: there was a man between it and her.

He had a spear in his hands. No, *the* spear. Captain's tasseled half-spear, black, engraved, crusted with age and history. He looked up from it as Zhang came into view. He spoke, but she understood none of his speech.

She raised her sword and took a stance, the wood and bark dropping to her feet. In that moment, she knew what she was.

Then she heard noise behind her. Two more soldiers, unsubtle, took up positions at her flanks. And two more came into the clearing from the other side.

I still know what I am, she thought. *I am a captive.*

***

Xin Ban's eyes narrowed. They had walked miles out of their way to avoid the gate, and yet guards still waited for them.

They were fanned out across the road. Bronze breastplates and helms reflected the midday sunlight. Three women and one man, they held tall spears with barbed crossbars in one hand, and little round shields in the other.

Now what?

Now we just walk. This is a city, full of people going places.

What if...?

Find my sister, find Oona.

Nothing we can do now.

The conversation had become completely silent and seamless. Xin Ban did not know which thoughts were hers, and which her friends'. Only Fum was left out, an unknown mind. They were glad to have one normal person with them, someone who had to communicate, who had secrets.

One of the guards raised her hand. It seemed either a greeting or a direction to hold. Her voice dispelled the ambiguity: "Stop where you are."

Hitaian. They were getting used to the language again; Fum did not prefer Greenlander. The language of their inner speech, though, Xin Ban could not quite detect. Was it a language?

"I said stop."

Xin Ban did as she was asked and looked around to see if Fum had also complied. He was twenty feet behind, frozen in place and half crouching.

He looks furtive.

He will get us in trouble by looking guilty of something.

"How can we help you?" Xin Ban said.

"Trouble in the city," the guard called. Her voice bounced between the houses on either side of her, mud daubed buildings with tile roofs. "Strangers with weapons are an unwelcome sight. What is your business here?"

Tell her.

Say nothing.

Run. No, nowhere to run. They have bows over their backs.

"Just travelers," Xin Ban offered. "Dangerous out there. We've come up from Hong on our way home. To the Starfall."

"Ah, Starfallers. You might have said." The guard seemed to relax and her fellows did the same. Spears pointed at cocky angles rather than right at the sky, and shield arms relaxed. "As I said, trouble in the city. All the rooming and eating houses are closed. You would do well to go around to the south."

"Trouble?" Guarl said. "Violence?"

"Nothing serious," the guard replied, but she looked impatient. "You should move along."

Xin Ban offered a weak wave and then led the way south, turning away from the guards. Guarl followed, and Chess, with Vault coming last. He kept his head down and his sword out of sight. Xin Ban could feel his movements, his desire to declare himself, his restraint.

Fum was still the unknown. Coming up last rather than first, having shrunk back at the signs of danger, he followed at a short distance. Vault could hear him and so Xin Ban could hear him.

"A moment," the guard said, and all her companions came back to alert.

"Yes?" Vault asked, now being the nearest to her.

"You have The Blood," she said. "And so does he."

Xin Ban turned around. She saw Fum shrinking into his skin. Despite having no special connection to him, she could almost feel his terror.

Vault spoke. "There is Blood at the Starfall. We renounce our ranks and ties, though. All are equal at the lake. Simple pilgrims."

"I have seen you before," the guard said to Fum. "I am Sela. Sergeant at arms. This is my squad. Now how would I know a Starfaller?"

"Common face?" Fum said. His voice trembled.

"Uncommon, rather," she said back. "Distinguished. A tall man, well-fed in a hungry place. Old yet healthy for it. You are no Starfaller, man. Take him."

Take him? Why? For what? Never mind. We can't allow it.

Guards had weapons leveled now. They advanced, cutting Fum away from the friends, pushing Vault away to the south and Fum to the east.

Fum turned and ran. His feet slapped on the road, hard-baked dirt erupting in puffs of dust under each of his footfalls. Two of the guard followed; the others turned to face Xin Ban, Whilla, Guarl and Vault. They came on with spears down.

Terror rose up. It was all falling apart too fast. From a peaceful encounter to an arrest, weapons ready – conflict! – and nothing to do but submit or fight. Xin Ban did not want to fight. She did not want to kill. But she also could not let these people hurt her friends.

Something rose up with the terror. It was not love but it glowed blue. All four young people exuded the light from their skins. One of the guards lobbed his spear but it was weak. The weapon wobbled forward and skittered along the ground.

The ground.

Feet, legs, armor, weapons.

The light went out and touched them, all of them, even the guards running after Fum. Light did not need to run; it flashed from here to there and never seemed to cover the distance between. Where it touched, things changed.

In a moment, Xin Ban seemed to come around even though she had never been unconscious. And the scene she surveyed made her nauseous.

All of the guards had merged into the road. They moaned or screamed or sobbed, torso emerging from hardpan and legs lost somewhere beneath. Their armor and helms and weapons had fused to them. They would die soon. Xin Ban hoped so because the alternative was much worse than dying.

We killed again.

It was the god.

It was us. We did this.

We can't go on this way.

"We have to go on. Somewhere. Get Fum." Xin Ban pointed the way he had run. "We need to get him and disappear. Now."

In The Sand

Chans reclined on a large square of silk in the shade provided by more silk. He was separated from the sand by a pile of pillows in purple, red and orange. "What attack?" he said.

Myrsa stood outside the shade, her feet touching the hot ground. Her eyes narrowed. "Great One, it is plain you were attacked. You lay there as if taking your ease but there is blood on your clothing. Under that tunic is a bandage that has soaked through. Others of your company pretend not to limp."

Chans smiled. Of course the facts were impossible to hide. His interest was in who would take the time to dispute them. "To gainsay a Prince of the Blood, even a regent, might be costly."

"We are face to face, Great One. Nobody overhears us. Plain speech seems worthy."

Chans nodded.

"Then, it is as plain to you that Resp's treachery was organized by others as it is to me that you survived it."

"You admit it."

"Yes," Myrsa said. "And you will thank me for it."

Chans arched his brows. At the edge of his vision, between Myrsa's feet, workers began to file out of the quarry and into their little village. A trick of perspective had them walking right on the horizon, a little line of black ants against a fading orange sky. "I might prefer to have you flayed for it."

"You might. Except that he plotted against the regency. After what Dllyx did, he did not trust The Blood any longer. And, more: he did not trust you. What brother would come back from exile to confuse the succession?"

"Get to the moment where I thank you."

Myrsa nodded, a little too quickly. "He would have done some fool thing. It was those who serve Caiph that led him to this foolhardy action. We convinced him that some common rabble were Tomblands Guard ready to revolt. We convince the slaves themselves they were a match for real soldiers.

Then we threw him in your path, hoping for this outcome: a rival eliminated, our alliance preserved."

Chans stroked his chin, trying not to show that his wound still pained him. She was right about the bloody bandage under his clothing. "Hoping."

"Yes."

"But either outcome would have suited your needs. Me out of the way and a malleable boy left to the throne – a coup."

Myrsa nodded, slowly this time.

Chans dragged himself to his feet, restraining a grunt. It seemed a great effort to rise. "Hitaian rulers stand in the path of a sandstorm. They accept all manner of attack and rebellion. From their people, from their siblings, from their children. Clumsy attacks we do not tolerate."

"No, Great One."

"I will reward your boldness. I will allow you to go on living."

"A gracious deed, Great One." Myrsa hardly sounded grateful. She went on quickly: "And there is another matter. My Mistress wishes to speak with you."

Mistress? "I thought you were mistress of Caiph. Or is Caiph mistress of you? Do you invite me to speak with a god? Perhaps you offer to help me ascend."

"You seem to have risen well enough on your own," Myrsa said. "A long way up from soft pillows. Repose suits you, and now you seem a little gray. Shall I bring water?" She waited until he waved her off. "I am nominal head of our order. The women hear my words. But I hear the words of another. Few ever see her or even know of her. This is a great honor she bestows."

Chans leaned against a tent pole. It bowed against his weight and he thought better of it. "She honors me? Well enough that none can hear us. It would shame me to have to follow Dllyx' example. Murdering priests and Gravetenders – and her a King." Myrsa failed to blanch at the threat. Chans thought his own thrust weak. Pain made it hard to concentrate, to play the game of words and implications.

"As you like, Great One. You honor her by accepting her invitation."

"I have not accepted."

"Of course. The woman you brought out here: the guard who served Dllyx as captain and her brother before that as animal handler."

"What of her?" In the distance, the line of workers had finished their peregrination. The horizon was still except for some heat-shimmer.

"Lovely scars she has. I can see why a man of your stature would be enamored of her. She is too old for sons, and this makes her a wise choice."

"More clumsy threats?"

Myrsa followed Chans' gaze, turning to scan the horizon. "It is not Caiph or her houris that threaten you, Great One. It is the position you have elected for yourself. No place safe now in all the world, and never again can brother banish brother. Now brothers will slay one another as they always have, always before Ynn, knowing that the sand sometimes spits up relicts. She will not survive as Gravetender. When Jul comes to power, she will wind up on a stake just as her predecessor did."

Chans elected silence. He stood as tall as he could and crossed his arms. Blood spread out from his side, making his cotton tunic stick to his skin.

Myrsa's face was blank. "But she could come to the temple."

"Make a whore of her?" Chans shouted, hands sudden fists, and advanced a step onto the sand.

Myrsa did not move. "No. Only keep her safe. In the shade, in the dark, away from harm. We would see more of you, Great One. Know more of you. Come to temple. Bring your lover to live there, safe from Blood games. Jul is crude but he knows how to hurt you. His mother taught him better than you think."

Chans gradually calmed, resuming his cross-armed posture in the shade. "I am not certain she will accept such protection. I shall have to talk this over with her. And with your mistress."

"Then you do accept our invitation, after all."
Chans grunted.

***

It is time to play.
The day had been long and boring. Jul ruled the palace.
Slaves jumped to obey. He did justice, talked about taxes,
heard reports from farmers and animal husbanders. He ate
without a care for poison, alone now as highest of The Blood,
absent any rival.

And all of that was desperately boring.

His toy sat next to him. His throne was too big for him but
he would not let her share it, so she sat by him on the dais, feet
drawn up under her body. Jul slid down from the throne and
held out a hand to her. Warro reached up and took it. She
stood facing him, eye to eye.

Jul's heart did a strange turn in his chest. He thought of
Xenia and Chans, of the smell of their rutting, and went a little
woozy. Saying nothing, he led the girl out of the audience
chamber. The back exit led into a hallway through the
residences. They walked silently, hand in hand. Slaves
scurried out of their path. Some ducked into other passages,
going a long way around to avoid Jul.

Cruelty and caprice, those are the marks of a ruler.

He ignored the turn that would have led to his own
chambers. Instead, he took Warro all the way through the
palace and out into the stable yards. The cheetah run was
empty today. An elephant paced in a narrow stall: two steps
forward, two back, over and over again. It paid no attention as
Jul and Warro passed.

Voices whispered ahead. Past the shack where Jul had once
raised jackal pups, a crowd had formed. Their attention was
fixed on a pole just inside the horse track. Thirty slaves and
servants looked up to the body fixed there. Nobody saw Jul.

"This is justice," he said, pointing with his free hand. He
turned to look his toy in the face.

She did not grimace or flinch, only looked at the bloody woman hung by her wrists. When she moaned, there was a twinkle in Warro's eye. Maybe the faintest amusement.

Jul said, "I let the cheetahs eat her feet. Tomorrow I will let them eat her calves, and then her thighs. Every day she will lose a little more of herself until she is gone."

"What was her crime?" She turned to meet his gaze, a vague half-smile on her lips.

"She deprived me of my justice. Murdered a criminal. She hangs in that one's place."

"You have a bloody mind, My Prince."

Jul could not hear if she meant 'bloody' in the proper or the common sense. He could not hear if she mocked him. He hardly cared. Watching her made his breath come ragged. This demonstration was meant to make him feel in control of her, to cow her. Usually inflicting pain on others made his heart slow down. It made the world take on sane proportions. He glanced at the dying Master and hoped to feel the peace that usually came on.

Warro squeezed his hand. "I thought you wanted to play. My Prince." She added the last as if it were an afterthought.

Jul turned and dragged her back into the palace, all but running. She caught up quickly and jogged along beside him, that half-smile still on her face. This time he took the turn that led to his own rooms. Guards took up station at the door as if he had summoned them. With the heavy stone doors shut behind him, Jul thought he could breathe a little better.

"These are not the King's chambers," Warro said.

"No."

She turned to face him again. Standing close, almost breathing into his mouth, she said, "Who is left to bar you from them?"

"Chans will be back."

"And what if he found you in your mother's rooms? In your grandfather's rooms? He left you, after all, to defend the city and The Blood from rebellion."

Why is she standing so close? I can feel the heat of her body.
"I... I prefer it h-here. This will be the King's chamber. Mother changed it and so can I – hers was not her father's room. They tried to make me soft. This place was full of furs and cushions. Look what I have done."

He watched her turn, taking in the bare stone floor, the bed of simple maple, walls ornamented with knives. There was a long table against one wall. A collection of blades rested on its dull surface.

"This place makes you strong?" she said.

"It does not weaken me."

"It makes you cruel. Do you wish to be cruel to me now?" Warro stepped close again.

Jul took a step back and bumped into the door. It hardly noticed. "I do. I... I want..." He found it hard to speak. His tongue wanted him to stutter and his mouth was as dry as the Yellow Sea.

"What do you want?" She came close again, her chest touching his.

"I want to cut you." The words fell out like blood from a shallow wound and spattered on the ground between them.

"Go on, then."

It would be a simple thing to squeeze around her, to take a few steps to the table. A knife would feel nice in his hand. The wood grip would be cool and his hands were hot, sweating. A simple thing.

Instead, he grabbed her by the waist and pulled her closer.

"Is that what you want?" she said.

"No. Yes."

"I could teach you. A new kind of play."

"You could?"

"Yes. But not here."

"Where?"

"When you are ready, really ready, I will take you to the temple of Caiph. This is just a child's body and not prepared for such mysteries. But at the temple, I will take the form you want. Whatever you want."

"I..."

"When you are ready." Warro leaned forward and put her lips against his. They were cool and soft and tasted of sweet wine. Then she pulled away. She took a few steps back and sat on his bed. "Do you still want to cut me?"

"I have thought of little else. But now..."

"You should have kept the pillows and furs. You are weak. You might as well be weak and comfortable."

"I am not weak."

Warro slid back on the bed and kicked off her sandals. "You think my feet would not look better with some scars?"

Jul licked his lips. "What game is this? My heart, it dances like a dervish. This is no good."

She wiggled her toes. "Very good. Come and play with me, Prince Jul."

He strode to the table and grabbed the first knife he could touch. It had a backwards curve for skinning fish. When he turned back to the girl, he saw she was smiling.

"Where will you start? This skin is fresh and tender." She pointed to one shin.

Jul's pulse filled his head. The world went gray and swimmy. There was a feeling in his loins like pain and pleasure all at once. For the first time in his life, he stood with a knife in his hand and a victim in front of him and had no idea what to do.

"Get out," he said.

"If you like." She dropped to the floor and padded towards the door.

They had played this game before, though. He knew she could no more leave than he could let her go. "Stay. Help me. I need you."

"How do you need me?"

"I wish I knew. I need you like Chans need Xenia. I need you like a pup needs it mother, like a knife needs blood. Help me." He started to cry then, an un-Kingly thing to do. Far off in his mind, he swore those were the last tears of childhood.

Warro came back to him, held him in her arms. When he shut his eyes, it seemed she was much bigger than him, able to enfold him, wrap him up like his mother had done when he was just a babe. Jul's lust began to recede as he wept and he saw something under it, something that his fantasies had covered over like sand covers a tomb: fear.

He saw how afraid he was because that fear receded with the lust. Safe in the arms of this little priestess, held in the embrace of someone who meant him no harm, he could see his burden for the first time in its absence.

"Thank you," he said.

***

Stars glared down from a black sky. On a night like this, far away from the city, the crisp air of the desert was like no air at all. Xenia felt like she floated through the sky itself, like she was part of it. Up there, between the stars, was a strange mist only partly visible. Not clouds, not part of the sky but something in-between.

The gods are watching.

That was superstition, of course. Xenia did not believe in either Gods or gods. These people who made Kings of themselves were just mortal women and mortal men. She had been in Dllyx' bed and she had been in Chans'; she had even once seen Moburu shit into a chamber pot.

Chans lay beside her now. His breathing was shallow and even and she imagined he might be sleeping. His flesh was warm. That mattered. The sand gave up its heat quickly and they had only silk for coverings. A night like this wanted skins.

Safe.

Chans promised her safety. A place of refuge deep under some crusty old temple to a god that was imaginary. Safety from a malignant child.

I will show him safety.

Xenia had helped her patron become a King in her own right when the King before her had tried to marry her off. She had killed monsters in the Preserves. Had survived Moburu, a man who saw no other people in the world but only prey. Ten years later, all the Gods, Kings and monsters were dead and she lived yet, laying on her back in the midst of the tombs, staring at the sky.

The sky stared back, each tiny star the cold eye of a god far away. Watching, judging.

I will not go. I will not hide away.

But there were few choices for her. Chans offered her a home among the tombs as a fake Gravetender. That would be hiding as much as going under the temple. He skirted along the edges of wedding her and that would be another kind of hiding. Men were fun but not what she wanted from life. And as Princess-Consort, she would be immune to danger from any but the child prince.

She wanted more.

Beside her, Chans snored once and then awakened. He smacked his lips. Xenia hoped he might go back to sleep and leave her alone with this sky but he did not.

"You are awake."

"Yes. It is too cold to sleep."

"We could make our own warmth."

She sighed but kept that inside. "You are hurt, I am tired, and you hardly mean it."

"She speaks truth."

"Go back to sleep."

He was quiet a moment. Xenia listened to him breathe. Her own eyes began to grow heavy. But he spoke again. "Blood knows how to hurt. Blood learns early to find what you love and kill it."

"I know that, fool. I have been in the palace longer than you have."

Chans was quiet again, perhaps encountering this truth for the first time: he had spent most of his life away from the intrigues but she had survived them all.

"I am sorry," she said.

Chans took her hand. His skin was warm against hers. That seemed to be the way of it. Women's heat was directed inwards, towards the womb, while men's heat went out from the body to warm all that it touched.

"You have not heard my words," Chans said. "The Blood is a danger to you because it looks for love and kills its object. The stripling would hurt you because that would hurt me. Because I love you."

Xenia froze inside. All her thoughts left her head.

Her mouth tried to frame a word. "Love?"

"What?"

"You love me?"

"Yes."

Love. A dangerous thing, a game for children and puppies. Not a thing to be sanctioned among The Blood. The word scarcely had meaning except as a warning, denoting an attachment best cut away.

But Xenia was not of The Blood. Just as common as sand and never mind the silver kilt Dllyx had given her to wear. Her family would not murder her for love.

Unless she bore Ergol a child or two.

"You cannot love me," she said, regaining her composure. "Too dangerous. Go back to sleep."

"I am awake now. Once awakened, a man has trouble sleeping again, much as he might wish to. But we can talk more on this when there is light in the sky."

Breaking

Vault trudged ahead of his friends. Fum was somewhere even farther ahead but Fum was not his problem.

We killed those people.

He struggled to have his own thoughts on the matter but it was hard. His friends' minds had infected his thinking quickly, making him lose track of himself. Even their dreams were blended into one seamless nighttime madness.

I am glad we killed them. They would not worry so over our corpses.

He was aware of a need for revenge. And also that those guards were not the people who had murdered his parents. More, though, he felt his friends' distress at killing again. Xin Ban, especially, suffered inside. Their whirling mind had contained this flavor before. Dreams of a dying man needing mercy, of a spear-thrust. And also of Gareth: of his shame, his pain. Something terrible had happened to him. Something unbearable. Increasingly, Vault had to bear that thing with them all.

He glanced around at low houses built of clay bricks in red and gray. A silver cat watched him pass from a rooftop, eyes lazy and insolent. This part of the city was tending into poverty as the road ran out towards the Tomblands and the Yellow Sea. Nobody had decided to go this way, towards home; the choice was collective and unconscious.

A voice came from one of the doorways. At first, Vault imagined it was only the noise in his head, the spinning, dust-devil thought. But he turned and saw a woman half in the shade, leaning out into the sun.

"You. Child. Step in here, and quickly."

The woman wore a ruined shift of old cotton. It was threadbare, desert-stained, and had inky splotches on the sleeves. She had coarse gray hair and gray skin.

"Who are you?" Vault said, voicing the collective mind.

"No-one you know," she said back. "Who you are is more important. There is a prophet in here who insists you have something important."

"What?"

"Blood."

That word rested heavily on Vault. It was a burden his friends had not borne yet, one his mother had tried to free him from. Fum had tried to spare him Blood politics, too, and the inevitable murder that came with his lineage. He could hear their thoughts, his thoughts, chewing on this weight now.

"A prophet?" he said.

"You know him. He held you by your ankle the day you were born."

Gravetender. The group mind lingered on the name.

"Come in," the woman repeated. "Hurry."

Vault heard voices from behind. A troop of guards. He made a decision. They all did. He stepped past the woman into the shade. The room was dark and smelled of flint. A hole waited in the floor, a blacker patch of darkness.

"Down there?"

"Only if you want to live."

He did. He wanted to live, and he wanted to fight. For all the pressure on his mind, he wanted to survive long enough to get revenge.

Vault went to the hole and felt his way down the stairs. In the dark, the Gravetender met him, throwing a meager light in his face with a tallow candle.

"Ah," the man said. "I knew I would see you again. Built you a tomb, after all. The Blood never learned to read the tombs."

"Read?" Vault said, but it was really Whilla asking. *She will learn to read, and then learn to read.*

The strange woman sealed the ceiling behind them, then moved a bit of what Vault had taken for rock. A plaster construction made to conceal this space should anyone stumble on the trap.

She saw him gaping and said, "Good to know an architect, sometimes, even though I am not the best of students. Wyrrn, you can call me."

"Save that for later. For now, rest until daylight."

"Daylight?" This time it was Xin Ban giving voice to the group mind. "But isn't it already day?"

"Yes," the Gravetender said. "But only in Hitai."

***

"Slaver?"

There was a word Zhang knew in Greenlander. This Southron soldier had mistaken her for a Hitaian, just as most Greenlanders did.

That hardly mattered. The rest of his speech was lost on her. Her Greenlander was far worse than his and she imagined his was rudimentary. Conquerors rarely took the time to learn the languages of their subjects.

Still, she had a certain national pride that had survived maltreatment and exile. "Xunian," she said, using the speech of her home lands.

"Xunian?" a new voice. A dark-skinned woman pushed into the clearing. The man frowned at her but she ignored him. "What is a Xunian fighter doing this side of the Gray?"

"Good question," Zhang said. "For my part, trying to get back across with my hide and a few spoils."

Her counterpart noticed the body. Gareth breathed slowly, still not awake to his new condition. "Gruesome trophy."

"He is no spoil of war. Just a mistake. Saved his life, for now, but could not save his arms. He is unlikely to be grateful. What of you?"

"Mercenary, like you. Unit was lost in Carday. These people found me and set me to work. I will make Lieutenant soon. You should come with us. The Emperor knows what to do with good soldiers."

"My fighting days are behind me," Zhang said, but she knew that for a lie. These people were not about to let her leave. Even now, they were drawing into a tighter circle.

The dark soldier conferred with her leader a moment. He looked less annoyed now and his hand moved away from his sword.

"That was not really a friendly invitation, soldier," the woman said. "More of a polite order. One way or another, you and this wounded child are coming with us. She knows what to do with soldiers: put them in the fighting pits, in the army, or in the ground."

"The Emperor?"

"Yes."

"Fine," Zhang said. But you carry the boy. I am getting old for such things."

"Fine," the soldier agreed. "We will also carry all those weapons. I would like to keep getting older."

They shared a polite laugh like two dogs over one bone when neither do was hungry. "Tell me your name," Zhang said.

"Rugli."

"Zhang."

"We are going to be good friends," Rugli said, but Zhang did not believe her.

Stories

"That's good work." The master set down Korina's hinge plate. "We may make a smith out of you yet."

Korina suppressed a smile, knowing how much even the simplest praise had cost Kass. The woman was more sparing with praise than the winter with warmth. "I will not start shopping for my Journeyman's leathers just yet."

Kass laughed, a robust sound like an anvil rung incautiously. "See that you don't. But I think you can be left with simple work. Braggi." She called an assistant from the back room. He had been relegated to running ores while Korina took his station at the bellows. "Apprentice Korina will need a firewarder while she completes this list of supplies."

"Yes, mistress," the boy said. He was a tall lad, too thin. His hair was orange where it was not grimed with soot. There was a white patch just above the nape of his neck. He took up his bellows and poker and checked on the fire.

"I am honored," Korina said.

"Yes," Kass replied, turning to her own work.

Korina knew she was only pretending not to watch, giving an illusion of privacy where none was really possible. She had lived most of her life in her forge, sleeping alone, eating alone, but she also knew about life in the longhall. Parents might rut in the same bed with their children with their neighbors in view. To feign sleep, to become deaf and blind, these things were good manners.

Korina checked the list, though she had it memorized. The runic language of the North had not been easy to learn even to a basic level. It was full of characters that stood for things rather than sounds, and each character could have various meanings depending on what others surrounded it. Chalk on slate was a rough medium making for fuzzy lines. But the next line of runes suggested a large hammer head for breaking rocks. Rounded on one side and pointed on the other.

"So much iron could buy a kingdom," she muttered.

"Less," her firetender said. "Matreus, the Northmother, is said to have bought these forgelands from Winter. A thousand years ago, for a steel sword and helmet."

"Stories. They used to be so important. I grew up with such tales. I will need to attend to this work but, perhaps later, you could tell me more of these tales. This place... I would learn all I can of it. Of you."

Kass said, "Fairy stories to frighten children. What is worth knowing about us is in front of you."

Braggi blushed and looked away.

"She is right," Korina said. She went to the shelves behind her and collected four two-ounce ingots. They would form the round face of the hammer. "Steel is what I came for. Still, the fears of a people are worth knowing."

Braggi blushed more fiercely. Korina knew she was not perfectly observing the rankings here and blushed herself. Even so much disagreement was too much. But then Braggi surprised her.

"Begging pardon, new mistress, but she isn't right. I mean she is, of course she is, only the stories are as much true as false. No help with smelting, but with living..."

Korina glanced at Kass' back. Kass had returned to careful ignorance. Korina took a moment to appreciate that show of manners and respect. For Braggi, she had no response. Her language skills did not extend to discussing the nature of allegory, so she worked iron with hammer. Rolling, folding, massing. A little heat, just enough that she could mate the masses into one.

Hours later, Kass tapped her on the shoulder.

"Huh?"

"Eloquent as a rutting moose, Southlander. You lied to me." What? When?"

"The day we met. That misfortunate hour that spawned off all the hours between."

"How have I offended?"

Kass laughed. "You said you were not a slaver. Remember?"

"No lie," Korina said, returning her attention to the steel. The hammer was half done now. Korina recalled little of the time spent on it.

"Look at your boy."

She did. He was washed out, half there. His face sagged and his shoulders followed. Korina could not remember him looking so tired, not even after the day one of the oxen had died in the traces. He had run all the ore for the day by hand and never complained.

"Are you ill?" she asked him.

"Sorry, new mistress. Only tired."

"After half a day? You must be ill."

Kass took her by the arm and led her to the rear door of the smithy. Outside, she pointed to the sun, low on the eastern horizon.

"I do not understand," Korina said, but she did really. The same happened all the time at home. Concerned family would stop her to make her eat, waking her not from sleep but from work.

"Morning, fool. You worked through the night. Fine for you. Die how you wish. But the master must consider the apprentice. You'll kill the boy."

"This has not happened. Not with steel. Not here. I apologize. And to the boy. You are correct."

"You are not the first to lose track of the time or to work too hard to impress her teacher."

"Is that what you think this is? Well, you could be right." She had been about to contradict Kass and, worse, bring gods into the matter. But no good could come of that.

"Go and sleep now. Tell Braggi to do the same. He proved his worth last night. He will never run ores again."

Korina might have protested that she was not tired but that, too, seemed a profitless conversation to begin. So she went indoors. Braggi was slumped against the anvil stand, eyes half shut already. "Go and rest," she told him. "I will clean up here and join you soon. You ought to have told me we had gone too long. I have a way of getting lost in the work."

"Sorry, new mistress, but I did say so. You could not hear me. But I could not stop, either. When the gods demand of us, we obey. Only flesh, us."

"Gods?"

"You did not know? You could not hear me over the voice of your blue mother. She stood behind you all night and told you what to do. She kept telling you to put aside the hammer and build the crown. Why she spoke our tongue I couldn't say because she wasn't the blue ghost of Mithodroxes' myth."

"Mithodroxes is no myth. I met her myself. Twice."

Kass spoke from the doorway. "Don't let Whestle hear you chattering such nonsense. We've no time for such bear scat."

Braggi flushed and hurried away to make a nest among sooty furs at the back of the room where three other children were just rising to start their labors.

Whestle, though, entered the front door at just that moment. "Someone is taking my name."

"Ah, forge-master." Kass stood up straight and brushed snow from the front of her apron. "We were just discussing the value of myth. So much better to rely on things we know are true. The melting point of iron. Where to find the best blue ice. How many pounds of wood to make a pound of charcoal."

"Oh, my dears," Whestle said, grinning. "We focus so much on the work I have neglected the rest of your education. Not much to do about it now. Orders to fill. Who made this hammer? This is good work. Kass, listen now: just because something is a myth does not mean it isn't true."

"Nonsense and lies," Kass said.

Korina opened her mouth in surprise, but Kass had always felt free to speak to her trainer how she wanted. She was a journeyman, ready for her own apprentices, and more: she was part-owner of this forge. Korina promised herself she would work harder at remembering the web of rankings and relationships that made this place run.

"What lies?" Whestle said, hanging her cloak on a hook in the front room, away from the worst of the smoke.

"Swords made of walrus tusks. Ironworkers living forever. Metal from the sky. Men who are women. Winter taking shape as a bear or a walrus or a seal. The worst kind of nonsense." Kass actually raised her voice, her tongue sharpening.

Ironworkers living forever? Korina thought. *Like the Bronzeworker? Tears of bronze, a wedding gift to a mortal wife...*

"Braggi!" Whestle called.

He shuffled up from the back room, rubbing his eyes with grimy fists. "Mistress?"

"Oh. You look tired, boy. Can you do one job for me?"

"Always, Mistress."

Whestle turned to look at the front door. Through it. Out past the wall. "Kass and Korina are not to rest today until you have walked them into the peat bogs. Show them the holes, the pits."

"Yes, Mistress."

"Holes in the marsh?" Kass said. "What will that accomplish? Waste of time. I could build the heavy chain Master Durpiz wants of us."

"I'll do it. Only go and look," Whestle said. "And reflect on the story of Kilrovexen."

They left right away, bundling up in furs as they went. The chill outside was like a kick in the back. Korina felt fatigue settling into her muscles, in her arms and shoulders. Away from the forge-fires, the cold felt like anguish.

Braggi set a hard pace. He had long strides and youthful vigor despite the marathon of work they had done. He would be hard to keep pace with when fresh. They slogged through slush, broke through an icy crust over shallow puddles where awnings and rooves prevented snow from piling up. Everywhere the snow was broken it had grime around the edges, soot from a hundred forge-fires.

Brick and stone buildings crowded for space and Braggi wove his mistresses through them, a tangled path leading farther from the mountain, farther from the warmth of the earth. Korina started to shiver even though she sweated under her furs. Her hands groped their way under her clothing and her teeth champed. "Is it far?"

"Not so far," Braggi said, but the sun was well clear of the horizon when they reached the walls and farther before they found what Whestle wanted them to see.

Light glistered from patches of snow, ice, dark water in pools. The ground out here was black and loamy, rich. In a warmer place, it would be planted year-round, giving two or even three crops. Here, it was barren, cut for fuel rather than food.

Braggi stood over a hole ten feet on a side and as deep. Square, tooled.

"So what?" Kass said, barely looking. "A hole in the ground. They are all around us. What makes this one special? People cut the peat to burn."

"I trust Mistress Whestle," Braggi said.

Kass glowered. "Now we've seen it and we are all the wiser for it. Let's go back to the forge. I miss the fire."

Korina agreed with all her heart. Just thinking of the fire made everything seem worth it. All her life, the losses, her poor father, the war, all of it made sense in the light of the forge-fire. She turned away, back towards the walls just visible in the distance. All around, dead grass poked through snow or ice and the holes were plainly visible: hundreds of them, all ten feet by ten. Some were eroded by time and some were fresh.

Kass started to walk and Korina followed. Braggi, the leader before, now ran to catch up. They had walked a thousand paces when an anguished cry rose up.

Korina spun to see who had shouted. Braggi looked surprised and Kass annoyed; neither seemed distressed and besides, the voice had been manly and deep. It came again, from her left. Nobody was there... but there was a hole. Korina ran to it, stopped before the edge. She crouched and peered down.

At the bottom, in the dimness and shadow, an old man picked up a shovel and a pick. The pick was stuck in the wall as though thrown there. He used it to climb out of the hole.

Now he stood in the light of the waning morning. He was tall, over six feet. His hair was braided in the way of Northerners – Northern by the reckoning of Deyklaveyn, the half-barbarian seal-hunters who lived on the backs of sleds. Most of his braid was white, only a little yellow left in it to make it seem silver. He had a great unkempt beard full of peat, mossy at the ends, and madness in his eyes. He saw Korina and raised the pick.

What he roared was lost on her, some Northern dialect, but she felt his intentions clearly and backed away. She put up her empty hands. "Sorry to startle you. Sorry."

Some of the fire went out of his face but he kept the pick up like a weapon.

Braggi came up beside Korina, hands palm-down in front of him. "Just back away," he said. "He cannot hurt you but he might frighten you."

Korina did as he said, slowly. "Why can he not hurt me? That pick or that shovel could both split my head."

"He is just a spirit, a wandering ghost."

Kass coughed, or maybe laughed. Korina could not tell the difference. "Ghost. Madman, more like. Either way, get away from him."

The man seemed to lose interest when they were a few paces from him. He put the pick over one shoulder and the shovel over the other and strode off into the peat bog, into a rising mist, and was gone.

"Who is he?" Korina said.

"Just a mad fool," Kass answered, turning back towards Deyklaveyn. "Madder than us. Every night climbing the walls to get out, if you listen to the stories the guards tell. He turns away from the fires. Let us turn towards them."

"Not a fool, a ghost, a lost man," Braggi insisted, running again to catch up. "He is what Whestle wanted you to see. Or who."

"Who?" Korina said, the question a misty puff of air in the cold, quickly lost behind them.

"Who?" Braggi repeated. "Who? He is Kilrovexen. Or was."

Kass stopped in her tracks. She turned to Braggi, balled her fists. "Kilrovexen is just a story. A tale to frighten children to their beds."

"Begging your forgiveness, mistress, he is as real as we are. You saw him. Out digging in the peat bogs, searching for his lost daughter. For Helnedrexenon, the lost girl. She kept her bargain with Winter. Married a walrus, disappeared from all sight. Her father was damned to roam these bogs for all time, forgetting his wife, forgetting Helnedrexenon's sisters, forgetting himself. There he went, into the mist, to live out his damnation."

Kass roared at him, "Just a story. A damnable story!"

Braggi just lowered his head, stared at the snowy peat between his boots.

"A story, and I'll prove it." She stalked off back away from the city, into the mist that had risen around the lost man. "I will find him and ask his name."

Korina ran to her, put a hand on her arm. Kass stopped where she was, glowered at the hand until Korina snatched it back.

"Sorry," Korina muttered, "only it is true. All of it is true. He is no ghost and no story but a real man in real anguish."

"What do you know of it?"

"Not so much, this is true. Only, I know the name of the sister he forgot. I do not know about marrying walruses or damnation. Is that the word? Damnation? Like a curse? Of these things, I have no knowledge. But the sister, I have met her. She came for the birth of my brother at the Starfall, and now she lives in the desert in the house of another story we tell to scare children."

"You are angering me," Kass said.

"Sorry, again," Korina said. "Sometimes it is good to be angered. And sometimes people can only say what they know."

"Say it, then," Kass said, "and be done with it. Say her name."

"Mithodroxes. Her name is Mithodroxes."

In the growing fog, that pained cry came again. Like a man being stabbed. It went on for minutes. Kass ran into the mist, chasing the noise, but never came any closer. Korina and Braggi followed her around the bogs for hours.

Kilrovexen, by guile or magic or luck, stayed always out of their vision. He made no more noise. The fog burned away as the day aged, revealing the same winter scene: a peat bog, ice, snow, and hundreds of identical holes dug into the ground.

"We should go back," Korina said. She felt frozen through and through. Soaked with sweat, shivering, lost. Exhausted. "We should get back to the fires and sleep."

Kass turned on her and Korina thought she would rage some more, but Kass looked as tired as Korina felt. "Yes, I think you are right."

Korina offered a hand and Kass took it. Braggi looked everywhere but at the pair of them as they walked hand in hand back to the forge town. At the gates, Kass let her hand go and Korina was glad to get it back under cover, but glad also to have offered a small comfort.

Back at the forge, Whestle watched them without comment. Korina and Braggi stripped off their furs and boots and bundled up with fresher ones at the back of the forge. Korina was asleep almost before she was done crawling into her little nest.

Asleep and dreaming.

Anguished cries. A blue lady. And a crown of steel.

Emperor

She stood on a bit of rock that rose out of the grass. Trees loomed on the horizon behind her, a wall of them fifty miles thick; grass waved with a somnolent wind, hissing gently all around. The sea was somewhere to her left. She could smell it: rank, salty, full of associations. And here was the road.

This was one end. The other was in mountains many days of travel north of here. At this end, the road was not worthy of the name. A few bits of rock jagged by fracture then rounded by erosion hid among the high grasses, as hard to find as a desert fox.

"Empress. This place is desolate."

That was Fum. Or what she had taken from him: the courageous man, the worthy warrior. He stood behind and to her left. Other soldiers and assistants stood away to the right, as insignificant as the grass. Kilba, her treasurer; Maes, the wise woman. Pikemen and logicians.

"You would prefer to be where the resistance is." She kept her gaze locked on the north horizon while her feelings, her blue feelings, drifted down into the stone.

"You know I would, Mistress."

"Yes."

The blue feeling sank deeper, drifted, searched for purity. For an aspect, an abstraction, a pure form. The *roadness* of the thing under her feet. She directed it, or perhaps was directed by it. Full of languages and all their implications, those no longer seemed like opposite propositions.

It found what it wanted and took hold of it. Beneath her feet, the tired, worn, broken thing shook loose of time. There was a road and it was mixed with age, with ages; with dirt, heat, ice, compression, the movements of the world beneath it, energy from the sun and stars and the tug of the moon on it.

The god inside her grabbed hold of the pure thing that was the road and caused it to rise above all those other things the way it had cause brave Fum to rise out of the tangled, complicated man he had been. It surfaced as a whale surfaces: slowly, tentatively, but eager for air. She half expected the road would blow steam from long-submerged lungs then settle back down beneath the surface.

It remained where it was. Clean, solid, smooth, shining.

Fum's jaw dropped open. The Emperor could practically hear it. Her work done, she turned and confirmed it with her eyes.

"A miracle. This road will carry us to our enemies and on to glory."

"Just so," she said. A breeze caught hold of her hair and it waved like the grass all around. "To begin, a small village in the mountains. The most dangerous of my enemies dwells there, a maker to my breaker. Contamination to my purity. While it exists, the world continues to be imperfect."

"Then we will shatter it into pieces."

She smiled, feeling none of it. A united world lay in her back trail and chaos along the path ahead. She had refined herself many times and might have to do so again, using the god within to perfect the form without. Painful self-sacrifice, costly, and always the result of such chaos. "Shatter it, yes."

"Emperor?"

A rustle of disorder from behind. A guard captain came at nearly a run, his path still visible through the tall grass.

"What news is it?" she said.

His skin was light to her dark, his stature tall to her short, hair thin and lank to her kinky waves. An opposite, a form almost as refined as her own.

"A prisoner, Emperor. Two of them. Nearly."

Uncertainty. He would need more painful refinement. Imperfections were not to be tolerated. The blue thing under her skin trembled, hungry.

She could see them now, pushing aside grass as they came. A disorderly mass of troopers with someone between them. A woman. Dark and strong, stoicism hiding something deeper. They pushed her along but she made it seem she came at her own pace, of her own volition. Two women pushed her harder when they came close, hoping to throw her to the ground, but she only took one longer step and stayed on her feet. The woman's hands were tied in front of her with a leather thong.

"This woman... is she one of the slavers?"

"No," said one of the troopers. "From over the sea. A mercenary. Good one: had all these weapons."

Emperor glanced at the array of arms. A black spear with an ill aspect. A steel sword. A longer, keener sword of uncertain metal. A bow stave as tall as a man in some strange wood. All these things were tinged with lake-magic, with chaos. The blue inside of her withdrew, recoiled.

"Two prisoners, you said?"

"Yes," the captain said. "Here is the second."

He came dragged between two men. One had his arms around the boy's chest, the other around his knees. Her eyes glanced around the scene, confused: it looked wrong. It *was* wrong. She realized he had no arms, only blackened stumps.

"A local? What did you do to him? I ordered no abuses of the living."

"Soldiers are difficult to control," Fum said. "You make a tool of them and they become that tool. Asking a hammer to be an awl..."

"We did not do this thing," the captain interjected. "She did." He pointed at the woman from across the sea. "The Xunian."

Xunian. Emperor was a Xunian, Xunian enough to know the word carried very little information. A huge continent full of diverse people reduced to that one term. Might as well say *barbarian* or *foreigner*. "You mutilated the boy? What kind of enemy might he have been to deserve such treatment?"

The woman's eyes went wide, the first break in her stoic demeanor. "What language do you speak?" She used her own native tongue and now Emperor knew where she had come from and, perhaps, why. "I have never heard it, but I understand it."

"Later, I will instruct you. I use the first tongue, the pure form of speech. Accept this for now. And answer my question."

"Him?" The woman glanced back at the ruined boy. "A slaver had him. Bound his arms too tight for too long. When I found him they were rotting, killing him. I saved his life. How he will live with this, if he does keep living, well, that's up to him."

Emperor followed the glance, examined the boy more closely. He was too thin. Tall and shaggy with a hint of beard around his chin. He was colored like the forest people she had just conquered but there was something off about him. He stank like the sword.

"This boy has bathed in the lake," she said. "Him and this sword." She pointed to the black metal, the dubious blade.

Fum crossed his eyes and smiled. "The road brings us enemies faster than we can walk upon it."

Fool. A useful fool, maybe. And one of my own making. She forgave him with that thought and moved on. "Can you wake him?"

None of the gathered courtiers was a medic. Her wisdom-speaker intoned, though: "The body takes what rest it needs. If you mean to kill him, he needs no consciousness. And if you mean to let him live, still he needs no words to sway you."

Emperor grunted. "Bring him, then, only more gently. Do you not know how to make a litter? And bring me that sword."

The captain took it from its bearer and proffered it on the flats of his hands.

Emperor was careful not to touch it. She did not know what such a thing might do to her. Her blue rider twitched inside her and she coupled its will to hers. Together, they explored the hilt, the wrappings, the blade.

Metal. Chaos made its own form of purity in the world, reducing variety by combining forms. Iron and soot made steel in the forge and the metalworker made alloys but the lake god made something else: a progenitor form. Metal. And this metal, this progenitor form, was mixed with more than that.

Emotions were warped into the mix, soiling it. A kind of misguided love, a compassion twisted into a weapon, twisted into *this* weapon.

The boy. She could feel him in there. Rage, loss, shame, all used in a horrific, pained compassion.

Compassion for who?

The worst thing in the blade. A monster lurked in there. The lake had reached out and made it. One driven man, much like the maker of the blade. A familiar feel to him. He had been a monster before the lake touched him. The blue god could feel that, knew it. At the core of his soul, he was already a pure form, already refined and uncomplicated. Then he had met the god and something else. A cat of some kind. An unwilling victim of the lake's smithing, an element to smelt into this alloy.

"Repulsive. All of it. This thing should not be."

"I will melt it down for you," the captain said.

"No. Wait."

He held his pose, sword held flat under the yellow glare of the aging day. She held hers: questing, questioning. The blue god did not want to intercede here. This was dirty magic, evil magic. But she could fix it.

She reached in. The god did, she did, and what was the difference? They took hold of the man inside and made him rise up like the road had risen from the countryside all around, a high, straight line through the chaos of terrain and life.

He rose up in this way, a vessel filled with air bobbing to the surface of a lake.

It took a moment, no more. He flopped to the ground in front of her, prostrate on the road. A tall naked man, one of the slavers like brave Fum. Very like him. Made of muscle, hands like the blades of shovels, hair tight to his scalp. A face made for squinting at far horizons, a chest made to hold a heart that never knew fear.

Fum stared down at him. "Moburu. I thought they had killed you. At least, I hoped so."

Emperor glanced at Fum and then glared. There was a thing she thought had been burned away in the crucible. He would need another agony of refinement.

Fum feared his brother.

***

It was not a good feeling and not a familiar one.

Fum knew what he was: some kind of distillation, a reversal of potential. Something he might have been but never had. He did not remember fear. He was the part of himself that had always disregarded it, been immune to it.

But he knew it.

His brother lay there across the road and Fum felt fear.

Moburu was a magnificent savage. He was totally bereft of any empathy or remorse. He could not tell one person from another any more than the man at the feast table cares which leg of meat he chews on. He only rips the flesh off with his teeth. Fum had been made fearless but Moburu had been born that way.

"Brother. Welcome back to the world. It seems you have been robbed of a few years." Fum knelt to help Moburu to his feet.

Moburu needed no help. "It is true. I feel as youthful as the day Father exiled me, only also just as weak."

"Weak?" Fum raised his eyebrows in surprise. Moburu looked as spectacular as ever. He was over six feet tall while the average was closer to five. He had his father's extravagant musculature spread over a more generous frame, resulting in a build like a graceful animal. Moburu in his prime had been as strong as three men – and he seemed to have regained that prime.

"Weak. I have been robbed of something." Moburu stood and tested the air. His eyes fell on the diminutive emperor. They raked across guards armed with spears, over his brother – now almost as splendid a figure as Moburu himself. "I have been away too long. Or perhaps been cast backwards into history. Is this not the Old Hitai road, restored to perfection? But who are these foreign soldiers?"

"You belong to me now," the emperor said, almost purring. "This whole land does." She approached and put her hands on

Moburu's chest. "I know you, Moburu. I know you like no other can. Not even your brother."

"Brother?" Moburu's eyes scanned around him again, settling on Fum with some uncertainty. "Fum? Is that you? You have grown and I am diminished."

"This is the emperor, Moburu. She will perfect you as she has perfected me. She will perfect Hitai and all the world."

"Oh, no," she said. "This man is already exactly what he is, what the gods made him. And he will follow me." She stepped away and turned her attention back to the sword. It was a charcoal gray now rather than black. "I know what he wants. Don't I, Moburu?"

"I am disadvantaged," he said.

Fum felt that little shiver again at the top of his stomach. Moburu looked at the sword, pretending to look where the little woman looked, but really he was evaluating his setting, his enemies, his chances. Fum mattered to him as much as any other man, which is to say not at all.

"You are perfect," the emperor said. "And what you want is vengeance."

Moburu froze. "How could you know?"

"I told you. I know you inside and out. I set you free from your steely prison so I can help you get what you want. We will go to the Starfall and burn it to the ground, destroy the god in its lake. Then on to Hitai to take back what is yours by all rights."

"You do know me after all."

Fum watched his brother make a decision. His memory was spotty for some things and still he had grown up with this man. He recalled every instance, every encounter, but absent the shades of terror Moburu inspired. And, minus the clouds that feeling created, he had an even clearer recollection. He knew what Moburu was thinking better than his brother knew himself.

"You know how dangerous he is," Fum said.

"Are you afraid for me?" the emperor replied. She did not break her concentration.

"You made me to have no fear. You did not make me to not know when fear is appropriate. You would not sleep with a viper or leap from too great a height or ride a lion into battle and you ought not take Moburu lightly. He will bide his time and then snatch up a sword or a spear or a fistful of air and kill all of us in glorious battle."

She nodded, eyes closed. "Almost done." She hummed, muttered. The sword grew lighter still. Another being flopped onto the road, released from the metal.

A jaguar.

Two hundred pounds of angry cat slid into existence surrounded by pikes and flesh. It assessed its chances much as Moburu had done but, rather than stillness, it chose frantic motion. Claws dug into fresh stone as the animal sprang into a run, weaving away between people. Away, into the grass, where it was lost to sight.

"Now this is only a sword," the emperor said. "Give it to Fum. This other one, give it to Moburu. It wouldn't do to play favorites."

The Xunian woman said something but Fum could not understand it. Some clicking dialect from over the sea.

"No, not yours. But perhaps you can earn it back." The emperor turned now to the injured boy. "Service to me, voluntary service, can be rewarding. Here I have two of the foremost warriors on this continent, and I suspect you might rank among them." She touched the boy's face with both hands. Dangerous, nearly as dangerous as the sword. "This will take me some few moments. In the meantime, Fum, why don't you try to murder your brother? You always have wanted to and you will never get a better chance than now."

Fum's eyes went wide once more. Before he even knew he was surprised, Moburu was on him with the Xunian's steel sword. A brutal overhand slash would have done for him, but Fum brushed it away with his own new weapon. It was heavy, cumbersome even, and it rang like an ingot when struck. It nearly shivered out of his hand.

He struck back, a low jab for his brother's belly. All that fear, a decade or more of it, had transmuted into rage. Moburu twisted aside, slinging his weapon around in an arc as he went. Fum ducked under it and kicked for his ankles. Moburu dove to his right side, tucked into a roll. Fum spun and lunged. His brother reversed course suddenly, as if unaffected by momentum or gravity, stepped behind Fum, and jammed two feet of steel into his back.

Fum's legs stopped working. Blood spattered to the road beneath his feet. He was dead, he knew that. The sword stuck out through his diaphragm, keeping him from breathing. The pain was intense, almost overwhelming, and darkness crashed in around the edges of his sight.

Death.

The one thing he had always feared. He could remember it now, the constant companion. Fear of poison in his food, of a knife in his back, of betrayal, of love – all fear of this moment: the moment of death.

And now he had no fear of it, none at all.

He could draw in no more breath but he had half a lungful to spit out. A word, maybe two. Last words. And he said what he felt.

"Ahhh... Thank you."

***

Gareth opened his eyes.

They seemed muddy, full of the little sandy crystals that formed during sleep. Light bleared through them. He wanted to rub them but his arms would not move.

He was in pain.

It rolled through him in waves. Like a fever, a shivering ache that started in his fingertips and rippled through his arms into his back. His stomach hurt as though he had been clenching it for a long time and his teeth ached for maybe the same reason.

Above, indolent clouds scudded through a crystal blue sky as if his pain did not matter.

Somebody said words that meant nothing to him. There were people, a forest of legs. He was on the ground, on his back. The world was hard, stony, but also warm. It seemed to fit him. To nurture him. The people had weapons and armor. They seemed alien to him, foreign.

He tried to push himself up into a sitting position but his arms still refused his commands. He tried to mutter a request for help. His dry throat produced no sound.

Then a woman was with him, kneeling, staring him in the eyes. She was a beauty, a rare thing, fey and feral. Her eyes were orange, bright and keen, her skin deep brown like varnished wood. He could see little else, wanted to see little else.

And she was like him.

He could tell right way. Through a sweating wave of pain, he held the thought in his mind. She, too, had swallowed a god.

What do you want?

She did not answer, did not seem to hear. So, not the same god. She was not like his friends. She was not his friend.

"There is a spirit in you, a god," she said. "Where did you get it?"

The words were strange but he knew them. In the habit of speaking Greenlander, he used that language to reply. "Starfall."

The woman beamed but, behind the radiant smile, there was something else. Something calculating, maybe something fearful. "Delicious. Fum, it seems we repaired the road for nothing." She stood and turned, leaving Gareth to stare at her calves. "Ah," she said. "It seems Moburu is the greater, as I thought. I might have been able to perfect your brother, Moburu, but there is no need. You are the one. You were made perfect."

No. No, he was not. I perfected him.

"I will serve you, to a point," Moburu said. Gareth knew his voice like he knew his own. It was deep, sonorous. Like a lion calling out his range. "Do you know that point?"

"Intimately," she said. "Now, what should I do with this boy? It seems he has taken on the god of the lake. The god that refused you and then used you. The one that trapped you in that sword."

"It looks like you have already done as you would. Why take off his arms and let him go on living? Did you eat them? Feed them to him?"

"He came to me this way," the woman said, sounding hurt. "I can be cruel but only when it is needful. You will come to know me."

"Huh. Feed him his legs, then. What do I care?"

"You aren't afraid of him?"

Hitaian. Moburu spoke Hitaian. The woman did not. She spoke something else. It was Hitaian to Moburu and Greenlander to Gareth. He worked over that problem, knowing he understood the words, knowing there was a meaning in them too monstrous to digest. He tried to roll way from the meaning. He turned onto his side and came face to face with a corpse. A man who looked much like Moburu. His face was flat, affectless in death, eyes open to the next world. His blood pooled all around him. It was warm where Gareth touched it.

The dead man's arms stretched in front of him. The right hand loosely gripped a sword hilt. Gareth's sword. The one his sister had made. Gareth lay now on the fingers of the left hand. Fingers, hands, arms. His stomach tightened and tried to vomit, but there was nothing inside. Retching was hardly more painful than being.

Why did you take...

"Afraid? The worst he could have done was kill me. Now what can he do? Look at him, trying to puke up his guts. Kill him, do not kill him. What does it matter? Is there a scabbard for this sword?"

Another woman entered Gareth's field of view. She knelt and took the sword from the dead man. She held it gently, not in a stance. In Hitaian, she said, "Live through this moment, boy. And the next, and then the next. I took your arms, not this woman. It was that or let you die. In truth, that slaver took them with his ropes."

He knew her then. His first tormentor and his last. Hate stronger than pain raged through him. It made his face hot. He tried to strike her but had no fists to hit her with.

"That it is, boy. Hate me. Do it. Hate keeps you alive. It kept me alive through... well, not worse than this. Just hate."

Hate.

I hate you.

He knew he could do something with that feeling but he couldn't remember what. No, not hate: love.

"Are you finished with my litter? Put him on it, then." The woman, the small one.

Gareth felt himself lifted and put onto an itchy frame. It was made of leaves and branches and hemp ropes and cut into his back.

Her again: "Carry him back the way we came. Time enough for the Starfall later. It seems the god is no longer there. Hitai will be an easier conquest for it." She loomed into view, blocking out some of Gareth's sky. "It seems we are to travel together, young man. We should get to know each other. What shall I call you?"

He tried to speak but still had no words.

"Oh, you poor boy. Bring him clean water. Help him to drink it. You see? I can be kind, too, as it is needful. Soon you will come to love me, as all my people do."

Love, yes, that's it. That was just what he needed to do. Hate Zhang and love this new woman. Someone poured water into his throat. He choked on it, spluttered, but still relished it. Coughing was for the living. The dead choked on nothing. Later, with the woman still at his side, he managed to speak.

"Gareth. Call me Gareth."

Friendship

Jul woke up and wondered why. He was warm. The room was quiet. It was dark. The only thing breathing was him.

But it shouldn't be. He remembered. The girl, Warro. She had climbed into his bed with him.

"Let me be with you."

"Like a woman is with a man?"

"No. Like a friend is when a friend needs her. You are not ready for the other things. Not yet."

Now she was gone.

Jul slid out from under the skins of lions and zebra. He slipped on his clothes: pants and a jerkin in the style of his great-uncle, with a dagger in his belt. Barefoot, he creaked open his door and padded into the hallway.

Guards watched him from obdurate eyes.

"Which way did she go?"

A sullen woman pointed the way with her chin. He might have her beaten, but maybe the beatings caused the bad blood less than the bad blood caused the beatings. Warro was helping him see things differently and Jul was unsure he liked what he saw with his fresh eyes.

The indicated direction took him down into the servants' quarters. Hard to walk through that place like a King, not without guards. He was just a boy alone. Putting one hand on the dagger his uncle had gifted him offered little comfort. A servant stopped in front of him, on her way from somewhere to somewhere else. She had a ewer of water on her head.

"I am looking for a girl," he said.

"The Prince need not look in these low places to satisfy such needs," the servant said. One hand went to her mouth and she blushed and went pale at the same time. "We would dishonor you, my... Prince?"

Jul blushed along with her. "No, not like that. A girl from my retinue... a friend... she came this way. I think."

"Oh. With apologies, young Prince. I think I saw the one you mean. A stranger. Went to the stairs to the slave quarters. Only, please, let me go down there for you. Not fitting..."

But he was already gone, walking quickly on his toes. The servants' quarters were a warren of bad smells and uncomfortable noises. People pretended not to see him at every turn. If Chans' stories were right, the last time a King had come down here, he had left behind a trail of corpses.

Jul took his hand off his dagger.

His heart raced by the time he found the stairs into the lower levels where the human chattel lived. The smells were worse. Two men waited at the bottom of the steps, eyes downcast when they saw who was coming. Others dropped into crouches. Tallow candles lit the way. There were no windows: neither daylight nor ventilation came this low.

Jul was close on her trail now. He could follow her passage by the people glancing along her path. There were no walls, only great columns between the floor and the low ceiling with bits of fabric strung up between them – goat hide, wool, a little cotton. In the night, most of the slaves slept. A few rutted and a few more watched the ways – Jul could not have said why.

Another stairwell.

Are there levels lower than this? Are there people down there?

He descended into the dark. No tallow candles.

Candles need air to burn.

He had hardly paid attention to Wyrrn. Had hardly seen any point in it. But he knew this thing. Where candles cannot burn, people cannot breathe. Was there air down there?

He proceeded quietly, listening for some clue as to his way. The stairs were cold on the soles of his feet, and rough. Cut from bedrock rather than carried into place. Air moved past his face. It smelled like loam and old flowers. With it came the sound of low voices. Jul froze in place. He wanted to run down there, to call out her name: *Warro! Warro, come back to me!* But something restrained him, some habit of caution.

"...ready. I think so. We think so."

"Bring him, then."

And an echo that might have bounced up the walls in the dark or might have been in his head:

bring him bring him bringhimbring
ready I think
bring him

"We will bring him. He is innocent. You could let us have him. Pay us."

"I will taste his blood. If the Blood is bad, you may have him. But I think he is his father's son, after all. Ynn had good blood, good Blood."

blood blood bloodblood blood

This was one of the deep places. Wyrrn had told him stories when he was younger, stories to frighten him, to get him ready for the real nightmares that came with life in the palace. Monsters lived in the ground. The Gods went into the sky but monsters would dwell forever under the earth, under the sand. Some of the great tombs would have passages into the low places. Krim, the eater of souls, he lived down here.

Maybe Ynn was down here, too. A whispered voice might be any voice. Or his mother. She was a monster, not fit to ascend into the sky.

You are being a baby. These are just voices, and they sound like a conspiracy.

He knew he should keep going, push down the stairs and confront whoever was there. That is what a brave king would do. Ynn would do it. He would smash their heads open with his scepter.

But Jul was just a child. His dagger was steel and sharp as could be and he had killed before, but that was different. Then his blood had been cold. His heart had not been thundering in his head. He had won with a trick, not in real combat. Steel was rare and costly, good for buying his life but not for selling it dearly.

He backed away, back up the steps. He left his heart down there in the dark, knowing Warro was down there, selling him to some conspirator. They wanted to drink his blood and maybe to eat him. Perhaps the heart of a King could give them power or imagined power.

The voices receded. He came back up into the relative light of the slave quarters.

"What are you doing down here?"

Jul jumped and whipped out the knife. Teeth bared, he whirled around – and came face to face with Warro.

"Jul, why are you down here? This is no place for a Prince in his bare feet. You soil your name. Is it that you have come to care for the slaves? Let me show you how to care while observing propriety."

He kept the knife between them and Warro almost walked into it. "Stay back."

"What is this? Let me help you."

"No. I heard you plotting down there. Planning to cut me open and take my blood. You were going to eat my heart."

"What are you talking about? How could I be down there and up here at the same time? I came to minister to these people. I am a priest, Jul. For everyone. Is someone down there, in the dark? Their candle must have gone out. Just a root cellar. Come on, I will show you."

She went behind some animal skins and borrowed a candle. The flame shortened noticeably as she came to the head of the stairs.

"I am not going down there," Jul said.

"You need not. I will go and you can see all the way to the bottom, if the candle stays lit."

It did. Rough stone walls ended at a dirt floor, a chamber full of second-rate vegetables. Nobody down there but her. Nothing to make a noise at all, never mind a voice. "You must have heard echoes or imaginings, My Prince. And no wonder. Your life terrifies me. I could never live as you do. Come back to bed and let me rub your back until the nightmare goes away."

He looked at the floor and twisted one foot nervously against the ground. "I heard bad things."

"I know you did. But there is nothing there. Come on. We should leave this place quickly."

Warro took his hand and he let her. It felt good, after all. He must have imagined it. Nothing else was possible.

***

The stairs loomed. They seemed to ascend forever. Xenia knew that, inside, they descended again perhaps farther.

"I feel ill about this."

"Ill?" Ergol took her elbow and pulled her along.

He was strong. His brutish father had passed that along, the legendary strength of his dynasty. "Ill. Uneasy. Nauseous."

"I will not let anything bad happen to you."

"Something bad is happening to me," she said. "I am being buried before my time. For politics."

"For love."

"I want to live under the sun, not under the ground."

"More likely to die there. I made a mistake, thinking I could re-order the way things have been here for a thousand years." He walked a little faster.

Xenia trotted to keep up for a few steps and then pulled away. "What hurry to go down into the dark? Not such a bad fate for you. For a *man*."

"What they ask of me is bestial. I will endure it."

"Endure. For politics."

"For love."

"For love," she spat. He stopped and she strode past him. The stairs made her legs hurt, made her breath short – too short for more arguing. Ergol, with his bulk and his ruined foot, came more slowly. Ponderously and quiet.

Near the top, she rested. He was twenty steps behind her now. She turned to look out over the city.

Cursed place.

Ten Tomblands Guard stood vigil at the foot of the steps. Their spears were ready, shields buckled. Hitaians had noticed the royal entry into the city and a few gathered in a ring a few paces wider than the guards'. Twenty, thirty. They wore animal skins or undyed wool and left their heads uncovered. Gray people with gray dreams.

The city itself was beige and brown. Dull. Everywhere things were splashed with paint to try to make them seem lively but paint faded in a few days, grew dusty, wore away, and what was left behind looked brown but it was really gray.

But the sun!

In a pearl-blue sky, she blazed with fearsome heat. Xenia wanted to stare, to see something that was alive and not gray.

Ergol caught up to her. From two steps below, he said, "Yes, for love. And for love, you will come in with me."

"Never again to see the sun."

"Do not speak foolish words. To see the sun later, when I have resolved these family matters. Ynn was a monster and his daughter a snake. Her son is no better and cannot be saved. The hyena cannot tolerate the lion."

"Really?" She took her eyes off the sky and put them on Ergol's face. So much light made him seem dim, dark. "You mean to kill him?"

"End his line, make my own in my own way."

"You would become a God. For what?"

"For love. Will you come with me?"

She turned and looked at the last few stairs, leading out of this world and into a new one. In that world, men became objects of worship and the price was standing stud as priests ordered. The price was murdering his own family. All this, with godhead only the means to an end.

"*I* am the end," she said, and resumed her climb.

***

Jul closed the door behind him. It shuddered in its frame. It was a final sound and he shuddered along with the door.

"We will be late," Warro said.

"Kings are not late. Others make time around them."

"You are a Prince today and perhaps a King tomorrow."

"Perhaps?"

She took his hand and pulled him with such gentleness that he hardly knew he was being led. "The King rules Hitai and the priests rule everyone lower. They are expecting us."

"Mother never trusted priests. Especially your priests. She said they presided over serpents and was glad she had no snake to charm."

"Snake-charmers, yes, a crude joke beneath your intelligence."

Jul pondered on that while making it seem he was walking along the hall under his own power. They passed a pair of guards walking from one duty to another. He thought he saw a smile on a man's face, a fey, fleeting expression. When he turned to check, the man had gone past him and Jul could see only the back of his helmet.

Warro squeezed his hand. He squeezed back and paid attention to his path. It led out of the palace through the front doors, down steps of granite quarried from the mountains. Some had green flecks in them. Ancient vermidion, so old it had sunken into the stones. Jul thought of all the feet that had walked down these stairs since Hitai had been a nation. Thousands. Thousands of thousands. Numbers only Wyrrn could imagine.

A chariot waited for him. His driver was a hard man with hard features. "Great One," he said. Jul boarded and the man lashed the horses into motion. Two big, gray mares whose hooves made a loud noise on the cobblestones. Once onto the dirt roads of the city they sounded less violent but the whole chariot rumbled and rattled until Jul's teeth hurt from the sound and vibration.

Warro followed in a second chariot and three more came as flankers. A team of young guards trotted behind, struggling to keep up. None of them had more than eighteen years.

Jul had not been out into the city since the last uprising. The noise and discomfort distracted him from his nerves. It was not good for a King to be nervous among his people. The sweat on his palms was unseemly. He wished he had his sword at his hip but Warro had talked him out of it.

"A King rules with his presence, not with his weapons. Go and be present."

"I do not know what that means."

"It means to be who you are without doubts or hesitations. It means to not pretend you are a King. Be a Prince. Be Jul. Remember how it feels to be loved."

"The sword is a part of my office."

"But only a thing, after all."

It hung from a hook on the wall of his chambers. He could imagine it dangling there, casting a shadow on the plaster. Sharp but scabbarded. He tried to imagine it on his hip instead. A comforting weight, a knowledge of power. He could defend himself.

The temple rose above the houses around it now. Another few minutes and he would be safely inside. He tried to stand on the platform of the chariot as though he were not exposed, as though he were already surrounded by walls with his sword to protect him and Warro to love him.

Hitaians started to line the streets. A few here and there at first come to the sound of chariots rumbling by and then more and more until they seemed an unbroken line. News of their travels went at the speed of voice and rumor and that speed seemed magically faster than the speed of horses and wheels. As long as they only watched, Jul could be happy. He maintained his pose of confidence while increasingly not feeling it.

Then the last of the obstacles was behind them and the temple was in full view. There were Tomblands guards on the stairs and two people just cresting the summit. At the base, a crowd had gathered: Old Hitaians with their hands full of stones and bits of broken masonry. They murmured and grumbled. Then, hearing the chariots, they turned all at once to face Jul and his entourage.

"Another of the princes!" one shouted, a woman with age lines like scars on her face. She threw her stone. It bounced from the front cowling of the chariot. Then there was a barrage.

The horses screamed and bolted. They trampled through the crowd. The wheels bumped over a body. Jul heard bones snapping under his feet. The jolt tossed him into the air. When he came down, the chariot had moved on. He fell into the dust, twisting his leg. Stones landed all around him. One struck his temple and Jul blinked away blindness and pain.

The other chariots raced into the growing mass of people. Someone lifted Jul and carried him. He shook his vision into focus enough to see greaves and boots and knew this was a rescuer rather than an abductor. Rescue was a kind of humiliation but he could do little about that now.

There were stairs under him, and then the man carrying him fell. Jul hit the ground again. He broke his fall with his hands. The stone stairs were warm and slick with sticky blood. He looked up to see one of the Tomblands guards pulling her spear from Jul's guard and aiming it at his face.

"Strike!" That was Ergol at the top of the stairs, his face a desperate mix of grief and joy.

"Stop!"

A louder cry, from the base of the steps. Everyone turned to see who had shouted with a voice like thunder.

Warro.

"You have spilled blood on the temple steps. You invite wrath into your lives. Cursed! Your children will die and your lines will break. You!" She pointed at the woman with the spear. "You – your womb is dry."

The Tomblands guard doubled over as if in pain, her eyes wide. "What have you..."

"And you!" Now she pointed at Ergol, who had come partway back down the stairway. "Betrayer. Usurper. Take another step and Caiph will revoke her protections."

"Not our gods!" The cry was from one of the gray people. He picked up a bit of stone and cocked his arm to throw it.

Warro stamped her foot and the ground shook. The man fell down. The crowd panicked and ran. Jul, on the stairs, felt nothing.

"What are you?" he said.

"I am yours," Warro answered in her normal voice. "Shall we complete our journey, My Prince?"

"In there? With him? Past all these guards?"

"Nobody can hurt you while you are with me," Warro said.
"I am afraid of you."
She smiled. "Come on. Mistress is waiting."

Hael

Sorubers had their own kind of afterlife. Fum's teachers
had made him read about it although even they mocked the
idea. When a Soruber died, if they had been good in the world
below, they went to a great hall in the sky to drink the gods'
mead and fornicate. But if they were bad, they went to a place
they called Hael.

In Hael, they were tormented with fire and dogs with two
heads. Perhaps it was because their land was so cold that they
made the torment of their afterlife hot. Fum was not hot, but
he felt he might be in Hael now.

He lay in a dark corner under a blanket that smelled of
mildew. The space was underground, through a secret
stairwell beneath a hearthstone. A brazen trick.

I used to be brazen.

The thought alarmed him. So hard to rest with no courage.
The children were right; his son was right. He was a coward.
The darkness frightened him but, if there were light, the sight
of rats or just the disrepair of the place would frighten him.
His own thoughts frightened him.

And then there was the pain.

It had started suddenly just an hour ago. A sharp outrage in
his back, in his chest. Nobody in his family ever died
peacefully, of natural causes, but he knew about heart attacks

This could be one. Or poison. Or a heart attack caused by
poison.

The pain had faded, though. It lingered but seemed unreal,
the property of another man. He watched himself feel it.
Wondered what it meant. If he died, could he face Krim or was
his heart overfilled with fear?

He watched himself fear for his self and a remote part of his
mind noted no concern for his son. None for the woman he
had once loved, for his friend, for anyone at all.

When you grow up among The Blood...

But that was not everything. He knew he was selfish, but he
had some regard for others. Or else why send Jac away so long

ago? Why traipse through the Preserves to the Greenlands seeking to save his little brother, to reunite with Vault and Jac?

In the dark, under his smelly blanket, a man who once might have been king of Hitai but for a little courage more, he had a revelation.

I am dead already.

The thought offered comfort. The dark was still bothersome but what has a dead man to fear of the dark? What does a man living in Hael have to fear of a mythical monster with a hunger for souls? He slept a little and dreamed blankly, bleakly.

Then they came for him. The impossible Gravetender. The woman with inky sleeves who reeked of sweat, desert and vellum. The children on the edge of womanhood and manhood. It was his son who told him in a voice full of disdain: "Time to go."

"Go where?"

"Away." Vault turned to go then stopped, shoulders rounded and head down. "The old man won't say."

Fum sat up. Vault's weak candle showed the tracks of rats through old dust and little else. Fum wanted to speak, to explain. "I..." There were no more words. He had been glib, once. Reckless with his tongue.

Vault left, no curiosity evident in his father's abortive revelation. Fum followed. This was his life, now: following behind like an irrelevance. Like a ghost.

The pain came along with him. It had moved from his body into his head, the seat of his soul. It was like a helmet rang with a sword-blow and yet still as if removed from him. Like a memory of pain, a headache he had once endured after a night of drinking. A story to tell his grandchildren, if only a dead man could live so long.

He climbed the trick stairs into the house that existed to disguise the basement. Light flooded through gaps in the ruined door and Fum checked his internal sense of time.

Did I sleep so long? It seemed only a few moments.

***

Whilla looked at the door. It looked like the same door. Broken and repaired, held together with little scraps of wood and scavenged nails, but it was not.

The sun shone through it.

Through a thousand little cracks and gaps and crevices, sunlight streamed in, highlighting motes of dust that swirled and danced like leaves in a storm wind. But outside should have been night.

Whilla knew the confusion of her companions. Guarl stood dumbfounded and Xin Ban's mouth hung open. Vault looked away and looked at the door again to see if it changed. She could see what he saw now, saw her vision double and triple and blur until she blinked away the feeling, the knowledge.

I am myself.

A futile thought, a panicked thought. Her self was lost so long as her friends were nearby and staring at this impossible door did not help.

"Go on, then. Pull it open."

The Gravetender. The old one, the old man impossibly reborn in his old body, stood behind her. Whilla had not seen him before but Wyrrn had and Wyrrn was a teacher. A storyteller.

"There is nothing for us on this side of the doorway." He was an impatient sort and that came through in his voice: hurried and nasal.

Whilla stepped forward and pulled it open. More dust swirled in. She expected the smell of sand and flint but got hay with it. Her eyes adjusted slowly to the light. Her mind adjusted more slowly to the lack of familiarity.

Outside should have been a city of wattle and daub, of crude plaster, of thatched and tile rooves competing for space and all lined with cats. A city on the edge of a desert. But outside was a pastoral place: rolling fields at the end of a long summer with hay rolled up into great bales. A few structures stood near the horizon: brick houses, a granary dark against a bright sky. Cattle murmured to one another from someplace behind the ruin Whilla occupied.

"Impossible."

That was Xin Ban's voice and everyone's sentiment.

"Things that happen were never impossible," the Gravetender said. "They were always certain."

"This thing seems especially nonsensical," Wyrrn said from deeper in the hovel. And, behind her, Fum groaned.

For two days he had lain in the dark, holding his head and moaning. Whilla had let him be. He was no good to anyone. A risk and an annoyance, a coward when bravery was called for.

If The Gravetender spoke truly, and the view through the door seemed to confirm his words, then this was a new world outside. Was there value in dragging a useless coward into the new world?

They moved, all four of them as one being. Out of the dark and into the light of this strange place. The air felt warm despite breeze that moved through Whilla's hair. And moist, almost heavy. Thick gray clouds promised rain.

We are far from the desert.

"Ho, what people?"

A voice from around the side of the hovel.

"Strangers in the dell, Derig."

"More strangers?"

They spoke Hitaian. Whilla thought their accent was a little strange but the words were clear. The Gravetender strode around to meet them. "Not strangers. Companions of mine."

"Oh, Chief Builder. You surprised us. Companions? From where?"

"Far away, but they are good workers. I need help with an especially tricky bit of stonework."

Whilla followed him around the building. There were two people. A woman and a man, both with the appearance of royal Hitaians but in strange dress: robes and heavy shoes, felt hats, bent crooks in their hands. Cows followed behind them, twenty of them.

"Come with me now, young ones. We have work to do." The Gravetender beckoned and Whilla followed, eager to be away from the dark place they had hidden in for so long but also afraid of her new dislocation.

And something was missing. Something ineffable. Something vital.

Xin Ban was there with her, in her mind, in her feelings. And Guarl and Vault. But part of her was empty, too.

Fum emerged behind them. He peered at the sky, at the passing cows, at the bales of hay. "New world. I knew it, I always knew."

"Knew what?" Wyrrn asked him. She took his hand to lead him along.

"The legends said our people came up from the south. I went down there looking. Looking for us. For some sign of our passage. I found none of it. No people like mine. The Blood had never been through there. I knew we had come from somewhere else. I never imagined it was through a door in the poorest part of town that opens on a new season."

"The legends, the histories..." Wyrrn spoke softly but Whilla heard with four pairs of ears. "They need much amendment. A lot has been altered to protect certain secrets."

"What secrets?" Fum said.

"Here is one. I know there are more. I can see their edges but not yet the whole shape of them. The old man alludes to many more."

Whilla took that old man by one arm and asked him directly. "What is this place? Why have you brought us here?"

"Fum is wrong," The Gravetender said. "His people came not from this place, but from one like it in the same manner. The Tomblands link many places. They shuffled out of there a thousand years ago. My people brought them, helped them escape a disaster, and we had a compact. Ten centuries it lasted. Now I have brought you out from under the rim of a disaster with proportions you cannot imagine and with no compact or contract, only a thin hope."

"What hope?"

"Only the hope that I saw the manner of your death correctly."

Fum stopped. Whilla, with the combined senses of four people, noticed him fall behind. She turned to see what was the matter despite a strong urge to just leave him there.

"I feel fine," he said.

"So keep walking." Xin Ban.

"Yes, of course." He made his feet move again. "Only for the last few days I have been in terrible pain. For no reason, as if I had fallen from some height onto a hard surface. It started in the back of my head but occupied all my body. And as we stepped through the door, the feeling was lost."

Whilla stopped then just as Fum had. That was it, exactly. She had been feeling something and lost the sense as they left her world. Pain, too low to really notice. She flexed her shoulders, rolled them. Opened and closed her fists.

Guarl looked at her and said, "Something terrible has happened to Gareth."

***

Xin Ban had troubled dreams. She lay under a workbench made of wood, her friends in unlikely places all around her – draped over a stool or in a window ledge. Her dreams were their dreams. Vault dreamed of bloody vengeance. Being asleep he could not consider her more peaceable desires, her dread of killing. Whilla thought of Gareth and surmised a grim fate for him. Guarl dreamed mostly of Xin Ban in ways that made her uncomfortable.

Her own dreams were a sick blend of these other minds and their dreams, too, were blends of all the others.

She woke in a fever, groaning, sweating.

This can't go on.

They had killed those soldiers. Fused them with the road, with each other. And all around them, things would continue to change. Mostly plants and animals but maybe people, too. Innocent people, guilty ones, what was the difference?

Eyes wide, mind alert, she dreamed of Whilla's spear, of all their hands pushing it into that dying man. He had been guilty. He would have died anyway. They had done him a mercy. And still she was stained by this, horrified by it.

Xin Ban stumbled to her feet. She lurched outside and threw up in the grass under stars she did not know.

Behind her, the Gravetender stood over his table staring at plans etched on vellum scrolls. A man just like him stood at his side. A few years younger but otherwise identical. Neither of them seemed to notice the bit of clay on the table holding down a corner of a scroll. Red clay that produced a dim orange light, hardly noticeable with the competition of a weak candle.

She threw up again then wiped her lips with the back of one hand.

What might happen if the god inside them took hold of that clay, or ahold of the men fussing over their plans? Or the sheep in the pen behind the workshop?

What if it did to their bodies what it was doing to their minds?

I have to leave. Gareth was right. Better mutilated than this.
***

Moburu stood over Gareth's little body in a trampled-down area in tall grass under a starry sky. *So weak.* Without arms, he seemed tiny. His eyes moved in some dream, probably a horrible, fever-addled one. *I could just kill him and free him from this... degradation.*

That was what this was. A humiliation, a lessening. Moburu had barely known Gareth, had met him at his birth and again when Gareth had joined him to the sword. That had been a degradation, too, of sorts, but Moburu felt no special rancor about it. In war, one killed or died.

Only the boy did not kill me. Is that why I stay my hand now?

The woman was nearby. Meat roasted over a fire, awakening Moburu's memories from before... before...

When I was a man and ate mainly the flesh of predators.

He had not been awake in a long time. For a few moments, when Whilla had hit him with her spear, knocking the Jaguar out of him, but that had lasted only as long as it had taken Gareth to merge him with steel instead. Before that, he had been lost in a dream of hunting.

Awake.

He felt good. Strong. The years, Empress had left those in the steel. He was young, virile, and capable. His hands were big and hard. His eyes sharp, his mind astute.

Am I remade or reduced? Do I miss the dream? Do I miss the jaguar?

He put his back to the child and strode into the main camp. There, soldiers stripped meat from a gazelle. A woman offered him some and he declined it without words. If he knew their speech, he would have said that he only ate beasts that ate other beasts. There was only one such animal nearby.

Empress sat on a rock, staring south.

She takes what she wants. Father would have been proud of her as he was never proud of me.

That was a weak thought and he put it down. He walked up to her, interposed himself between her and the horizon she stared into. "What is the child to you that you have not killed him yet? You are without mercy. I see that. All mercy, all compassion, you have set these things aside. And this armless weakling, you let him go on breathing."

Her eyes did not focus on him but remained locked on that distant point for a moment. Then she seemed to *arrive* back in her body, in this time, and notice him. "Once," she said, "There was being and non-being. Then being broke apart into order and chaos. Chaos sought to erase the lines between things and order to draw them. There are dogs and wolves and this is orderly; there is you and there is this sword and that is orderly."

"The boy, then, is chaos."

"Yes." She stood and scented the air like a fox. "There is meat. Will you not eat it?"

"No."

"I understand. You are an orderly man. The greatest of hunters. Deer are beneath you."

"The boy is beneath you, then."

She waved at one of the soldiers. "Bring me meat, and then bring me the bow."

Moburu waited while the woman ate, her attention returned to the horizon. Later, when he was sure she had forgotten him, she picked up the bow from the rock beside her. "String this."

He took it on both hands and tried to bend it. It had the form of a bow stave but barely flexed at all. He put more effort into it, and more, and then grunted with the effort.

"When he had his arms," Empress said, "that weak boy could bend the stave easily. He could slip loops over the ends. I inhabited his mind and saw him remembering it. He killed with it."

"I can do it." And he could – but it cost him a great deal of effort. He took the string she proffered and looped it over the ends, turning the stave into a bow. She passed him an arrow, too, and he nocked it, tested the draw. "Impressive. Is this why you have not killed him? Perhaps you imagined he might work it with his toes. I saw a carnival freak do this, once."

"You are a fool, Moburu, but I did not bring you here to think through problems. I brought you here to be my soldier. Perhaps my foremost."

Perhaps. He glanced around for the mercenary woman. There she was, eating meat from a bone and pretending not to look his way. She still had the sword in which he had been trapped. "If you told me, I would not have to think. These implications and imprecations. I have a tactical mind but your actions defy reason. Win. Murder him."

"I have won. My enemy is not the child, Moburu. It is the god that lives in him. I thought I would have to march all the way up to their little lake colony and shatter the god where it lived. But the god shattered itself. He is not the god."

Moburu peered into the dark towards where he lay, unguarded. Any wild thing might sneak up in the shadows and snap his neck, drag his carcass away to feed its pups. A glimmer of understanding crept into his reason and he felt an urge to go stand a watch over him.

"You see, yes? The god that made you its tool, one fifth of it resides in that child. Kill him and free it to rejoin its other parts. Keep it trapped in that body and it is weak. Malleable and weak. It cannot even wipe its own ass without help. It is broken. With it locked into this little body, I can pass over the village and ride straight for the city, with you at my side. Crush the palace, crush the tombs. We will regroup in Hong and then ride north, an arrow through these prairies."

"I see now. I will stand over him, then."

Empress made no sign she heard. Her eyes went back to the horizon, a dark line against a dark sky.

Into the World

Vault snuck away.

Of course he could not leave without Xin Ban, Whilla and Guarl being aware of it. They knew. They had but one mind between them and, while it was as conflicted as any other mind, it had reached a decision.

It was the cows that did it. Yesterday morning, one of the local people had come to The Gravetender with a story of two cows fused together. Still alive, they had screamed through the morning until confused villagers had silenced them with hammers to their heads. Two living things smashed into one monstrous abomination. Death.

Xin Ban abhorred killing. They each did in their way but her strongest. And so long as they stayed together their strange nature would act of its own will, would corrupt and contaminate, would destroy.

That is why it took five of us and not one of us.

Yes, Vault saw the truth in this group thought. It was too powerful to stay in one place. It needed to spread through the world, to be within beings with minds who could guide it to good purpose.

Vault had a purpose. He would wield the blue god as a weapon against invaders, take Hitai from the cruel people who ruled it, and find what happened to his parents and his sister.

Alone.

He walked across the pastures, gathering dew from the grass onto his bare feet. He stepped over some evidence that cows had passed this way. It took just minutes to reach the strange door that sometimes opened on a storehouse for farm equipment and sometimes on a whole new world.

The Gravetender awaited him there, leaning against the door frame. "You are doing the right thing."

"All part of your plan?"

"There is a plan that I follow. I try to account for all the variables."

"Variables?"

"This door will open onto your home for another hour and then fall out of alignment. You should go now."

Vault put his hand on the wood. It felt warm and never mind the cool of the morning. How many suns shone upon it? Onto how many worlds might such a door open?

He could still hear his friends' thoughts and see their visions. The Gravetender stood there, too, leaning on his work bench. This doubled vision felt strange always and all the more so because the Gravetender was in each.

"What are you?" Vault said.

"A question. Ask yourself."

"I'm asking you. What are you? A person? A god? Did you do this to us? You came to our village when we were born. You came to the Starfall and put something into us."

"I told you, boy. I only build the tombs. I place the bricks on the markers, and for that I have to be able to read the markers. You have more free will than I do. Which is not to say very much. The door is shut but will open at your touch – for a little while longer."

"What happens if I stay?"

"You know that," The Gravetender said. "I do not. Only that if you stay in this world much longer, I built your tomb in vain."

"And that would ruin your plans."

The Gravetender sighed and rubbed his head. He had restored his headdress. Wyrrn had insisted on it. "You are angry. When terrible things happen, we seek to know why. Who to blame. Blame me if you like, if it helps you. It does not hurt me. But I say again, I have no plan of my own. Go now. Or stay. But decide."

Vault went.

He pulled open the door and went into the disheveled room. Rats scurried away at his presence. "How do I close the way? Do I just shut..." He turned as he asked the question and found it not needed. Behind him was not the cool day of a faraway world but harsh white daylight.

He wished it were night so he might look at the stars and wonder which one his friends were on. At the Starfall he had learned all the legends of a dozen peoples and they all spoke of other worlds visited after death, and they all put those worlds in the sky. The tombs of his ancestors were great machines meant to send the dead into those worlds.

He grabbed the door then and pulled it shut, then pushed it open, and did this three times knowing it would only ever open for him into Hitai.

If the dead went to these other worlds, he had come to the wrong place to find his parents.

He went out into the street. It seemed empty of people. Quiet.

Quiet.

So quiet. In the world and in his head. Mentally, it felt like he had been pulling on a rope for so long he had not noticed when the person pulling the other way let go. A kind of freedom, of effortless selfdom, had taken over without his notice.

If felt lonely. Parentless, friendless, and alone in his own space, he walked along the road towards the palace, no particular plans in mind.

***

Xin Ban came to the door not long after. She passed through it without comment. She had been with Vault for his conversation with the Gravetender, had *been* Vault, and had nothing new to add.

Vault's mind was missing from hers as she pulled the door open. She felt both diminished and restored by this.

I wonder if this is what it feels like to give birth. To lose the presence of the other while gaining back your body?

Through the door now, into the same broken room Vault must have encountered an hour ago. He re-entered her experience but vaguely, like the call of a wolf from across a valley or the ripples left behind after the passage of a fish. The others, Whilla and Guarl, were gone abruptly as if severed with a knife.

But not gone.

It has been so long since I had my own ideas...

Her friends had been part of her thinking for months now. She could not hear them directly, but they were still part of her. Vault's anger; Whilla's regrets; Guarl's thoughtfulness and growing desire.

These thoughts were a comfort. Vault had wanted his own mind back but Xin Ban had grown used to being who she was as part of a collective mind. Giving it up was necessary but not what she wished.

The streets were dusty and bright. She could hear wind in the eaves, the mutter of conversation from a nearby market. A cat mewing on a roof. It all seemed loud to her, and intrusive.

Where to go? Free to roam all of the world, and no direction.

There was only one place she wished to be. She missed her mother. Now, absent the confusion of her friends' motives and wishes, she missed her mother with a longing intensity that shocked her.

One place to go, then. Only one.

Home. Home to tend the nets. That was what her mother had whispered to her so long ago, when they had left the village for the first time: *"come home again to tend the nets."*

Xin Ban turned left towards the Tomblands, towards the Yellow Sea, towards the Starfall.

***

Whilla stood at the work bench. Her fingers trailed along lines on a map. One of the Gravetenders watched from across the table.

"See where these two lines meet?" he said.

"I see. But what are they? The lines? Are these hills, or roads, or rivers?"

"Not as you would understand them. These lines, the blue ones, are waterways. The red are terrain elevations. Deeper red, lower elevation. Roads are double black lines."

"What, then?"

"What the lines are is not of much consequence to you. Not yet. The confluences, though... Are you well?"

Whilla had stepped back to lean on the wall and put her hands to her head. "It's nothing," she said. "Just the last of them leaving. Guarl." She rubbed her temples then came back to the table.

"It is a difficult thing you do," the Gravetender said. He put both hands flat on the table.

"What do you know about it?"

"Well, more than you think. These lines. My mind flows along them. I am not a person, you see. I am the Gravetender. All of the Gravetenders. All of them at once. We are born into ignorance much as any person and then grow into this sure knowledge of ourselves and our purpose. When the ways are open, I know what the others of me know."

"That seems much to contain."

His eyes stayed on the map. "Much. All of their hopes and fears. Ambitions. And the centuries. The losses."

"Losses?"

"I had a daughter. I think. Or that might have been the other one." He touched his head. "No headdress. That means I live here, and the other one had a daughter. Well, he was his daughter, and he was her son. They were both murdered. He was murdered."

Whilla rubbed her head again. "I apologize. You do know how I feel. Do they ever kill? The Gravetenders? Do they make you guilty with their actions?" She thought of Xin Ban and her remorse; of Gareth and his concern that he not impart his shame onto them all.

"Ah, guilt. Well. It has been a great long time since we took any action beyond our project. I seem to have brought in some intentions from your world, though. The accords have failed there. Revenge is not in our plans."

"What is the plan?"

"In these lines, these confluences," he said. "Where these lines touch, these are places where worlds might touch – with just a little bit of help. These are the plans."

"To what?"

"To a great machine."

Machine. Not a familiar word, not a known meaning. "I don't understand."

"For now, look for all the confluences. This map is all the confluences for a thousand miles. Learn them. Tomorrow, after you rest, we will go to the sites. You can learn to recognize them."

"Learning to read. How did you know? Fifteen years ago, could you see this time?"

"Oh, no," he said. "Only one moment, one instant of your life: the time that your spirit or, um, soul, for want of a better word... the moment it rejoins the lines that make these points."

"You see the time when people die."

"Yes."

"I'm sorry. I am sorry for you."

"Thank you," the Gravetender said.

The Taste of Blood

Ergol reclined with Xenia beside him. The bed was soft and clean and the room brightly lit. White walls reflected warm yellow light. The room had a door, a table, furs on the floor.

A glorious prison.

On the heels of that thought:

No more a prison than the palace.

Someone rapped on the door – an unnecessary courtesy in this place. Ergol hoped he was doing the right thing. Xenia rolled off the bed and pulled the door open.

"Myrsa," she said. "Nice of you to visit."

"I wished to see that you are comfortable," Myrsa said.

"Yes," Ergol said, standing. "Very comfortable. Such a soft place. Safe."

"Safe. That is what we agreed? One day and you complain already. Well. There is someone I wish you to meet."

"Is he to make a contribution?" Xenia said. Her hands went to her hips like an angry governess, but her feet were in a fighter's stance.

Myrsa smiled. "Not that sort of contribution. My superior wishes something of him. Again, not that," she said, at Xenia's sour expression.

"What, then?" Ergol said.

"I will let her explain." She took his arm and Ergol let himself be led out into the hallway.

Xenia followed but Myrsa turned to stop her.

"Where I go, she goes," Ergol said.

"She will not like what she sees."

"All the more reason. Do not put me in situations she will not like. In every way but a completed ceremony, this is my wife; this is a Queen of Hitai."

"As you like, then," Myrsa said.

Xenia's expression did not improve. Ergol put her to his back, led again along the hallway by Myrsa's gentle touch on his arm. They came to a stairwell leading higher in the complex but she led him past it.

"We are not going up?"

"No. Down."

"I thought we were as far down as it was possible to go."

Myrsa halfway smiled. "Not so far down as that. We can descend a little further. Come, now."

Soon she was proved right. Another set of stairs led down to their left. The stone walls here seeped out gentle moisture that pooled on the floors and the air tasted sour. The torch on the wall opposite the stairs gave off more smoke than flame.

"What is down there?" Ergol said. The stairs went down five steps into darkness and then were lost to sight. "It smells bad."

"Ergol..." Xenia touched his shoulder. "There is not much in this world that frightens me. Not after surviving your father. But this place... I do not like it."

"Neither do I." He looked at Myrsa.

"I have never gone down there," she said. "Not all the way. She usually finds me in the higher levels, wherever I am. Before a year ago, she was a legend. None had ever seen her. Down in the dark must be all the things she needs to live. A wonderland none have seen but her. And you are about to see it. The only mortals ever to do so, to my knowledge."

"An adventure, then?" Ergol said. Xenia tightened her grip on his shoulder.

"Go on. She is waiting."

"Who is she?" Xenia asked. "This legend."

"'Mistress' is the only name I know for her. She has been here since the temple was built. She is not Caiph but has her ear. The rest, you will need to learn. Go on, now. It is only a flight of steps, after all."

Ergol stepped down onto the first. The world did not change, except for growing a little darker. The walls were too close for Xenia to come at his side. Down another step and he pulled at her hand.

"I do not want to go," she said.

"I thought-"

"I changed my mind. Whatever down there is no threat to your fidelity. I cannot save you from it. It is beyond both of us.

Go on. Go down there. Better still, come back up. We will go back into the daylight and face the fates together. I would rather reave the north with you than go down there."

He let go of her hand. The next step was harder than the first two because it was a lonely step. The fourth was harder still. He reached the place where he could see no further and kept going.

"Chans," Xenia said behind him, and her voice seemed far away. "Chans, please come back. Give her what she wants and then come back to me."

He put one hand on each wall. The walls were close, and they were warm. No condensation here. His footfalls made little sound, the echoes soft and subtle. He felt for each step before taking it.

After what seemed a long time, his foot found the next step much too soon and he almost lost his balance, jarred by the impact.

A flat floor.

He turned to look back up the steps but there was nothing. Either he had come too far or else some unnoticed curve in the stairwell had cut off the light from view. Turning back to the room before him, Ergol felt around with his hands, finding nothing. A few halting steps out onto the floor revealed nothing more.

Then light rose around him. Cold, blue light. It came up slowly, not hurting his eyes. He slowly took in the room.

It was fifty feet across and roughly circular. The floor and walls were flat, featureless stone, blank obsidian. No doors. One chair, right in the center.

A woman sat on the chair. She seemed ordinary enough. Light skin, like a Greenlander if not quite a Soruber. Silver palms. Thin, dark hair. Her face was plain and hard to place in an age group. More motherly than grandmotherly.

"Thank you for coming to visit," she said.

"I had little choice, and little information to make one."

"Nevertheless. Please, sit."

Ergol was about to protest that there was just one chair but now there were two. One rested just in front of her, facing her. It was cane with a fabric cover. Ergol moved it back a foot and sat down, still appraising his host. "What may I do for you? Mistress?"

"Almost nothing, in fact. Merely allow me a single drop of your blood."

"Blood?"

"You carry a knife, yes? Take it out. Prick your thumb."

"A small thing to do. Blood, though. It seems so weighty. Why would you have this of me?"

She did not move, did not smile, did nothing but speak. "Is it too high a price for my protection?"

"I cannot say, in fact, as I do not know the use you would put my blood to."

"Let me show you what I am protecting you from, then."

Behind her, the wall filled with light. No, not just light: an image. It was the temple, seen from outside. People fought in the street. Soldiers, Tomblands Guard. He expected they would be fighting Hitaian commoners but the commoners fought alongside them. Men and women in strange armor came at them with spears and swords and large round shields. They marched in ordered ranks. When one fell, another stepped into her place.

"Chariots," Ergol called, as though he were among the fighters. But he was not. No chariot rolled into the ranks. They did not break but only pushed ahead, forcing the defenders back.

"The city will fall," Mistress said.

The wall went dark. "Is this happening now? I have to get up there." He turned to find the stairs but there were none, only the same blank wall all the way around. "You cannot keep me here while they die."

"You knew what this was about," she said. "We preserve your line. We need it. Give me a drop of your blood."

"Then you will let me fight?"

"No," she said. "You cannot save the city. You can only preserve your line – if your blood has the right taste to it. Give it to me."

In a daze, he drew the knife from his boot. Murder flitted across his mind: he might stick this knife in her head, kill her. But it was clear to him he had wandered out of reality, into the realm of legend where myths walked and talked and abstractions were real. So he pricked a thumb. Bronze held little sharpness so he had to saw at it. When the skin opened, it was more than a pin-prick.

Blood trickled out. He held out his hand, hearing his life patter on the obsidian floor.

The thing before him touched his wound with a finger, then touched that wound to her tongue. At last, her face showed an expression. She smiled.

"In three weeks, that scene will play out above us. Nothing you or I can do to stop it. Your line must continue, though. This is true. If Jul proves untrue, The Blood must continue some other way."

"You will taste his, too. That is why he is here."

"Yes."

"And if his is true? Why would it not be?"

She pointed behind him, and he turned to see the stairs just where they ought to have been. "In that case, you may spend your blood as you wish. On your woman, on your city, on sport. You and I have the same wish in this: that you go free."

He turned to argue that she had admitted he was a captive, but the room was once again dark – except for the mildest bit of light from the stairwell.

Legends

Korina sat on the roof of the forge. The tiles warmed her from below, making the chill of the night endurable. She clutched sooty furs around her and looked into the sky.

The stars this far north were like a splatter of paint along the south horizon, a wild spray of faint color all washed out into cold white. Along the northern horizon, vague green and blue fires danced and played.

The boy would have a story about the lights. Ghosts or gods or poor lost men searching out their daughters.

"You are ready, or as ready as we can make you."

Kass, earlier that day, had put fists on her shoulders and smiled into her face. Korina had smiled back, stretching her face to match her teacher's.

"You are dreadful at smiling but good at working. You are no master, mind you, nor even really a journeyman. We will just certify you won't burn down your own forge. The rest is up to you."

They would even let her recruit an apprentice if one would go with her. For Kass, the idea of apprenticing to a hedge smith was like being consigned to Hael but there were many young people here and few forges to inherit.

Korina heard Kass down there right now, grumbling over her fires while Korina stared at the sky. Nobody came and went in a few weeks. Not in Deyklaveyn. The lake spirit had put something into her, one final drive or compulsion. She had been its first love, its first unwilling servant. Now here she was at the edge of the world, staring north – beyond where the maps went, where people wore whale fur and hunted walruses and great white bears.

Where people married spirits.

The boy was full of stories and they were true. Helnedrexenon's father really did haunt the bogs by night, digging and digging in search of her. Kilrovexen had lost two daughters. Korina had met one of them. Mithodroxes knew the future and talked with God. So why not the other? Why not Helnedrexenon?

Forge a crown. Her dream told her that. The spirit whispered it. *Put down the hammer and forge a crown*. But her eyes stared at the aurora in the north and wondered what gods dwelled there. What metals waited to be mined. What destiny could be carved up there where the cold had driven away all the people, murdered all the farms and holdings.

She tugged on her beard. It was matted and filthy with cinders, sparse and black as her hair. It felt good to tug on while thinking ponderous thoughts.

Forge a crown. Why make a circle of steel when one might build a kingdom and rule it – and be free?

I am not made for thinking. I am made to wield the hammer.

She might make a home, and she might do more. She might find Helnedrexenon and her winter god.

Korina heard a whisper behind her. She did not turn to look. The whisper was known to her now. It was a blue shadow that cast no light, the color of lake-water in the old days when her forge was new. And she could hear it whispering.

Helnedrexenon....

***

Into the dark. Jul did not like it. It smelled like the root cellar at the palace and it was full of the same whispers. Warro held his hand and that should have helped, only he had seen her differently since the night in the servants' quarters, since that day outside.

She had frightened a whole crowd. Town people ready to fight soldiers and soldiers ready to fight back; his uncle's people set to murder him, had all turned to look at her and done as she said out of fear.

Why should I feel any differently?

After a few steps the light was gone completely. Jul counted on Warro, trusting her to know this stairwell.

"This is my birthplace," she said.

"This temple? I imagined."

"No, this very stairwell. I came into being here. Mistress breathed out. The breath became a wind and the wind bore me into existence. I arose from here into that hallway above. Snuffed out the torch. Myrsa found me and I became the tool that was needed."

Jul had stopped and now Warro tugged on his hand.

"Come on, silly. Only a little longer."

"I am afraid," he said. "You are not helping. What is this story of being born in a wind? Are you a god to be born so or a mad person to think it? Or is it all some game or some trick? I know you came to seduce me for some purpose."

"Just ten years old, more or less, and already so wise. So wise and world-weary and cynical. I was made to love you, silly boy. Come on."

He let himself be led because there seemed no good alternatives. In Caiph's temple, he was as good as a captive. All the guards had stayed outside as was tradition. Even one of the whores could get in his way, could stop him from leaving, assuming he could find his way to a staircase leading out in the first place.

"That is good," Warro purred. "Just a little longer. A few more steps."

"I see light."

"We are there. Carefully, now."

They came into a room as big as any at the palace. The floor was covered in animal skins and the wall with trophies: skins, heads, antlers, bits of armor, weapons. A woman stood by a mounted lion, one hand on its chin. It was posed standing on its back feet, front paws in mid-swipe.

Jul thought the woman posed as carefully.

She wore a floor-length gown in green with sandaled feet poking out at the bottom. Gold bands adorned her arms. Her hair was straight and flat like an Old Hitaian, her skin somewhere between their gray and his black. She seemed older than his mother but it was hard to tell.

"Welcome," she said.

Warro let go of his hand. As he watched, she stepped onto an empty podium and posed much like the lion. "What do you want?" he said.

"Not much, child. First, to make you welcome. Do you like my chambers?"

"Where is the light coming from?"

"What?"

"There is gold light all around us as if from the sun, but there are no windows. No lamps or candles. Why is there light?"

The woman frowned briefly and then smiled so fast Jul doubted what he had seen. "Trifles. You know this room is not real and I know I could have what I want from you without being polite. What if we both just agree to pretend?"

He did not understand. The words all made sense but their meaning seemed just a little out of his reach. "Do you mean the room is magic?"

"Yes." She came closer, covering the space between them without appearing to move very much. Then she had his chin in her hand just as she had held the lion's. "Does that make you more comfortable?"

"Comfort is for the weak," he said, feeling a lot less brave than he wanted to sound. "Soft settings make soft people, and soft people cannot rule Hitai."

"So I have heard. Nothing soft about you, then. Good. You like your rooms, I hope. A bed and a girl who keeps you warm. Nice food to eat. I hope we are not weakening you. I could find you a cell with a floor made of knife points and a bed too hot to touch."

"Threats. What do you want?"

"Just a taste of your blood," the woman said, letting go of his chin. She moved behind him.

Jul turned to follow her with his eyes, and noted the doorway was gone. Even though his situation was really no different, still it was disconcerting. He had gone out of the real world and into a realm of monsters. And this one wanted to bite him.

"I need my blood."

"Why?" she said, crouching down to his level.

"It... keeps me alive." He remembered some talk from Wyrrn about it. Blood flowed through the lungs and into the heart, carrying air into the body to balance out the other elements. With this woman staring at him, it seemed silly to try to repeat.

"Surely you can spare just one drop. A boy as strong and hale as you can bleed a little and feel perfectly well."

"You cannot have it. You are some sort of monster. I am a King of Hitai and I say no. No blood for monsters."

She smiled again. "Your mother was a monster. This I know. And I fear you are one, too. I sent my... girl... to blunt some of your ambitions. To tame you a little. Not too much. And still I see the monstrous in you."

"I want to leave."

"And you shall. When you give me a drop of your blood. A knife in your boot, just like your uncle. Yours is steel. It will do the job better. Come, now. Your mother took plenty of your blood. Gave it to servants and slaves. Let me have a drop."

"No."

"Hm. I could take it."

"Do it, then. But I will not give it to you."

She stood and went to the podium where Warro stood. She was not Warro anymore. Now she was a huge salamander with blue and red stripes and huge claws. When the woman touched her, the salamander dropped to all four feet and trotted towards Jul.

"Cut yourself," she said. "Just your thumb. Just a little drop of blood. Or else Warro here will take all of it. Waste it, mostly. Out here, we do not need food."

He whipped out his knife but did not slice his hand. He took a stance, ready to receive the salamander. He understood none of this byplay, but fighting was no mystery. You fought or you died; that was the way of The Blood.

The beast swatted the knife from his hand with no effort at all. Then it was on him, knocking him to the floor. He should have landed on soft furs but instead struck bare stone. He struggled, grappled with the salamander.

It put one claw in his face and scratched, and then he was free.

Jul rolled onto his feet and, crouching, glanced around the room again. Now it was bare. Black stone walls, black stone floor. He watched the salamander trot over to the strange woman and offer its bloody claw.

She touched one finger to the blood and then to her mouth.

"Oh, this will not do. Not one bit of it."

Jul backed away. The look on her face was not savory. Even with nowhere to go, distance felt better.

"Your grandfather father is not your grandfather, little boy," she said, stepping easily in his direction. One step seemed to cover a lot more ground than it should. She took him by the throat and lifted him up. "This we knew. He put his wife out like a sow, a breeding program of his own. This we knew. The bad news is, though, that neither was he your father."

"Ynn. My father was King Ynn."

"Oh, no. Your father was some petty noble. Ynn saw too clearly, I think. He had his own plans for The Blood. Unless Dllyx did it to thwart him at the end. Either way, we are set back two generations, all the way back to his brother."

Jul wiggled, struggled, kicked. Nothing helped. The hand on his neck was like brass. He struck the woman's wrist and it was like punching old tree branches.

"Such a waste." She tossed him aside. "Still, we are not monsters, are we, Jul?"

He got to his knees and rubbed his throat, saying nothing.

"I suppose I could send you back up the stairs. Back into a soft life. Warro wants you, you know. She loves you."

"She does?"

"Oh, yes. Warro, do you want the boy?"

The salamander sat back on its haunches. It looked at him with one eye and then the other.

"That is not Warro. It is some illusion." Jul got to his feet.

"Yes, of course it is. And her, too. Warro, take him."

This time, the beast did not stop with a scratch to the face.

Elders

Ergol climbed stairs. It was a slow and painful activity but he did it stair by stair, flight by flight. The hallways in between were a kind of relief. They all stank of old ruttings and, behind some doors, he could hear fresh ones in progress. Those made him cringe inside but it was still better than stairs.

"What did she do to you?"

That was Xenia.

"She tasted my blood and told me it was good. And that means we are stuck in this pyramid, trapped in this tomb while the city burns."

"I thought that was what you wanted. I followed you here through the desert, through the real tombs, and you promised me a life here."

He stopped, turned to face her. "I do want that," he said, softly. "I want a life with you. I want to do the right thing, and that's the rub. Up there, it is no revolution, Xenia. It is an invasion. The boy cannot lead our people against invaders. I have to get up there."

"I should have gone with you. Down that staircase. I... The dark... I never felt such fear."

"No matter now. The city is about to burn, if it is not just more witchery. I have to try to stop it."

"I will come with you. I will never leave your side again."

He smiled and strode on. Now she took her place beside him. He struggled to match her pace. They finished the staircase and moved down another hallway. This one had all the doors open. Young people lounged on beds. Some read scrolls; one prayed at a small altar.

Two priests came around the corner. Women with skirts to their knees in the style of Masters' kilts. Their hands were empty but their eyes were laden.

One said, "You should come below with us. Let us see to your needs."

"Just going up for some air," Ergol said, not slowing.

"Such is not permitted," the priest said.

"Priests do not rule Hitai. The regent does. Move aside."

The hallway was not wide enough for Ergol to pass them. They stood in his way, firmly. He still did not slow. One of them took a stance as if to stop him. But she was just a mortal woman of ordinary stature and Ergol had the body his family had given him. Wide, heavy, low-centered. He kept going, pushing the two women into the walls with his hands as he went.

Xenia danced over the tangle of arms and legs they made and watched his back as Ergol found the next stairway up.

More priests piled out of doorways in the next, final hallway. These corridors were short, only three doors on a side. Still, soon there were nine priests blocking up the way and three more coming up behind.

He could not see the next stairwell but surmised it was around the next corner. And there were too many of them now, too many to get past without hurting someone.

"Stop!"

He turned at the voice. It was Myrsa, finishing a headlong rush up the previous stairwell.

"Stop. Come back. Too much is lost if you go out there, My King."

King?

"Explain yourself," he said. "And make these priests move away from me. I mean to go and flesh will not stop me."

"Stop," Myrsa repeated. "Everyone stop. The boy. The King's Nephew. He had an accident in the lower chambers. Fell down a staircase in the dark and hurt his head. He did not survive. Ergol. My King, there is nobody left to assume the throne but you. You are the King of Hitai, not the regent."

He thought this over, taking silent seconds to ponder. "War in Hitai. King or regent, no matter. The place of the ruler is on the field of battle. Get out of my way. Now your *King* demands it."

"If you go," Myrsa said, "Xenia will die."

"A threat?" Xenia said. "You threaten your Queen?"

"No." Myrsa put up her hands, palms out. She spoke still to Ergol. "You misunderstand. Mistress showed you some scenes on a wall, yes? The future. A thing that cannot be changed. It has already happened, like a tree that has fallen over a road you have yet to travel. She told me your line depends on staying here. If you go, your line is lost. Xenia is lost. Not our doing; the fates or the gods."

Ergol stopped to think again but Xenia pushed at him. "Go. Get up there. I am coming with you. If I die, well, I am a warrior as you are. I have lived well. I have loved you." That last she choked out.

"Well, then. Myrsa, thank you for your hospitality. And for solving my political problem. For the murder of a Prince of The Blood, well, do not make me come to enact justice. Stay out of my way from now on." He walked into the mass of waiting priests, pushing and elbowing. They offered resistance until he put his elbow into a woman's face. She dropped to the ground, face broken. Then they backed away.

More stairs. A doorway. Daylight. He was outside.

On the deck outside, his guard captain argued with more priests. They saw Ergol emerge and went silent.

"Spears," Ergol said. "Chariots. We ride south. Invaders come, an army of them. We fight them in the Preserves or we fight them here, street to street – and lose."

"Yes, Great One," the captain said.

Ergol took him by the elbow and they clattered down the long single staircase towards the street.

From below, from somewhere in the ground, came a noise like a shriek and like thunder. The temple shook enough to throw Ergol off-balance. Xenia fell into his back and he steadied them both.

The noise grew louder and louder. It took minutes, shaking the world such that it was impossible to safely descend any more steps. People fell all around him. Ergol sat on the stair he was on so that he would not fall.

"What is it?"

He could barely hear Xenia over the noise from below. Below and growing closer. Inside the temple, rising up, bellowing as it came.

The bellow became a roar as the door flew open above. He heard it slam against the wall, clatter to the ground. The word was:

"Blood!"

She swept down towards him. The woman from far underground, from the realm of monsters. Her legs were made of smoke and her eyes of fury, and she came for him.

***

Guarl reached the eastern end of the city. It seemed nearly empty, except for the cats. He had seen two soldiers earlier in the day, both running south and west.

But, here, now, he was alone.

There were buildings to either side. A granary and one of Hitai's ubiquitous temples. A cat sat on the roof of the latter, pretending not to watch him pass. Ahead, out of the shadows of city buildings, lay immense golden fields.

He could feel two of his friends nearby. All but Xin Ban. Whilla was the faintest, moving away. Vault was nearer but also too far away to read clearly. For the first time in months, his mind was his own. And one thought was particularly clear:

I am in love with Xin Ban.

That was a thought he had needed to push down on, to push away almost constantly. If he did not thrust the feeling aside the group mind had done it for him. And, down there in the darkness, the thought did not wither and die like a sun-starved plant but only grew stronger and deeper.

That they could not be together was obvious. That changed nothing of his feelings.

He stepped into the grain field before him, trying to keep to the rows rather than trample the crop. The grains were high here. They smelled rich, as though he were gaining sustenance just through the air they filled.

The world was out there. It was under his feet and it rolled on forever ahead, behind, to either side. His mother had told him, months ago now, about the day of his birth. About the Gravetender and the White Witch. He could all but remember the day based on her description.

Held aloft, turned in a circle. *He will see all of the world.*

He had seen much of it already. Hitai in brief. The Preserves, the Greenlands. Roads and towns, plantations, animals and birds and insects.

Why not see the rest of it?

I have to get away from the people I love. Far away. As far as I can.

And nowhere was farther than Lurk.

He came to the end of a grain field and kept going, only his weapons and the clothes on his back to sustain him. His heart hurt because his love, all his loves, faded in his mind with each step.

Each step a benediction.

Each step a prayer.

Each step absolution.

Each step into the future.

Then the feeling in his chest changed. It was sudden, violent. It hurt. He was shaken, terrified. An alien thought rose through his mind and out of his mind:

"She returns."

He stopped and looked behind him. Whatever was back there, whatever terror had just stepped into the world, it was too big for him. The thing inside him, the blue thing, the god – it hated her. But he felt nothing of his own.

Whoever she was, she was the past. Xin Ban was the past, too. The future lay in front of him, past these fields of grains. He put his feet back into motion, heart pounding, and tried to slow his breathing.

***

I had a name once.

Empress stood on a palanquin born by six men who embodied strength. Ahead of her, Greenlander chariots had stalled into her massed ranks of shield and spear bearers. No good among the trees anyway. Oxen died in their traces. Drivers struggled against gut wounds that left them screaming but helpless. On the left flank, the last little elephant raged against a tormenter: a woman with a bow who stayed always a little out of its vision on the left. Its skin was made of arrow fletchings.

My name... I lost my name.

At a gesture from her hand, her men advanced her palanquin a little closer to the action. The Hongian archers had already broken and run. Wolf-hunting dogs lay scattered among the trees, bloody and broken. The last effective unit left on the field was heavy infantry. Short swords and small round shields but heavy armor – too heavy to effectively run. They were surrounded now on three sides. Her own infantry had spears with long metal heads, hard to hack with swords. The spears pushed the remaining resistance into a shrinking circle. Broad bronze shields kept her soldiers protected where the occasional soldier snuck a strike between spears.

Sixteen times I have distilled myself. Sixteen times I have left behind everything weak. This is my seventeenth self. I have no name but Emperor.

"Dress those lines," she called. "Archers, help finish that elephant. Reserves. Finish encircling. This is our time. Do not kill more than you must. Save me some recruits."

That always made them nervous. Loyalty was the issue and enemies could not be made loyal. But she did it again and again: took out the hate and offered them service. All of these soldiers fighting for her had been enemies once.

Moburu waited off to her right. His sword was bloody. So was his mouth. She wondered if he had been hit in the face or if he had eaten the flesh of one of the fallen. He restrained himself now, though. An encirclement was no place for an honor-warrior, for single combat.

On a rock ahead and to the left, Zhang stood and watched the proceedings. She, too, came from an honor tradition that left little room for organized fighting.

They have their uses.

And I will use them.

It was nearly done. Another hour at most and the battle would be part of history, another conquest.

Then everything changed.

The ground seemed to rumble under her feet, only she was not standing on the ground but on a platform feet above it. Nobody else appeared to notice. Her stomach went tight. The thing in her felt something, tried to tell her something.

A presence. She could feel it, north across the woods, across the fields. Something old. Almost as old as the god she had taken in, as old as the one she battled.

"First there was nothing," she whispered. "Then there was order and chaos. Finally, when the worlds were made, there came evil."

Nobody heard Empress but herself.

"Sound the retreat," she said, and a horn-bearer blew three short blasts. The encircling troops were confused but obeyed. She could hear their comments, their querulous talk. They came in good order. The Hongian Greenlanders, suddenly reprieved from what must have seemed certain death, regrouped into ranks and fell back slowly.

Moburu came to stand under her gaze. "Are you mad? How is this a part of your plan?"

"Something changed," she said. "Something unexpected awaits us in Hitai, in the city. We need a new plan."

"What thing? What waits?"

"Evil."

Epilogue

Sun shone in Gareth's eyes. He squeezed them shut but that was no help; light just smashed through his eyelids, giving him a bright red view that made him a little queasy.

He hung from a wall like an ornament. The height was another factor in his closed eyes; the drop looked as sickening as the interior view of his eyelids.

Above him in a little stone viewing box, Emperor and her aides sat on wooden chairs. To his left and right hung banners in lime green, a color he had never witnessed before on a fabric. They draped more than ten feet and were hardly moved by the breeze that tickled his brows.

Breeze through a building.

The top was open to sun and sky. Walls of stone higher than anything in Hong, anything outside the Tomblands, enclosed benches to seat thousands.

The noise of those thousands was as deafening as the sunlight was blinding. He wished he could squeeze his ears shut.

The rope around his chest made it hard to breathe. It itched and cut which at least was a distraction from the itching of his new stitches.

"You should be dead."

Blithe had told him that. She called herself a surgeon.

"Seen wounds like this and even survivors. This field surgery, though. A mess. Lucky."

Her table had been less comfortable than this perch on the wall. She had cut away more flesh and jabbed him with needles. All through that harrowing pain, he had nurtured his hatred. It was easy to do. Hatred wanted to grow like weeds in a barley field.

The crowd screamed, their dull roar turned sharp. The first contenders had entered the arena. He cracked an eye.

Across the sandy floor from him, at the longest range of his bow, two big cats sauntered through an open gate. They stretched in the noon heat. Each was as big as a lion. Emperor's animal keepers seemed to have painted them orange and black, striped them for effect, or else they were part zebra.

A fighter came out of the gate under his feet. She passed right through his shadow. His perspective was strange, staring right own onto her head, but he knew who she was. Who else could it be? She had Korina's sword in one hand. Her leather armor had been set aside for something gaudier, some lacquer-work costume in red and gold.

The cats saw her and stopped their languorous exploration of the ring. Their ears perked, tails dropped. They trotted forwards as if with one mind.

Zhang let her sword trail her as she took almost prancing steps, circling to her right.

I hope she wins.
I hope she survives because I'm going to kill her myself.
I'm going to kill her for the Emperor.

Keep reading for an except from *For An Uncertain Future*, a collection of three short stories set before the events of *For Love of Their Children*.

Your opinion matters. Visit my author page to rate this work and leave comments.

To Spare Her the Guilt explores the origins of the enigmatic Mithodroxes.

Heln came around a pair of thorny evergreen bushes and found her sister, Mithodroxes, looking down onto the frozen lake. Her reflection was just a shadow in thin water atop ice. Sunlight screamed off the surface like an arrow: cold white light, colder white ice. All Heln saw, though, was blue: a blue fog that hazed around her sister's pale face, her yellow-white hair. Thin, oozing, perhaps not part of the world at all – it was like moss trying to grow through the bark of a tree. Mithodroxes had the end of a string in one hand. The other trailed down to a hole in the ice that had mostly frozen back over. Ice beaded the string itself.

Heln pushed Mithodroxes' shoulder. "Hey – time to go. Father will be waiting." She was much like her sister: tall, blonde, too thin. Her faded blue eyes matched the clear summer sky.

Mithodroxes did not respond, did not look up from her contemplations.

"Drox, not again. Not now." Heln hung her own brace of fish from a nearby tree branch, then took her sister by both shoulders from behind and shook her energetically.

"What?" the girl said.

"Are you with me now?"

Mithodroxes stood up and brushed her hair back from her face. It was too straight to want to stay braided and Heln's shaking had loosened it. "Where else would I be?" she said, pulling her line out of the water. The hook was empty, bait stolen.

"Wherever you go when we talk to you and you do not hear us, when we touch you but you feel nothing." Heln looked down at her, hands on hips and mouth stern.

"I do not know what you mean."

But she did know. Heln was sure of it. Sometimes in the night when the sounds of Mother and Father rutting woke her, Heln would sit up to think. Mostly to wonder if she would rut as her mother did one day, perhaps with Rigel. He was her age, sixteen, well old enough to marry if still boyish in many ways. And while she sat awake, wondering in the dark, sometimes she would realize it wasn't really all the way dark, and her parents were not alone in making noise in the night.

"Let's just go back," Heln said. "I have enough fish for us both." The blue mist was gone now – it always cleared when Mithodroxes was forced to focus on the real world.

"I'm tired," she complained.

Heln knew why: it had been another long night of congress with that blue smoke. It had only cleared when Heln prodded her sister awake with one foot.

"You're only a child," Heln said. "It is very late for a child of eight years to still be awake."

"It won't be dark for hours," Mithodroxes whined. "And you are only a child yourself. Mother says so – until she marries you off. She says Dank or Jull could make a woman of you."

Heln looked sharply at her but the girl did not seem serious about picking a fight: she rubbed at her eyes and then put up one hand to be held. Heln took it and they started the walk home together.

***

Home was a long hall built from thick logs and half buried in turf. Blue-green grass grew from the roof and sturdy ivy up the walls, a sheen of snow over the whole affair. Their father, Kilrovexen, stood outside the doors at the end of the hall, arms folded in front of his chest. His braids were neat and orderly, yellow hair fading to white at the temples and letting more scalp show than last year. He hid a smile as he saw his daughters clambering up from the glade at the bottom of the hill but Heln saw it.

"We brought salmon," she said, and held up her brace. Five fat fish hung from her line, enough that holding them high for Father's approval was strenuous.

"You should have been asleep an hour ago," Father said. "Your mother has worried." That was probably true. If Father ever worried about anything, he never said, but Mother was a different kind of animal: a deer to Father's bear.

Heln came close enough to look up into his face. While she was tall, he was still taller, maybe always would be. She opened her mouth to speak, to take the blame, to smooth him over as she always smoothed him over. But Mithodroxes surprised her.

"Sorry, Father. It is my fault. I lost track of time as I often do, sitting by the lake. And Heln will not tell you those fish are all her catches. I brought nothing."

Father's eyes widened a little. It took him a moment to speak. "Nothing? I should say you have brought truth. Your truth and your sister's little dishonesties are the same. Come inside, now. The sun is nearly gone and the cold will grow teeth."

He went first and barred the door behind them. Inside smelled of smoke and meat, the odors part of the log walls now, part of the furs marking off each family living area. A pair of tallow candles gave just enough light for anyone needing the privy trench in the night. Those sat in pots on the central hearth.

Heln led Mithodroxes to their family area. Two other sisters were already asleep in the pile of furs on the soft ground. They were aged between Mithodroxes and Heln, just as blonde, just as tall and slender. Their mother was from the same mold. She sat on a wooden bench with a flagon of mead in one hand. The weak tallow light just showed her eyes raising to meet Heln's. She said nothing, though, only set aside her cup and her robe. Heln let Mithodroxes get into bed next to Mother, her behind, and Father last of all.

Only in the heat of so many bodies pressed together did she notice how cold her hands and feet were, how her face was numb with it. A few stalls away people rutted in the night and that was a warm sound, a comforting sound, as much as the noise of her family breathing together. Mithodroxes breath evened out, became shallow; her father snored soon after; her mother stayed awake but relaxed. Heln was close to drifting away herself when Mother whispered in the dark:

"We have to move south, Heln. You must help me with all these girls. There is no more time for growing up."

"Why, Mother?" she whispered back. "Why must we go?"

"We all are to move. The cold... nothing will grow here, now. Not enough to keep us. Too many summers with not enough warmth, too many winters with too much ice. The elders decided while you were gone."

The bar across the front doors kept the bears out. Great white ice bears roved the tundra and came here too often, drawn by the smell of food – both the stuff cooked by Heln's family and friends, and the meat they were all made of. She lay in the dark listening to the sounds of life, wondering if her mother would speak again, and wondering too if a bear would try the doors tonight.

Of course she had known, had seen with her own eyes how the lake never thawed out anymore. How the bears came more and more often, drawn by the promise of easy meals because their usual prey had wandered south ahead of the glaciers. And she had heard the elders speaking in corners, never so quiet as they thought they were. The knowledge did not stop her grief. At least her tears were warm.

Sleep came close again and she put her face into Mithodroxes' hair, clutched her close, hoped to keep her here tonight – out of the arms of her foggy blue lover.

Get the full story in For An Uncertain Future, here:

https://www.amazon.com/Uncertain-Future-stories-universe-Children-ebook/dp/B0775HY69D/ref=asap_bc?ie=UTF8